Also by Antoine Vanner

Britannia's Wolf
The Dawlish Chronicles
September 1877 - February 1878

Britannia's Reach

The Dawlish Chronicles

November 1879 - April 1880

by

Antoine Vanner

Nicholas Dawlish R.N.

Born: Shrewsbury 16.12.1845

Died: Zeebrugge 23.04.1918

Prologue

Puerto Plutarcho,

Upper Reaches of the San Joaquin River

Northern Paraguay

June 6th 1879

A single shot woke Daniel Greenough, one only, distant, followed by shouting, and then three more in quick succession. He reached out in the darkness, feeling for the girl by his side – Pilar, was it? Or Beatriz? Or maybe Catalina? There was little to distinguish them. All were young though few were willing.

"Que pasa?" he asked, "What's happening?"

It did not alarm him that she was already gone, for they often were before dawn broke, but the noise was increasing, a low roar, as if many voices were raised in anger and there were more shots, and closer. He was fully awake now. He reached for the revolver he always kept beneath his pillow, thought better of lighting the oil lamp, found the trousers and shoes cast down by the bedside and pulled them on.

There was more shooting, ragged fire punctuated by brief silence. Alarmed now, Greenough padded from his bedroom and through the house. There was no sign of the girl. He paused behind the main entrance door – the key had been turned and the bolts drawn back, the girl must have done so when she left – but he did not open it.

"Que pasa?" he called twice, softly at first, then more loudly, for the guards on the veranda outside might not have heard him through the iron-bound wood.

He was frightened now, for the noise of distant shouting was louder now and the shooting almost continuous. "Que pasa?" he called again and again there was no answer. Heart beating wildly, he cocked the pistol, then opened the door. A single wall-mounted lamp cast a semicircle of yellow light towards the top of the steps leading up to the veranda. There was nobody to be seen even though there should have been one sentry there through the night. Three more should be patrolling the perimeter.

"Ramirez? Williamson?" he called out, remembering that he had seen both guards earlier.

No answer.

Greenough moved towards the steps and called out "Schirmer?" for the hulking German corporal should also have been here. It was then that he looked down and saw the body slumped at the bottom of the steps, the head drawn back at an impossible angle to it, the throat a dark gash and the eyes locked open. The blond hair and moustache identified him as Williamson. Terrified, Greenough turned towards the door, glimpsing the outline of another body just beyond the circle of light and a dark pool spreading from it, then froze as a single shot blasted splinters from the doorpost by his head.

And then, suddenly, a crowd, a mob, was rushing from the darkness, up the steps from the garden, and flowing from right and left along the veranda, ragged men and dishevelled women with upraised machetes and poleaxes that did daily slaughter in the stockyards. Their hatred rose in a single voice and Greenough knew he could expect no mercy. He rushed for the door, found it still half-open, somehow got through. The first of his assailants was reaching it reached it as he swung it closed. He got his shoulder against it and somehow shot the upper and lower bolts. A window over to his left shattered, then another to his right, but he knew that they could not get past the bars. He emptied the pistol towards them, losing count of the shots, and as the hammer clicked on an empty chamber realised that his ammunition was in his bedroom. He must hold them at bay, he told himself, for Culbertson and his men must surely be drawn here soon by the noise of riot. But then he heard the sound of splintering wood as the door was attacked. It was vital now to reload.

His hands fluttered uselessly in the empty drawer. The box of ammunition had been here – he had been sure of it – but he pulled out another drawer and found that it too was empty. Behind him the shutters on the bedroom window gave way under hammer blows and hands clasped the bars within and tried to drag them from the frame. They were calling his name now – some still called him Señor, and others Don Danielo – but the words now conveyed no respect, only hatred. He rushed from the bedroom, into the darkness of the corridor beyond. And there something slashed across his face.

There was no pain, not immediately, but the hand he clapped to his cheek found the flesh wet and flapping. He staggered back into the bedroom and saw the girl *silhouetted in the door, the knife – a kitchen knife – in one hand, a small cardboard box in the other." You want this, Señor?" she said, then turned and threw the ammunition into the darkness behind her. And then she too was gone and as Greenough felt the blood running between his fingers, and despair rising in him, he heard her draw back the bolts to admit the mob.*

Culbertson must be on his way, La Guardia cannot allow this to happen, he told himself as they pummelled him half-senseless. Hope did not die in him until they dragged him outside, half-conscious, and began to pull his trousers off.

"Yo en primera!" the girl screamed, "Me first!"

She might have been Pilar or Beatriz or maybe Catalina, but it didn't matter which as she began to hack.

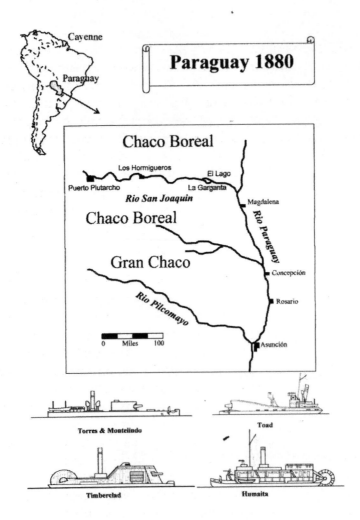

Cayenne

Paraguay

Paraguay 1880

Chaco Boreal

Los Hormigueros   El Lago

Puerto Plutarcho   La Garganta

Rio San Joaquin

Magdalena

Chaco Boreal

Rio Paraguay

Gran Chaco

Concepción

Rio Pilcomayo

Rosario

0   Miles   100

Asunción

Torres & Montelindo

Toad

Timberclad

Humaita

1

Thursday February 12th, 1880 – the ninth day since the Hyperion Consortium's flotilla had left Asunción, the most powerful force seen on South America's river systems for a decade, crawling north towards revenge and reconquest.

The Chaco Boreal lay westwards, to port, vast, arid and sinister. The afternoon heat shimmered above its brown and dusty scrub and there was no sign of human activity. Reports had been received earlier of Reducción mounted patrols even this far south and Commander Nicholas Dawlish wondered if the flotilla was even now under observation. Tall, slim, in his mid-thirties, his dark hair and the beard below the livid coin-sized scar on his left cheek flecked with grey, he sat writing up his journal at a chart-strewn table under an awning on the upper deck of the *Humaita*, the most powerful of the sternwheelers. Sweat soaked his light cotton clothing and dripped from his hand on to the damp page. *Progress generally satisfactory today*, he noted.

But progress had been difficult since Concepción, the last major town before the Rio San Joaquin. Few vessels could make more than six knots in still water but the adverse current and the drag of the towed barges together reduced overall speed to half that. The Rio Paraguay's swirling and muddy waters were shallow in places and vicious with snags. Most of the pilots were unfamiliar with the river this far north and groundings were frequent. The laden barges caused most problems. If they carried troops it was a relatively easy matter to bring one of the shallow-draught sternwheelers alongside and transfer them temporarily to it. The barge would nudge free under increased buoyancy, the steamer would take it under tow again and the troops would transfer back once deeper water was reached. The problems were greater when stores were carried, demanding backbreaking effort to lighten the grounded craft, and the delay would be so much the longer, fuelling the impatience and tempers of Murillo's staff.

Dawlish glanced again over the previous day's entry and hoped that it was not a portent of trouble to come. A dozen conscripts, emboldened by drink, had refused to reboard when the flotilla had finished loading firewood at Concepción and had barricaded themselves in a warehouse. Their mutiny lasted half an hour. General Aquino ordered a six-pounder to blast the door down, then personally led a dozen of his regulars through the breach. The ringleaders were shot out of hand and the remainder beaten brutally. They lay now in one of the transport barges, useless for anything other than as examples to their fellows.

Journal updated, Dawlish stood up and moved towards the bridge. The helmsman, Mauricio, seemed to know his business, for the craft had avoided grounding so far. He was an Argentinean, a veteran of the great war on the river in the sixties. Since Asunción he had been imparting the complexities of sternwheeler handling to the hulking British seaman who stood by him.

"Getting the hang of it now, Egdean, are you?" Dawlish asked.

"It's tricky, Sir, powerful tricky," Jeremiah Egdean said, "and the lingo don't help neither, though I'm improving."

The *Humaita* was close to head of the flotilla, a hundred yards astern of the decrepit monitor, the *Montelindo*, which led it. Forging ahead in the van, the monitor was little more than a heavily armoured raft, its decks nearly awash, smoke belching from its thin smokestack, firewood piled high abaft its single turret. Its engine was somehow still running, though no doubt tonight, as on previous nights, it would demand further repairs to keep it in service. Most of the crew was on deck, for the hot and cramped conditions below were untenable except during action.

"Take the journal below, Egdean," Dawlish said. "Stow it in the usual place."

The seaman, a reassuringly familiar figure in this wilderness, disappeared to Dawlish's personal cabin. It directly adjoined the main saloon, which had been converted to accommodate maps, files and the administrative support that the expedition's fighting vessels demanded. The *Humaita*, normally a passenger vessel on the Asunción to Buenos Aires run, towed no barges and, due to her superior power and handiness, served as Dawlish's flagship.

He looked down from the bridge to where the foredeck had been strengthened to carry a shielded three-pounder on a swivel mounting. Its recently trained Paraguayan crew was lounging inattentively. On seeing Dawlish they stood lethargically to their weapon. A Gatling was mounted in a shield above the steering platform, manned by a two-man crew, both Indians. These weapons, and the rifles of the sixty regulars who slept on deck, comprised the sole armament. The steamer was unarmoured but for the low sandbag ramparts laid along the deck edges.

Dawlish moved towards the stern and looked aft over the thrashing wheel. The flotilla straggled downstream for over a mile until the last vessels were lost beyond a bend. There were eleven paddle-steamers in total, most towing two or three barges, several of them Paraguayan government vessels, as was the *Montelindo*, but all of them, like the human and military freight they carried, financed by the Consortium. Three were sidewheelers. Dawlish disliked them as vulnerable, their beating paddles opportunities for even the most incompetent enemy gunner.

The conscripts, cowed and spiritless peons whose reliability was even more doubtful after the mutiny at Concepción, sweltered in open barges while the regulars were accommodated under awnings on the decks of the steamers themselves. They slept where they could, for the decks were laden with supplies and stacked with firewood. The heavier equipment – the artillery and the munitions – was carried in barges. Several of the barges were also devoted to extra firewood, one was laden with coal for the two vessels that needed it and two were equipped to carry mules and horses. Aft of the *Tacuari*, the large sidewheeler that accommodated Murillo and his staff, Dawlish spotted the *Pilcomayo*, the small steamer that towed the flat-top barge carrying Grinling's carboys and other paraphernalia.

Getting this flotilla mobilised had been an impressive achievement. Almost five thousand men were on the river. The impressment of craft to carry them would have brought trade north of Asunción to a standstill even had the threat represented by the Reducción not already done so.

One vessel stood out by its appearance from all the others – the squat and blunt-bowed craft that chugged purposefully against the current half-way down the flotilla. The absence of paddles showed her to be screw-propelled and dark smoke billowing from her twin buff stacks identified her as the only coal burner. Her black hull and white upperworks gleamed nonetheless, a tribute to the professionalism of her British crew, temporary mercenaries, but still governed by naval discipline. She lay low in the water and occasionally, as she ran into the wake of her predecessor, a wave ran over the bow and broke against the curved breastwork that screened off the deck and armament. The *Toad*, late of the Royal Navy, now Consortium property, was not only the smartest vessel in the flotilla but also carried the heaviest weapon.

And though Dawlish, on extended leave-of-absence from that same Royal Navy, commanded the naval component of the largest riverine force in South America, the fact would never appear in his service record. This assignment was private.

"Commander Dawlish, Sir! Magdalena's in sight."

Dawlish looked up, recognising the drawl of Travis, the American captain of the *Humaita*. His yellow complexion attested to years of fevers on this river. He had risen no higher than Petty Officer in the Union's Mississippi Flotilla before peace had sent him to seek his fortune further south but his sense of discipline marked him out from his Paraguayan counterparts. It did not however extend as far as removing his cigar when addressing a superior.

"Signal Fourteen," Dawlish said. "Standard night-time deployment."

Travis spoke briefly in Guaraní to a deckhand. A moment later the steam whistle blasted twice to draw attention to the red and yellow-striped flag being run up the improvised signal mast. One of Dawlish's first innovations had been to institute a simple signalling system – just twenty commands, each designated by a single flag. Even this much appeared too complex for many of the steamer captains, and confusion was common. Given the distance the flotilla was strung out along the river, and the difficulties of manoeuvring with the barges in tow, it would be another two hours before all craft were moored. There would be confusion, probably a grounding or two, and the *Montelindo* and the *Toad* would assume defensive positions upstream. The night would give an opportunity for drunkenness and desertions and there would be inevitable problems with stores. Getting the vessels underway in the morning would be similarly difficult. Control of this semi-disciplined and resentful force on a river too treacherous to allow night sailing was little short of a nightmare.

"Magdalena's sure changed, Sir," Travis said. "Looks more like Vicksburg in '63 with all them earthworks."

The town consisted of little more than a wooden jetty and a cluster of shacks and decrepit warehouses on the eastern bank but Dawlish's attention was fixed on the defences. Commanding the river from the sixty-foot bluffs on either shore, the sloped faces of each redoubt were some twelve feet high. Brown-clad Paraguayan regulars moved on the parapets but the guns below them were invisible. The position was a superb one for blocking southward movement and the rapid construction of the earthworks represented the only success so far against La Reducción Nueva.

A heavy figure in a grey linen uniform, a plume in his wide brimmed hat, waited on the jetty. A group of officers and a ragged platoon were drawn up behind him. Dawlish guessed his identity even before Travis told him.

"Colonel Silas Culbertson. Cavalier of Old Dixie. Don't want to show his face in the re-United States no more." Travis spat, aiming for the cuspidor by the helm. As usual, he missed.

The platoon came haphazardly to attention as Dawlish descended the gangplank and a half-dozen civilian musicians struck up a tune that was just recognisable as "Rule Britannia". Culbertson advanced to meet him, hand extended.

"You are welcome, Sir," he said gravely. "Your fame precedes you. Your arrival seals the doom of our enemies". He grasped Dawlish's hand and shook it slowly. "This day will be remembered as the commencement of a great campaign".

He smelled of alcohol. Sweat ran between the folds of flesh on his livid face and neck, staining the uniform below. His eyes were small and blue and piercing – intelligent and ruthless eyes at sharp variance with the over-courtly manner.

Dawlish responded with reserve. He met Culbertson's officers – a mixture of Paraguayans and foreign mercenaries – and went on to inspect the guard of honour now inexpertly attempting a salute. His initial poor impression changed as he came closer. Unkempt they might be, but all had a lean muscularity that indicated fitness and there was a hard set to their faces. Their weapons, Winchester repeater carbines, were well maintained and all carried long knives in their belts. They wore high canvas leggings and spurs on their boots.

Culbertson sensed Dawlish's reluctant admiration.

"La Guardia Hyperion, Sir – not regulars," he said, omitting the "H" in the Spanish manner. "Twenty-four carat sons of bitches, every one. Handpicked by myself – every self-respectin' nationality under the sun! You there!" He prodded a lean, grizzled sergeant. "Tell the Commander what you are and where you've been."

"Gelb, Sir." His English was still guttural enough to betray his origin. "Sergeant, Magdeburg Cuirassiers, 'fore I left Prussia. An' I served later with Stuart, Sir. I was with him at Yellow Tavern."

Dawlish felt the man's pride.

"You see, Commander? The cream, the very cream – one of Jeb Stuart's own. And you, Son?" Culbertson gestured towards a flaxen-headed, flat-faced giant.

"Sprokkelaar, Sir. From the Kingdom of the Netherlands, Sir. And there, Sir, I was…"

"That's enough, Son. The Commander don't need to know your whole breed, seed an' generation."

"All horsemen, then?" Dawlish asked, as they passed on down the line.

"I ain't got nothin' else, because nothin' else is worth a damn in this terrain. They've served with me since the Consortium first came to the Rio San Joac – Germans and Dutch and English and Danes and Spanish and Paraguayans and assorted Latinos and whatnot – why, we've even got a few Yankees!"

"All survivors of the revolt?"

"These gentlemen didn't take too kindly to being evicted, Sir. Got a mighty big score to settle, all of 'em, can't wait to get upriver again. But now, Sir – let me show you the eastern redoubt."

The sloping track leading to the fortification was steep and Culbertson lagged. Dawlish slackened his pace to keep level with him and noticed a slight limp.

"An old wound Sir," Culbertson said, with a somewhat theatrical wince. "A relic of the late War of Secession – I stopped a bullet at the stormin' of Fort Pillow. But worth it, Sir! Worth it to earn the thanks of General Forrest! You know of the gentleman? A genius Sir, a veritable genius!"

The earthwork was embrasured to allow two sixty-eight pounders to dominate the river.

"Armstrongs, Sir," Culbertson said, "They'd been in the Asunción dockyard since the end o' the Tripartite War. Hercules himself would have been proud of the job we did to get them here."

They were mounted on mats of hardwood logs and a buried shed by each weapon sheltered the charges and shells. The earthwork's sloped walls had firing steps on their inner faces so that rifle fire could be brought to bear on the ground down to the river. It had been burned clean of vegetation. Dawlish could not but be impressed. The labour needed must have been immense – not that Culbertson would have any problems securing a workforce, he imagined. La Guardia

Hyperion would have ensured that the local population co-operated effectively if not willingly.

"A professional job, Colonel." Dawlish said, looking across the shimmering river towards the other redoubt. The sun had dropped low over the Chaco and the weapons there were silhouetted against the reddening sky. "I shouldn't want to run any vessel past here, armoured or not."

"Just what them sons o' bitches up the San Joaquin think too." Culbertson's eyes gleamed. "We've got them bottled up, damn right we have! And now it's time to settle the reckoning."

A whistle-blast drew their attention to the jetty. The *Tacuari* was securing alongside. Dawlish and Culbertson started back to meet it. Murillo had arrived.

*　　*　　*

The staff-conference in the *Tacuari's* saloon that evening was presided over by Don Plutarcho Murillo. It did little more than confirm the arrangements already agreed in Asunción.

A small regular garrison would continue to hold Magdalena as a base to fall back upon should the advance up the San Joaquin falter. Culbertson's Guardia would be embarked however – the *Ipora*, one of the more powerful sternwheelers, and her two towed barges, one with improvised ramps and stalls for horses, had been earmarked for them. Among the conscripts there had been more deaths from fever but they were to be expected, and there would be more to come. There was nothing that could be done about it – they were poor and underfed and unhealthy to start with, born only to toil and suffer and die. A single steamer was released to return to Asunción, towing two empty barges, the fuel and fodder on which had been consumed. It would return with further supplies.

In two days the flotilla would leave the main river and turn off, westwards, into the Rio San Joaquin. A monitor, a gunboat, ten paddle-steamers. A battalion of regular Paraguayan infantry – almost twelve hundred men. Three battalions of unwilling and half-trained conscripts, upwards of a thousand men each after desertions. Three troops of Culbertson's Guardia Hyperion, almost four hundred men. And horses, mules, artillery, food and munitions and more besides. All paid for by a company registered on the London Stock Exchange. Its shares had been trading at less than a tenth of their nominal value when Dawlish left England.

Murillo, in black frock coat and starched collar, correct as ever despite the warmth and humidity, presided over the meeting. He kept the minutes himself in a thick ledger, his eyes enormous behind thick-lensed pince-nez. The language of record was English. Even here, on the edge of the wilderness, planning a war of reconquest, he looked the part of a sober and responsible company official. He concluded by passing the book for signature.

"A business formality Gentlemen," he said accentlessly. "A necessary formality. The Board will require strict reckoning at the end of this affair."

They signed in turn. Aquino, overall Army commander, with a half-literate scrawl. Culbertson put C.S.A. after his name, though the Confederacy had been dead for fifteen years. Tinsley's small, cramped signature omitted his rank, Major, and his affiliation, Royal Artillery. Dawlish merely initialled. No rank, no RN.

"That concludes the night's business," Murillo said. "I will be dining alone. I wish you good evening." He closed the ledger with a low sigh, and reached for another volume from the pile before him, his brow furrowed in concentration.

Dawlish, leaving, saw Culbertson sidle up to Murillo. His voice was low but could just be overheard.

"The goods you requested are waitin', Don Plutarcho," he said. "Two of 'em, neither a day more than twelve. Fresh but willin' I'd say. Only speak Guaraní but I don't suppose you'll hold that against them."

For the first time Dawlish, disgusted, saw a smile pass over Murillo's thin lips. He would certainly not be dining with the others tonight.

Two days after leaving Magdalena the flotilla left the Rio Paraguay and turned west into the Rio San Joaquin. The width seldom exceeded a hundred yards and frequent sandbanks made the navigable channel even narrower. To either side was low and arid scrub, interspersed with stands of forest. In places the banks were marshy and covered with tall grasses. The few waterside villages all seemed deserted, their occupants having fled over a hundred miles westwards to La Reducción Nueva. Burned roofs and empty doorways testified to the efficiency of the lightning punitive raids that Culbertson had mounted from Magdalena in recent months.

Dawlish would have liked to have placed the only armoured vessel, the monitor *Montelindo*, in the lead, but her low steering position and sluggish manoeuvring capability were drawbacks on this difficult waterway. Instead, the *Velasco*, the smallest and shallowest-draughted of the sternwheelers, led the advance. Her captain knew the river well – she was Consortium-owned, one of the vessels that had carried supplies up-river to the settlements before the revolt and had exported their produce on the return journey. Like Dawlish's *Humaita*, which followed her, she had nothing in tow but she did carry a full complement of troops. She nosed forward cautiously, for flooding might have drastically altered sandbar patterns, skirting around shallows and seeking the swirling eddies of the deeper waters on the outsides of the bends. The monitor, the *Montelindo*, followed in the *Humaita's* wake, her low-mounted helmsman slavishly following the sternwheeler's movements. The *Toad* took its place astern of her. The other paddle steamers followed, their tows streaming astern.

The first night's halt passed without incident. The conscripts were landed to cut wood for the steamers' insatiable furnaces and to bury two more of their number who had died of heat-stroke in the open barges. Surrounded by deserted and inhospitable terrain, which the enemy might well control, none showed any tendency to desert. The flotilla was underway again an hour after daybreak and by mid-morning had moved a good six miles upriver.

From the *Humaita's* upper deck, fifteen feet above the water, Dawlish had a clear view across the dry, brown Chaco. A lookout atop the signal mast once reported a cloud of dust on rising ground to the south and Dawlish went aloft to examine it through his telescope. The air above the scrub quivered from the heat and it was impossible to be categoric. It might have been a dust devil – or a small group of horsemen keeping pace with the flotilla. Sooner or later it must be the latter. He returned to the steering position.

"*La Garganta's* ahead." Travis pointed to a low scrub-covered ridge. He had taken the helm himself for the next section of the river, leaving Egdean and the Argentinean, Mauricio, to watch and learn.

Dawlish had hardly used his Spanish it in over a dozen years and it brought with it memories of folly and humiliation he would prefer to forget. This word eluded him. "*La Garganta?*" he asked.

"The Gullet. Where the San Joac passes through them hills."

The river narrowed between high, green-enshrouded banks and the current quickened, slowing progress to less than walking pace. The Gullet was well named, for where it gouged through the ridge the river was scarcely forty yards wide. Its surface seethed with vortices and eddies.

"He's taking it well." Travis's tone conveyed his admiration for the skill with which the *Velasco's* skipper, a hundred yards ahead, was steering his sternwheeler, thrashing and swaying, through the racing waters. "But it ain't easy – No Sir! I'll lay you ten to one, Commander, that we'll see at least two groundings before we get the rest through."

Dawlish glanced astern towards the wallowing *Montelindo* and hoped her engine would not choose this moment to break down again. He would feel safer once the monitor's lumbering menace had been carried safely past this obstacle.

"Our turn now!" Travis's air was that of a man taking on a difficult task he knew he was good at. He winked at Egdean. "Just watch this, Jerry – when we next come up, I'll put you on the helm!"

Dawlish and Egdean watched with respect as Travis took the *Humaita* beating at full power into the Gullet, nudging the unwieldy craft against the torrent, now avoiding an eddy, now taking advantage of another, the wheel spinning and counter-spinning through his hands as he somehow clawed slowly upstream.

And then, suddenly, they were through, the ridge and the Gullet left astern, the current slackening. The troops lining the side galleries, who had been silent and apprehensive as the vessel had lurched and shuddered in the narrows, cheered spontaneously in recognition of a danger past.

"That's how it's done, Gents!" Travis said. "Just remember, Jerry — your turn next time."

Directly upstream of the Gullet's constriction the river widened into a placid lake-like section, eight hundred yards broad and extending onwards for three miles or more. High reeds and grasses showed the low-lying southerly shore to be marshy, but on the opposite bank firm brush-covered ground sloped towards low hills to the north. As the *Humaita* thrashed forward into this calm pool Dawlish looked astern. The *Montelindo* monitor was yawing sluggishly in the Gullet, three hundred yards distant, almost at a standstill, her tired engine all but beaten by the current. The *Toad* had dropped back, cautious lest the monitor lose way completely and drift down on her. The *Montelindo* might well require assistance.

"Slow down and circle," Dawlish said to Travis. "Make ready to pass a tow to the *Montelindo*. Signal the *Velasco* to stand by. We may need her help also."

It was a manoeuvre they had executed several times earlier on the main river — a three-inch hawser was strung along the port side for such an eventuality. Travis bellowed orders and the *Humaita* lurched into a shallow turn to port as her whistle blasts advised the *Velasco* of her intention.

The *Humaita* had almost completed her first half-circle, with her bows facing downstream towards the *Montelindo*, now four hundred yards away in the Gullet, when a yell from the signal-mast startled

Dawlish. The lookout's pointing finger directed his gaze to the southern shore.

A mass of vegetation, a floating island, was detaching itself from the reed beds. As it moved out into clear water and gathered speed the covering greenery began to fall away. The outlines of a black vessel became unmistakable and a bow wave was starting to cream about its stem. The decks were almost awash and as its disguise was dragged free by the rushing water a single circular turret was revealed, two stubby muzzles protruding from it, just abaft a tiny armoured conning tower. Heat shimmered above the low funnel aft.

Dawlish's stomach knotted with the sick realisation that La Reducción's single monitor, the *Torres*, that providential relic of the Tripartite War, the *Montelindo's* identical sister, had trapped him by the expedient of fuelling with bone-dry timber that was practically smokeless.

The monitor surged forward into area between the *Humaita* and the point where the pool emptied into the Gullet. Shouts of alarm rose from the troops on the sternwheeler and confused scurrying followed as officers ordered them to take cover behind the sandbags. The two vessels were less than a hundred yards apart now and Travis was flinging the *Humaita* over to starboard to avoid collision. It was obvious however that she was not the quarry, for the *Torres'* turret was rotating slowly towards the Gullet itself – Dawlish could hear the metallic grinding of the training gears.

The *Montelindo* was almost stationary in the narrows' high current. Another fifty yards and she would be in calmer water, but for now she was trapped. There was panic among those of her crew who were on deck as they saw the path ahead blocked by the enemy monitor. Struggling bodies clustered around the two hatches leading below and a few splashes alongside showed that some more timorous souls preferred to take their chances in the river.

The *Humaita's* armament was puny – the three-pounder could make no impression on what Dawlish knew to be four inches of British iron on the *Torres'* turret, and the Gatling even less – but he yelled nonetheless for the gunners to engage. Rifle shots were already ringing out – the regulars on the lower deck were starting to blaze ineffectually at the surging black vessel.

The waters aft of the *Torres* foamed and its forward motion slowed – the screw had been thrown in reverse to bring the vessel stationary directly upstream of the Gullet. The range was almost point blank, the guns now trained at ninety degrees to the monitor's axis – the *Montelindo* must be filling their sights. The *Torres* was suddenly engulfed in billowing grey smoke as its twin one hundred and ten-pounders blasted simultaneously. An instant later an orange flash erupted on the forward face of the *Montelindo's* turret, scouring the open deck of all life, before it too was enshrouded in smoke.

Dawlish flinched as the double wave of sound, deafening and painful, washed over the *Humaita* but his mind was racing over the alternatives. Running upstream was useless – the only hope, a desperate one, lay in boarding. The turret's gun-ports were the weak point – if only he could get troops across, then their rifles could wreak devastation inside that metal box.

The *Humaita* was still turning tightly and scarcely eighty yards lay between her and the monitor.

"Straighten out", Dawlish yelled to Travis, "lay her alongside!"

As she came bow-on towards the monitor the *Humaita's* three-pounder fired, the shell exploding uselessly against her adversary's armoured flank. Dawlish tore his eyes from the enemy. In the Gullet the smoke was drifting clear of the *Montelindo*. To his relief there was no obvious damage – the turret's armour seemed intact, though the bodies on deck were gone – but the bows were swinging over and the monitor was starting to drift beam-on to the current and to move downstream. He realised with horror that the helmsman must be stunned from the shells' impact – worse still, the engine was still on full ahead and driving the bows towards the northern bank. The *Toad* was eighty yards downstream of her now, stoutly breasting the current. Dawlish's heart leapt as he saw her weapon elevate. She was obviously trying to bring it to bear, but the *Montelindo's* intervening bulk blocked her aim.

The enemy monitor was close now – scarcely fifty yards from the *Humaita's* bows – and Travis was swinging the helm over to turn her parallel and lay her alongside. He had signalled for astern revolutions and the paddle wheel stilled momentarily, then ground into reverse, and the vessel decelerated rapidly. Dawlish tugged his revolver from its holster and yelled instructions to the troops on the lower deck to hold their fire until they could board.

"Stand by the Gatling!" he called to Egdean. "Start firing as soon as you glimpse the turret embrasures!"

The seaman heaved himself up onto the platform above the bridge and crouched behind the gunner and loader. "Espera, muchachos! Espera!" he growled. "Solamente cuando yo lo digo! Y no mas que seis balas cada vez!" His accent was still broad Sussex but his message was unmistakable – short bursts, and only when he called for them. But the turret gun-ports, the only point of vulnerability, were turned away for now as the monitor's guns trained on the Gullet.

Troops were milling in the *Humaita's* bows, some resolute, others terrified, all excited, as a lieutenant, assisted by a sergeant, tried to prepare them for boarding. The three-pounder fired again – as uselessly as before, though it raised a cheer from some of the troops. The stern wheel was still thrashing in reverse, killing the *Humaita's* forward motion.

The *Torres*, still stationary, fired again towards the Gullet, her weapons' report ear-shattering at this close proximity. Immediately the waters astern boiled and she lurched into motion again, surging forward past the *Humaita*, so close that Dawlish could see the rust streaks on her sides and the remaining reeds that had disguised her still bound to the turret and decks. An instant later there was a flash and an explosion in the Gullet. The shells had struck home again on the *Montelindo* and when the smoke engulfing her cleared Dawlish saw that her bows were lodged in the northern bank. She lay beam-on to the current for a moment and then began to rotate, and dragged free, drifting sluggishly downstream towards the *Toad*. Smoke still gushed from the funnel but the engine seemed to have fallen still. The *Toad's* path was blocked as the stricken *Montelindo* bore down on her – and it was now that her manoeuvrability saved the gunboat from collision.

She spun on her axis and headed downstream ahead of the drifting monitor. The *Montelindo* heaved as her stern caught on a sandbank and her bows swung against the northern bank. There she remained, jammed diagonally across the river at its narrowest point.

The *Humaita* was at a standstill now and the *Torres* was accelerating away from her. Rifle fire crackled from the sternwheeler and then, suddenly, the monitor's helm was thrown over and it was doubling back in an ever-tightening circle. The turret was swinging slowly around and in seconds the unarmoured paddler would be at its mercy.

Dawlish staggered as the *Humaita* leaped forward under the full revolutions Travis had signalled for. He grasped the bridge screen for support as the paddler accelerated, turning tightly to port inside the monitor's circle, his gaze locked on the two dreadful muzzles gaping from the turret ports and rotating towards him. He heard Egdean urging the Gatling crew into action and the weapon chattered as it was cranked into life, spraying the monitor's deck ahead of the turret, then reaching back towards the embrasures – and then falling suddenly silent as it jammed. Egdean's exhortations as to short bursts had gone unheeded, with inevitable results.

For almost a half-circle the two craft slewed in unison, the sternwheeler inside the monitor's greater arc, but the turret creeping ever further round to port. Dawlish steeled himself for the detonation…

The *Humaita* lurched to starboard, out of the circle, as Travis threw in full rudder. The sternwheeler passed directly ahead of the monitor for a moment, scarcely fifty yards beyond her bow, and moved outside her circle, safe momentarily from the turret's guns. Travis was now heading the *Humaita* up the pool at maximum revolutions. Ahead of her loomed the leading sternwheeler, the *Velasco*, which had turned back, unwisely, and was beating downstream towards her. The rifle fire had fallen silent, the troops on the lower deck cowering behind the sandbags as they waited in terror for the shells that would tear the unarmoured paddler apart.

"We can't outrun her," Dawlish yelled. "Head for the bank!"

He glanced over his shoulder to see the monitor pulling out of its circle. The turn was so tight that almost half her deck was awash as she heeled. Then she was straightening out again and running directly for the *Humaita's* stern. Her speed built up – she had at least a knot's advantage, maybe more. Her turret, though rotating, was still not bearing, but she did not need it – her momentum was weapon enough.

With a rending crash the *Torres'* low bows came smashing into the paddle wheel, throwing chunks of wood and iron skywards. Still it ploughed on, thrusting and tearing up the *Humaita's* central axis and only stopping when the turret itself ground against the disintegrating superstructure. Men screamed as they were thrown on the deck or against bulkheads by the impact – Dawlish himself was hurled against the bridge-screen – or were mangled in the wreckage.

The two vessels, paddle-steamer and monitor alike, stayed locked for an instant in that terrible coitus, and then shuddered as the aggressor's screw reversed and it commenced its withdrawal. The stricken *Humaita* heaved and shook as the *Torres* rasped from her vitals. Her entire after-portion dropped as the monitor's bows tore free and water rushed into her gaping wound.

Dawlish, dazed, found himself being pulled to his feet by Egdean. "This ship's finished, Sir," he said. "She's a-going fast."

They struggled towards the rail across the canted deck. Dawlish noticed remotely that Travis was lying motionless by the wheel, his head at an impossible angle to his body and blood running from his mouth. Mauricio, the helmsman, was crouched over him, his face ashen.

"Save yourself, Amigo!" Egdean shouted. "You can do nothing for him!"

The planking beneath them was already tilted at thirty degrees and the after end of the upper deck – what remained of it – was almost awash. The inclination was increasing and it could be only moments before the water reached the glowing boiler amidships. A creaking overhead told that the smokestack was about to come crashing down and from every side came the cries of panicking men throwing themselves into the water. Order and discipline, what there had been of them to start with, had collapsed. There was no need to order "Abandon Ship" – the surviving crew and troops were taking their own decisions.

The doomed craft jerked as it settled yet lower in the water. Dawlish pushed the Gatling crew ahead of him down the ladder leading to the forecastle. Egdean followed, assisting the stunned Mauricio. They scrambled over the deserted three-pounder mounting and on to the bow. Normally almost awash, it was now raised six feet or more above the water and the area beyond was teeming with swimming – and drowning – figures.

"Jump, Man!" Dawlish shoved the gunner off.

"No puedo nadar! No puedo, Señor!" the man screamed as he fell, and then he too was one more among the splashing, despairing bodies.

Dawlish paused for an instant before he leaped himself and he saw the *Torres* surging forward again, heading upstream now and straight for the *Velasco*.

"Now, Sir! Jump or it'll be too late!" Egdean was shouting from the water, already a long way from the dying vessel's rising bow.

The *Humaita* shuddered once more beneath his feet and Dawlish threw himself outwards. He went under, kicked to the surface and struck powerfully away from the settling craft. The water was crowded with bobbing heads, many clustered around floating wreckage. He threaded his way between them, shutting his ears to the cries around him – for many of these men could not swim – until he was on the outer periphery and clear of the danger of being dragged down.

"Over here, Sir!" It was Egdean.

Dawlish swam towards him and as he drew near turned and trod water. The *Humaita* was starting her final slide, the bow rearing ever higher and exposing the flat bottom. The waters lapped higher along the shattered wooden superstructure. The funnel wrenched free and disappeared in a sheet of spray. There were still men on board, desperate wretches who crawled ever higher along the sloping deck and who clung despairingly to any handhold. Then, as the rising waters found the boiler, a muffled internal explosion burst the craft asunder, scattering timbers and bodies even as it disappeared in a cloud of steam. Debris rained through the air, flinging up spray as it smashed down among the survivors. Dawlish instinctively clapped his hands over his head and went under for a moment.

He surfaced, spluttering, and shook the water from his eyes, then rotated slowly to get his bearings, only to witness a second massacre.

The *Velasco*, powerless to assist her sister in her death agony, and confronted by the monitor rushing towards her, was turning upstream in a frantic effort to run before it. Futile rifle fire crackled from the sandbag ramparts lining her bulwarks and she was heeling over as her flailing stern wheel drove her into a turn.

These efforts were hopeless. She lay beam-on to the *Torres* at the moment of impact, her high wooden upperworks towering over the low armoured-raft that crashed into her midships. Even five hundred yards away, and surrounded by the screams of drowning men, Dawlish heard the rending of wood and iron as the paddle steamer's fragile structure disintegrated and the *Torres* cleaved straight through her.

The *Velasco* did not sink – she collapsed into the water in a torrent of wreckage while the monitor, her momentum hardly checked, her armoured decks and turret unscathed by the impact, forged on upstream and disappeared round the bend at the head of the pool.

Egdean was swimming towards him with a splintered piece of planking. "Grab this, Sir!" he called. They hung on to it, heaving for breath.

There were fewer heads visible in the water now and the cries for aid were more like moans, exhausted and hopeless. Dawlish looked downstream to the Gullet, towards which the sluggish current out here near the centre of the pool was carrying himself and Egdean and the other survivors. The *Montelindo* blocked the passage of the *Toad* and the other vessels downstream of her. The *Torres'* escape was assured.

Dawlish shut his ears to the cries around him. Survival, his own survival, was the first priority if he was to avenge this disaster. He hung on grimly to the plank and tried to ignore the recognition that he had been tried and found wanting at this first encounter.

It was not how he had visualised it on that wet November day in Sheerness when he had been introduced to the Consortium and had first learned of La Reducción Nueva ...

3

When he stepped ashore from H.M.S. *Lightning* on a cold and wet night in November 1879 Commander Nicholas Dawlish was chilled beneath his oilskins. The small, fast craft had been conducting rough-weather torpedo-launching trials in the Solent. Egdean, his helmsman, had coped expertly with the short, vicious waves and the bridge had been constantly drenched with spray. But for all his discomfort Dawlish felt a glow of satisfaction. The trials had gone well, very well, and the "Dawlish Cam", his own invention, demonstrated its ability to improve depth-keeping capability significantly. There was every chance now that it would become standard on all British torpedoes. His skill on the lathe, which had often previously aroused the amusement of fellow officers, had stood him in good stead in his experiments. And this was only the beginning. He already had improvements to gearing and propeller shapes in mind to increase speed and range.

A cab was waiting, ready booked, to carry him through the deserted, rain-lashed streets of Portsmouth and towards his small rented villa in Southsea. The prospect of hot food, a chapter or two of Trollope by the fireside and Florence's embraces afterwards had never seemed more attractive.

Just outside the dockyard gates the cab overtook a large figure, hunched against the rain as he strode forward. Dawlish recognised Egdean and signalled to the driver to pull over.

The seaman touched his cap. "Good evening, Sir."

"Where are you going," Dawlish asked.

"My church," Egdean said. "On Kingston Road, Sir, in Buckland"

"You're going to sing?" Dawlish knew of his convictions.

Egdean nodded. "Hymns, Sir." The rain was streaming over his face.

"It's too far to walk on a night like this," Dawlish said. "Get in."

"Thank you, Sir." The seaman climbed in.

As the horse trotted on there was an uneasy silence, broken only by Dawlish's observations about the weather and Egdean's awkward agreements. In Africa they had together survived duties too sensitive ever to speak of – had indeed supported each other more closely than brothers might have done – and yet the social gulf that separated officer and rating was still so wide that even respect and goodwill could do little to bridge it.

As Egdean was dropped off Dawlish said "I'll send the cab back for you. The driver will wait for you. He'll have been paid." He waved Egdean's embarrassed thanks aside. It was the least he could do.

Dawlish leant back as the cab turned towards Southsea and realised that he had never been happier. Life was good with Florence and his time – almost two years – as Deputy to the Senior Instructor at H.M.S. *Vernon*, the Royal Navy's Torpedo and Mine School had been one of achievement and satisfaction. Previous experience had rendered him uniquely suited to the position and his duties were not confined to courses and lecturing. *Vernon* was the centre of British torpedo development and his role was pivotal in turning the unreliable and capricious weapon of earlier years into a deadly instrument of war.

Florence, he knew, would be full of her doings today with Miss Agnes Weston in their efforts to convert an old public-house into a Sailor's Rest. Miss Weston, a cheerful and determined spinster who had adopted seaman's wellbeing ashore as her cause, had previously set up a similar establishment in Devonport. It provided cheap meals and beds for enlisted Navy personnel and had proved popular and successful. Florence's enthusiastic commitment to establishing a similar one in Portsmouth had earned her the praise of senior offices and the grudging admiration of some of their wives even if many more still pointedly avoided her. She had never disguised the fact that she had been a servant – nor had Dawlish either. By their marriage he had invited social rejection, and she had faced a succession of petty slights, but neither had regretted their decision.

The cab turned into Albert Grove and Dawlish was surprised to see a Hansom waiting outside his home, its driver sheltering inside, rain running in sheets off the cover on the horse's back. The passenger it had brought might perhaps be the building contractor coming to plead about his expenses, for Florence had brought the same meticulous energy to the public-house conversion as she once had to feeding refugees.

The door was opened, not by the housemaid, but by Florence herself. As always, he thrilled to see her, and tonight she looked lovelier than ever, her golden hair piled up elaborately and her restrained but flattering silk gown showing off her tall figure to perfection. Her bony features and large mouth might have been ugly had it not been for their mobility and for the sweetness of her unfailing smile – and for her habit in private of pulling humorous faces. She rubbed his cold cheeks between her hands and kissed him lightly. He was suddenly reminded of the icy roads of Thrace on which their bond had been forged during a nightmare flight ahead of a merciless enemy.

"You're frozen, Nick," she said, pulling off his coat. Her accent was slightly different now, more cultured, than when they had first met and he suspected that a part of her housekeeping money had been diverted to elocution lessons, though pride would never let her admit it.

"You've got a visitor," she said. "An oldish boy, but a real charmer."

"I've got to be careful about leaving you alone then, Florence!"

"He said you know him well, Nicholas. Topcliffe's his name."

Dawlish felt a surge of excitement – and fear. His contacts with Admiral Sir Richard Topcliffe had been few and formal over the last eighteen months, meetings at trials and demonstrations. Powerful and secretive, his position undefined, perhaps indefinable, Topcliffe had little to do with normal naval operations. Dawlish had carried out assignments for him before, most recently a brief but action-filled secondment to the Ottoman Navy. It had won him the *Vernon* posting, a plum one. If Topcliffe was here tonight the visit was neither casual nor purely social.

"Take me to him, Florence," Dawlish said.

She looked at him in surprise, recognising the terrible seriousness that had descended on him. She pressed his hand, then led him through into the parlour.

Topcliffe set down a glass of wine – Florence had been looking after him well – and rose from a deep leather armchair by the fire. He advanced with hand outstretched. His dark civilian attire and dignified mien made him look like a clergyman. It was hard to associate him with a certain event on a summer's night on London's Victoria Embankment ...

"So good to see you, Commander," he said. "You must forgive my unannounced visit, though indeed I have been splendidly entertained by Mrs. Dawlish in your absence."

"You're most welcome, Sir." Dawlish gestured for him to sit again.

"You will appreciate, Commander, that only a matter of the gravest importance would force me to intrude. I've no doubt that your wife has arranged a splendid dinner to warm you on such a miserable night and I hesitate to keep you from it." He looked to her with a smile, holding up a hand as she started to speak. "No Ma'am – I really can't stay to dine. I need no more than ten minutes with Commander Dawlish and then I'll be on my way."

Florence ushered both men to the fireside, recharged Topcliffe's glass and set another down by Dawlish's side. As she faced him, her back to the Admiral, she winked and pulled a mock-serious face, and then she left the room, once more the personification of dignity and discretion. Dawlish felt uncomfortable.

"A most impressive woman," Topcliffe said. "I know of her work for the Sailor's Rest, for seamen's families' welfare too. You're very lucky, Commander, very lucky."

"It is a pleasure to see you again, Sir," Dawlish knew that Topcliffe had not come merely to compliment him on his wife.

"And you, Commander, and you," Topcliffe sounded genial, "though it is, I believe, time to think of your next step on the ladder."

So this was it. As it had happened before. The bait. Dawlish felt his heart thumping and let Topcliffe continue.

"Your work at *Vernon* hasn't gone unnoticed and you've not been forgotten. How old are you, Commander? Almost thirty-four? I thought so. A little young for Captain in peacetime but it's been known – Fisher has managed it, for instance."

Twenty years before Dawlish had cowered with Jacky Fisher in a muddy ditch, waiting to join that murderous assault on the Taku forts, their first taste of action. And Fisher had instructed at *Vernon* before him and was now obviously headed for greatness. He'd had as little family influence as Dawlish. But Dawlish had Topcliffe for support – though only if he was ready, once again, to pay the price. Whatever it might be.

"I'd welcome service at sea again, Sir," he said. "This life here is pleasant but I'd relish my own command."

"There are opportunities aplenty in the offing." Topcliffe sipped his wine. "Every month sees another new ship gliding down the slipways. A command isn't unthinkable, Dawlish – plenty of other contenders of course, but you're being borne in mind."

"I'm glad to hear it, Sir" Dawlish was unsure whether to say more.

"But to change the subject," Topcliffe continued, "what's your opinion of Rendels, Commander?"

The reference to an obsolescent class of steam-gunboats came as a surprise and Dawlish could not guess where the question was leading. But on his answer, he knew, could depend his future career that, Topcliffe had just made plain. His mind raced as he sought to order his views on these unlovely vessels, named after their inventor.

"Useful craft inshore or in an estuary," he said. "Ideal for coast defence. Powerful, very powerful, even against an ironclad. One big weapon and a small crew. Rather too complex, I'd say – the hydraulics need damn good engineers to keep them in condition. Manoeuvrable - that's their substitute for armour. Cheap too. Not that I'd recommend building any more – the torpedo boat does the same job a lot more effectively."

"Bravo!" Topcliffe said, "You've summed them up well. We've more than two dozen Rendels in service and they're quite frankly a liability nowadays."

"They're to be stricken, Sir?"

"Not quite yet. But let's pose a tactical problem for a moment – purely academic, mark you. How would you rate a Rendel's chances against a turret monitor? An obsolete unit, I mean, American Civil War vintage?"

There was nothing academic about any question Topcliffe ever posed, Dawlish knew, though he could not imagine where the Royal Navy might be confronted with such a situation. And he knew

Rendels only by repute as easy berths that seldom left major bases. He pondered for twenty seconds before answering.

"Pretty evenly matched, I'd say. The monitor would have weight of shell, plus armour. The Rendel would throw even heavier metal but she'd lack the armour. But with a good helmsman she'd be nimble enough to keep in a blind-spot." He paused, thought further and then said: "With a good crew – a British crew – I'd put my money on the Rendel. But if I wanted a quick decision I'd forget the Rendel and rely on a torpedo boat."

Topcliffe shook his head. "No torpedoes," he said, smiling. "No room for fast manoeuvre – river room only. And, by the way, what do you know of Paraguay?"

Dawlish looked at him in surprise. "In the heart of South America, is it not?" he began. Topcliffe gave him no encouragement. "Tropical... landlocked... hasn't it got a major river system?"

Topcliffe smiled. "The Parana-Paraguay," he said. "It extends from the Plate Estuary to the deepest recesses of the continent."

"And involved in a major war with its neighbours a decade and more ago?" Dawlish was beginning to see a tenuous link to Topcliffe's earlier talk of monitors.

"The Tripartite War." said Topcliffe. "A hideous affair. Neither the American nor Franco-Prussian contests approached it in intensity or duration. For six years Paraguay withstood the Tripartite alliance of Brazil, Argentina and Uruguay. The dictator Lopez was a lunatic, little doubt of it, but he had method in his madness. He'd built up a powerful army and a modern river-fleet. His ships and his fortresses contested every mile the Tripartite ironclads advanced up the river system."

"Bloody, I understand, Sir."

"Slaughter, Dawlish, carnage pure and simple. When Lopez lost his warships canoe-loads of his troops launched themselves on the enemy vessels and all but overwhelmed them. When he lost control of the rivers he retreated into the Gran Chaco wilderness in the west. He held out there for two years more before the Brazilians ran him down and killed him in 1870."

The outlines Dawlish already knew. "What's hard to fathom, Sir," he said, "is how such a tyrant could evoke such devotion to the death."

Topcliffe shrugged. "Hardly surprising in Paraguay," he said. "It's got a unique history. Until a century ago the Jesuits ruled it like a private commonwealth. It was like a gigantic, benevolent beehive, with property communally owned, the fruits of labour shared and an effective militia to protect it from outsiders."

"An Eden?"

"A well-controlled one. And it couldn't last. The Jesuits were expelled and their missions – the Reducciones – were destroyed by the Spanish and Portuguese. And yet the Indians never forgot the Jesuits, or the way of life they represented. They retained some inkling that an earthly paradise, free from outside oppression, could be theirs. Lopez exploited that feeling. And so could any other charismatic leader again in the future."

"And would that be of concern to Britain?" Dawlish asked. There must be a link. Topcliffe had not sought him out to deliver a history lesson.

"We can talk of that again," said Topcliffe, smiling. Dawlish sensed that he was pleased to have aroused his curiosity. "I see an excellent encyclopaedia on the shelves behind you, Commander. I commend volume ONT to PEN to your attention this evening. Its perusal might prove of value when I introduce you to some friends of mine tomorrow."

"Here in Portsmouth, Sir?"

Topcliffe shook his head. "I understand that your launching trials ended today, Commander. They were going satisfactorily, I believe."

Dawlish nodded. The tests were shrouded in secrecy, but that made it all the more likely that Topcliffe would know of them.

"Then you'll have no problem in joining me tomorrow on an excursion to Sheerness Dockyard?" Topcliffe asked. "I'll be meeting some friends – indeed one was already asking after you."

"A friend, Sir?"

"Lord Kegworth certainly hasn't forgotten you – considers himself indebted to you in fact." He dropped his voice. "A friend worth having, Commander."

"I'd be most honoured to see his Lordship," Dawlish said. "And yes – I do believe I can spare the time. Do we travel together?"

"By the seven-thirteen to London. I'm lodging with a friend in Portsmouth tonight. I have the tickets. And by the way, mufti if you please. The business is private."

There was a gleam of satisfaction in Topcliffe's eye as he moved to the door. Dawlish helped him with his coat and ushered him under an umbrella to his cab.

Topcliffe leaned out and spoke before he tapped for the cabby to proceed. "Present my compliments to Mrs. Dawlish," he said, "A splendid lady. You were both lucky to meet."

The cab crunched over the gravel and into the wet darkness. Dawlish turned indoors, wondering what he had just been committed to.

4

It was eleven-thirty before they reached Sheerness in a chill downpour and were directed to a small graving dock in a remote corner of the dockyard. The main party was there ahead of them. Even at a distance Dawlish recognised Lord Kegworth's portly figure in the small group clustered under umbrellas by the dock's edge.

Kegworth shook his hand warmly. "It's too long since we've seen you, Dawlish," he said. "And Agatha sends her regards. She hasn't forgotten what you did for her – nor have I."

"She did as much for me, My Lord" Dawlish said. In the chaos of an army's collapse he had saved Kegworth's stout, myopic, clever daughter and her companion from death – or worse. They in turn had nursed him when fever and delirium had almost snatched him on the dreadful retreat that followed. One of them he admired and respected, the other he loved and married.

"Agatha's a remarkable girl." Kegworth spoke with bemused pride. "I'm damned if I can understand those X's and Y's and squiggles of hers but the Royal Society seem to think highly of those papers she keeps sending them. She's set on being the first woman Fellow, you know!"

Dawlish noticed that Kegworth had avoided congratulating him on his marriage. It was inconceivable that he might refer to the embarrassing fact that his father-in-law was His Lordship's head coachman and that his two brothers-in-law were employed about the stables. However genial Kegworth's tone there could be no weekend-invitation for Commander and Mrs. Dawlish.

Topcliffe drew Dawlish away to introduce him briefly to the other members of the party, all apparently civilians. Dawlish missed most of the names but Sir Herbert Mellish was well known for his industrial and financial interests and Don Plutarcho Murillo was hardly a name to be expected on a wet quayside on an English winter's day, even if he did look like a consumptive London clerk.

"If this is H.M.S. *Toad*," Kegworth said, gesturing towards the squat vessel in the dock, "then she's well named. An uglier ship I've never seen. I can see now why they're referred to as 'flatirons'."

Seen from above the Rendel had indeed got the proportions of a clothes-iron, her beam a fifth of her 75-foot length, her bows pointed and her stern rounded. The low forecastle sloped slightly aft to a curved breastwork that extended across the ship, a hinged port in its centre allowing her single gun to protrude through it when ready for action. The breastwork ran around the entire deck, higher than a man, but the superstructure was negligible. There was a low casing above the engine and boiler rooms, a conning tower, a tiny accommodation with an open steering platform mounted atop it and two thin funnels side by side. Her draught was shallow and she was flat-bottomed. Two huge screws, each with a large rudder abaft, were visible under the stern's flare.

The hull was streaked with red lead. Plating had been removed forward to allow repairs. A shear legs was rigged over the bow – something heavy needed lifting in or out – and a canvas shelter had been located under it, blocking the armament off from sight. Sounds of activity came from a group of workmen there.

Dawlish was roused from his private examination by a gentle touch on his elbow. It was Kegworth, questioning him.

"No, my Lord," he answered. "I've never served in one."

Topcliffe was explaining the Rendel's features to the others. "Not just twin screws," he was saying. "Twin engines, compounds, totally independent. They're the secret of her agility. If they're reversed against each other she can circle in her own length – all but spin around. Even with both engines full ahead she can turn in three times her length. That's why the gun can be aimed by lining up the entire boat on the target."

There was only the slightest hint of a foreign intonation when Murillo spoke. "But the gun," he said. "I don't see the gun."

"Nor will the enemy, until it's ready for action," said Topcliffe. "It's on a Moncrieff disappearing mount."

Murillo looked blank.

"You'd better explain, Topcliffe. We're not all sailors here." Sir Herbert's accent was flat, its origin indeterminate, not that of a born gentleman. There was a rawness about him, more than a hint of the ambitious tradesman made good.

"The gun lies down in the hull itself, below the waterline. That's its protection," Topcliffe said. "Hydraulic rams raise it into the firing position when it's needed. Once it's been fired it drops back into the hull again and another hydraulic ram – it's hidden right up in the bows – loads the next charge and shell through the muzzle."

"And the gun? How large?" Murillo's voice was devoid of any enthusiasm.

Topcliffe closed his eyes for a moment, concentrating, and then said: "Armstrong nine-inch. Two hundred and fifty-six pound shell. One hundred rounds stored. It's heavier than many line-battleships carry. Without the hydraulics it would be impossible to serve such a large weapon with a small crew."

And Dawlish was reminded of other weapons on disappearing mounts, and of the stomach-churning fear he had somehow masked as the merciless Russian twelve-inchers heaved themselves above their armoured breastwork, his own ship filling their sights as she forged towards them, her ram lost beneath an incoming wave, then rising again, the pointed horn lifting. …

"And the vessel is definitely up for disposal?" Sir Herbert's question drew Dawlish back to the present.

"Decidedly," Topcliffe said. "Most of the Rendels will be scrapped over the next few years. But the *Toad* will go first - she's an exception, doesn't belong to a class like the *Ants*, one of a kind. She was built for the Greeks, but they ran out of money before she was completed, and we took delivery instead."

"But she's in good condition?"

"Perfect, and scarcely five years old. But as Commander Dawlish will assure you we can much better defend our coasts and harbours with modern torpedo boats." Topcliffe looked pointedly at Kegworth. "A word in the right place and the *Toad* can be sold off immediately."

"And the price?" Sir Herbert asked.

"Modest," Topcliffe said. "Little more than scrap value."

"And a crew?"

"Don't underestimate our records system, Sir Herbert. There will be no problem in tracing discharged seamen with Rendel experience, or in providing leave of absence for serving hands who might be induced to volunteer."

"We'll get our death if we stay in this drizzle," Kegworth said. "We can continue the discussion over lunch at the Railway Hotel. The craft looks suitable to me anyway."

"The Consortium Board must decide that," said Murillo.

"My dear fellow, we are the Board," Kegworth said affably. "Now do let's hurry back to the warmth."

Dawlish assured the others that he would follow and then crossed over a gangplank to the *Toad*. He stepped carefully across the clutter of cordage, metal sections and tools typical of a vessel under overhaul and found his way under the tarpaulin in the bows. The bottle-shaped Armstrong muzzle-loader lay retracted in a large pit along the centreline. It was flanked by the two huge pistons and by the massive scissors arms that would raise it into the firing position. Workmen were fitting new brass feed-tubing to one of the pistons.

"Delicate work," Dawlish said to the foreman. "It must need a real craftsman's skill. I can see you need a fine eye for tolerances and dimensions to get it right."

"Indeed you do, Sir," he said, "though this blasted rain don't help none, what with the blessed tarpaulin crampin' us. But it's got to be a fast job, even if it's a big one."

"Extensive, is it?" said Dawlish.

"Total overhaul of the hydraulics, Sir. We finished reinstalling the rams yesterday – they've been in the machine shop for reboring and lapping. Tricky it was to drop them in. Now all the pipework's got to be replaced and she's had a new main pump as well. What with the engines havin' been rebuilt, and now this, she'll be like new again."

"And needed soon, you said?"

"Needed urgent, Sir, though God knows why. We've been workin' all hours."

Dawlish thanked him and moved aft. A companionway led to the engine and boiler rooms. They were immaculate, with every significant item of equipment either new or recently overhauled. He retraced his steps and followed the others to the hotel, deep in thought.

For a representative of an obsolete type, marked down for immediate disposal at little more than scrap value, somebody was spending a lot of money – Admiralty money – on the *Toad*.

*   *   *

"Don Plutarcho's proposition did not impress us when he first laid it before us a decade ago," said Lord Kegworth. "Had it not been for his vision – and his persistence – the Hyperion Consortium might have been still-born."

Lunch was over and they were sitting over coffee in a private dining room. A coal fire glowed agreeably, dispelling the chill seeping in from outside. There was a pleasant aroma of brandy and cigars.

Murillo shrugged dismissively. "A simple insight Gentlemen," he said. "Ten years ago my country was devastated and empty beyond European comprehension. The remaining population was exhausted and starving. Probably less than a quarter of a million – one sixth of the pre-war figure. A country of women – perhaps thirty thousand adult men left alive. We exiles who returned to form the new government even discussed legalising polygamy. Settled areas were reverting to wilderness. And yet the land was rich."

"The opportunity was unique," Mellish said. "Only investment and labour were needed."

"Easy to say with hindsight," Kegworth added. "It cost Don Plutarcho effort enough to convince us at the time."

"My family had lost everything." Murillo's voice was bitter. "Our estates in the east laid waste. Our river-steamers on the Buenos Aires route expropriated and sunk. Our trading posts looted. My father and brothers murdered by Lopez. My mother and my sister..." He stopped, then resumed in a voice devoid of emotion. "I escaped by virtue of my position at our London office – but I fear that by then the credit of the house of Murillo was only a memory in the City..."

"A memory, but not forgotten," Kegworth said. "I was on the board of one of the British companies that did business with the Murillos before the war. The memory did at least guarantee Don Plutarcho a hearing – not an enthusiastic one initially, I'm sorry to say – when he came to me with his tale of a three thousand square mile land grant on the San Joaquin River, in the North West of the Chaco Boreal Province. He said he only needed investment to turn it into a veritable Golconda. I introduced him to Sir Herbert – and that was the genesis of the Consortium."

"Half a dozen companies now, but the Hyperion Livestock, Tallow and Meat Packing Company Limited was the foundation." There was a hint of satisfaction in Mellish's voice. "Registered in London with myself as Chairman and Don Plutarcho as Managing Director. Until a few months ago Hyperion beef was being marketed at Smithfield."

"Quite an achievement, Sir." Dawlish was impressed.

"The cattle went downriver live on Hyperion barges to the Plate Estuary, were slaughtered there in Hyperion shambles and reached Britain chilled in Hyperion ships – we took a gamble on ammonia refrigeration from the start, and it paid off." Mellish's face was flushed with pride now, though from his pallor Dawlish guessed that he never came closer to the San Joaquin than the balance sheets. "The dividends were the talk of the City – and were nothing to what Hyperion will deliver once our canning plant is operating on the San Joaquin itself and the live transportation can be eliminated. That's why the current delay is so infuriating and so costly."

"Stock quality was the major concern initially." Kegworth's pride matched his fellow director's. "The local cattle could live on almost nothing but the meat was tough and stringy. A cross with my own Shorthorn stock proved very successful - we sent out a dozen bulls to start with and the breed's been refined since. Several of my tenants, cowmen and the like, were induced to settle on the Rio. The terms were attractive - several took their families. The settlement manager and the overseers were recruited in Britain and North America. Some skilled tradesmen for the workshops came from Sir Herbert's Birmingham factories."

"And so, Commander Dawlish, you come to sense the root of our problem - the labour supply," said Murillo. "The country was almost depopulated. Supervisors we could recruit outside Paraguay, but we needed labour - peons. Not just men to work with the cattle. Men to clear the ground for the settlement and build the accommodation and the jetties and the warehouses and the workshops. Men and women to plant and harvest the food to feed the others. We needed hundreds to start with and thousands more as time went on. As of six months ago the settlement comprised more than fifteen thousand souls, men women and children."

"Where did you find them?"

"My own estates in eastern Paraguay provided many, mainly Guaraní Indians - docile, obedient people. Others we shipped north from the Argentine – the inducement was attractive. But for the cattle we needed horsemen and we were thrown back on impressing the Guaikuru of the Chaco."

Murillo paused, as if uncertain if to continue on this topic. He looked towards Topcliffe and from the corner of his eye Dawlish saw the Admiral nod slightly. He recognised the signal that he himself could be trusted to hear more.

"A degree of... of coercion was necessary." Murillo said. "The Guaikuru are semi-nomadic and regular labour has never been to their taste. They are however excellent horsemen – ideal for our purposes. We offered them splendid inducements – but it was quite hopeless. They were gone in a few weeks. The government at Asunción was agreeable to our taking stronger measures but was too weak to provide the necessary forces. We had no option but to expand our own gendarmerie – La Guardia Hyperion, as we called it. We were lucky enough to secure the services of an American, a Colonel Culbertson. He developed it into a most potent force, recruiting foreigners as well as Paraguayans."

"I do believe that the discipline they imposed was most beneficial," Kegworth said. "I understand that the previous way of life of the Guaikuru was irregular and feckless, if not indeed downright immoral. It was replaced by useful employment for an adequate wage, accommodation in secure camps protected by the Guardia and acquaintance with the most modern agricultural and industrial methods. We laid the foundations for a modern economy in the centre of a wilderness."

"But there was widespread disaffection in the beginning," Murillo said. "Overseers murdered. Cattle driven off into the Chaco. Occasional minor rioting. A warehouse burned. Damage to steamboats. Colonel Culbertson was obliged to make significant examples of the perpetrators."

"Regrettable but essential," Mellish said. "And the workers themselves were the greatest beneficiaries once they realised the benefits of co-operation. By the mid-seventies Hyperion was in profit. The main settlement, Puerto Plutarcho, had tripled in size and we were obliged to order new steamers to cope with the growing trade. The Government at Asunción, with which Don Plutarcho maintained excellent relations, was happy with the increased revenues and most co-operative in supplying extra labour – convicts and the like. The Guardia was well capable of maintaining control."

"A veritable paradise in the wilderness." Kegworth refilled his glass. "A recreation in modern terms of the earlier Jesuit missions, the Reducciones, but free of the baleful influence of the Church of Rome."

"Which brings us to La Reducción Nueva," Topcliffe said.

"The serpent had entered Paradise." Kegworth sighed. "An alien influence – Heaven knows where it came from – was at work."

"There was little to warn us," Murillo said. "For months Culbertson's network of informants had been reporting the prophecies of someone called El Pobre – the Poor Man – about an approaching day of deliverance. It seemed unfocussed and harmless. I frankly disbelieved that El Pobre was a real person."

"You can't blame yourself, Don Plutarcho. None of us took it seriously." Kegworth shook his head, as if still disbelieving.

"We felt secure," Murillo continued. "The haphazard lawlessness of the early days was over. The peons were outwardly docile and respectful. The settlements had never been so productive. And then, on the night of June the Sixth, the entire San Joaquin exploded in revolt."

"A significant date," Topcliffe said quietly. "The anniversary of the decree abolishing the Jesuit missions in 1755."

"There was a concerted plan," Murillo said. "The Consortium land-grant extends eighty miles along the San Joaquin and there are eight sub-centres in addition to Puerto Plutarcho. The rising was simultaneous. Isolated Guardia troopers were butchered, barracks attacked, arms seized, overseers murdered..."

"Dreadful, dreadful," Kegworth said sadly. "Even the settlement manager – an Englishman, who had spent years in Brazil – was a victim. The unfortunate fellow was subjected to mutilation of a most indelicate nature. It seems they resented his somewhat free manner with the younger Indian women." He shook his head, still clearly upset. "Poor Greenough was from a good family too – a clergyman's son."

"And yet there was little destruction of property." Murillo, obviously no great admirer of the late Mr. Greenough, cut him off. "No burning, no cattle maimed or driven off. Warehouses and workshops left intact. The rebels appropriated, but they did not destroy. A steamer managed to escape downriver with several of the foreign overseers and their families. Culbertson was cut off but he managed to fight his way out and cross the Chaco south-eastwards to the main Paraguay River with the Guardia survivors. When the news reached me in Asunción I believed at first that it would be a matter of Culbertson returning with the support of Government troops and reasserting control."

"The next developments were the most alarming," Topcliffe said, "and they induced my old friend Kegworth to seek my advice – in a private capacity of course. The rebels seized two Hyperion steamers and followed downriver hard on the heels of the fugitives. They arrived without warning at the small settlement of Magdalena on the Paraguay River – an unimportant place in itself, but it had served as a base for Brazilian forces in the last stages of the Tripartite War."

Dawlish recognised the name – he had spent most of the previous evening poring over the map in the encyclopaedia, while simultaneously fending off Florence's curiosity.

"The present Paraguayan Government had a nominal garrison at Magdalena – a few men guarding a large store of obsolete artillery and munitions and other equipment left over from the war. An abandoned British-built monitor was tied up at the jetty – there had been vague plans to take it to Asunción and to refurbish it when funds permitted. Most of the garrison fled at the first shot, the remainder threw in their lot with the attackers and Magdalena was looted. When the rebel steamers headed back up the San Joaquin they took every movable piece of equipment with them. That included the artillery – fifteen Parrott twenty-pounders and a handful of smaller pieces – and enough small arms to equip several battalions, as well as all the munitions they could lay their hands on."

Topcliffe paused. Dawlish already guessed what was coming. "Worst of all they had the monitor in tow."

The pieces were falling in place.

"Asunción recognised that it was confronted with a major regional rebellion," Murillo said, "but it took a month before a punitive force could be equipped and organised. Two steamer-loads of regular

46

troops were despatched upriver while Culbertson drove up through the Chaco with a mounted column. The steamers got little further than the mouth of the San Joaquin before they were driven back – one steamer sunk, the other badly damaged."

"Impressive, very impressive," Topcliffe said.

"Somehow the rebels had got the monitor operational," Murillo continued. "I say 'somehow' – there's no doubt that the machine shops and slipway at Puerto Plutarcho were more than adequate for its repair, but there had to be some controlling influence. Somebody with professional knowledge, somebody with the ability to train a crew. And not just on water. Culbertson's column penetrated to the vicinity of Puerto Plutarcho before being repulsed. He ran into substantial defences – half-completed earthworks, trenches, redoubts. The place was being readied for a siege by land or water – once again the hand of a professional. Culbertson fell back on Magdalena and concentrated on strengthening it to stop any further advances downriver."

"And so the rebellion was consolidated." Topcliffe spoke with grudging respect. "The Republic of Paraguay has neither the finances nor the resources to crush it. At present the government commands but a single decrepit monitor, the *Montelindo*, a sister of the rebel unit. The San Joaquin settlements have become a virtual state – La Reducción Nueva. It's well organised, well defended, well led and self-sufficient. It's consciously modelled on the Jesuit missions – even their monitor is named the "*Torres*", apparently after a Jesuit who once organised the Guaraní militia."

"And El Pobre – was he a real person?" Dawlish was fascinated.

"There's little doubt of that now," Murillo said, "though we don't know who he is. He appears to command total loyalty from the rebels. He has convinced them that their salvation lies in La Reducción and that if they can defend it long enough it can establish its independence."

Kegworth shook his head. "I still wonder if some infernal Jesuit influence is at work."

47

"No, My Lord," Topcliffe said, "not the Jesuits, but a power still more sinister. In a continent where every second petty rebel with ambitions of dictatorship styles himself 'El Supremo' a leader who is content to be known as 'The Poor Man' is dangerous indeed".

He withdrew a folded paper from his inner pocket and smoothed it on the table. It was covered in bold hand-blocked letters.

"These handbills are passing southwards along the river," he said. "There's a lot of millennial nonsense but the final words can be strictly translated as *"Arise! You have nothing to lose but your chains!"* – words that make me believe that these simple Indians have been exposed to Socialist thinking of the most malign nature."

"Socialists! We've invested too much on the San Joaquin to let a gang of Jacobins rob us of it!" Mellish's plebeian vowels were more noticeable as he grew indignant.

"Just imagine, Dawlish," Kegworth's tone was grave, "that our five shilling shares stood at fourteen and sevenpence halfpenny before the news reached London? And today they're trading at fippence three farthings!"

"They'll come back, My Lord, they'll come back!" Mellish said with passion.

"The Consortium has raised the finance – against the expectation of future profits, mark you – to restore order," Murillo said. "The Asunción government is cooperating to the full with troops and its remaining monitor – but the funds are being supplied by us."

"But the government's monitor alone will decide nothing," said Topcliffe. "On current showing it will be outfought by the Reducción's unit. That's why the Consortium will be purchasing the *Toad* from the Admiralty. She'll be at the heart of the riverine flotilla that will carry the forces up the San Joaquin for the reconquest of the territory. You, my dear Dawlish, as you probably have guessed, are being offered the command of the naval component."

Dawlish looked at him in amazement. "But this is a private matter," he said. "No British interest..."

"Ah, but there you're wrong Commander," Topcliffe cut him short. "Britannia's reach is not just political or military alone. What higher interest can there be than consolidation of Britain's commercial interests?"

"A generous cash gratuity also," Mellish said. Then, perhaps fearing some hesitation, he added "And five-thousand shares."

Kegworth laughed. "So you're still buying up shares, Mellish?"

Topcliffe ignored him. "And as to formalities, Dawlish – the necessary leave of absence is easily arranged. You'll have the chance to expand your experience in a way given to few officers by fighting your own private war – a squalid little war, admittedly – but your own nonetheless."

Dawlish looked around the table. At Kegworth beaming and nodding kindly, encouraging acceptance. At Mellish, sizing him up as he would an investment, and obviously ready to chance his luck on him. At Murillo, remote and cerebral, plotting cold vengeance and profit on the San Joaquin. At Topcliffe, the cold glint in his eye telling what was the price of promotion.

There was no choice – not if he wanted advancement. He had known the satisfaction – no, the joy – of his own command. But when he had paced his own bridge then, his faced numbed by Black Sea spray, the deck beneath his feet had been that of an Ottoman ironclad. But the next time that deck should be British, the crew his countryman, his rank the goal of twenty years of dedication.. He had made up his mind the night before even before he knew the details.

"I'll do it, Gentlemen" he said. "I'll take the job."

And that was how he came to be floundering in a muddy river three months later, surrounded by the cries of drowning men.

5

Dawlish and Egdean struggled on to the southern shore a half-mile above the point at which the lake funnelled into the Gullet. They left behind the debris, the bobbing heads and the cries of despair and drifted on their backs towards the bank, cradled by the tepid water.

Mud clutched and sucked at Dawlish's knees as he staggered through the low reeds by the water's edge. He gained dry ground before throwing himself down to regain his breath. He looked back along the shore. Small groups of exhausted survivors were struggling to safety.

"Gather them," he said to Egdean. "Then get them back downstream. I'll get boats sent up to rescue anybody still alive out there."

"Aye, aye, Sir." Egdean lurched to his feet and set off at the best pace he could manage.

Dawlish turned from the devastation on the lake and glanced towards the Gullet. The *Montelindo's* bows were jammed solidly against the northern shore. Her hull was heeling over under the force of the current, men swarming over it in obvious confusion. He needed to be there.

The intervening ground was open but rough. Coarse grass and thorny scrub lacerated his feet and calves as he hobbled along, regretting that he had cast off his shoes in the water. He avoided the swampy shoreline, aiming to cut off the bulge of land that lay between him and the point of the *Montelindo's* discomfort. A low ridge lay ahead and he limped towards it, ignoring the agony that increased with every step.

What he saw from the crest was far worse than he had feared. The *Montelindo* lay diagonally across the river, effectively blocking it, the current forcing the bows and stern ever more firmly against the bank and sandbar that held them. Fifty yards below her the sidewheeler *Coimbra* had seemingly piled into the southern shore and was firmly lodged there, a plume of white steam shooting from a vent pipe amidships and her whistle screaming. The troops she carried were milling on the bank with no obvious indication of order or purpose. Small figures, officers perhaps, scurried between them like frightened ants. Occasional single shots rang out, stopping all movement briefly until chaos again asserted itself. The conscripts were failing their first test. The *Coimbra's* two towed barges, urged by the current, were whipping lazily from her stern in midstream. It could not be too long before the tow cables broke and launched them downstream to threaten Murillo's vessel, the *Tacuari*, which had moored to the southern bank a hundred yards beyond and which seemed to be landing her troops in good order. The *Toad* was holding station in midstream a little beyond and the remainder of the flotilla had drawn haphazardly in to the banks further down. Two boats had reached the *Montelindo* and three more were being rowed painfully towards it, against the current, from the *Tacuari* and the *Toad*.

Too late, Dawlish heard a movement behind him. As he turned there was a rushing of feet and he found himself flung to the ground by a blow between the shoulder blades. Stunned, he was just beginning to realise that somebody was kneeling on his back when his hair was grabbed and his head jerked back violently. Something unmistakably metallic and sharp brushed against his throat. Terror surged through him and he had to force himself to breathe. His head was pulled further back and a scuffed and dusty pair of boots, tarnished spurs and stained leggings moved into his view.

The unknown legs bent, one knee touched the ground and now Dawlish saw the pockmarked face and small black eyes of Capitan Obregón, one of Culbertson's troop commanders.

"No es un peon de la Reducción," he said with a sneer that told that he had known so all along. "Es el comandante Inglés." He did not signal to Dawlish's captor to release him.

Dawlish tried to speak but could only croak. Shame and anger coursed through him.

"You see now that it is not just La Guardia that flee before El Pobre, Comandante." Obregón spoke in slow, careful Spanish so Dawlish could not but understand. "Even the officers of Her Majesty Victoria must escape him like drowning rats".

He looked away, spat deliberately, then nodded to the man holding Dawlish to release him.

Dawlish scrambled to his feet with as much dignity as he could manage and found himself surrounded by a half-dozen of Culbertson's troopers. He stood before them wet and ragged, his impotence mocked by their bandoliers and carbines and air of ruthless indifference.

"The Colonel sent us to search for you," Obregón said. "With Señor Murillo he waits for you on the *Tacuari.*" There was a hint of a sneer around his thin lips. "They will welcome the advice of such a distinguished naval officer now that the Rio San Joac is blocked."

Obregón turned and strode down the ridge towards the Gullet. Dawlish stumbled behind him, flanked by the other troopers, his humiliation compounded by the obvious efficiency of Culbertson's response. He had already landed his men on foot from the *Tacuari* and had thrown them in two screens along the shorelines. Dawlish and his escort encountered the southern group advancing forward through the scrub in open skirmishing order. They moved cautiously from cover to cover, carbines at the ready, silent and alert, their quiet advance in stark contrast to the scenes of confusion among the conscripts.

Obregón and his men left Dawlish a hundred yards from the *Montelindo*, turning from him without a word and padding back into the scrub. He limped towards the hillock above the narrows from where Murillo, Culbertson and Tinsley were surveying the blockage. None of them moved towards him, though Tinsley looked nervously at the others, uncertain of how to comport himself. Despite the heat and dust Murillo's white suit was spotless, his necktie perfectly knotted and his spectacles gleaming. It was the sweating Culbertson who greeted Dawlish.

"It do smart, don't it?" he drawled, with a wink. "A bunch o' peons and illiterates and some old ironmongery and the old story of watches not posted. And then, Sir, lo and behold, we've got dozens o' poor souls splutterin' their last and meetin' their maker in the middle of the San Joac. I know the feelin' Commander Nick, I surely do. Them Reducción boys are a sight cuter than they look – assumin' you even spot 'em in the first place."

Murillo regarded Dawlish's bedraggled form without a flicker of sympathy. "You have lost the *Humaita* and the *Velasco*, Mr. Dawlish," he said quietly, emphasising his civilian title. "You have allowed the expedition to be surprised and its progress interrupted."

Dawlish fought down the urge to explain like a schoolboy, knowing that the next thirty seconds would determine whether he had any future role in the venture. His position was indefensible – he had already accepted that himself – but he forced himself to speak calmly, fearing even so that his exhaustion and disappointment would come quavering through.

"The responsibility is mine, Sir," he said. "I cannot shirk it. It gives me no satisfaction to lose two ships and see men die."

"Indeed, Mr. Dawlish. And the expedition?"

"Recriminations should wait, Sir. The need now is to rescue the survivors and to dislodge the *Montelindo*. It's imperative that we get her and the *Toad* into the lake as quickly as possible. That is what I will now set about doing."

"You assume too easily that you still have command of the riverine forces, Mr. Dawlish," Murillo said. "Why should you retain your position after this debacle?"

Dawlish moved closer and looked him straight in his weak, lens-magnified eyes, conscious of Culbertson sniggering to his right and Tinsley glancing away in embarrassment.

"Because I'm still the most competent naval officer between here and Buenos Aires." He infused more confidence into his voice than he felt. "And because your next option, Lieutenant Holmes of the *Toad*, excellent though he is, has never commanded anything larger than a single third-class gunboat, and your next choice again, Calles of the *Montelindo*, is a drunken incompetent who hasn't seen action since the Tripartite War. I'm the best you have available, Señor Murillo, and if you think otherwise I'll be happy to convey your views to the Consortium Board."

The silence that followed was endless. Murillo's gaze did not waver and his voice was devoid of emotion when he finally spoke. "Proceed as you propose, Mr. Dawlish," he said. "You retain the riverine command for now. Report progress at sundown."

He turned and walked away, flanked by two troopers.

Tinsley bustled forward. "A bad business, Dawlish'" he said, "Very bad indeed – but Don Plutarcho took it very well in the circumstances. Very well indeed, very generously, even magnanimously, I might say."

His brow was furrowed with concern, his cadaverous features set in grim disapproval. "A great respecter of authority, but a damn fine gunner," Topcliffe had warned Dawlish, "when he doesn't see ten sides to even the simplest problem, that is. But he'll be wanted if you're ever to see El Pobre off the premises."

"You'll be needing clothing, Commander," Tinsley said, as if announcing a revelation, "and boots too I fear, and your feet will need some attention if those scratches are not to mortify. I've no doubt they can fit you out on the *Toad*."

"Thank you, Major. It's good to have the sympathy of a fellow Englishman." Dawlish's tone of irony went unnoticed.

"I must return now to the *Tacuari*. General Aquino is establishing a defensive perimeter and I must see to its progress". Tinsley made to leave, then paused. "I'm sorry about this, Dawlish," his tone was solemn. "But I trust you'll be thankful to the Almighty for your deliverance."

"You'll oblige me, Tinsley, if you'll locate a battery on the ridge," Dawlish said. "Until we can get the flotilla past the narrows it would be better than nothing for discouraging any further attack from upstream."

"If General Aquino approves, Commander, if he approves. I'll put it to him. The line of command must be observed, you know." And then Tinsley departed.

Dawlish ignored Culbertson's half-mocking offer of a cigar and hobbled painfully down to the *Montelindo*. The monitor's stern was grounded on a shallow sandbar ten yards from the nearer shoreline and the bows had burrowed into the overhanging vegetation on the opposite bank. The hull shuddered and heaved under the force of the current, its deck heeled-over and its flank lifted on the upstream side to reveal the green-slimed curve of the bilge.

"We're all of us glad to see you've come through, Sir," said a pleasant English voice.

It was Purdon, the *Toad's* first officer. He was Dawlish's own choice, a slight, blond Sub-Lieutenant on leave of absence from the *Lightning*.

"The *Toad* is unharmed?"

"Fighting fit, Sir. Lieutenant Holmes sent me with a dozen men to check the situation here. The old *Montelindo's* well jammed, but with a spring to this bank and the *Toad* to push from just abaft the bow and we'll have her freed in a trice, Sir – if we can get her crew to work, that is. A quarter of them jumped overboard and I doubt if many made it. The current is truly fierce."

"How many boats here? Five? That's good." Dawlish's mind was racing. "You'll be so kind as to take four up into the lake – it won't be easy getting them past here, but you'll manage. Recover whoever you can from the water – I doubt if there'll be many. Leave the gig to me – I'll check the position on the *Montelindo* and then cross to the *Toad*. Signal to her to come upriver and take station just below here. Without her we'll never clear this mess."

The gig carried Dawlish across to the grounded monitor and the coxswain, a British seaman from the *Toad*, took off his own canvas shoes and insisted that he have them. The comfort they afforded his lacerated feet was minimal but they made him look marginally less like a vagrant when he stepped on to the *Montelindo's* canted deck.

Confusion reigned there. Not only had many of the crew abandoned ship but Calles, the captain, had ordered the boiler to be blown down and the furnace damped to avoid explosion should the vessel come again under fire. Clearly shaken, almost to the point of hysteria, he stammered his assent to Dawlish's order to get the fires rekindled and steam raised once more. It would take at least six hours.

The first concern was to clear the channel. This would necessitate dragging the *Montelindo's* bows free from the northern bank and into midstream, then freeing her stern from the sand bar. Dawlish explained his plan quickly to Calles, who calmed visibly once he found that someone was ready to do his thinking for him. Together they ascertained that a sufficiently large cable and adequate blocks were available for fashioning a spring. Made fast to a strong-point on the foredeck, this should suffice to drag the bow free. One of the *Montelindo's* two boats had disappeared downriver but the other was still lashed to its mountings. Dawlish directed that it be launched and used to run the cable from the bows to a point diagonally upstream on the southern bank, where a large tree offered an anchorage point. With the *Toad* pushing from downstream to counter the current, and the spring taken under tension, it should be possible to free the bows and swing them upstream. The *Toad's* efforts, supplemented by the *Montelindo's* own power, should then suffice to get her free and into the open waters beyond the Gullet.

Satisfied at last that Calles was getting his remaining crew to work under some semblance of discipline, Dawlish again boarded the gig and had himself taken downstream to the *Toad*, which by now had edged past the intervening vessels and was hovering just below the *Montelindo*.

The *Toad's* holystoned decks and gleaming brasswork presented a welcome contrast to the chaos upstream. As he stepped through the lowered shield in the armoured breastwork and acknowledged Holmes' welcome, Dawlish saw with satisfaction that the Armstrong nine-inch had been raised to the firing position and that its crew were at action stations. The engines panted softly, driving the twin screws at minimum revolutions and holding the Rendel's ponderous bulk stationary against the current. Holmes took him immediately to his tiny cabin and within minutes he had not only pulled on dry but ill-fitting clothes but had explained all that would be required of the *Toad* once the *Montelindo* had run its spring and raised steam. Until then the gunboat should drop downstream and moor alongside the *Tacuari*. Darkness was now little over three hours away and it was unlikely that the Gullet could be cleared before morning.

The next hours found Dawlish regretting that he had not recruited another half-dozen junior British officers, or even experienced seamen, in addition to the *Toad's* complement. The task of sorting out the chaos into which the flotilla had fallen required only determination, initiative and the most rudimentary organisational skills, yet these qualities were all too lacking in the mongrel crews that manned the ill-assorted collection of vessels. The officers of the impressed civilian craft were generally amenable, if incompetent, but those of the government vessels were sullen and resentful, their enmity almost palpable. The burden of organisation fell therefore on the few men who could be spared from the *Toad's* complement. There was one boon however. Egdean arrived back with a knot of survivors, who already appeared unquestioning of his authority and won over by his gruff kindness. The troops among them returned to Aquino's force but the crewmen of the sunken steamers were sent with Egdean, after a hurried meal, to assist with the freeing of the *Montelindo*.

By nightfall a mixture of cajolery, suggestion and outright threats had ensured restoration of some degree of order. The paddlers and their barges were anchored in midstream to discourage desertion by their now-terrified conscript loads, their fears increased by the debris, some draped with corpses, that drifted down from the lake. Individual exhausted and terrified survivors from the lost vessels, who had somehow reached the shore, came straggling in. Purdon's boats returned from the lake, laden with another three dozen. He was then set to supervising the running of the spring.

"It's done, Sir," Purdon reported to Dawlish just before eight o'clock. He had achieved more in three hours than Calles and his crew had managed in the whole afternoon. But though its fires had been relit the *Montelindo* had raised insufficient steam pressure. Efforts to dislodge her must await first light.

Dawlish found himself friendless when he arrived at the *Tacuari* for the evening's council. Tinsley ventured a few conciliatory remarks but fell into embarrassed silence in the teeth of Murillo's icy politeness and Culbertson's hearty sarcasm.

Murillo adjusted his spectacles, opened his ledger and called the meeting to order. "You may report our losses, Mr. Dawlish," he said. "Be as exact as possible."

It was a painful summary: two paddlers, the *Humaita* and *Velasco*; the three-pounders and Gatlings they carried; nineteen crew, including one experienced river pilot; almost forty regulars and more than twice that number of rifles, as well as assorted munitions and stores. Dawlish omitted the loss of his own reputation.

"And the valuation, Mr. Dawlish? The Board will need a full valuation."

Dawlish felt his temper rising, knew he must control it. But still he said "We've more urgent concerns Don Plutarcho, we've got to …"

Murillo cut him off. "Urgent concerns indeed. And all of them thanks to your good self, Mr. Dawlish."

Anger and humiliation seethed through him, but somehow Dawlish kept silent and listened as Culbertson reported that his troopers had established pickets a half-mile upstream on either bank. Their horses had not been landed and he was unwilling to push them out further on foot. Tinsley had established a pair of Parrott ten-pounders on the ridge just south of the lake's exit, but not the full battery that Dawlish had suggested. Even this much had proved difficult since Aquino's regulars found it beneath their dignity to clear a path or throw up earthworks with any degree of enthusiasm and the conscripts sent to assist them, frightened and confused by events, had proved even more useless, despite the usual resort to flogging.

Murillo heard them out, then turned again to Dawlish. "How soon will the river be cleared?"

"By midday at the latest." It might even be sooner. And then the advance could resume, slow and infinitely more cautious than before, with the *Montelindo* now in the van.

"Midday at the latest, Mr. Dawlish, and noted," Murillo said, writing in the ledger.

Dawlish retired to sleep on the *Toad*, vainly trying to shut out the memory of the day's failure and of his own misjudgement of the enemy. He had left Portsmouth, left Florence, left the comfort and delight of the home they had made together – the only one he could call truly his own since boyhood – for this humbling. As sleep came he felt something growing within him demanded a settling of accounts. El Pobre was only a name to him but the commander of that monitor was an almost palpable presence whose intelligence and skill had shamed him.

And only that man's elimination could wipe away the stain of this day's failure.

6

The operation to free the *Montelindo* started at dawn. Her boilers had raised steam and the *Toad*, her vertical stem padded by a hastily woven rope fender, was lodged against a point just short of the monitor's bows and pushing steadily. The cable-spring was secured by a block and tackle to the mooring bits in the monitor's bows and ran diagonally across the river to the massive tree opposite.

Murillo and his staff had gathered to watch from the slope to the south as the climbing sun dispersed the remnants of mist over the river. Dawlish stood a little apart and saw with satisfaction the first shudder that ran through the *Montelindo's* hull as the *Toad's* 1200 horsepower dislodged the bow from the soft riverbank. The Rendel's twin screws lashed the waters astern to froth as she strained to hold the monitor against the current while the sudden slack was taken up on the spring and the gain was held. The squat gunboat, slowly pushing her own bulk, and the monitor's, against the flow, seemed almost to burrow into the *Montelindo's* flank.

Slowly, ever so slowly, the *Montelindo's* bow arced out from the northern bank and a clear channel began to open. It would now be only a matter of time, of slow tensioning of the spring under Purdon's direction, and of judicious manoeuvring by the *Toad*, until the monitor would be lined up with the current and her own screw could be brought into play to free her completely and take her upstream. Within the hour the *Montelindo* would be in the lake to cover the expedition's advance.

It was then that the bombardment commenced.

The howitzer's report, a sharp crack that reverberated across the forest and surged across the river, came seconds before Dawlish heard the scream of its plunging shell. There was no time for thought – instinct told him that it would strike close, very close, and he flung himself down, fingers clutching at the earth. Almost instantly the ground heaved beneath him. A searing gale blasted across his back and needles of agony shot through his ears. He lay concussed for a moment as earth and pebbles showered on and around him, then staggered to his feet, remotely conscious that he was unharmed. He stumbled past something red and torn, unrecognisable as the Paraguayan officer who had stood there a moment before, and past the reeking crater that the shell had torn in the slope. Beyond it he saw a tattered Culbertson supporting Murillo, whose blackened face was disfigured with crimson, while Tinsley, shaken but seemingly uninjured, was rising unsteadily behind.

"Get back quickly!" Dawlish yelled. "Take cover!"

He dragged Tinsley to his feet, pulled his left arm across his shoulder and started to drag him down the slope. There was a small ravine ahead, the course of a dried rivulet scarcely five feet deep, but it offered some protection and he made for it. Culbertson followed with Murillo and they had just blundered into its cover as the next explosions sent tremors through the ground beneath. Two shells fell in quick succession, closer to the river this time, one almost in it, and throwing up fountains of soil and gravel.

"At least two weapons," Tinsley gasped, struggling to regain his breath as twenty years of artillery experience asserted themselves. "Reports too close together for one. Howitzers – probably twelve-pounders. Range – I'd say under three thousand yards. Indirect fire – from somewhere to the north east – over there, beyond that ridge."

There was nothing to be seen – he was pointing to the relatively open scrub and thorn-covered ridge that rose above the lake's northern shore beyond the narrows. It seemed innocuous and yet, somewhere behind it, sweating howitzer crews must even now be ramming and sighting, readying for the next salvo.

"They're a-watchin' us and a-callin' the range from the ridge, signalling back to the guns in the valley behind," Culbertson said, moving crouched along the gully towards them with surprising agility. Obregón followed. Murillo had been left behind to nurse a gash on his forehead, a Paraguayan officer attending him. "Me and Aquino, our boys are goin' to have to flush them out on foot. Major Tinsley Sir, I'll be obliged for some covering fire from them Parrotts o' yours up there ... Heads down!"

The commingled scream of the next shells plunging towards the river was lost in the roar of their explosions. One threw up a plume of mud and stones from the nearer bank while the other fell just short of the *Montelindo's* bows, showering Purdon and the group labouring there with spray. The monitor heaved as a wave rolled back from the point of impact and the spring jerked and tautened before parting with a sharp crack that was audible on the ridge above. The freed cable whipped back towards the bows, a writhing three-inch lash, and scythed across the foredeck, sweeping Purdon and his crew into the waters downstream. The *Toad* was still pushing but her efforts could not match the current that now caught the *Montelindo's* bows and swung them round to crunch again into the northern bank. The Rio San Joaquin was once more blocked.

"I'm withdrawing the *Toad*," Dawlish yelled to Culbertson. "Her decks can't take plunging fire! The *Montelindo* will just have to sit tight until you clear the ridge!"

"I'll trouble you to shift my boys across, Commander Nick," Culbertson suddenly seemed ten years younger, enlivened by danger. "A troop will do, and two companies of conscripts to draw the fire ahead of them. I'll have 'em mustered a mile below here in thirty minutes".

He's enjoying this, Dawlish thought and he said "You'll have the boats, Colonel."

Culbertson turned to Tinsley. "Lay whatever fire you can on that there ridge, Major, just enough to keep their heads down, wherever they may be. You see that there dead tree, half-way up the slope? Save your shrapnel until my boys pass it, then lay it down on the crest. An' you see that line of scrub, further up? You cease firing when they're passing it and they'll do the rest."

He heaved himself to his feet, signalled Obregón to follow with Murillo, and broke into a shambling run down the slope.

Dawlish also left cover, racing towards the cluster of open boats at the riverbank. He reached them just as the next salvo crashed down, this time mercifully short, throwing up harmless plumes in the river. He found chaos by the water's edge, with all who had not fled in panic cowering under any available cover. It took precious minutes and the threat of his pistol to muster a crew to take him the necessary forty yards across to the *Toad*, which was still straining hopelessly to shift the *Montelindo*. He stepped on board the gunboat to be confronted by Purdon's bruised form slumped exhausted behind the bulwark, his shirt shredded and his chest and midriff livid from the blow dealt by the flailing cable. Purdon was surrounded by a groaning cluster of lacerated men also plucked from the river. He struggled to his feet as he saw Dawlish.

"I'm game, Commander." His face was taut with pain and his teeth were gritted. "Nothing's broken."

The next ten minutes saw all but the most essential crew stripped from the *Montelindo*, leaving only her commander, Calles, and sufficient men to operate the turret and its weapons should the enemy monitor reappear. The unseen enemy kept up the shelling, a salvo every two minutes, the vessels in the narrows clearly their target. Most projectiles burst on the banks or in the river, but one exploded spectacularly on the *Montelindo's* armoured turret. It did little more than scorch the metal and concuss the crew within but it sent a hail of splinters clattering against the *Toad's* breastwork as she dropped away slowly from the monitor. She drifted downstream with the current for fifty yards before one screw on full ahead and the other on full astern swung her on her axis and pointed her downriver. The Gullet fell quickly astern and Dawlish, looking aft from the steering platform, saw that no more shells were falling. Whoever was directing the fire from up there on the ridge knew better than to waste munitions on the *Montelindo's* armour and was content that its grounded bulk should block all passage.

The day had started badly, but it got worse.

Culbertson's troopers landed on the northern bank and within ten minutes moved up to the limits of the existing picket line. But it took almost three hours before two reluctant and terrified conscript companies were issued with ammunition, herded into boats and ferried across from their barges. And all the time the shells screamed down, individually now, and at irregular intervals, throwing up fountains from the river and blasting craters in the banks, causing negligible casualties but bringing activity around the *Montelindo* to a halt.

With the *Toad* moored safely downstream her commander, Holmes, supervised the transfer of troops while Dawlish saw to it that the unarmoured steamers and their barges were moved further downriver. The Gullet appeared to be at the limit of the howitzers' range but he shuddered to think of the havoc they could wreak on the scantily protected transports should their unseen firing locations be shifted closer. Purdon, bruised but mobile, accompanied Dawlish, scribbling down his orders and handing them to relays of messengers, for the complexity of the operations exceeded the simple flag-signalling system's capacity.

Tinsley's two ten-pounders on the southern ridge were obviously out of the howitzers' range, for they were never targeted by them. Both weapons opened fire across the river in mid-morning, their fused shells falling along the crest of the ridge on the opposite bank. There was no sign of life among the scrub and after the range was registered they fell silent. But now a more vulnerable target was presenting itself for the enemy.

Tinsley had repeatedly signalled for further munitions – without them he could manage only a half-dozen salvos. Aquino responded by driving a ragged snake of conscripts up the slope from the river, dragging shells, powder and the battery's two remaining weapons. There was no path and the manhandling through the thorn that littered the fissured incline was slowed yet further by the heat. The first munitions had however all but reached Tinsley's guns, and the other two ten-pounders were half-way up the ridge, when three enemy two-round salvos, and three only, slammed progress to a halt. The shells plunged down around the straggling column, none scoring a direct hit, but flinging up columns of dirt and thorn scrub. Injuries were minimal but the noise alone – the screams of the plunging missiles and the crashes of their impacts – was enough to panic the terrified conscripts into headlong flight. They streamed back down the slope, leaving it strewn with discarded supplies and two forlorn artillery pieces.

"Mighty impressive canoneering," Culbertson remarked to Dawlish. "They've one damned fine observer up there on the ridge somewhere an' callin' the shots. Beats me though how he's correctin' the fall so mighty quick – too fast for runners. Pretty smart for a bunch o' peons, ain't it?"

Dawlish nodded and with sick apprehension watched the attack now being prepared on the northern bank. He was standing with Culbertson on the opposite slope above the river, a mile below the Gullet, and the position afforded a wide panorama of the disaster about to unfold.

Led by Obregón, the Guardia troopers advanced up the slope and beyond the existing picket line in open order, moving cautiously from cover to cover. They halted some three hundred yards beyond the narrows, fading quickly into invisibility among the scrub. The two conscript companies followed, their ranks open to start with, but bunching together as they progressed. By the time they passed through the Guardia line they were concentrated into half-a-dozen conspicuous clusters, partly obscured by clouds of dust. They moved haltingly, came several times to a complete stop, then lurched forward again as the sounds of shouting, and once of a single pistol shot, signalled the success of Aquino's officers in persuading them to press on. In this manner they passed the line of Obregón's troopers and on into the thinning scrub beyond, their pace ever more hesitant.

"It's about time for Tinsley's shrapnel," Culbertson said.

The wavering clusters of conscripts were drawing level now with the dead tree — the agreed marker. As they did so a twin report announced Tinsley's ten-pounders opening simultaneously from across the river. He had ranged them well — that Dawlish had to admit — for their fire came crashing down close to the crest, orange flashes blasting out dozens of small iron balls through the surrounding scrub. There was still no sign of an enemy but the conscripts halted and a few began to run back down the slope, only to be driven back up it again as they reached Obregón's positions. Somehow the reluctant groups of uniformed peons were again herded towards the crest as Tinsley dropped two more rounds on it. The Guardia troopers were on their feet now, moving behind the conscripts' two open ranks like beaters at a grouse shoot.

The crash of Tinsley's next salvo falling on the crest drowned out the sudden sharp ripple of rifle fire from the brush below it. It tore jagged rents in the first rank of the advancing conscripts. From a hundred or more unseen points on the fissured and thorn-shrouded slope the Reducción's hidden troops poured a vicious and continuous fire into the half-trained wretches advancing towards them.

There was no instant flight. Many attackers stopped as if paralysed, bewildered by the hail that hurled down comrades to either side. Others blundered forward, only to halt or throw themselves down after a few yards. There was firing from behind them now, though less intense, as Obregón's troopers moved cautiously forward. They came level with the aftermost ranks, which had ground to a total stop, and the Guardia officers made examples of the waverers. These ranks lurched into motion again, crouched and terrified as they turned and again moved on reluctantly up into the bullet-torn scrub.

The firing continued and now there was little to be seen of the leading ranks – those still unwounded had flung themselves to the ground and those who came behind were doing likewise as soon as they entered the zone of fire. More and more of them crowded into this ragged strip of hazard as the Guardia troopers drove them forward mercilessly. A few fired wildly up the slope at their unseen tormentors, their unaimed shots as ineffectual as the four salvos that Tinsley's ten-pounders laid down on the ridge's crest before their supplies ran out.

The panic began at no single point – it was more a simultaneous general stampede, as if every terrified conscript still capable of movement had decided to turn and run for his life. Lashed by the fire of the Reducción's hidden riflemen above them, and even on their flanks, they blundered back through the scrub, weapons abandoned, some few dragging wounded comrades. They rolled in a wave against the line of Guardia troopers that briefly held firm and dropped their leaders in a ragged volley before themselves losing cohesion and joining in the headlong rout. The fire from above lessened and died, leaving the slope littered with abandoned casualties. The first panting survivors were now streaming back past their original starting line.

Culbertson's face had paled and he could not disguise the tremor in his voice. "It's goin' to be a slow and bloody job takin' that slope – but we'll have it by nightfall," he said. "I'll be obliged for you to shift more men across, Commander Nick."

"You don't want to take the slope, Colonel," Dawlish said. "You want to destroy the howitzers."

"How, Goddamit?"

"Mortars – and Tinsley has them. They're still on board one of the barges downriver. They'll far outrange those howitzers."

"Outrange them?" Culbertson snarled. "Damn easy if we could see the Goddamn howitzers – but we can't."

"No," Dawlish said, "but I'll wager Professor Grinling can." He was already scribbling out the order that would bring the *Pilcomayo* upstream with its cargo of acid, scrap iron, goldbeater's skin and, he hoped, the key for reopening the Rio San Joaquin.

7

The basket creaked as Dawlish shifted his weight and directed his telescope north-eastwards, probing the valley beyond the ridge for any sign of the Reducción's howitzers. He marvelled at the vista presented – no ship's mast, however high, could provide such a vantage for observation. His single earlier experience of a balloon ascent had been six months earlier, at a fete on the Downs above Portsmouth. At half-a-crown for fifteen minutes he had shared a basket with Grinling, a frightened clergyman and a delighted Florence. The sight of the city and dockyard spread before him, and of the Solent stretching beyond, had been memorable enough for him to seek out Grinling again before he sailed for Buenos Aires and to recruit him for the expedition.

A ripple shivered through the goldbeater's skin of the canopy as the balloon rose higher in the sodden afternoon air, straining lazily at the cable still being paid out from the winch on the barge four hundred feet below.

"She won't carry us much higher, Commander." Grinling was a small, balding man of indeterminable age, with the air of a harried bookkeeper. His eyes bulged in his thin face and his Adam's apple bobbed nervously as he spoke. The hint of Cockney in his voice belied his title of Professor. "She's getting sluggish, Sir. She can't support much more cable."

"We're high enough."

Dawlish steadied his glass against a suspension rope. The ridge that had witnessed the previous day's bloody repulse was revealed from this height as a narrow, scrub-covered plateau devoid of any sign of life. Whatever forces or observers the Reducción's commanders had deployed there, or on the slopes below, had taken cover at the first sight of the balloon rising slowly above the river. The shallow valley beyond, which must surely shelter the howitzers, was a mile or more wide, and covered with lush vegetation, its canopy obscuring the ground even from an observer at the balloon's height. The howitzers had been silent since sunrise, for no target worthy of them had presented itself, but there could be no doubt that they nestled somewhere among the foliage of that innocuous green valley, waiting patiently for the next attempt to free the still-stranded *Montelindo*.

Dawlish lowered the telescope, took off the seaman's Sennet hat he was reduced to wearing and wiped away the salty perspiration that ran down and stung his eyes. The winch had stopped paying out and the balloon swayed gently against its tether. Far below, its barge was moored against the northern bank, a mile downriver from the Gullet, with the winch in the bows and the decks crowded with acid carboys, scrap iron and retorts. Iron and acid together produced hydrogen but generating enough to fill the balloon was a long and slow process. Close to it, squatting on a mattress of logs on level ground some fifty yards from the water's edge, was Tinsley's thirteen-inch mortar, one of the three carried by the flotilla, semi-antique trophies of Sevastopol that he had located in some forgotten corner of Woolwich Arsenal. Heavy and clumsy, though still serviceable, it had a trajectory high enough to clear the ridge and a range sufficient to dominate the entire valley beyond. It had been landed during the hours of darkness and was flanked now by pyramids of shells and powder charges. Its crew, Paraguayan regulars in grey uniforms who had benefited from a fortnight of Tinsley's drilling before departure from Asunción, were at their places. The gunner officer himself paced nervously back and forth, waiting for the first message from above.

*   *   *

It had taken three rancorous hours at the previous afternoon's conference in the *Tacuari's* hot and airless saloon to gain support for this approach. A full hour was wasted in recrimination before Dawlish's proposal was considered. Murillo had presided, his head bandaged and his face drawn in pain, yet more disconcerted by the morning's reverses than by his own discomfort. A grimy and dishevelled Tinsley found himself blamed by Culbertson for the failure of the infantry assault on the northern bank which, he claimed, would have surely succeeded with more effective artillery support. Tinsley in turn complained petulantly about the failure to supply him and about the cowardice – yes, he would use the word, contradict him who might, though nobody did – of the conscript forces and about the unwillingness of Aquino's officers to persist after encountering a few volleys of rifle fire. The mere mention of the conscripts diverted Culbertson's fury and he raged that if they had been better led, not to mention better trained to start with, the northern crest would have been cleared by mid-morning, all observation posts eliminated and the howitzers forced, by their resulting blindness, to retreat. Aquino sprung to his feet at this and the two stood face to face, quivering with anger, until the grey-visaged Murillo stilled them. Glowering, they resumed their seats.

"Every day of delay is costing the Consortium one thousand, one hundred and sixty sterling," Murillo said. "I need your suggestions for clearing La Garganta and resuming the advance."

Only Dawlish spoke. He sketched a rough map to explain his proposal.

Culbertson laughed. "Tomfoolery," he said. "I heard tell o' the Yankees trying this on the Peninsula in '62 and all it resulted in was wasted shot."

Tinsley pursed his lips, furrowed his mottled pate, sucked on his pipe, looked even more gravely knowledgeable than usual, shook his head slowly and said nothing.

"You're the artilleryman, Major" Murillo said.

"Unconventional," Tinsley said. "Superficially attractive but unconventional in the extreme." He sucked his pipe again. "I understood that the balloon was for strictly naval purposes. I'd personally be loath to stake my reputation on such an innovation."

Only Aquino was supportive. He had few enough men as it was and all present had seen the quality of the conscripts. He doubted that he'd ever get them moving up that slope again even if he were to shoot one half to encourage the other. Comandante Dawlish's solution was worth a try.

Murillo's approval was only finally secured when Dawlish sent for Grinling. The man's poor grammar and deferential manner did little to convince Tinsley, who insisted on addressing him indirectly through Dawlish. Murillo treated him with similar contempt but his questions were penetrating and he seemed convinced by the answers. And as he inclined towards support Culbertson shrugged and said there might be something in it.

"You're in agreement, Major Tinsley?" Murillo asked, pen poised above the minute-ledger.

"I'm not accepting observations from a fairground showman," Tinsley said. "If you're determined on this course, Sir, then I'll need professional support." He glanced towards Dawlish, and it was obvious that it pained him to do so.

"I'll go up," Dawlish said.

And so it was settled. Grinling scurried off to charge his retorts with iron scrap and sulphuric acid. Dawlish and Tinsley, coldly polite after their skirmishing, agreed the details for moving the siege-artillery's barge upstream to the agreed landing point, where Aquino would muster several companies of conscripts to assist in the unloading.

The night's long labour was enlivened half-a-dozen times by shells from the unseen howitzers. They fell around the Gullet, lighting it with brief and thunderous flashes that caused no damage but inconvenienced Holmes' efforts to lay a new spring from the *Montelindo's* bows to the opposite shore. The *Toad*, potent but fragile, lay out of range downstream, waiting for her hour, while four hundred conscripts, reverting to their more usual role of beasts of burden, laboured to drag the mortar up a timbered ramp from the waterside and into position. On its barge the balloon slowly bulged into shape as hydrogen hissed from the bubbling retorts. Dawlish satisfied himself that preparations at the Gullet were advancing satisfactorily and then snatched four hours' sleep, conscious that the following day would decide the fate of the expedition, and with it his own hopes for promotion half a world away.

*   *   *

Dawlish ignored his faint nausea – the balloon's lazy swaying was having an effect that no sea had had for more than twenty years – and scanned the valley again. He found no sign of activity. There was no alternative – the bait would have to be risked. He picked up a green flag and swept it horizontally three times. An ant-like figure far below attracted Tinsley's attention and Dawlish repeated his signal when he saw his gaze directed upwards. Tinsley spoke to his own signaller, whose semaphored message was acknowledged a few seconds later by a blast on the *Toad's* whistle. The gunboat nudged into midstream, heading for the narrows, chugging past the moored paddlers and barges and across the invisible boundary of the howitzers' range.

He shifted his focus to the northern ridge, where the invisible observers must even now be noting the *Toad's* movement. He quickly took in the Consortium deployments. On the northern shore two companies of Aquino's more reliable troops were in a grove-sheltered defile at the foot of the slope, hidden to anybody on the crest. South of the Gullet Tinsley's ten-pounder battery was now protected by more substantial earthworks, strengthened during the night. Along the banks, out of howitzer range, untidy bivouacs and smoking fires showed where troops had been landed from the transports.

The *Toad's* whistle blasted again, deliberately inviting the enemy's attention as she moved upriver. Ahead of her, in the Gullet, figures swarmed on the *Montelindo's* bow as Purdon, bandaged and aching, but still mobile, drove his working party to tension the spring. The stricken monitor had received further fuel under cover of darkness and the boilers had been brought to full pressure. Boyson, the *Toad's* chief artificer, had freed the turret's bearings, jammed since the *Torres'* first hit, and it could be rotated again.

The whistle screamed again and this time its sustained wail drew response. As the last reverberations died away Dawlish heard a distinct report from beyond the ridge. Another followed almost immediately. He suppressed his impulse to look to the river, to the likely target, and swung his telescope towards the valley. The image swam for a moment as his eye adjusted and then he swept the carpet of dusty foliage that filled the valley floor. His heart jumped as a flock of rising birds suddenly blurred the disc of vision, lost just as quickly as he swept on.

He paused, moved back – and there they were, by God! The birds were rapidly scattering but below them rose a yellowish-grey cloud that was already thinning and dispersing as it rose above the treetops.

Grinling had seen it too. "There!" he yelled. "In line with that dead tree on the crest!"

Dawlish pushed the telescope into Grinling's hands and lifted the prismatic compass hanging around his neck. Intent only on fixing the bearing, he ignored the scream of the two howitzer shells falling from their apogee towards the river. He could see no trace of a clearing and only the faintest trailing smoke-wisps now drifted above the forest canopy, but it was enough.

Three hundred and eighteen degrees.

The range was more difficult – not more than three thousand yards, but how much less? It must be a guess now, for the telltale smoke was lost and the wheeling birds were settling to new perches. He held his gaze fixed on the spot and heard remotely Grinling's cry of delight as the shells fell harmlessly on the northern bank, slightly astern of the surging *Toad*. Two thousand yards to the ridge's crest and nine hundred – no, eight hundred – beyond that. It would have to do for the initial shot.

Dawlish pulled a notebook and pencil from his shirt pocket and scribbled, reducing the bearing by half a degree to compensate for the balloon's offset from the mortar. He tore the page loose and stuffed it into a tin canister attached by a ring to the thin coir rope running from the basket to a point on the ground close to the piled munitions. It dropped down the line and seconds later Tinsley was scanning the sheet, then hurrying to the mortar and directing the training himself, mimicking Dawlish's earlier use of the compass as his hand signals directed the crew that strained to align the massive weapon. Two blocks and tackles connected its cradle to nearby trees and successive tensioning and loosening rotated its mass ponderously to the correct bearing.

On the river the *Toad* had now reached the Gullet and was manoeuvring close to the northern bank to lodge the rope fender on her bows against the *Montelindo's* flank. Seen from the balloon, her open decks, well protected by their iron breastworks against light low-trajectory fire, seemed hopelessly vulnerable to the unseen howitzers' plunging shells. Dawlish knew that at this moment the concealed observers on the crest must be redirecting fire towards the narrows. If only Tinsley could hasten!

He looked down. The bearing was set, the elevation adjusted, the crew had withdrawn a dozen yards and only Tinsley and the chief gunner still hovered by the mortar. Then Tinsley too stepped back, looked up to the balloon and waved a green flag in a wide arc. Only when he saw Dawlish's acknowledging signal did he nod to the gunner, who retreated several paces and then jerked the lanyard.

Dawlish clapped his hands to his ears as flame and smoke vomited from the muzzle. A ripple ran outward through the ground from the three-layer log mattress as the mortar's half-ton of iron heaved downwards. Then the shell, a sixty-pound spherical case packed with powder, roared upwards and high into the sky above the ridge. "I can see it," Grinling shouted as it reached its zenith, a black dot that hung still for an instant before commencing its downward plunge. Dawlish did not see it, for already his telescope was aligned with that dead tree on the ridge and focused on the surface of the treetops beyond, and so, as the mortar shell arced high, he caught a glimpse of another cloud of yellowish smoke rolling up through the foliage there.

The howitzer and mortar shells must have passed closely, seconds before the great iron sphere smashed down through the trees beyond and to the right of the invisible howitzers' billowing smoke, gouging deep into the soft humus before the last fraction of smouldering fuse consumed itself within the case. An orange flash was half lost among the trees, and then a plume of earth and shattered wood rose skywards, stood still for an instant like a frozen and muddy fountain,

73

and then fell back into the smoke-filled crater the shell had blasted in the forest canopy.

"We've got the range advantage," Dawlish said, more to himself than to Grinling, yet not daring to admit the vulnerability of the *Toad* in the half-hour ahead. He swayed his glass slowly between the smoking point of the mortar's impact and the rapidly thinning traces of the howitzers' salvo. "A half-degree less, back two hundred yards..."

His attention was drawn by Grinling shouting "They've missed the *Toad* again, Commander!" as the howitzer shells fell harmlessly in the river just downstream of the straining gunboat, which was now lodged firmly against the *Montelindo's* bows and pushing strongly. Two feathery plumes rose from the brown water but they were close, very close. The next salvo might well smash through the gunboat's deck or sweep away the crew on the *Montelindo* that was now hauling in on the bar-tight spring, capturing each gain the *Toad* made in urging the bow against the current.

If this work was not to be interrupted then it was essential that those unseen observers on the ridge be inconvenienced. Dawlish scribbled again, adding to the range and bearing corrections for the mortar the request for the ten-pounders in the southern battery to open fire. The message dropped down the coir rope.

Now they could only wait, Dawlish forcing himself into calm and Grinling fussing nervously with the basket-suspension ropes and jettisoning a ten-pound sand-bag to counter leakage from the canopy.

It was an artilleryman's battle now - on both sides.

8

The crew had sponged the mortar, rammed in the bagged charges and two men were carrying the next shot towards it with tongs before Tinsley received the aiming correction that had reached him down the coir rope. He waved confirmation of receipt to Dawlish, instructed his signaller to semaphore the southern battery to open fire and then turned to the mortar. He gestured for the shot to be held back, then crouched behind the weapon, intent and absorbed, his prismatic compass held before his eye, as he directed the fractional movements needed to shift the squat monster into its new alignment. At last satisfied, he hovered thoughtfully about the elevation mechanism, then shook his head and reached inside the maw, pulling out one of the half-pound silken pouches of powder. The coarse elevation adjustment offered no further scope for range correction and the charge-weight must now be fine-tuned. He checked the shot's fuse, then nodded to the loaders. The sphere was manhandled over the muzzle and dropped in.

Dawlish turned his glass to the southern ridge beyond the Gullet. A small figure atop the earthwork sheltering the guns was waving acknowledgement of Tinsley's signal. Behind the elongated bank of brown clay, embrasured for the ten-pounders' muzzles, the Paraguayan gunners completed loading in a flurry of movement. Dawlish could almost sense the battery commander's excitement as he saw him sweep his sword down, the signal to open fire. The ten-pounders crashed out together. Their shells screamed over the *Montelindo* and the straining *Toad* and exploded along the northern ridge. Shrapnel was being used and one shell burst in the air while the other detonated on impact, both lashing the scrub-covered crest with hails of half-ounce balls.

If nothing else this should keep the observers' heads down and prevent further correction of the howitzers' aim. Sufficient munitions had been dragged up to the battery during the night for this bombardment to continue for another seventeen salvos. Dawlish's satisfaction was suddenly curbed however by a report from the far valley and by the sight of another swirl of tell-tale smoke rising above the forest. Blinded or not, the howitzers were firing again and Dawlish, apprehensive but impotent, looked towards the inevitable area of impact in the Gullet. His heart leapt as he saw that a ribbon of water had opened between the *Montelindo's* bows and the northern bank – and the tensioned spring was holding as the Rendel gunboat strove to rotate the monitor into the current.

Not now! he wanted to yell, *don't let them hit now, so close to success!*

He heard the howls of the plunging shells for an instant before they detonated on the southern bank, feet from the water's edge and in line with the monitor's stern. A shower of mud and pebbles rained on the *Montelindo*, scything down a figure on the deck, but doing no further damage. The monitor was almost bow-on to the current and the brown waters boiled round her stern as her screw was engaged, thrashing furiously to release her from the imprisoning sandbar. The *Toad* had stopped pushing, leaving the tensioned spring to hold the monitor's bows and she was nudging forward to deploy a towing cable. Another five minutes and both vessels could be in the lake above the Gullet.

Grinling pulled excitedly on Dawlish's sleeve and pointed down. Tinsley was waving confirmation that he was ready for the next shot. Dawlish focused again on the sea of treetops beyond the ridge. The howitzers' smoke had disappeared but the gaping scar torn by the mortar's opening shot gave a point of reference. He heard the mortar's roar and the rush of its soaring shot recede and die as it sped towards the summit of its parabolic flight, but his gaze did not flinch from that patch of forest where the howitzers must lurk.

There was silence for a moment. It was broken then by the roar of the southern ten-pounders as they again raked the observers' ridge – and suddenly that distant green canopy seemed to heave and thrash as a pillar of earth and flame and foliage blasted up from it. Birds careered upwards in demented flight and a ripple trembled outwards across the treetops as if from a stone cast into a pond. It was impossible to judge exactly, but the impact must have been close, very close, to the howitzers.

Dawlish felt a surge of delight – now was the time to make the position of those unseen tormentors untenable. The message he sent rattling down the rope read "No correction. Sustain fire". He allowed himself to survey the Gullet while Tinsley's crew sponged and loaded and rammed far below.

The *Toad* had passed upstream of the *Montelindo* and lay stationary some fifty yards ahead of her, a towing hawser linking them stern to bow. The waters seethed astern of both craft as their screws churned against the combined resistance of the onrushing current and the grasping sandbar. The hawser dipped and jerked, throwing off sparkling showers of droplets. Suddenly the monitor was free, wallowing forward as she broke loose from the shoal. A wave of brown water rolled across her low bows and lapped around her turret as she surged towards the *Toad*. Dawlish smiled with approval as Holmes took up the slack and resumed the pull. Slowly, at little more than walking pace, the two vessels moved towards the lake. From the southern ridge the ten-pounders crashed out again, their shells scouring the opposite crest with shrapnel seconds later. Their report was lost in the crash of Tinsley's mortar blasting again on its previous bearing.

Dawlish trained his glass again on the smoking crater punched in the forest by the last mortar shell. He had it in focus a moment before the green canopy slightly beyond it was torn by a volcano of flame and climbing earth. Once more a convulsive wave of lashing treetops ran out from the point of impact but this time the central column of smoke did not disperse, but rather thickened and grew. Orange flame flickered around its base, at first half-glimpsed through the surrounding green, then growing as the blaze quickened in the dry underbrush. The new crater was an expanding inferno within a minute of the impact, the tinder-dry vegetation around it flashing into combustion before the searing waves of heat thrown out by the advancing flames.

At this moment Dawlish knew that, whether directly hit or not, the howitzers' position had become untenable. He could imagine the frantic efforts to limber up and withdraw, the wild-eyed terror of the draught animals, the near panic of the crews and the rising despair of the commander, whoever he might be, - and he had been good, by God! – when faced with this combination of plunging death and blazing forest. A long blast on the *Toad's* whistle drew his attention to the lake. The *Toad* and the *Montelindo* had passed the funnel-point where it emptied into the Gullet and were almost stationary in calm water. The squat gunboat was drawing back to slip the tow. Her whistle screamed again in triumph, telling the vessels downstream that their passage into the lake was clear.

Dawlish smiled grimly. The invisible artillery had inflicted torment enough and there was time for one more shot to speed them on their way. He looked down to the mortar and saw the crew stepping back from it, loading complete. The lanyard whipped under the gunner's jerk and the massive weapon was obscured by a belch of flame-cored smoke. This time Dawlish allowed himself to follow Grinling's pointing finger and to catch sight of the black speck that hung for an instant a half-mile above the forest before being lost to invisibility as it accelerated into its final plunge.

The explosion was slightly short and to the left of the previous impact, and on the margin of the blazing circle of forest. Before its column of earth had collapsed it had created a new focus of conflagration. The afternoon breeze was faint, almost imperceptible, but it was enough to drive a crackling and smoke-billowing flame-front back towards the intervening ridge. It gnawed hungrily through the sun-parched vegetation, the shimmering air above it laden with ash and circling birds. Suddenly, the wall of flame was rent by a series of yet brighter flashes that threw up gouts of earth and splintered timber. Seconds later Dawlish's ears were assaulted by an irregular and staccato series of reports.

A savage feeling of exultation thrilled him and he yelled to Grinling; "We found them! It's their ammunition!"

It was safe to assume now that the howitzers would not be soon again in action – time now to conserve the mortar's supplies. As Dawlish scribbled this message the Parrott ten-pounders raked the northern ridge again. He paused to see the result. The fuses must have been set somewhat too long, for both shells exploded among the scrub on the crest, rather than in the air above it. As the smoke cleared he caught sight of movement in the undergrowth, brown and grey-clad figures flitting in retreat upwards towards the ridge, clear evidence that the hidden observation post which they had protected so well was being abandoned. The Reducción's riflemen who had driven the conscripts back in such blind panic the previous day were withdrawing into the valley beyond.

Dawlish glanced towards the defile at the foot of the ridge where Aquino's two least-distrusted conscript companies sheltered restlessly, curious as to the outcome of the bombardment, the rising column of smoke rising above the crest from the valley beyond fully visible to them. A small victory was within their grasp now, a petty triumph that could bolster their confidence and repay their grim commander for the support he had given Dawlish at that hostile conference on the *Tacuari*. The message thrust into the next canister to Tinsley detailed the opportunity.

Clear of La Garganta, no longer linked by the towing hawser, the *Toad* and *Montelindo* steamed slowly up the lake. To starboard lay the inferno of smoke and flame a mile north of the water's edge, the howitzers that would otherwise have disputed their progress now silent and impotent. The monitor leading, both craft moved upstream, past the areas of the *Humaita's* last plunge and on beyond the point where the *Velasco* had been so brutally dismembered. Dawlish scanned the banks through his glass, fearful lest the rebel monitor emerge again from concealment in the reed-shrouded margins, and he searched the meanderings of the river that lay shimmering and silvery beyond the further end of the lake, just under three miles distant. There was no sign of movement, yet somewhere beyond there the monitor must lie in wait between dusty, scrub-covered banks.

The *Montelindo* pushed forward until it was three hundred yards short of the upstream narrows of the river's entry, then slowed and dropped a bow anchor. Nothing could now enter the lake without coming into the point-blank range of her two one-ten pounder turret weapons. The *Toad* nudged in towards the southern bank and anchored four hundred yards astern of her, well placed to bring her nine-inch Armstrong to bear on any intruder passing the gauntlet of the *Montelindo's* guns. Three long blasts on her whistle signalled that the lake was secure.

Figures were crossing the northern ridge now, darting furtively from cover to cover as they fled into the valley beyond. This was the first time, Dawlish realised, that he had seen enemy troops. From this height they did not look much different from the conscripts.

The southern battery lashed the northern crest for the last time. The fuses had been shortened and the shells burst in the air, their myriad balls scouring the scrub and mowing down several of the running figures. The impetus of the retreat was lost as the men dived into any available cover, oblivious of Aquino's companies pouring from the ravine below the slope and moving up it in three ragged lines.

Dawlish could pick out Aquino himself, a heavy figure plodding remorselessly ahead of the front rank, an unsheathed sabre in his right hand and a revolver in his left, disdaining to glance back to check if he was being followed. The conscripts' packs had been discarded for more rapid movement and they carried their Springfield rifles with bayonets fixed. They moved cautiously through the scrub at first, hunched and fearful, half-shamed, half-inspired by the resolute and bull-like figure forging ahead and sullenly aware of the officers following behind them with drawn pistols, but their pace quickened as they realised that there was little opposition.

They were more than halfway up the slope, and well past the furthest point reached by the earlier assault, before the first shots crackled back from the crest. A handful of retreating riflemen had spotted Aquino's advance and paused to delay it. The front line wavered as a man fell to this uncoordinated fire but Aquino kept moving forward, breaking into a shambling trot that was surprisingly fast for so heavy a man. The line strung out through the scrub behind him surged forward and Dawlish, high above, caught the sound of their yells as they crashed through the brush. The second and third lines lurched after them, the realisation that this rush could be easily and almost bloodlessly triumphant somehow communicating itself to them. The rifle fire from the crest was spasmodic, the shots few enough to be countable, and though they dropped a few individuals in the now charging front-rank the impact on the overall onslaught was negligible. Still no weapon had been discharged by Aquino's men, nor had they yet sighted the scattering of riflemen who still crouched among the scrub on the crest, covering the retreat of their fellows into the smoke-filled valley beyond. Fatigue slowed the attackers' pace as they panted up the slope and gaps opened in the line as the first well-concealed but now-abandoned trenches and rifle pits were encountered among the brush, forcing detours, but the overall advance was not halted.

Aquino was first on the crest, some twenty men at his heels. He had borne somewhat to the right in the final hundred yards and so outflanked the remaining riflemen on the ridge. They saw him too late as he crashed towards them, sabre upraised, the conscripts behind him forgetting their terror as they charged with lowered bayonets. A few riflemen swung to face them but the remainder broke and ran, racing towards the flame-wracked valley beyond. Dawlish saw the sabre and bayonets rise and fall and flash in the afternoon sun and he heard the crackle of the last small-arms fire as resistance ended.

The crest was taken, the Gullet passed and the Reducción's artillery countered, though possibly not eliminated.

Dawlish felt no joy in this small victory. It had brought the Consortium's forces to where they should have been two days earlier, but poorer now by two irreplaceable vessels and by several score of expendable men. He turned to Grinling and saw that he was shaking and on the point of nausea.

"They was killing those men like animals, Sir," His voice was hushed. "They was holding their hands up, surrendering like, and that General Aquino Sir, that General, he just chopped ..."

Grinling looked away and Dawlish recognised the distress of a decent man confronted by the unspeakable for the first time. He hardened himself to it and snapped "It's not your business, Professor Grinling."

Then he softened and said: "It happens. It's a madness, a release ..." and he stopped, knowing that this words were meaningless to this innocent civilian whom he had plucked from a world of fairgrounds and fetes.

"You've done well, Professor," he said gently. "Without you we'd still be on the wrong side of La Garganta. We'll go down now."

The canopy shuddered as the winch rope tautened and the descent to the barge commenced.

*　　　*　　　*

As he toiled upwards the slope seemed to Dawlish more thickly clad with scrub, the perspectives shorter and more claustrophobic, than had appeared from the balloon's Jovelike vantage. Tinsley, smugly triumphant at the mortar's success, and already self-convinced of his own wisdom in agreeing to use of the balloon for spotting, was a few paces to Dawlish's left. General Aquino strode ahead, drawing their attention, with the easy contempt of the victor, to the shortcomings of the enemy's empty trenches and rifle pits.

They had passed beyond the killing zone of the previous day, where swelling corpses lay half-concealed in the undergrowth, their presence betrayed by loudly buzzing flies and a growing stench. They waited their turn to be tumbled into a shallow grave by the parties of their erstwhile comrades working further down the slope. It was almost dusk and Dawlish was eager to press on to the crest to view what Aquino had found there and then get back to the river as quickly as possible. The night must be used to ready those units of the flotilla still downstream of the Gullet for passage into the lake at first light.

The deserted observation post, when they reached it, shocked both Dawlish and Tinsley. The competence – no, rather the ingenuity – of its purpose, layout and construction was almost as intimidating as the initial fall of the howitzer shot. Dug into a slightly protruding bulge of the ridge, some fifty yards below the crest on the forward slope, roofed with earth-covered logs on which scrub had been carefully replanted, its narrow viewing slits provided a two-hundred degree view of the Gullet, the river downstream and much of the terrain to either side. The shrapnel that had showered down around it might have continued for a week without inconveniencing the occupants and nothing short of a direct hit from Tinsley's mortar could have eliminated it. The entrance, a winding, log and earth-roofed trench that followed the contour of the slope, was concealed in a thicket some fifty yards away. Constructing it must have been the work of days, days laboured to realise the vision of a professional.

The interior was furnished with two cots, three stools and a table, all roughly hewn from wood and lashed together with split cane. It smelled of stale sweat and of the rotting fruit spilled from an upturned basket in one corner. But it was the gleam of copper that excited Dawlish's attention, the sheen of the exposed end of wire that protruded from the thin cotton-wrapped and tarred cable that terminated on the earthen floor and snaked back along the access tunnel. Something, almost certainly a Morse-key, had been hurriedly torn from the end as the unknown observers had made their escape.

"Consortium wire," Aquino said, taking the bare end from Dawlish and fingering it thoughtfully. "There would have been much of it up the San Joac. The distant cattle-stations had telegraph lines back to the main settlement."

"And this wire," said Dawlish, "where does it end?"

Aquino shrugged. "Who knows, Comandante? Somewhere in the valley, near the howitzers. It was buried, maybe weeks ago. It will have been overgrown. We'll never find the end. Does it matter?"

"No," Dawlish said. "It doesn't matter".

But he knew it did, not for itself, but for what it implied. An enemy who conceived this observation post perhaps weeks ahead, who dominated the Gullet with indirect fire controlled by telegraph, and who coordinated the bombardment with that savagely effective attack by the monitor, was no mere naive and messianic visionary, however much he might call himself "The Poor Man".

Tinsley was speaking. "And the prisoners Colonel? Could they enlighten you?" But he pursed his lips in old-maidish disapproval as Aquino smiled, shook his head slowly and asked "What prisoners, Major?"

"Regrettable, very regrettable, General," Tinsley said hurriedly, "but understandable in the circumstances. Regrettable but understandable. The right decision, Sir, the right decision."

They emerged into the sharp and brief golden light that so often precedes the sudden nightfall of the tropics. Far below, Tinsley's crews were already straining to shift the mortar back to the water's edge. Smoke was rising from the bivouacs as Aquino's troops, elated by their small success, prepared their evening meal. Somewhere among those fires was the grim tent where the expedition's two Paraguayan surgeons plied their butcher's trade on wounded recovered from the slope. Dawlish shuddered and hoped he would never have need of them himself. Several of the steamers were moving slowly upstream, positioning themselves for the morrow's passage of the Gullet. Closer, at the foot of the slope, the last victims of yesterday's slaughter were being tipped into a trench and covered with soil.

Dawlish plodded down the slope, suddenly aware of his fatigue and of his disgust at the business he had voluntarily undertaken. And he thought of Florence, not just as in her good works in Portsmouth but when she had risked all so selflessly in Thrace to succour the abandoned. He was glad that she was not here and that he did not have to justify himself to her.

But he pushed these thoughts away and told himself that it had been a successful day. Another long day lay ahead and he consoled himself with the promise of sleep.

9

It took the whole of the following day to bring all the vessels through the Gullet into the lake. The paddle steamers were unhandy in breasting strong currents and the barges they towed worsened their manoeuvrability. Long centipedes of stumbling, sweating men on either bank helped drag each vessel through the two-hundred yard stretch of racing water, step by painful step. Dawlish watched from the southern shore, leaving direct control to Purdon, whose role in freeing the *Montelindo* had given him a special feel for the Gullet's shoals and eddies.

The *Toad* hovered in the quiet waters upstream, available to re-enter the narrows to tow a vessel through in an emergency, yet ready to support the *Montelindo* should it come under attack. The monitor still lay moored near the head of the lake, her turret dominating the upstream entrance. Only once did the Rendel gunboat have to intervene to drag free a paddler which was losing the battle with the current. It drifted downstream, pulling screaming men with it over the rough paths on either shore, crunching and splintering its flailing stern wheel on the southern bank before coming to rest on the same shoal that had so firmly entrapped the *Montelindo*. Its draught was considerably less than the monitor's however and a tow passed from the *Toad* sufficed to haul it clear and into the lake, where repairs commenced immediately on the wheel's damaged wooden blades.

On the southern ridge Tinsley fussed over the re-embarkation of the ten-pounders. Culbertson sent out Guardia cavalry patrols both south and north of the lake, scouring the scrub for any signs of Reducción forces. They found none living, though in the charred and still-smouldering terrain to the north Obregón's patrol discovered the twisted remains of an ammunition limber, shards of exploded shell casings and the calcified remains of three men and half a dozen mules. Of the other elements of the battery there was no trace. The howitzers still survived somewhere ahead in the thorny scrub of the northern shore, threatening future torment. A whole day of cautious reconnaissance showed only that the Chaco was empty for twelve miles ahead alongside the lake and river – a hot, dusty near-desert of brush and cactus, broken only by stands of quebacho and the occasional red, stumpy anthill, the domain of peccary and jaguar and armadillo and a hundred varieties of colourful bird.

The full implications of the death of Travis, the *Humaita's* American skipper who had known the river so well, hit Dawlish at the conference he called for the flotilla's officers in the early evening. The last of the steamers were now moored in the lake, their human freight again packed into the barges or slumped exhausted on the decks, ready for the move upstream at first light. The Reducción was still some hundred and fifty miles upstream - eight day's steaming if all went well - and Dawlish wanted to ensure that all the vessels' skippers were aware of the need for a speedy but cautious advance. The *Toad*, on which he had now established himself, provided the venue for the meeting, but its accommodation was too small to contain the slovenly group that assembled. They gathered instead on the small stretch of open deck abaft the Armstrong mounting. Dawlish's newly remembered Spanish was improving, but he still did not trust it for a conference of this importance.

"Most of these men have been on this river before, Colonel," he said to Culbertson, whom he had reluctantly invited to participate. "Ask them to imagine that if they were commanding the *Torres* monitor where would they choose to attack us next?"

He gestured to the three charts laid end to end across a packing case before him, charts drawn with infinite skill by a British surveyor in

Consortium employ in those prosperous days when livestock-laden steamers had slipped down the San Joaquin to the distant Plate.

Culbertson withdrew his cheroot and spat on the holystoned deck. On Dawlish's right Holmes, the *Toad*'s commander, stiffened and breathed in sharply. The sweating colonel translated in Spanish too rapid for Dawlish to follow easily. He drew little reaction from the circle of bored and weary faces on the periphery of the circle of light cast by the lamp slung overhead. Dawlish recognised the one who finally spoke as Cabrera, the *Tacuari*'s captain, a mournful-looking man with an unhealthy yellow complexion and sunken eyes. Serrano, the fat skipper of the *Ipora*, Culbertson's transport, sniggered next to him and looked round at the others, his expression inviting them to join in.

"He says he's only a merchant skipper, Commander Nick," Culbertson drawled, eyes gleaming with smug malice, "an' he reckons that sort o' speculation is best left to professional naval gentlemen employed for the purpose."

Cabrera was looking Dawlish straight in the eye, his face a mask of dumb insolence.

Dawlish resisted the urge to strike him and said instead: "Tell him the *Torres* is waiting somewhere upstream. It'll probably be half-covered in a reed bank or lurking round a bend." As he spoke he could imagine the workings of the mind of the rebel commander, whoever he was, that cool, ruthless intellect that had already used the ancient monitor to such devastating effect. "It'll be striking at the transports and the troops, not at the *Toad* and the *Montelindo*, if its commander can help it. If Captain Cabrera hasn't thought already about where that might happen then I suggest that he starts now."

There was a note of mockery in Culbertson's translation, just as surely as in Cabrera's response. Several other skippers nodded agreement as he spoke. "He says it's impossible to judge these things," Culbertson said. "The river just changes by the month - currents, shoals, shiftin' channels, snags, differin' depths. It's been a year, an' more, since any o' them has been this way. I guess,

Commander Nick, that as a professional you recognise these sort o' problems."

"Señor Cabrera's problems, yes, all too well." Dawlish struggled to disguise his fury. "I understand that the last time he descended the San Joaquin there was no contest in his race with El Pobre's forces. Tell him his problems aren't my sort. Officers of the Royal Navy sail towards the sound of the guns, not away from it."

"You can't tell him that, and I won't," Culbertson said quietly, the hint of mockery gone. "The bastard doesn't have the sand to slit your gizzard like a man but he'll be quick enough to run his boat aground on every bar between here and the settlement to spite you. These greasers are proud as Satan and twice as mean. You need him, Commander Nick, him and the whole damn cowardly gang of incompetents and cut-throats."

"Tell him then that the *Montelindo* will be leading the advance from now on. The *Toad* will follow and then the transports. You can ask Capitan Calles how happy he'll be to head the flotilla."

The monitor's captain would not be happy to do so, and he said so volubly. Dawlish understood even before Culbertson translated.

"He don't know the San Joac, nor the currents, nor the shoals nor the snags. And he ain't too happy about his own monitor neither, nor how to handle it. He never did see the damn thing before Don Plutarcho had it hauled out of the scrap yard and prettied up." There was a cold edge of contempt to the colonel's voice now and despite his dislike of the man Dawlish recognised the realism of a professional.

"The fact is, Commander Nick," Culbertson dropped his voice, "that Señor Capitan Calles o' the navy o' the Republic of Paraguay never ventured further north before than Asunción. Neither did he ever command anythin' larger than a scow until a few months back - and now he's only skippering the *Montelindo* because his brother's wife is warming the bed of El Presidente himself. That little skirmish with the *Torres* a few days back satisfied all the longings he's ever had for glory afloat."

In the silence that followed Dawlish could feel himself the focus of the hostile reluctance of the sallow faces before him. He had known that he could expect no enthusiasm, no commitment, from this group that had been thrown together by greed and compulsion, but it had been a cerebral, intellectual knowledge. Now he could feel their reluctance as something so palpable as to be almost touched and smelled. He confronted a group that hated the river, the expedition, the Consortium and himself and which made no effort to disguise the fact. Only Holmes and Purdon and their sparkling *Toad*, so misplaced in the heart of this dusty wilderness, represented a tenuous link to the certainties that had sustained him since boyhood. Glimpsed in the shadows behind Culbertson, their disgust at the truth he had uttered just barely disguised, the two young British officers embodied the discipline and determination that had inspired him since the example of others had first taught him to keep fear in check.

But Culbertson had been correct, Dawlish knew. He needed this gang of cowardly incompetents and they must come with him whether they liked it or not.

"Tell Captain Calles that he'll have Captain Cabrera as his pilot for the *Montelindo*. I understand he knows the river well." Dawlish's voice was raised, for he meant his tone of command to be heard and unmistakable, even if his words were as yet incomprehensible to most of his hearers. "Tell Cabrera that his mate can quite competently skipper the *Tacuari* until we get to La Reducción Nueva. Tell Cabrera to shift his traps to the monitor tonight so that we can cast off at first light."

Cabrera was already protesting before Culbertson had finished translating.

"Tell him to shut up," Dawlish said. "If he's not satisfied then let him tell Don Plutarcho that he's not prepared to put his knowledge of the river at that gentleman's disposal ... Oh No? He doesn't think that's necessary? That's as I thought. And I trust that Captain Calles is happy with the arrangement?"

The answer was more than Dawlish could have hoped for. "He's got a favour to ask of you, Commander Nick," Culbertson said. "He seems to be mighty impressed with Lieutenant Purdon."

"And rightly so. The *Montelindo* would still be jamming the Gullet if it wasn't for his exertions."

"He'd like him as his first officer," Culbertson said. Calles was grinning and nodding his head by his side. "He reckons that Purdon might benefit from seein' how an ironclad is handled in the navy o' the Republic."

"Compliment Captain Calles on his acute perception." Dawlish turned with studied gravity to the two British officers. "Mr. Purdon - I trust you find the proposal one that will be to the benefit of your professional skills? You do? Then to business. Colonel Culbertson, would you kindly tell these gentleman that we'll set the order for their vessels in tomorrow's advance?"

*　　*　　*

Upstream of the lake the San Joaquin snaked across an ever-more featureless plain. The width was seldom more than seventy yards but in this season the depth was adequate for the flotilla, except at the bends, where shoals and bars necessitated careful manoeuvring through the vortices and ripples at the outer rims. For the most part the banks were low, often fringed with stands of lush green vegetation that sheltered capinchos, water-hogs, but beyond them the dry scrub of the Chaco reasserted itself. Along some lower-lying sections the river slowed and broadened, the main channel meandering through wide expanses of high reeds. It was these stretches which demanded the most cautious progress lest the *Torres* lurk there, repeating her previous disguise.

The *Montelindo* led the advance, guns loaded, turret permanently manned. This was rotated, on Dawlish's instructions, and under Purdon's supervision, once per hour to ensure that the training mechanism was operative. If it stuck, as it did twice, the entire flotilla was brought to a halt until it was freed, the *Toad* taking station upstream until the huge iron cylinder could grind round smoothly again.

The *Toad* maintained station a hundred yards astern of the monitor, Egdean now often at the helm, picking up from the regular quartermasters the technique of steering with screws as well as rudders, the key to Rendel manoeuvrability. The big seaman was showing the same instinctive mastery that had made him a helmsman of genius on fast torpedo boats. Dawlish spent much of each day on her steering platform. From it he could survey the arid Chaco Boreal slipping past and fret silently over what each new bend or expanse of gently swaying reeds might conceal. Strung out along the river downstream, the transports followed, vomiting wood-smoke, lucky if they made three knots against the current.

The *Tacuari*, Murillo's paddler, was last in line, the presence on board of General Aquino and a half-company of Paraguayan regulars providing the skippers ahead with an incentive against straggling. Half of Culbertson's Guardia troopers were concentrated in the *Ipora*, the steamer following the *Toad*, their horses sweating and champing under a palm-thatch awning on the barge that lurched in its wake. At any time some twenty beasts stood saddled, though with loosened girths, and with Spencer carbines thrust in bucket holsters ahead of the right stirrup, water-canteens and sabres before the left. Their riders smoked, gambled and drank coffee under an awning close to the rickety wooden drawbridge structures amidships which allowed fast loading and landing. The pockmarked Obregón, who had looked at Dawlish with continuing contempt since their encounter at the Gullet, endlessly scanned the scrub to the north, searching for the surviving howitzers. Small and slowly moving dust-clouds to the south indicated Reducción patrols keeping pace with the flotilla and observing its progress but they represented too elusive an annoyance to justify chasing.

Dawlish already regretted that more acid had not been carried for Grinling's balloon. It sagged on the deck of its barge, some halfway down the convoy, half-collapsed, lessening by the hour as the remaining hydrogen seeped through its canopy. The ascent at the Gullet had cost almost one third of the acid brought with the expedition and what remained was being conserved against the unknown demands of future operations upstream. Were it possible to keep the balloon permanently aloft, towing it as the flotilla moved ahead, then both Chaco and river could have been viewed like an open map and any possible ambush detected well in advance. In Britain Murillo had only agreed with extreme reluctance to the expense of transporting Grinling and his contraptions half-way across the world, his obstinacy only overcome by Topcliffe's support of Dawlish's arguments. Now Dawlish realised that he had erred only in the modesty of his demands. He had underestimated the capability that the balloon could bestow on him and so, for the sake of another score of carboys of sulphuric acid, he must scrimp and husband that capability and fear the surprises that each twist of the swirling San Joaquin might bring.

Twice per day, morning and afternoon, the *Toad's* crew ran through the complete sequence for loading, raising and mock-firing the nine-inch Armstrong. The majority were discharged British seamen with previous service in Rendel gunboats, known personally to Holmes, Purdon and the petty officers, all of these still serving, their leave of absence arranged by Topcliffe. Dawlish made it his business to know them too and already the distinct personalities were emerging: Morgan, the quiet Armstrong gunner, and his mate Jarvis, who spent his leisure hours with Egdean in Bible study; Hilliard, the Gatling gunner who took an artistic pleasure in his daily stripping and oiling of his weapon; Wilcox, the stoker whose talentless banjo-strumming was patiently endured by his shipmates in moments of repose; these and two dozen more. They had crewed the gunboat on the long tow from Sheerness to Buenos Aires, wallowing in the wake of one of the Hyperion ocean steamers, its low decks often awash. Thanks to the attentions of Boyson, the grizzled artificer petty-officer, the main engine and hydraulic systems had been kept operative, despite the quantities of water shipped. Within a week of its arrival at the Plate the gunboat was fit to head upriver under its own steam. "Them compounds - they're like my children, Sir. Why wouldn't I look after them?" Boyson had answered when Dawlish had complimented him on the achievement.

Dawlish now was kitted out like the crew in simple duck garments and Sennet hat – for though both Holmes and Purdon had been eager to lend him more seemly garb neither were of his height. All he had brought with him from Britain had been lost with *Humaita*: his clothing, his shaving tackle and, worst of all, the silver-framed photograph Florence had pressed into his hands as he departed, showing her smiling and slim and lovely as she posed by a plaster balustrade in a Southsea studio. He missed scarcely less keenly the few volumes of Trollope and Macaulay that had given the odd quarter-hour of pleasure before he had drifted into sleep in his tiny cabin. Other than the crew's penny dreadfuls there was nothing to read on the *Toad* after he had finished Purdon's *Jorrocks*. Tinsley had provided little comfort when Dawlish swallowed his pride and approached him. "You'll find food for thought here, Dawlish," he had intoned as he lent him *"Oh Fearful Hour! – Meditations on the Last Judgement"* by the Rev. O. Slope M.A. Oxon. "I trust you'll return it - it was a gift from my dear wife. I've no doubt you'll profit from it."

On the morning of the third day after leaving the lake Dawlish was watching the gun-drill, the smooth efficiency of these evolutions a welcome contrast to the shortcomings that otherwise characterised the flotilla's progress. In essence the actions involved in loading and firing the weapon were no different to those that sweating gun-crews had accomplished by raw muscle power at the Nile and Trafalgar and for three centuries before. But now the size of the weapon, though still a muzzle-loader, had increased to gigantic proportions and hydraulic force was employed to mimic human endeavours.

Unloaded, the massive nine-inch cannon - eighteen tons including its mounting - lay on its metal cradle below deck level, hidden from view by the hinged iron plates that lay flush with the deck above, its muzzle aligned with the semi-circular trough on which the silk-bagged powder charge had been laid. At the command of Morgan, the gun-captain, who stood on a small platform immediately behind the gun, the loader on his right threw over a lever. This fed fluid from a hydraulic accumulator to a leather-padded rammer piston that slid along the trough, thrusting the charge deep into the barrel and compacting it. As it reached the limit of its stroke it tripped a valve that diverted the hydraulic fluid to the other side of the double-acting rammer, withdrawing it from the barrel.

On the opposite side of the trough the other loaders had already used tongs, suspended from a short jib-crane, to lift a conically pointed shell from a storage rack. As the rammer hissed out from the barrel they swung the two hundred and fifty-six pound shell across and lowered it gently into the trough. While they snapped the tongs free from the shell flank one of the opposite loaders was screwing in the percussion fuse to the shell's nose while his assistant changed the cover on the rammer, this time to a leather-padded cup that would fit closely over the conical point. The loaders stood back, their chief confirmed with a hand signal that the shell was armed and at the gun-captain's command the rammer was again energised. The polished shaft advanced, more slowly now as it encountered the shell's huge weight, and the great missile disappeared into the barrel to rest on the propellant charge. The loaders readied themselves for the following round, on one side manhandling the next bagged charge to the side of the loading trough, on the other manoeuvring the crane to pick up the next shell from the rack. The gun-captain adjusted the firing-pistol that would ignite the charge through the firing-port at the breech.

The weapon was now ready. A blast on the whistle clenched between the gun-captain's teeth warned the crew both above and below decks to stand clear. He pulled the lever to his right and activated the twelve-inch diameter rams to either side of the Moncrieff scissors-action gun cradle. The great black weapon heaved upwards, leaving the loaders below, pushing open the hinged plates overhead that had sheltered it so that they flanked it like iron walls. It emerged on deck, the muzzle aligning with the gap in the armoured breastwork to point dead ahead along the vessel's axis. The gun-captain, carried with it on his platform, and blinking as he emerged into the light of day from the loading compartment's gloom, threw another lever. Now two axial pistons ran the weapon out along the cradle's polished slides to gape through the breastwork and over the bows. All that now remained was for the gun-captain to adjust the elevation as it was fed to him by telegraph indicator by the commander on the bridge, using the handwheel to his left to feed or bleed fluid to the small cylinder that raised or lowered the barrel, reading off its angle as it moved a small pointer across a graduated brass scale. He would then raise his arm to confirm readiness for firing. Aiming of the weapon was not his concern, but rather that of the commander and the helmsman, who must swing the entire vessel to bring the weapon to bear on the target, juggling screw revolutions and rudder to align the craft and judging the exact moment to order firing. An electric bell, activated by the commander, would give that order.

The mock-firing drill ended at this point but in action, on command, the gun-captain's lanyard would snap the firing-pistol. As the shell blasted from the barrel the monster weapon's recoil would be absorbed against its own two axial pistons, driving their mixture of water and glycerine back into the hydraulic accumulator. The gun-captain's whistle would blast again, warning the loading crew below to stand clear, and as he threw his lever over again the entire mounting would sink below the deck under its own weight, charging of the hydraulic accumulator. As the huge gun settled, the rammer, now covered in a soaking fleece-covered sleeve, would plunge into the muzzle, sponging the smoking barrel free of the last traces of smouldering propellant. The loading sequence could then commence again.

"Two minutes and fifty five seconds for the whole cycle," Holmes said, snapping his watch shut. "I've assumed thirty seconds for aiming the ship, Sir. In action I'll guarantee you a round every three minutes for up to ten rounds."

"And then?" Dawlish asked.

"By then the *Torres* will be at the bottom of the San Joac."

"And if she's not?"

"Then we'll need to be pretty nimble in staying out of her fire. By then we'd have exhausted the first shell rack - assuming we're using glass-hard Palliser armour piercing - and it would take just over four minutes to rig the loading crane over the second rack. But then we'd be ready for another ten rounds."

"If you keep hitting," Dawlish said, "the *Torres* will be..."

His words were cut off suddenly by a distant crack that reverberated towards them across the scrub to starboard. Another followed almost immediately.

The sound was unmistakable.

La Reducción's howitzers were somewhere to the north and far overhead, at this instant, their shells would be climbing towards their apogee before plunging towards the river.

A new agony was beginning ...

10

Time stood still in the seconds before impact.

Cold reason told Dawlish that the shells might be dropping straight towards him. A rising panic, instantly suppressed, urged him to fling himself beneath the nearest cover. Instead, he stood impassively, forcing himself to analyse the situation. A glance upriver showed the *Montelindo* churning purposefully ahead between low, brush-dotted banks, the river ahead clear. A glance aft showed the *Ipora*, Culbertson's sternwheeler towing the barge that carried his troopers and their horses, forging past a lone high tree. It was bare and lightning-blasted, on the southern shore – the sighting mark, by God! The other steamers were strung out downstream. On all sides low and scanty scrub, no reeds along the banks, no dominating ridges, a bad place for an ambush were he the Reducción monitor's commander...

And then the howitzers' shells landed.

The first was harmless. Its feathery plume rose from the water to starboard of Culbertson's craft as the second shell struck it just ahead of the thrashing paddle-wheel. Debris and splinters flew upwards as the missile tore into the wooden superstructure and then there was a flash, and smoke, and more debris blasting upwards and outwards. The vessel shuddered, its two thin smokestacks whipping, then lurched towards the northern bank to impact bow-on a moment later. It lodged there, held fast by the still-beating stern wheel. The towed barge surged forward under its own momentum and almost ground into the paddle before the current caught it and dragged it downstream. Straining on its towing hawser, it also swung in towards the northern bank and grounded in the shallows. Smoke, shot through with scarlet tongues of flame, poured from the ruptured point of detonation on the *Ipora's* upperworks.

Dawlish's mind raced as he strove to visualise the enemy's plan, to imagine and evaluate counter actions, to assign priorities. No small arms fire from the river side, no sign of the enemy monitor, not yet at least ...

"Signal the *Montelindo* to continue upstream," he said quietly to Holmes. If the *Torres* was in the vicinity then Calles and Purdon must block her advance downriver.

Two blasts on the *Toad's* whistle relayed the order.

"Other vessels to drop downstream." Four long blasts screamed the instruction.

There would be confusion, perhaps grounding, as the paddlers swung about in the narrow waters, all of them as vulnerable as Culbertson's *Ipora*. They must not pass that marker tree. The howitzers, smarting from the repulse they had sustained at the Gullet, had outstripped the flotilla as it moved upriver. They would have ranged on that tree, perhaps have registered live rounds on it the previous day, would be sure of the range ... and what had Tinsley said about their range as they had cowered in that gully under the fury of the howitzers' first salvos? Three thousand yards? Not that it mattered. In this low and featureless country the howitzers would be invisible behind even a low screen of scrub. The *Toad's* Armstrong had the range and weight of shell to obliterate them with a single round but there was no way of locating them.

And then, in one terrifying flash of inspiration, Dawlish knew there was only one way to eliminate these weapons. It had to be immediate, ruthlessly grabbing the initiative from the howitzers if the flotilla's progress was not to be endlessly harassed by them and by the unknown but brilliant gunner who deployed them.

"Drop back, Mr. Holmes," he said. "Take me alongside the *Ipora*."

Holmes stepped towards the double telegraph and pushed the handle for the port engine to full ahead and that for the starboard for full astern. "Full starboard," he told Egdean, who was on the helm. The wheel spun through his hands as the engine room responded. The waters astern boiled as the gunboat's screws thrashed at maximum revolutions, one urging the craft forward, the other striving to drag her astern. The squat craft shuddered, her forward momentum stilled, and spun about on her midships axis. As the bows momentarily faced the northern bank Holmes rang for full ahead on the starboard screw. Still she swung over and seconds later both screws were urging the gunboat downstream towards the stricken *Ipora*.

"Well done, Holmes," Dawlish said, impressed, despite the urgency of the moment, by the skill of the manoeuvre. Nothing but a Rendel could have accomplished such a turn in confined waters.

The *Ipora* was close and Holmes was ringing for reduced revolutions. The sandbagged outer galleries of the stricken paddler were thronged but there was no panic. A bucket brigade was already in action and the flames seemed to be extinguished, although there was still much smoke. The stern wheel was stationary and the absence of escaping steam indicated that the boiler was undamaged. The next salvo might change that, Dawlish knew, glancing towards the blasted tree, no more than thirty yards downstream – too close for comfort. He forced himself not to think that the Reducción gunners must even now be ramming their next shells home and readying to fire.

The *Toad* bumped alongside the paddler and Dawlish, on the helmsman's platform, found himself on a level with the outer gallery of the middle deck of the superstructure. Culbertson was pushing his way towards him through the troops there, his face grimy and his uniform singed.

"We got the fire under control, Commander Nick!" he yelled, "but we're like fish in a barrel. Can you drag us free?"

"First land your cavalry!" Dawlish yelled. "We'll tow you upstream but you've got to land the cavalry first! There's no other way of eliminating those howitzers. We can't do it from the river."

"Goddamn you!" Culbertson's face flushed purple through the grime as he bellowed across the rail. "Goddamn you, Nick! Get us free! Cavalry can't charge artillery! This ain't Goddamn Balaclava!"

"There are only two howitzers, not..." Dawlish began, then cut himself short. There was no time to draw contrasts with the Valley of Death. And cavalry could charge artillery successfully from the flank – he knew it because he had done so himself on a blizzard-swept Balkan battlefield. "You've got cover, Colonel!" he shouted, "You'd have surprise! You'd be on top of them before they ..."

"Get us Goddamn off! You leave the solderin' to me and stick to the river!" Culbertson screamed, his face a paroxysm of anger. He was starting to climb the gallery rail, as if to spring across to the *Toad*. "Pass us a tow, you Goddamn English son of a bitch!"

"Put me alongside the barge," Dawlish said quietly to Holmes. Far off, above the clamour on the smoke-shrouded *Ipora*, above even his own pounding heartbeat, he heard the dual reports of the howitzers, but he shut them out. The next salvo was on the way.

The *Toad* nudged away from the stranded paddler and moved cautiously around its stern, skirting the great wheel and heading for the barge beyond. Horses stamped and whinnied there, terrified by the drifting smoke, straining at their halters. Culbertson struggled along the gallery to keep pace with them, battering a path through the press of men who were still flinging water over the steaming wreckage.

"Dawlish! You bastard!" he yelled. "I'll kill you if you desert us! Nick, you son of a bitch!"

The howl of the dropping howitzer shells drowned him out. They fell almost simultaneously, the first no more than three yards from the *Toad*'s starboard flank, throwing up a muddy geyser that showered spray over the foredeck. The second hit the stern of the barge. A tethered horse exploded in a mist of blood as the shell sliced through it and smashed down through the wooden deck before bursting in the space below. The planking heaved upwards, splintering and tearing loose, scything outwards and upwards in deadly fragments, driven by shards of broken shell and the explosion's blazing fury. Several horses were blown bodily into the water. Others, mangled and writhing, screamed amongst the wreckage of their stalls on the after deck. Flames licked through the brownish grey smoke enveloping the point of impact. It could only be seconds before the entire barge was ablaze.

"Draw in amidships," Dawlish said. "I'm going across. Leave me and then pass a tow to the *Ipora*." He spoke urgently, conscious of the fear lodged like a lump in his stomach and hopeful that it was not apparent to Holmes. "Don't start to pull her free until I've got the horses ashore - you understand? Once they're across it's imperative to get the *Ipora* upriver. Even a hundred yards is better than nothing."

There was more, much more, to say but now all must be left to Holmes' initiative since the *Toad* was edging up towards the barge. Dawlish swung himself down from the steering platform and hurried towards the bows. "Give me a leg up!" he shouted to two of the seamen and an instant later he was balanced on top of the armoured breastwork and poised to jump the four feet that separated him from the barge's deck.

Chaos confronted him there. Frightened horses, mostly uninjured, plunged wildly against their tethers. Smut-laden smoke, acrid and terrifying, drifted through their stalls. Shocked men, Guardia troopers, mercenaries of half-a-dozen nationalities, moved between them, still with discipline enough to attempt to quieten the terrified animals and fight the blaze.

Dawlish leaped and as his feet hit the barge's deck he heard the surge of the *Toad's* engines as she pulled away. He pushed forward between the stalls of stamping and whinnying animals. A trooper was rushing towards him, water slopping from the bucket he held. Dawlish grabbed him and yelled "Where's Capitan Obregón? Take me to Obregón."

The man was too dazed to comprehend and Dawlish shouted again. This time he understood and jerked his head for Dawlish to follow. They shoved their way through the knot of troopers at the after-end who were already trying to douse the flames. Several were using sabres to hack free the burning remnants of the palm-thatch roof and were casting them overboard. A gaunt figure in a scorched uniform strode between them, urging them on.

Dawlish half-recognised the raw features and sunken eyes - a sergeant, the German-American proud of once charging in a forgotten battle. "Where's Obregón, Sergeant?" he asked. "Where is he? Bring me to him."

"There, for all the good he is now," said the sergeant, gesturing behind him. The remnants of a man, bloody and unrecognisable, had been dumped against a stall. "Full in the guts he took it, a splinter." He flinched momentarily to avoid a shower of sparks thrown off as a section of blazing roof collapsed, then said: "Did the Colonel sent you, Sir?"

"That's right," Dawlish lied. "Colonel Culbertson couldn't make it across. He sent me in his place. Who's the senior man here now?"

"I guess I am. Gelb, Sir, Sergeant Gelb."

"Then you're going to get these horses ashore, Sergeant, all of them," Dawlish shouted above the din. "The saddled horses to be formed in a troop - you've twenty saddled? None of them hit? Good. You'll need your best men to ride them, and have the remainder tethered by the bank. Leave the rest of your men to quench the fire - we need to save this barge. You understand?"

Gelb did not hesitate or question Dawlish's tone of command and he quickly detailed the men who were to remain to fight the blaze. The remainder was sent to assemble the horses amidships.

"I'll need a hand with the drawbridge, Sir," he said. "I guess you won't mind?"

Dawlish hurried with him to the wooden structure on the starboard side, a large planked surface hinged to the deck and held almost vertical by rope lashings.

"Get the saddled horses and their troopers off first, Gelb," Dawlish said. "Leave a reliable man behind to supervise getting the other animals off. Once we're ashore you'll follow me with the troopers."

"And then, Sir?"

"We're going for those howitzers. You've got a mount for me?"

"That's Capitan Obregón's Carmelita." Gelb pointed to a bay mare stamping with the other saddled horses under the shelter by the drawbridge. "She's sweet tempered, used to gunfire. You'll need the sabre, Sir. We'll have to cut the bridge lashings."

Dawlish ducked under the hitching bar and cupped the mare's nose in his hands for an instant. She was quivering, her eyes straining, yet she seemed to calm slightly at his touch. An image of morning canters in Shropshire flashed for an incongruous instant through his mind as his nostrils caught the whiff of her sweat. He pushed his revolver back in its holster and heaved on the saddle girth, tightening it three notches, then pulled the sabre from the scabbard before the stirrup. It was heavy, with only a slight curve to the blade, the guard large enough to envelop his whole fist and the weight close enough to that of a cutlass to feel comfortable. He glanced back. In the clear space before the drawbridge Gelb had gathered a small group and was hurriedly selecting the men he wanted to accompany him. They hurried to the saddled horses and busied themselves with quietening them before unhitching them.

"We're ready, Sir," Gelb called. "Can you help me?"

He was standing by the lashings on one side of the drawbridge, sabre upraised. Dawlish hurried towards him and stationed himself by the opposite lashing. Gelb's picked troopers had freed their horses and a few were already mounted, their beasts circling and stamping and closely reined in, still terrified by the smoke and sparks drifting from the barge's after-end. Dawlish nodded to Gelb.

"Form up on the bank, Boys!" Gelb yelled in Spanish. "Single rank, you understand? You wait for Comandante Dawlish and for me!"

His blade flashed down and bit into the straining manila rope supporting his side of the bridge. Fibres sprung free and he hacked again. Dawlish attacked the lashing on his side with equal energy but it took half a dozen strokes before it parted, an instant before Gelb's. The drawbridge teetered at the vertical for a moment, then swung out with gathering speed and the outer end smashed down into the shallows between the barge and the riverbank. One plank sprang loose, and the thirty-degree ramp sagged in the middle, but it looked intact.

Now there was no way back.

11

"Go!" Gelb's command was drowned by the drumming of hooves as the mounted troopers urged their beasts towards the sloping drawbridge.

Dawlish crouched behind a bollard as the half-crazed horses surged past him, eager to escape the cracking flames behind. They cascaded down the incline, slithering, plunging, biting, then crashed in a cloud of spray into the muddy shallows and headed for the shore. One tumbled off the ramp's side, throwing its rider, and lay still in the water below, but the others were reined in on the bank, shivering and snorting. Dawlish ran for Obregón's still-tethered mare, loosened her and pushed his left foot into her stirrup. She was frightened, and she circled as he strove to mount, but he somehow pulled himself up, threw his leg across and found the stirrup on the other side. Obregón had been less tall than himself and the stirrups were short, but there was no time to remedy that now. He held the mare on a tight rein until he was at the top of the ramp, then gave her her head and she went clattering down. The waters at the foot hardly reached her belly and Dawlish urged her forward and towards the single line of horsemen stringing out on the bank. Gelb passed him, more assured in the saddle of his own black mount.

The howitzers' next salvo fell as they reached dry ground. Dawlish glanced back to see two fountains rising in the river beyond the *Ipora*. The *Toad* had moved towards her bows. With luck the wounded paddler might be under tow before the next salvo arrived - the salvo that must reveal the direction in which he must attack. The barge's deck was now alive with horses. The unsaddled mounts were free from their stalls and were being herded towards the drawbridge. It was important to be out of the path of their stampede. He urged his horse to Gelb's side and they faced the straggling row of riders before them.

Dawlish stood in his stirrups and raised his sabre, dismissing the small internal voice that told him how ridiculous he looked with duck trousers riding up from his canvas shoes to expose bare calves. Any show of hesitation would be fatal at this moment, for there was no bond of loyalty or discipline between him and the men before him. Many were no doubt frightened and confused, yet they retained sufficient cohesion and steadiness to have got their horses ashore from a burning craft. Given an example of confident leadership there was a slim chance of success.

"Por allá estan los canones de la Reducción!" he yelled, pointing behind him with the sabre, hoping that nobody would notice his uncertainty as to direction. "There are Reducción's guns! They'll reveal their exact position when they fire again."

"Y vamos a destruirles, Muchachos!" Gelb shouted in support, guttural but unmistakable in his resolve.

"You form on Sergeant Gelb and me. When we trot, you trot. Nobody gallops until you see Gelb or me do so, and I'll shoot the first man to pass me!"

It was impossible to gauge their reaction. Many faces were shaded by broad-brimmed hats and others were intent on controlling their frightened mounts. Beyond them he could see a small boat pulling away from the *Ipora's* side and towards the shore. A burly figure, unmistakably Culbertson, was standing in the bows. Departure must be hasty.

"Sabre or pistol, it's up to yourselves," Dawlish shouted. "There may be riflemen in the scrub. Ride over them, but keep moving! Head for the guns and kill the crews. Now follow me!"

He pulled the mare around and urged her into a fast walk, not daring to look back to see if he was being followed. He heard Gelb call "Vamos muchachos!" and then there was a sound of hooves, first a single beast's, then growing in volume.

The ground ahead was flat and brown and parched, the air above it shimmering in the midday's oven heat. From horseback Dawlish could see clearly across the tops of the low bushes, straggling and thorny, that littered it. Anyone crouching in that scrub could see him even more clearly but there was no sign of movement, no clear focus for his steady advance. His mare was calmer now and he headed her approximately perpendicular to the river. Gelb rode some ten yards to his right and the remaining troopers followed in an open line, six or eight yards apart, weaving to avoid the bushes but maintaining their dressing with reasonable precision.

Two hundred yards into the scrub now, and the noises from the river were drowned by the surrounding clamour of crickets. Sweat stung Dawlish's searching eyes. He was frightened now, badly frightened, knowing the target he must present, but he fought back the urge to kick the mare into a canter - she would be too quickly blown in this heat. How long since the last howitzer shells had fallen - surely it was when he had splashed from the shallows on to the bank? Four, five minutes? Surely it was time...

A sharp crack to his front and left, closely followed by another, gave the answer. Two separate clouds of smoke, the same dirty yellowish-grey he had seen from the balloon, were billowing up over the scrub at perhaps a thousand yards distance. Now at last he had a focus for his advance. He glanced to his right and saw Gelb standing in his stirrups, also transfixed by the sight.

No word was spoken. Dawlish pointed with his sabre to the thinning clouds and wheeled his horse towards them, urging her into a trot. Gelb spurred forward to keep pace and station, gesturing to the line behind to follow. Dawlish found his fear decreasing as the pace quickened and as the remote rational voice that reminded him of his persisting vulnerability was silenced by rising excitement. The noise of the crickets was lost in the rippling thud of hooves on the parched ground as the line of horsemen wove forward between the scrub.

They moved at a fast trot, too fast perhaps to Dawlish's thinking, if energy was to be conserved for the last furious dash on which success must depend. He reined in slightly and made a downward fanning motion with his sabre, then glanced back to see with satisfaction his followers dropping back.

Dawlish's heart was thumping with that mixture of exultation and fear he had known before whenever the die was cast and retreat impossible. The knowledge that injury and death were close realities was accepted and quickly ignored, his entire being concentrated on prevailing in the minutes ahead. He swung the sabre, gauging its momentum, conscious of his ignorance of its use from horseback. Too late to worry now - instinct must guide him. The mare - Carmelita was her name, he remembered - seemed to have caught his excitement and was straining forward, her eagerness different to that near panic that had possessed her when he had first mounted. The speed whipped away his Sennet hat and the sunlight was painfully dazzling, but there was no turning back and he screwed his eyes up against the glare.

Suddenly, eighty, maybe one hundred yards ahead, and to the right, rifle fire erupted. Smoke obscured the bank of thorn from which it issued. He heard a whinnying scream somewhere behind and the sound of a heavy body crashing to earth. He urged the mare into a canter and resisted the impulse to sheer off further to the left. "Canter!" he yelled, and to his right Gelb called too and the whole ragged line of horsemen surged forward, drawing level with the thorn bank and then passing it. A single wounded animal thrashed on the ground behind them, its rider pinned beneath.

This far from the river the scrub was sparse and Dawlish was heading on an almost straight course, crouched forward, sabre held low, the mare guided by only the slightest touch of the reins on her neck. He saw figures to his right, dashing from the cover from whence the fire had come, outflanked by the riders, running in a hopeless effort to keep pace, reloading as they ran.

Fifty yards ahead a clump of brush suddenly crackled with pinpoint muzzle-flashes that were quickly lost in drifting smoke. Their slugs screamed past and he knew he was untouched. He raced onwards, pulling the mare over to head slightly to the left of the brush, hoping that those lurking there were not armed with repeaters. His sabre was raised and that absurd sense of invincibility that has sustained cavalrymen through history was surging through him.

His path was to the left of the clearing smoke. Two figures in stained white burst from the scrub, their bayonet-tipped rifles upraised. One rushed to block Dawlish's path, rifle held high to thrust at him and the second was a few paces behind and fumbling with his weapon - a Martini Henry - and pushing a new round into the breech.

Dawlish rode straight at the nearer man, raising his sabre over his left shoulder. The man was stupid, Dawlish realised - he should be going for the horse with his bayonet, not the rider. He waited until he was almost on top of him before jerking the mare to the left. He could see the terrified eyes in the brown, flat Indian face as the man forced himself to stand his ground and jab upwards. The bayonet thrust uselessly upwards behind Dawlish. His right knee hit the Indian and he swung the sabre. It bit at the joint of neck and shoulder and then he was past, dragging the mare's head to the right and urging her at the second rifleman before him. This man had jerked his breech closed and was raising the rifle to fire but it was too late, for the mare was crashing into him, knocking him aside and jumping free when she felt the wriggling body under her hooves. Dawlish chopped down instinctively but the blood-streaked blade encountered no resistance. He heard more rifle fire, behind and to the right and glancing across saw a Guardia trooper jerk rigid in his saddle, arms flung out, then tumble. Gelb was drumming forward, the gleam of his upraised blade dulled with red. Beyond him the other riders were racing onwards, disregarding the firing that crackled and died behind them.

More figures flitted through the scrub another hundred or so yards ahead, breaking cover, clustering towards a low streak of thorny brush. Shots rang out, ineffective at this range against moving targets, but sufficient to crouch the oncoming riders still lower on their mounts. More men were emerging further to the left, all heading for that long clump of thorn almost dead ahead - and Dawlish knew with sudden clarity that the howitzers must lie beyond it and that any further frontal approach would be shredded in a storm of rife-fire.

"A la izquierda! Bear to the left!" he yelled, standing in his stirrups and glancing back, swinging his sabre to point some sixty degrees away from the present axis of charge.

"To the left, to the left, Boys! Follow El Comandante!" Gelb's voice rose clear above the beating hooves and he was lost in dust as he slewed his mount over sharply behind Dawlish. The line of horsemen bunched as they wheeled and Gelb bellowed for them to open out. Gunfire rippled from the line of thorn that was already dropping behind. The range was opening. Rifle rounds screamed ineffectually overhead, too high, or lashed into the low scrub that whipped at the riders' legs, but none found a mark.

Carmelita was sure-footed, a seasoned campaigner in this terrain, and neither she nor any of the mounts following were showing signs of fatigue. The thorn thicket was outflanked now and Dawlish searched for movement among the dusty brown and grey scrub that littered the ground ahead. It could only be moments now before the howitzers were revealed.

"Sergeant Gelb!" he called. "Ready to wheel right on my command!"

"Fall back, Navarro! You too, Plowright!" Gelb shouted, half turned in his saddle, his bloodied sabre pointing to individual riders. "Neruda! Draw in to your left! Sprokkelaar! Ignacio! Come level!"

Two orange muzzle flashes, and then sharp reports rolling across the plain, and rising billows of smoke, revealed the howitzers. They were closer than Dawlish had anticipated, perhaps four hundred yards ahead and to his right.

"Not yet, Sergeant. Not yet!" he shouted, fearing that a turn too soon would carry his charging line of horsemen straight into a screen of riflemen.

He resisted the urge to pull Carmelita's head over and plunge towards the smoke. Somewhere overhead the howitzer shells would be reaching the apex of their flight, pausing before plunging towards that blasted tree on the riverbank. Would the *Toad* have pulled the

Ipora free by now? Would those shells smash down on the Rendel's open deck?

"Another hundred yards, Gelb, then right wheel!" Dawlish yelled. "Leave the guns on our right. We're going to take them in the flank! Wait for my word!" His mare pounded onwards, weaving daintily around the larger bushes in her path.

The howitzers' thinning smoke was losing itself above the scrub and then it was time to shout "Now! Right wheel!"

Gelb carried the line around, bellowing commands he had learned on some distant Prussian cavalry ground, dropping back the right wing and speeding up the left until the whole ragged line was realigned and advancing on an axis that would carry it some two hundred yards to the left of the howitzers. Their position was marked now not by the thinning gun-smoke alone but by a rising cloud of dust. Suddenly Dawlish could see dark figures moving among the scrub, men and horses, maybe mules. He could sense their urgency, their controlled panic. They were limbering up, by God! They were abandoning their position!

Rifle fire opened from the right, as yet distant, but warning that the howitzers were still protected. Men were rushing from the cover of the thorn bank that the riders had outflanked, some standing in the open and aiming carefully at the horsemen outlined against the wave of dust rolling behind them. The range was two hundred yards and their shots were wild and still the troopers crashed forward. Other riflemen were running back towards the guns, some reloading as they ran, others fumbling to fix bayonets.

The ground was open here, the scrub meagre. As the last thicket was passed Dawlish finally saw to his right the weapons that had so tormented the flotilla. With squat barrels almost lost behind huge spoked wheels, the howitzers were at the centres of two knots of men who laboured to manoeuvre them into the traces behind stamping mules teams. Others were pushing a limber – only one, Dawlish noted, remembering the report of Carmelita's late master - and a mule-drawn wagon was already pulling away. A cry rose from the groups around the artillery as the riders burst into their view. Two men were on horseback among them and one's mount reared as he pulled it around and gestured towards the oncoming threat. Several men ran forward and dropped to one knee behind the first low bushes that offered cover.

Time now to make the last turn. "We'll right-wheel now, Sergeant!" Dawlish shouted to Gelb. "Straight for the guns - on your command!"

The line slewed round, the right extremity held back to a canter by Gelb's bellowed order and outstretched sabre, the left drawing ahead until the whole front rank had wheeled, then careered forward at full gallop into the last dash that would carry them among the enemy.

The nearest riflemen were less than a hundred yards ahead, their presence betrayed by muzzle flashes and rolling smoke among the isolated bushes hiding them. Dawlish knew that he was being shot at, but the reports of the rifles and the scream of the bullets slashing overhead were lost in the thunder of the hooves.

Eighty yards... Half a dozen men were running on the open ground between the bushes and the confusion around the howitzers, bayonet-tipped rifles in hand. A long scream came from somewhere behind Dawlish, followed by the crash of a body tumbling and falling.

Fifty yards... A thick patch of scrub ahead, high as Carmelita's shoulder, but Dawlish let her plunge through, ignoring the brush lacerating his calves. A white blur on his left, and too late the recognition of a figure rising from the thicket and the dark shaft of a rifle jabbing upwards. Dawlish lashed instinctively with his sabre across his body, but he was level with this attacker, and passing. His stroke was a clumsy one and the blade met only thin air. For an instant he was looking straight into an Indian face, its lips drawn back in a howl of rage and fear, and a bayonet point was swinging up and towards him. The muzzle flash was close enough to scorch his left shoulder with burning powder grains and the report near enough to send an explosive wave of pain smashing through his head, but he was alive, and plunging past, and breaking into the clear ground beyond the thicket.

Thirty yards... The faces and bandoliers and ragged clothing of the men bobbing from the bushes ahead were clearly defined, individuals now, not an impersonal presence. Gelb was pulling ahead, sabre trailing and low, ready for a forward cut. Dawlish's peripheral vision told him that the horsemen behind were drawing level with him. Their sound was muffled and he realised that he was part deafened by that near miss in the scrub. Rifle fire barked irregularly from ahead and somewhere to the left another horse went down in a thrashing cartwheel.

The riders smashed into the screen of riflemen. Dead ahead Dawlish saw a man rise from the brush, his foreshortened rifle almost invisible and aiming straight for him. Terror filled him but he could only jerk down to crouch along the mare's neck, his eyes fixed on that terrible muzzle. A tongue of flame, then smoke half obscuring the rifleman and Dawlish was filled with surging joy as he knew that he was safe. The rifleman knew it too, and knew also that he had no time to reload.

Only yards separated them and Dawlish thundered towards his attacker through the low scrub, raising his sabre. The man stood for a moment, swinging up his bayonet, but his nerve failed and he turned and started to run. Dawlish pulled slightly to the left and for a moment he was looking down and noting remotely the delta of sweat soaking the back of the man's shirt and the bald patch in the centre of his mop of straight black hair. Then the sabre arced down in a terrible slice that jarred Dawlish's arm as it met the skull beneath, but already he was past and had eyes only for the howitzers ahead.

The last obstacle was passed. The horsemen had punched through the riflemen's thin screen, losing another two in the process, so that few more than a dozen riders galloped across the open ground towards the chaos of artillery and carts and horses and mules and shouting men. Several riflemen ran terrified before the riders, weapons tossed aside in panic, and they were ridden or sabred down.

One howitzer was on the move, but slowly, its team of six mules ignoring the whips of their mounted drivers and maintaining a stolid plod. A hundred yards beyond it a handful of men, directed by a rider on a grey horse, was manoeuvring the second weapon behind another team and limber while a cart was moving off into the brush.

A single stationary horseman occupied the ground between the oncoming riders and the first howitzer, his brown mount skittish and stamping. He wore the semblance of a uniform, with cord breeches and black boots and a blue tunic, his bearded face shaded by a wide-brimmed felt hat, a long-barrelled revolver in his right hand. He glanced towards the nearing horsemen, then back towards the guns and then, with a perceptible shrug, as if accepting the inevitability of his fate, spurred to meet the attackers.

Gelb was nearest and pulled towards him. They were only yards apart when another rider cut in on Gelb's left, sabre extended beyond his horse's bulging eyes to skewer on the point. The bearded rider wheeled to meet him, reined in and fired twice, blowing him from the saddle.

Then Gelb was on top of the horseman. His first chopping blow missed but he caught him on the side of the head with the hilt as he drew back, and that threw him to the ground. Gelb's pace hardly faltered and he was almost immediately drawing level with Dawlish again and heading for the moving howitzer.

Consternation seized the drivers and gunners knotted around the mule team and artillery piece as the horsemen stormed down on them. Only a few were armed but the others' fear was contagious and they too deserted the beasts and scattered into the scrub. There were a few isolated shots, and one heroic soul flailed with a rammer until his arm was hacked through, but the advantages of shock and terror were with the riders. They spurred among the terrified gunners, thrusting and hacking and blazing down with pistols. Dawlish and Gelb were first among them, Dawlish ignoring the sobbing cry and upraised arms of the wretch on the leading mule and taking him through the chest on the point. He jerked his blade free, wheeled, then urged the mare around the head of the team and into the group that cowered beyond, uncertain whether to stand or flee. He chopped down on bowed heads, uselessly protected by clutching fingers, and was aware of other riders cleaving to right and left, and of bodies writhing under stamping hooves. For a seeming eternity the universe contracted to a chaos of screaming men and barking pistols and plunging mules and chunking blades, suffused by the smell of blood and fear and powder.

A small cold voice told Dawlish that this slaughter must be abandoned - this howitzer was his, but the other weapon remained and momentum must not be lost. He drew back, saw Gelb by the howitzer itself, leaning down and thrusting between a wheel's spokes, and he spurred towards him. A blood-smeared figure staggered from under the barrel as Dawlish came level with the muzzle, only to collapse with a wailing scream as Gelb slashed backhandedly across his face.

"Enough here, Sergeant!" Dawlish shouted. "Rally the men! Four to take this weapon to the river - the rest to charge the other!" He gestured towards the second howitzer.

Somehow, under the directions of that man on the grey horse, its crew had not panicked. They had got the mule-team hitched to it and were straining to drag it from the shallow pit in which it had been positioned. A dozen or so riflemen were crouched uncertainly on the open ground before it, fearfully conserving the single shots their Martini-Henrys would give them before they must resort to their bayonets. They were held in line by the grey's rider, who was clad similarly to the horseman whom Gelb had thrown down. He rode back and forth behind them, his mount close reined, pistol in hand.

Gelb's bellow's assembled the remaining riders – eleven, including Dawlish, all wearing a look of savage glee. Their blood was as yet uncooled and the minor wounds soaking irregular blotches on their uniforms were as yet unnoticed. Dawlish knew that they – and he himself – must charge again immediately, for within a minute fear and doubt would return. The cowering survivors of the gun crew scuttled away as Gelb selected the riders to lead the howitzer back to the river. The remainder pulled their steaming mounts into an open line.

Gelb looked enquiringly at Dawlish. "That fella on the grey horse", he said, "Neruda can take him. He's a good shot."

Dawlish nodded and Gelb spoke rapidly in Spanish. A lean figure pulled his Winchester carbine from its bucket holster and slid from his saddle. He moved to the howitzer and with infinite care steadied his barrel on the wheel, his right eye narrowed to a slit as he sighted.

The grey's rider flung out his arms and a scarlet crater exploded in his chest an instant after the carbine's report. The horse reared and he slid back over the haunches, crumpling on the ground and lying still. The riflemen saw their leader fall and they started uncertainly to their feet. Neruda ejected, fed in another round and fired again. A rifleman spun and fell and his companions started to run back to the howitzer.

Dawlish and Gelb spurred forward, the remaining horsemen surging behind them and Neruda vaulting into his saddle to follow.

Dawlish picked his victim, a short figure in a ragged shirt, who dropped his rifle and glanced over his shoulder as he ran. His face was a mask of despair as he saw horse and rider bear down on him, yet Dawlish's swing was clumsy, and he missed. He bore on towards the howitzer, crouching low, his sabre point now extended level with Carmelita's right eye. The mule team stood abandoned and the gunners were already disappearing into the brush beyond. A few irregular shots rang out and then, in front, Dawlish saw a running figure who suddenly turned, dropped his rifle, and raised his arms. His hair was grey, his face seamed and lined and he was sinking to his knees in an attitude of entreaty. Dawlish's mind registered willingness to surrender at the same moment that the mare carried him past and as his sabre smashed into the despair-filled face with a jarring impact. Carmelita swerved, almost unhorsing him, and crashed through a low thicket as he fought to regain his balance. He recovered, realised that the charge had left him behind, then saw the Guardia riders clustered round the howitzer beyond, whooping in triumph. The only riflemen and gunners visible were dead, their scattered bodies littering the open ground. Dawlish walked his mount towards the howitzer, threading his way between the corpses. He realised that his hands were shaking.

He looked down. Two men lay close together, both short, sunburned, of indeterminate age. One was crumpled and trampled, the other lay on his back, gaping sightlessly at the brazen sky. Their coarse cotton clothing was little better than rags and their feet were bound in hide sandals. One's hand was open, palm upwards, callused and rough, the hand of a labourer. They were no different from the despised conscripts on the flotilla's transports, little more than chattels. Yet something, somebody, had inspired them to stand and fight, however clumsily, against a vastly more potent and sophisticated power and in the name of a simple but powerful ideal.

He suddenly remembered the semi-uniformed horseman whom Gelb had knocked over. If he was alive, he might have answers.

12

The captured howitzer was on the move, two Guardia troopers flanking the mule team and dragging the leaders into a shambling trot. The cart previously seen escaping had been taken too, and it followed. The remaining troopers formed a loose screen, sabres sheathed, Winchesters at the ready.

Gelb cantered towards Dawlish.

"So you're alive, Sir," he said, reining in. His tone had a new hint of respect.

"We've got to move fast. Back to the river, back the way we came. There are still enemy over there." Dawlish pointed towards the thin line of scrub they had outflanked and which lay between them and the river. If a leader as resolute as those two men in uniforms still remained then the riflemen there could decimate this handful of troopers on their blown horses.

The first captured howitzer was far ahead, its track marked by a column of dust. Dawlish felt his joints loose with that release of fear and tension that always followed action and knew others must feel the same. This was the moment of weakness, of the temptation to relaxation of vigilance and resolution. And it must be thrust aside if the full fruits of success were to be reaped.

"We're too slow Sergeant!" he called to Gelb. "Have that team whipped up! And our losses? You're sure that none of them are wandering about dazed? Detach two men to search." Gelb spurred off and called orders and then, satisfied that a modicum of extra pace had been achieved, rejoined Dawlish.

"That man on the horse, the man in the blue tunic," Dawlish said, and he saw that Gelb had forgotten him in the ten-minute eternity since they had stormed down on the first howitzer. "The one with the revolver - he shot one of your men, then you threw him off his horse."

"The fella with the hat and boots." Gelb remembered now. "Black beard."

"I don't think you killed him. I want to find him."

They left the small plodding convoy and headed back, a trooper following. Wheel ruts in the dust, discarded weapons and birds already pulling at scattered corpses led them to the location of the clash. Whatever riflemen had survived had made their escape. A lifeless horse lay sprawled with its neck at right angles to its body. Its rider lay a few yards beyond, his clothing mottled with red blotches. He had been thrown but somebody had waited until the charge had passed and had then stabbed him repeatedly with a bayonet.

"Sprokkelaar," Gelb said. "Damn stupid Dutchman. He never was lucky."

It was the blue tunic that they saw first, a dark patch against the brownish dust, but there was no sign of movement. The trooper whom the horseman had shot lay a few yards from him, a huge exit wound blasted in his upturned back. Hatless now, the blue-clad rider showed closely cropped steel-grey hair above a tanned face and white-flecked black beard. The thought flashed through Dawlish's mind that this was how he himself would look in another five years and so there was some feeling of shared mortality as he dismounted. The man was lying on his side and a great bruise, purple and black, covered his left cheek and closed his eye.

Dawlish rolled him on his back and was rewarded with a soft groan and a flicker of the good eye. The tunic was double breasted and of poor material, and the brass buttons were plain, but the cut aped something military. Dawlish opened it and felt a strong heartbeat beneath the coarse cotton vest. "He'll live," he said to Gelb, who was squatting beside him after recovering the horseman's long-barrelled Colt from a few feet away. They dragged him into a sitting position and Gelb splashed water from his canteen into his face. Then, sensing that he was coming round, he forced it between his teeth. The man spluttered, swallowed and opened his eyes.

"I wouldn't move, if I were you," Gelb said in Spanish, laying the Colt's muzzle against his temple.

The horseman, dazed, and dazzled by the light, nodded slowly.

"There's a rope at my saddle, Commander," Gelb said to Dawlish, not turning his head. "He won't walk far but if we can truss him up we can throw him over one of the horses."

Covered by the mounted trooper, they bound the prisoner's hands behind him - long, delicate hands - and then lashed his feet together. He remained silent but Dawlish sensed that he was recovering fast and that a quick mind was already evaluating the situation and steeling itself for whatever ordeal was to come. Once he was secure Dawlish went through his pockets - an ivory handled penknife, a dog-eared booklet of trigonometry tables, a nickel-plated spoon and fork wrapped in oilcloth, a burning glass and, in the inner breast pocket, the real treasure, a leather-bound notebook with a silver-cased pencil in a loop in its cover. He flicked it open. The first page identified it as the appointment book of a Mrs. Hannah Farnsworth and the next half-dozen scheduled tea parties and dinners, the list ending abruptly a year before. But thereafter, in a different hand, the book was filled with neat, closely-spaced notes and calculations, interspersed with diagrams – all of them varying combinations of contours, hatchings and the unmistakable snaking line of the Rio San Joaquin. In every case straight lines fanned out from two dots to intersect the river. It was the record of half a dozen carefully chosen ambush points. And the language was one that Dawlish had learned in boyhood.

"A Frenchman, by God," he said, looking him in the face. It was square, with powerful features and a broken nose. Though lined, it had a sense of being younger than it appeared. There was a studied vacancy in the one open brown eye, the impression of a conscious effort by the owner to distance himself from the present reality.

"Who are you?" Dawlish asked in French. He felt rising frustration at the prisoner's abstraction.

He leaned down until their faces almost touched and said in slow French "I am a British officer. You would be well advised to speak to me rather than my associates." The Frenchman shrugged and Dawlish recognised the same gesture with which he had ridden alone to face the oncoming charge. This man was not going to talk readily.

They bundled him with difficulty across Gelb's mount. He offered no resistance or complaint. They secured him, head down, behind the saddle, hands and feet lashed beneath the belly.

Before they set off Gelb picked up the Frenchman's wide-brimmed felt hat from the ground. "I reckon it'll fit you, Commander. Sort of souvenir."

Dawlish took it. It was faded, but it still held its shape. He turned over the blackened sweatband. In indelible ink he read the name of the owner - "A. Greenough" - and remembered Kegworth's mention of the name in that impossibly distant inn-parlour in Chatham. Perhaps the prisoner's boots, dusty but well made, had also belonged to that same clergyman's son. Dawlish jammed the hat on his head and was grateful that it fitted and shaded his eyes comfortably.

The horses had regained their wind and a fast trot brought them level with the second howitzer, now halfway to the river. Three of the troopers who had come down during the charge had been picked up and were riding on the cart, two injured and the third whole, though with a bloodied horse in tow.

"They need to move faster, Sergeant," Dawlish called out but Gelb did not hear, for there was a sudden rifle fire from their left. They both reined in - it seemed to come from far beyond that line of scrub which they had outflanked and which had lain directly between the howitzers and the river. Dawlish concluded that troops had been landed from the flotilla. The firing was irregular and died away within minutes. With their howitzers captured, and their apparent leaders out of action, the Reducción forces were showing no evidence of wanting to stay and fight.

The green streak of vegetation that marked the river-line and the upperworks of the *Ipora* were just visible, the fires apparently extinguished, when Gelb's pointing finger indicated a cloud of dust rolling in from their left. Horsemen, moving fast.

"It's the Colonel," Gelb said. "See that crouch in the saddle? That's Colonel Si all right!"

Dawlish wheeled to meet the riders and Gelb trotted after, his prisoner bouncing across his horse's rump. There were twenty troopers and Dawlish begrudgingly acknowledged to himself that Culbertson had done well to muster this force from the chaos left behind on the burning barge.

Culbertson's raised hand brought his men to a halt but he cantered forward himself, reining in within a foot of Dawlish's mount. His eyes were bulging and his face inflamed. The veins in his neck pulsed as he spoke. "You bastard, Dawlish!" His voice almost a scream. "You bastard. You left us under fire!"

"We have the howitzers, Colonel," Dawlish spoke slowly, hoping that his words would sink in, yet knowing already that Culbertson was in no mood to listen. "We have the howitzers - you understand? No more shelling from cover, Colonel. We can move fast upriver now."

"Damn your howitzers, you son of a bitch! You took my troopers! That's what I understand! You Goddamn took my men and left us on the river to be shot at like fish in a barrel!"

"I can only apologise..." Dawlish's words were cut off as Culbertson spotted the bulk of the prisoner draped across Gelb's mount. "What in damnation is that, Sergeant?" he yelled.

"We got one of them, Colonel," Gelb smiled with grim satisfaction. "A horseman - seems he was directing them. Brought him down myself. Fancy sort, a Frenchman."

Culbertson jerked his horse away from Dawlish, skirted round and came level with Gelb on his left side, where the prisoner's head hung down. He reached down and caught the hair in his fist, jerking up and twisting savagely so he could see the Frenchman's face. There was a sharp intake of breath, the sound of a man forcing himself not to cry out.

"A Frenchman, are you?" Culbertson snarled. "Talk English, do you? Or Español? The lingo don't make no difference to me, amigo! One way or the other you'll be glad to talk soon enough."

"Leave him be, Colonel," Dawlish said. "I'll see no abuse of helpless men, whoever they are."

Culbertson jerked the Frenchman's head higher. The face now registered agony. "So you'll see no abuse, Commander Nick? And you'll stop me, I suppose?" His eyes were bloodshot with fury.

"Let go of that man's hair, Colonel," Dawlish said, his voice quiet and steady.

The Colonel paused, flung the prisoner's head from him and glared. "He's all yours for now, you son of a bitch," he growled.

"You'll order Sergeant Gelb to ride ahead of me to the river, Colonel," Dawlish said. "I'm holding the prisoner on the *Toad* until we have the flotilla sorted out. You have my word as a British officer that he'll be produced before Señor Murillo in the *Tacuari's* saloon at eight o'clock this evening. You understand?"

Culbertson's reply was to spit on the prisoner, then order Gelb to comply. "I'll see you in Hell, Commander Goddamn Dawlish," he snarled as he dragged his horse around, then spurred off to rejoin the larger group. They wheeled at his command and moved back into the scrub. Dawlish did not envy any wounded or straggling Reducción rifleman they might come upon.

Gelb had fallen into a smart trot but Dawlish drew level, eager to say something that might express his regret at having placed this brave, competent man into an impossible position with his own superior. His notice was drawn however by the sound of his own name being called. It came, weakly, from the prisoner, the words agonised and disjointed by the bouncing of the hanging head. At Dawlish's order Gelb reined in.

"Commander, Sir. Your name is Dawlish?" The captive was straining his hanging head around at an impossible angle to look up. "Thank you, Monsieur. You are a humanitarian."

"I am a British Officer, Sir," Dawlish said, feeling a little sententious, but unsure of how otherwise to answer and looking down into the face so awkwardly turned up towards him.

"And I a French one, Sir. Or at least I was until Sedan." There was still a hint of pride in his gasp. "Lieutenant Jacques Roybon. Late Twelfth Regiment of Artillery. And at your mercy, Commander."

Dawlish had at last met a leader of La Reducción Nueva.

13

Again the *Tacuari's* stuffy saloon. Again the same disunited, suspicious assembly, subdued and quiet, waiting for Murillo to lift his face from the minute book and open the council.

Three paraffin lamps cast a glare over the chart-spread table and shadows into the corners. Culbertson smoked a cheroot. Aquino cleaned his fingernails with a knife. Tinsley checked fussily in the sheaf of papers he always took with him to these sessions and scribbled busily on a memorandum pad, his brow furrowed in concentration. The clamour of frogs and crickets penetrated from the warm night outside, louder than the further-off sounds from the riverside bivouacs. Dawlish sat next to Tinsley, studiously gazing into the dark void beyond the open window opposite, pondering the choices he knew he might soon have to make.

On the gallery outside Holmes and Egdean waited with the French prisoner, his hands bound before him and his feet tied loosely enough for him to hobble. Another length of rope linked his belt to Egdean's to prevent a desperate plunge overboard. He had given little enough away since disclosing his name but Dawlish had gauged him sufficiently resolute to choose suicide rather than compromise his cause. Whatever might have driven Lieutenant Jacques Roybon, late Twelfth Artillery Regiment, to such desperate and inventive resistance in the Chaco Boreal, he almost certainly valued it above life itself.

Dawlish had arrived at the river to find that the *Toad* had indeed dragged the *Ipora* from danger and that the fire on the steamer and barge had been extinguished with less damage than could have been hoped for. Holmes had then taken the gunboat downstream to ensure that the other steamers were anchored in positions of safety. Thanks to his efforts, there had been no groundings. Tinsley was summoned immediately to take charge of the captured howitzers. American models, War of Secession vintage, twelve-pounders, he had assured Dawlish - just as he has surmised at the Gullet - worn but serviceable. Only a handful of shells had been captured but those carried for the expedition's ten-pounders could be used instead, if they were encased in leather bags, as they were of slightly lower calibre. Extreme accuracy would not be necessary in the type of operations envisaged at Puerto Plutarcho.

The prisoner had been brought on board the *Toad* under blindfold - Dawlish was not going to let an obvious artillery expert catch even a glimpse of the gunboat's Armstrong lurking in its pit. Cut free from Gelb's horse, he was too weak, dizzy and cramped to walk without assistance. He was lodged in the paint-locker under the guard of a cudgel-armed seaman who viewed him with even greater distrust when he heard he was French. His bonds were loosened and he was given food, for which he was politely thankful in good English, but he refused to answer any questions. The only other clue to his background came in the *Toad's* gig was they were being pulled across to make good Dawlish's promise to produce him on the *Tacuari* at eight o'clock.

"You shot well today - and back at La Garganta too, Lieutenant." Dawlish meant it. "They taught you well in France."

Roybon's bruised face was partly lit by the reflections of the lights of the moored steamers. "The Prussians taught me my best lesson," he said. "I was one of the unfortunates they caught in the chamber-pot at Sedan, and the inevitable followed. And Monsieur Thiers and his Versailles butchers completed my education." There was a hint of a smile, a bitter one.

"You're in that same pot again, Lieutenant," Dawlish pounced to exploit this chink. "However you got yourself mixed up with this Reducción Nueva nonsense is irrelevant now. You're obviously an intelligent man, a professional. You must know the whole Reducción business is doomed. You've put up a decent fight. The kindest thing you can do for those wretches who fight so well for you is to convince your associates to surrender now."

The Frenchman looked him directly in the face. "You cannot understand what we're trying to do for them," he said. "They've been nothing. They had nothing."

"Nothing but their chains. Yes, I know - I've seen your handbill. But you forget something. They've got lives to lose too, and wives, and children. If there's continued resistance I'll be powerless to stop excesses when the settlement is recaptured."

"For a British officer, you've found yourself fine company," Roybon said and then looked away into the darkness, giving again that impression of a man distancing himself from the present, preparing for the worst.

He spoke once more to Dawlish just before they reached the *Tacuari*.

"There was another mounted man," he said. "On a grey horse. He was with the other howitzer." He paused, then forced himself to continue. "Did he survive?"

Dawlish sensed deep sorrow. He shook his head. "He died well," he said. "A brave man."

122

For the first time Roybon's voice carried a quaver. "My parents would have expected as much," he said. "He was my older brother, Michel. Also an artilleryman."

"I'm sorry," Dawlish found himself saying. The remembrance of his own older brother James, his neck broken in the hunting field so long since, came flooding back. And Roybon suddenly seemed less an enemy and more a man.

The gig drew alongside the *Tacuari*. It was almost eight o'clock. Roybon had been delivered on time, just as Dawlish promised.

*   *   *

Murillo at last completed his perusal of the previous minutes and called the meeting to order as cold-bloodedly as if it had been in a City boardroom.

"Colonel Culbertson had a signal success today, I understand," he said, "though I believe some damage was sustained by one of our steamers. No doubt Commander Dawlish will be able to explain that. Colonel - if you please."

Culbertson smirked triumphantly towards Dawlish, then towards Murillo. "Can't say I can take all the credit, Señor," he said with a broad smile, all traces of the rancour of that encounter in the scrub apparently absent. "Old Commander Nick here, he did his bit too. I can't deny I didn't feel sore about being shot about by them Goddamn howitzers, and the *Toad* might have got to us a bit sooner once we were hit, but once she did get alongside - why, Commander Nick immediately agreed to help out when I asked him to take my boys ashore while I was taking control of the situation."

Dawlish listened speechless, his blood rising.

The Colonel beamed towards the others. "One thing you can say about these English gentlemen - you never do need ask if they can ride! I guess it's all that fox huntin' from an early age. Why, our sailor friend here rode as well as any of my boys, and better than many, and by the time I'd caught up with them - why, Gentlemen, they'd taken the Goddamn howitzers and an important prisoner with them."

Culbertson looked straight at Dawlish, his face a mask of geniality and only his eyes betraying the venom beneath. "You'd be mighty welcome to sign up as a Guardia trooper any day, Commander, any day you take a turn against the seafarin' life."

Even Murillo's thin lips creased into a weak smile and Tinsley turned and said: "You hear that Dawlish? You'll make a soldier yet."

Dawlish's heart was pounding, his face flushed, but he knew he was beaten. To challenge Culbertson's account in this gathering was to invite ridicule and an argument he could not hope to win.

"I'll stick to the river for now, Gentlemen," he heard himself saying. "There's still the *Torres* monitor to concern us and I doubt if Colonel Culbertson's troopers will deal with her so easily."

"The Commander's a mite possessive of his prisoner," Culbertson said, "Especially considering that one of my boys did the job o' knocking him down. But no need to dwell on that, is there, Commander Nick? I guess you've took him along tonight for us to take a look at - an' a damn interesting customer he sounds too. I guess you wouldn't object to us getting a sight of him now?"

Dawlish had Roybon ushered in.

"A seat for our guest - there, between these gentlemen" Murillo said.

Holmes pulled out a chair between Culbertson and Aquino. Egdean helped the trammelled prisoner sit down. Dawlish detected a degree of gentleness that implied that Roybon had earned both respect and pity since arriving on the *Toad.*

"That will be all, Mr. Holmes," Murillo said. "You may wait outside for the Commander."

Roybon was making every effort to maintain his composure. He placed his bound hands on the table before him, then looked deliberately round, stopping to stare into each face in turn. He nodded to Dawlish, not un-politely, as if to a formal business acquaintance. Tinsley looked away, avoiding meeting his gaze. For all the others there was an unmistakable hint of contempt in Roybon's look, despite the purple bruise that still disfigured one side of his face. Murillo stared back at him, eyes enlarged behind his thick pince-nez, as devoid of emotion or sympathy as a python's contemplating a rat.

"You see before you the representatives of a British business undertaking," he said to the prisoner in English. "We will deal with you on a business basis and you too will have a chance to profit from that business. You understand?"

A nod. Almost imperceptible.

"And so we start. Are you the man they call El Pobre?"

"A poor man, yes," the prisoner said, looking around the table with an air of defiance, "but not El Pobre, not The Poor Man. He's a better man than me by far."

"Smart, ain't he?" Culbertson drawled.

Murillo ignored him. "Are we to be honoured with your name? And your nationality? What you're doing here?"

"Jacques Roybon. Born a Frenchman and now - what? A citizen of nowhere and everywhere. But at present proud to serve La Reducción Nueva."

Dawlish had again the impression of a man who had gone beyond despair, a man who had known pain and was steeling himself for it again, a man who knew himself to be on the brink of the abyss and yet was even then still trying to define the meaning of his life and actions.

"La Reducción Nueva does not exist." There was a hint of shrillness in Murillo's voice, a glint of anger behind those thick lenses. "You may be referring to the Puerto Plutarcho settlement of the Hyperion

Consortium, Monsieur Roybon, to its livestock and workshops and facilities and employees - to that and nothing else!"

"But La Reducción does exist, Señor," Roybon said, "created by the very human livestock you shipped there. It exists as an objective fact, capable of defending itself, capable of holding its own against all you can send against it, capable of..."

Aquino, on Roybon's left, cut him off, smashing a fist into the bruise on the side of his face. He was thrown over towards Culbertson who lashed out with equal fury. "Steady up there, Sonny, steady up!" he said with laboured mirth. "Not even a smell of the cork and you're already fallin' around the place."

Roybon strove to stay upright, his bound hands clasped tightly on the table, a trickle of blood running down into his beard. Dawlish recognised fear in his eyes now, fear of yielding rather than fear of pain, fear he was trying to suppress.

"And your role in the plundering of the Consortium, Monsieur Roybon?" Murillo had not even blinked as Roybon was struck.

"In the liberation, Señor, only a small role. A little specialist advice, a little support. La Reducción doesn't need..."

And Culbertson hit him first this time even before Murillo began to repeat with rising shrillness: "La Reducción does not exist." There was blood now on the other side of Roybon's face, but still he tried to ignore his torment, his hands unmoved on the table before him.

"As I was saying Señor, La Reducción's forces..."

This time it was Aquino who reacted to a nod from Murillo, rising to his feet and dragging Roybon from his chair. His left arm clamped around his throat while his right pulled his pistol and jammed it against Roybon's temple. He looked to Murillo for instructions and was met by a beckoning jerk of the head. He half-pushed, half-dragged Roybon to the space at the table-end by Murillo's chair, then forced him to his knees. Dawlish recognised with sick impotence that Aquino was doing this without either pleasure or repugnance.

Roybon was an object to him, nothing more. Murillo, looked away for a moment, made a show of consulting a detail in the ledger before him, and then stared at the prisoner with studied remoteness.

Dawlish knew he could no longer keep silent, yet even as he spoke knew that his intervention was futile. "This type of treatment will get us nowhere, Señor Murillo." He put a hard edge to his voice. "This man is an ex-officer of the French Army and from what I've seen he's a gentleman and a courageous soldier. He deserves better than this."

Aquino ground his pistol muzzle against the prisoner's temple and simultaneously jerked a knee into his kidneys. Roybon could not suppress a gasp of pain.

"I fail to see that it is any of your business, Commander Dawlish," Murillo said. "This man is a criminal and may be treated accordingly. He can only help himself by co-operating with us."

Tinsley, lips pursed, was nodding silent approval.

"If you dislike these proceedings, Commander, then your objections can be recorded in the minutes," Murillo continued. "For the rest I would remind you that you have a contract of service with the Consortium and that you come recommended by Admiral Topcliffe himself. I trust that you would not wish to disappoint him."

Tinsley laid a hand on Dawlish's sleeve and spoke quietly in his ear. "No sense getting involved, Commander. These chaps have their own ways and we won't change them. We'd better stick to the job we were recruited for and leave them to it." Dawlish pulled his arm away and ignored him.

Murillo was talking slowly to the prisoner. "You are one of the leaders of this Jacquerie," he said, ticking off points from the paper before him, as if from a charge sheet. "You, no less than the others, are responsible for destruction of property, for disruption of a great commercial enterprise, for murder of its employees, for opposition to this legally-constituted force which has come to restore order. I have authority from the President of the Paraguayan Republic to execute you or any other rebel."

"Do it then," Roybon hissed.

Murillo ignored him. "I require certain information about the activities of your associates and about the disposition of your forces, Monsieur Roybon. If you co-operate you will live – even be rewarded, be sent downriver a free man, go where you like. Any refusal helps neither you nor your associates. The Consortium will prevail in any case, but your assistance might make it an easier process for all concerned."

He turned his thick lenses on Dawlish. "Nothing in that to offend your sensibilities I trust, Commander Dawlish? Your sense of fair play is not outraged? No? Then we can proceed. And Colonel Culbertson? You had some queries?"

"A few triflin' points for Monsieur Roybon," Culbertson said, positioning himself before him. The Frenchman tried to look away, as if fearing to provoke Culbertson with the contempt in his eyes, but Aquino caught his hair and forced him to look into the American's face. "Let's start with El Pobre himself. Just who the hell is he? And yourself, Sonny? An ex-officer, ain't you? I guess it's you who built them earthworks round Puerto Plutarcho? And who blasted the hell out of us back there at La Garganta?"

"I did. And I'm proud of it." Roybon spoke through gritted teeth.

"So you are, Sonny. And so you might be! And the monitor? Who's in charge there? Not some half-naked Guaikuru buck? And it sure as hell ain't some dissatisfied riverboat skipper. He's too damn good, whoever he is. So just where the hell did you all spring from?"

Roybon tried to look away. Culbertson stepped closer and slapped him backhandedly across the bruised side of his face. "I'm waitin' for an answer, Sonny," he said.

"Gentlemen," Murillo said, raising a hand. "Enough, Gentlemen, enough. We waste time. We can see that Monsieur Roybon is not in a mood to co-operate. I have no doubt that an hour or so of General Aquino's company will lead to a change of mood."

He spoke rapidly in Spanish to Aquino, too rapidly for Dawlish to follow, though the word "*rosario*" - rosary - stood out by its incongruity. Aquino's great loose mouth twisted into an assertion of agreement. He dragged Roybon to his feet and hustled him to the door, the pistol still ground against his head. Dawlish had a fleeting image of terrified but defiant eyes turned for a moment towards him and of an expression that went beyond despair.

"Don't say you weren't warned, Sonny," Culbertson called after him. Aquino shouted for assistance and a scuffle of feet told of the prisoner being dragged away along the dark gallery.

"The meeting is adjourned, Gentlemen," Murillo said, snapping his watch open. "Until – shall we say ten o'clock? That should be long enough. And – Colonel Culbertson? You might perhaps meet me about this afternoon's action. I'd appreciate more details." He stood and began busily to gather his papers.

"A bad business, Dawlish, a bad business." Tinsley was shaking his head and his voice was low. "The fellow was given every chance to help himself. I can't say but that I see Señor Murillo's viewpoint. He's not just in the right – he's absolutely right."

Dawlish looked at him. Tinsley was pale and agitated, the very picture of a man trying to rationalise his own sycophancy. The sight was enough to drive Dawlish to action he knew was futile, yet essential if he was to maintain his integrity. He pushed his way past Tinsley and stood before Murillo.

"I'd like a word in private, Señor," he said.

"I can hear you perfectly well here, Commander." Murillo peered at one of the papers before him and did not look up. Culbertson stood smirking behind him.

"You are forcing me to protest, Señor," Dawlish strove to keep the anger from his voice. "I appreciate that there is a campaign to be conducted. I understand that there must be losses. I know that there is a fanatical enemy to be beaten and that men must die. I've no cause to favour this Roybon – but he has fought decently. Cruelty to a helpless prisoner dishonours us, Señor."

"Is that all, Commander Dawlish?" Murillo closed his minute book and looked up. His tone conveyed suppressed impatience.

"It is not, Sir. If the type of callous brutality I've witnessed here is typical of what we may expect when we reach the Reducción – I beg your pardon, Puerto Plutarcho – then I can think of no more effective way of ensuring that the rebels resist us to the last man."

Murillo was quivering now, all but losing his effort to retain composure. "And now you will hear me out Commander." His voice rose shrilly. "You joined this expedition on the recommendation of two of Hyperion's major stockholders, Lord Kegworth and Admiral Topcliffe. I understand that the inducement offered went beyond the monetary compensation which the Consortium has guaranteed you – which is in itself generous enough. I have not enquired of either gentleman what that extra inducement may be – but rest assured, Commander, that neither will support you an inch further should your behaviour endanger the recovery of Consortium assets."

"So now you're threatening me, Señor Murillo?"

"Yes – and you're taking note, Commander Dawlish. You've been hired to lead the riverine forces, nothing else. You accepted the position without reference to moral scruples – and now, Sir, it's too late for them. You may have come highly recommended, Commander, but you've started the campaign in a singularly inauspicious manner. You've lost two irreplaceable steamers, several dozen men and a fortune in supplies. If you want to retain the esteem of your patrons I suggest you concentrate more on crushing the rebels and less on cosseting them."

He gathered his papers and swept out.

"There just ain't no sense in getting his back up, Commander Nick," Culbertson's voice was laden with mock sympathy. "But he does have a point – don't let this afternoon's little ride go to your head. Just stick to the river and quit preaching. Maybe you'll get a better hearin' from all of us once you've seen to that *Torres*."

He moved to the door and was followed by Tinsley, who looked guiltily towards Dawlish, seemed for a moment as if he was about to say something, but then joined the Colonel.

Dawlish was left alone in the hot saloon, humiliated and seething. He forced calmness on himself and then left to seek Holmes, his decision already made.

14

The *Toad's* gig nudged against the bank between the moored transports and Dawlish leapt ashore. Holmes and the seamen stayed with the boat, warned to be ready for a quick departure. No conscripts had been landed but the fires of the regulars' bivouac dotted the darkness for fifty yards inland from the bank. The smell of cooking food drifted towards the river, mingled with the tang of wood-smoke and tobacco. The sentry who challenged Dawlish on landing directed him towards a cluster of bell tents to the right, over which the fires threw a reddish tinge. General Aquino and his escort had gone there, and, *Si Señor*, they had a prisoner with them.

Dawlish loosened the flap of his holster and fingered the grip of is Adams revolver. It felt solidly reassuring, but he hoped he would not have to use it. Defiance had served him once today, with Culbertson, but he suspected that Aquino would prove less flexible. If he could but get Roybon back to the *Toad* he would have a position to bargain from – but the gunboat lay a full mile upriver. He pushed from his mind the enormity of what he was risking – the future of the expedition, his career, perhaps even his life itself. But the memory of Tinsley's craven acquiescence in the saloon drove him. Pride alone made any risk seem more welcome than identifying with that sanctimonious time-server.

A howl from the nearer tent, choking off into a gasping moan, quickened Dawlish's pace as he picked his way among the cooking fires and past the idling knots of sprawled and sitting regulars.

He knew that sound – the sound of reluctant capitulation to pain unimaginable, deliberately applied to tear strength and resolution from a courageous man. He had seen –

had known – such abuse of the helpless before at other times and places. The memories disgusted him and still occasionally haunted his sleep. He could not acquiesce passively to the like now. His heart was pounding and he forced himself to walk slowly. There could be no turning aside and only a cool determination could carry him through the endless minutes ahead.

A single lamp inside the tent threw the huge shadows of those within on to the outer walls. Two sentries, regulars, stood by the open flap but Dawlish ignored their challenge and pushed through the crossed rifles with which they sought to bar his passage. They hesitated, knowing him as one of the expedition commanders, but it was the anger and contempt on his face that made them think better of firmer resistance. There was another howl as Dawlish stooped and entered, and it distracted all attention from his arrival.

Aquino sat on a camp stool, his back to the entrance, and four of his regulars squatted or sat around the central pole, all half-appalled, half-excited by the groans and writhings of the bound and kneeling prisoner. A huge Indian soldier, stripped to the waist and sweating hard, crouched behind him, straining with an iron ramrod to tighten the rope that passed around the victim's head and press deeper the two expertly placed knots that bit into his eye sockets.

On the open Chaco Roybon had shown the courage to face a cavalry charge alone but now the *Rosario del Diablo* - the Devil's Rosary - was systematically destroying the last vestiges of his valour and resolution. The Frenchman's cry died to a long moan but at a nod from Aquino the Indian jerked the ramrod tighter still, grunting with effort. Roybon screamed and his body arced and strained but his hands were bound behind to his heels and there could be no relief. The torturer looked up expectantly towards Aquino and at another nod slackened the tension. Roybon's scream lapsed into gasping sobs.

"We can start again, Roybon," Aquino said, "The night is young", and at that moment he became conscious of the others looking past him, their attention drawn by Dawlish's presence. He turned to him.

"You should not be here, Comandante," he said quietly, with no hint of hostility. "This business, it is not for you. You do not understand it. It is not your way, but it must be done. You will be upset if you stay. Leave now please."

His tone gave Dawlish his opening. Talk of humanity must surely fail but there was a hint of the unspoken esteem that had grown up between him and Aquino since the delays at the Gullet. "He's my prisoner, General", he said. "It is my honour that is at stake – you understand, don't you? In my Navy, in my society..." He sought frantically in his Spanish vocabulary. "... in my brotherhood of arms, I am obliged to protect this man."

Aquino's gaze rested for a moment on the Adams' exposed butt, but there was no sign of fear in the small black eyes in the flat yellow face. He noticed a movement to his right, an officer's hand gliding slowly to a pistol holster, and he stilled it with a wave of his hand. "No need, Capitan Cardozo," he said. "Comandante Dawlish is my friend. He is just a little upset."

Dawlish shifted again, uncomfortably aware that the confines of the tent kept him within six feet of all its occupants. "I'm asking you to cut him free, General," he said. "You'll get nothing useful from him this way. He's too brave a man. You only dishonour yourself."

"The river, that is your affair, Comandante Dawlish," Aquino said patiently, even with a hint of concern that he should be understood. "But La Reducción – that is mine, and this man is the key to it. This questioning – I know it is not your way. I respect that. But that this method is necessary, that I assure you. He will talk – they always do in the end. Go back to your *sapo*, your *Toad*, and leave this business to me. I assure you that I will not mention this interruption to Señor Murillo."

Dawlish's heart was thumping and he forced himself to still the tremor in his hands. "You know I cannot accept this, General," he said.

Aquino turned to the Indian soldier, who stood with Roybon's head drawn back against him by its terrible bridle. He spoke curtly and the Indian twisted the rope free, to expose two black pits edged with purple. Roybon groaned and rocked his head as if trying to shake it free of agony.

"Look at him, Comandante," Aquino said. "He's in pain, but he's alive. The men we left downriver, his and ours – they have no pain, but they are dead. So too will others be when we reach Puerto Plutarcho. There are defences there – earthworks, batteries, redoubts – and this man has planned them. He hopes to break us on them. We must know of those defences, their weaknesses, their strengths, the disposition of their guns. If he does not suffer now then we must suffer then. His pain for ours."

"But you must get to the Reducción first, General," Dawlish said, grateful for rationality if not sympathy. "If I do not have him from you, then my services are ended. You know my ability by now. The *Torres* is still between us and the Reducción. Without me the flotilla will never reach there and any information you may get from him will be useless. But if ..."

The sudden crackle of small-arms fire somewhere in the darkness behind cut him short and he had a fleeting recollection, too late, of the clouds of dust from those Reducción patrols so far to the south of the river, so distant, so persistent, so apparently harmless as they shadowed the advancing flotilla in the past days.

The firing died. There were shouts, and a single piercing cry, then more shouting as men scattered from the cooking fires, tumbling over each other in their haste to pick up stacked rifles. Aquino pushed his way past Dawlish, shouting commands, sending his lieutenants scurrying to their posts with drawn pistols. The flame-lit circles of light died in smoke and dust as earth was kicked over them. A man screamed as an overturned pot scalded him and then rifle fire rippled again in a ragged volley from somewhere beyond the downstream edge of the bivouac.

The lamp-lit bell tent was briefly the brightest point in the camp but then Roybon's captor turned the wick down to extinguish it. In the instant before its glow died Dawlish saw that Roybon was still held firm. For one mad moment he thought of threatening the half-stripped Indian soldier with his pistol into releasing his prisoner but the sullen resolve on the flat face as it faded into darkness told him it would be useless.

Dawlish drew his Adams and hurried after Aquino. The moon and the distant lights of the flotilla gave scarcely enough illumination for dodging between the smouldering fires, discarded bedrolls and scattered cooking utensils. Isolated regulars were crouched with their weapons in the shelter of hollows or bushes but the General had gathered a group and was driving them forward through the darkened camp in a ragged skirmish line. His bellows had imposed silence on the advance, and bayonets had been fixed, but from the left and rear came sounds of shouting and panic.

And there was the enemy – identified only by flashes from dark fringe of scrub beyond the camp, and by yelled commands and some semblance of volley fire – eighteen or twenty rifles Dawlish guessed, spread irregularly over a sixty or eighty yard front. He fought down the urge to throw himself to the ground as unseen rounds screamed overhead or lashed the foliage to his side. He came level with Aquino. The General was striding forward, erect, hardly losing pace as he jerked a cringing rifleman to his feet and shoved him forward.

Dawlish forced himself not to crouch and strode forward on the General's right. Aquino showed no surprise at his appearance.

"I'm with you, General," Dawlish said. "Have you orders for me?"

"The right flank," Aquino ignored the spattering of dry earth thrown up by a bullet striking just ahead. "Capitan Cardozo, he's sweeping round that thicket to come behind them. Their horses must be there. Support him."

Dawlish left Aquino and broke into a half-run, his stomach hollow with fear and horribly conscious that his white ducks must make him a conspicuous and ghostly target. The firing had died down and the night seemed suddenly quiet, the threatening silence interrupted only by the crickets and the odd suppressed shout as a laggard was urged forward. The outlines of Cardozo's group were barely discernible ahead, their brown uniforms just light enough to stand out against the darkness as they moved forward slowly, reluctant to abandon whatever meagre protection a fold of ground or a cluster of baggage afforded them. Fifty yards further on Dawlish caught up with the skirmish line, a row of crouching, frightened men pacing cautiously forward with eyes fixed on the wall of scrub a further fifty yards ahead. He recognised Cardozo, a short, fat man whose agility seemed at variance with his rotundity, and fell in some five yards to his right.

Cardozo's teeth flashed in greeting. "A little further, Comandante," he hissed. "Then we charge. Wait for my word."

The line padded slowly forward, the loudest noise now the rustling of dry leaves underfoot, every member convinced that he alone must be the single focus of a dozen rifles in the thicket ahead. Here and there a bayonet caught the moonlight. Men glanced nervously to either side, half-hoping, half-fearing that their fellows were on the point of breaking and running back so that they too might join them with less shame. They stooped ever lower, choking back nausea as they waited for the cry that would hurl them forward.

Dawlish glanced to Cardozo and the fat regular shook his head. Not yet – a few yards more. And at that moment a single shot crashed out in the darkness away over to the left – a private close to Aquino, as they later learned, who tripped over a root and discharged his weapon. An instant later a ripple of rifle fire was rushing up Aquino's line as panicking men, their stretched nerves snapping, blazed blindly into the darkness ahead, then flung themselves to the ground, reloading and blasting off round after round.

Cardozo, realising that only decisive forward movement could save his troops from joining in the terrified fusillade, sprang forward with pistol upraised and shouted "Adelante!"

Dawlish was by his side, dashing towards the shadowy mass of brush ahead, and a half dozen troops did surge forward with them, but ragged volleys to either side told them they were too late. The panic had spread already to the right of the line and now Cardozo's own men also were firing into the darkness, then throwing themselves down to reload. Crackling fire continued to echo from the left and bright points of flame blazed briefly in the darkness. Aquino's wing had gone to ground and now Cardozo's was doing likewise.

Cardozo turned, his face drawn in fury. "The bastards!" he shouted. "We must get them on their feet."

He rushed back and Dawlish followed, briefly conscious that no answering fire had erupted from the foliage they had been rushing towards, and grateful for it. The significance of that silence eluded him as he flung himself on the nearest private cowering beneath a bush, fumbling ineffectually to reload. Dawlish caught him by the shoulders and dragged him to his feet. "The bayonet!" he yelled. "Go in with the bayonet." He kicked the man forward into a shambling rush, then pulled another to his feet, and another, driving them onwards into the darkness with blows and threats. Cardozo had several more moving forward and somewhere to the right a sergeant had restored a semblance of order and had mounted another ragged push into the brush.

A private stumbled from the shadows, intent on flight, his face a mask of fear. Dawlish barred his path and slashed his pistol backhandedly across his cheek, laying it open. "That way, you idiot!" he shouted and shoved the man towards the dark scrub, then himself joined in the half-hearted thrust – and still there was no answering fire.

He moved forward into ever thickening brush, thorn tearing at his legs, and heard the troops in front and to either side crashing forward. And still there was no response. The panicked volleys on Aquino's flank had died down and the loudest noises were the shouts of officers urging the line forward. They were deep in the thicket now, that same thicket from which the first storm of rifle fire had lashed the camp scarcely ten minutes before. But of the attackers there was no sign.

Cardozo was the first to reach the open ground beyond the line of brush, where the attackers' horses had been held – later, in daylight, they would find their dung and the marks left by the sack-muffled hooves. When he cried out his voice was full of anger and frustration. "Back!" he shouted. "Back! They've gone! Back to the camp! They've gone around! Back to the camp! Fast!"

And now the real chaos commenced as officers and sergeants fought to find their troops in the darkness, to re-establish a line somehow and to retrace their path through the shadowy scrub. There was isolated firing as confused and disorientated men blazed at shadows – one private was killed and two were wounded in these exchanges – and others had to be dragged from illusory cover, their hands shaking too violently to reload their weapons.

"Find El General, Comandante!" Cardozo called to Dawlish. "He must move his men back into the camp!"

Dawlish moved at a crouching run back through the thicket and emerged into the more open ground where the panic had first battened on the troops. He raised himself erect, knowing that he was in greater danger of being shot by terrified regulars than by Reducción forces, hoping that by showing himself he might be recognised. He slowed down. Shouting and the odd shot ahead told him that chaos reigned along Aquino's wing also. A figure suddenly raised itself from behind a bush ahead and he was swinging his Adams towards it when a voice said "Comandante Dawlish?"

He half-recognised the features of a regular corporal. "Take me to General Aquino," he said.

They were still searching for the General when the Reducción cavalry smashed into the camp some two hundred yards to their rear.

The twenty-strong troop had unleashed its volleys from the thicket and then had fallen silently back to remount the horses they had left beyond it. The stealth of their outflanking movement had been aided by the noise and panic in the brush and they remained undetected until they had reached the furthermost, upstream, edge of the encampment. The frightened cook who first caught sight of them fell backwards even as he cried out, a pistol bullet lodged in his chest. Only then did the troop break into a canter, fanning out among the tents. The terrified figures that rushed from them were hacked or ridden down. Stragglers from the earlier panic rushed towards the new incursion, thought better of it, wavered and fell back. There was a confusion of hoof beats, of shouting, of isolated shots, of men dismounting and remounting, of flames licking in the darkness, of horses whinnying. It was over in two minutes and then the rampaging horsemen were somehow regrouping and pounding away into the darkness.

Dawlish stood beside Aquino in the bell tent fifteen minutes later.

A match flickered in the darkness, then caught the oil lamp's wick. Wild shadows danced on the canvas walls as a private raised it to illuminate the floor. Of Roybon there was no sign, but his erstwhile Indian tormentor lay on his back on the ground, his head almost dragged from his shoulders and his throat a bloody chasm.

Aquino shrugged. "We'll settle accounts at Puerto Plutarcho," he said. "Their pain for ours."

15

It rained that night, heavily.

It rained for the next two days, a downpour that dropped the temperature ten degrees and turned the Chaco briefly into a vast muddy and scrub-studded lake and the Rio San Joaquin into a raging torrent that dragged two steamers from their moorings. Confined for the most part to open barges - for only the regulars could be trusted to bivouac ashore without fear of desertion - the saturated conscripts shivered under the deluge, hungered for warm food and caught the colds and fevers that would incapacitate and kill many among them in the period ahead. The *Toad* was endlessly busy, her manoeuvrability a boon in securing the two runaway steamers and in running additional moorings for others, her crew exhausted by the endless calls for support.

The rains ceased on the third day, though the current still ran fast and brown and laden with driftwood as the Chaco drained into the river through thousands of previously dry streambeds and gullies. Mists rose above the ground as it steamed and dried. Another day saw it as hard as if the rain had never been. It took longer for repairs to be made to the half-shattered stern wheel of one of the fugitive steamers, for clothing and equipment to be dried, for order to be restored among the demoralised and half-mutinous conscripts, for the current to slow sufficiently to allow reasonable progress upstream and for the bedraggled expedition to get underway again.

A full week was lost – and yet once it got moving the flotilla made steady progress westwards for the next four days. It advanced a steady twelve to fifteen miles per day, so coming within thirty miles by river of Puerto Plutarcho. A mood of sullen co-operation had settled on the expedition commanders after Roybon's escape. There was an unspoken recognition that the enemy in the field was dangerous, skilful and resourceful and that his destruction would demand an equal measure of cunning and ruthlessness. Aquino made no reference to Dawlish's intervention at the tent and indeed seemed appreciative of his role in rallying the panicking regulars. Sourly, but constructively, Culbertson proposed closer co-operation between the naval units and his Guardia cavalry. He was on home territory now, on the outer fringes of the Hyperion land-concession, and he wanted his cavalry patrols to reconnoitre ahead. Dawlish assented eagerly.

The system they agreed operated effectively from the start. The *Montelindo*, *Toad* and *Ipora* set off at dawn, moved ahead of the flotilla for two or three miles, the monitor leading and the paddler third in line, towing the scorched but serviceable cavalry barge with its landing ramps. The patrol was landed on the southern bank, never less than thirty Guardia horsemen, then moved forward, parallel to the river and up to five miles inland from it, while the flotilla continued upstream. Heliograph signalling was an innovation that Culbertson had never employed before but he grudgingly accepted a makeshift apparatus fabricated by Boyson, the *Toad's* artificer. Sergeant Gelb took charge of it and rapidly became adept at flashing simple messages back to the river from some slight eminence. A typical patrol would scour the bank for up to ten miles ahead, then drop back and rendezvous with the flotilla at a point close to the night's selected mooring place.

The terrain to the north was broken, seamed with brush-filled ravines running down to the river, the areas between bare and open. To the south the land was more regular, opening into the great plain on which the Consortium had established its herds. The scrub areas were broken by meagre grassland and stands of timber but there was no sign of human presence. Culbertson's patrols reported recently deserted settlements, small groups of huts and cattle-pens from where the Hyperion herdsmen had operated before the revolt. The buildings were intact but every usable item had been removed and fresh tracks showed that cattle had recently been moved upriver. The settlement names, ticked off as the advance continued, hinted at events and personalities lost forever in the tempest of El Pobre's revolt - Arroyo del Ingles, Llanura del Duelo, Estación Nicholson, Salto del Torro.

Clusters of huts along the bank, increasing in frequency as Puerto Plutarcho drew nearer, showed similar signs of recent abandonment. The *Montelindo*, sighting a spindly jetty extending from the shore, would slow down and nudge forward, the *Toad* on cautious station astern, the Gatlings on her upperworks ready to rake the huts and the Armstrong manned. Drawing closer, the same scene as before would present itself - the yawning doors, the single disconsolate dog barking from the jetty, the scattering of escaped hens scratching in the dust. A few miles upriver the tired and sweat-streaked Guardia patrol would be waiting at the water's edge, the horses drinking gratefully, the report once more of empty countryside.

The tension was heightened now on the two fighting craft that led the flotilla. The *Torres*, that deadly sister of the *Montelindo*, could not now be far ahead and each bend turned could disclose her lunging towards them. With Purdon now well established on board as titular First Officer, but de-facto Captain, the *Montelindo's* role was clear, to parry the initial onslaught with her thick armour, hammering back as far as possible with her one hundred and ten pounders, buying time for the nimble *Toad* to bring the Armstrong's smashing power to bear.

Purdon had driven the monitor's Paraguayan gunners hard, staging one loading drill after another, so that now something approaching minimum Royal Navy standards was being attained. Every night saw checking and repair of the turret's training system and of any restriction in the bearings that could spell jamming at a crucial moment. The crew had reacted first with resentment, later with growing enthusiasm, recognising that Purdon pushed himself as hard as them, catching something of his aggressive confidence and won over by his good humour and his attention to their food and welfare. Half the turret crew remained in the baking iron box at any time, the others resting under a deck awning, ready to scramble to their positions at a signal from Purdon or Calles on the makeshift bridge above the armoured conning tower.

On the steamers and barges that followed the troops were now at increased alertness. The euphoria engendered by the success against the howitzers had been quickly quenched by the lightning stroke that had freed Roybon and by the misery of the subsequent rain-soaked days. Even the conscripts now seemed to be taking their drills on the restricted decks more seriously – they might not have seen the frozen rictus on the face of Roybon's tormentor but they had heard of it. More than one had acquired a pebble and was obsessively honing his bayonet with it. The heat had returned to torment and parch them and with it, in the evenings, came the mosquito clouds that spelled itching discomfort. At the very rear of the flotilla, Grinling's balloon, now wholly deflated, was carefully spread out on deck, ready for quick filling, every part of its surface inspected and the abrasions carefully patched by the sweating aeronaut himself.

Contact came on the afternoon of the advance's fifth day.

At midday, from a low hummock rising above the plain some six miles ahead of the leading craft, the Guardia patrol flashed back another report of deserted countryside. It would press on for another two hours, then turn northwards for the river to meet the flotilla.

The *Montelindo* and *Toad* reached the agreed rendezvous point ahead of the *Ipora*. There was no sign of the anthills that might have given gave Los Hormigueros its name, just another deserted cluster of huts where the Consortium's steamers had once loaded cattle from a wooden pier jutting out across the shallows. The river was wide and sluggish here, with sandbanks dividing it into a single deep channel and several shallower ones. The *Montelindo* pressed on another five hundred yards and dropped anchor in midstream, her turret dominating the long stretch of open water ahead.

The *Toad* made fast alongside the jetty. Dawlish and Holmes were leaving the shelter of the awning above the steering platform, the prospect of coffee below a welcome one, when a distant crackle of rifle fire reached them. A lookout's yell and pointing finger drew their gaze to a cloud of dust boiling above the scrub some two miles distant. It was moving fast towards them.

Dawlish grabbed a telescope and swung himself above the awning for a higher vantage, balancing himself against a stay of the signal mast. The blurred disk of vision sharpened to show a knot of horsemen moving fast, dusty-uniformed troopers crouched low over their lathered mounts. Gelb was among them, and someone to his left was riding what must surely be Carmelita.

"They're being followed, Sir," Holmes called. "A whole squadron of them, look..."

There was not one cloud, but two, rolling through the dry Chaco and separated by some two hundred yards. The second group of horsemen was twice, three times larger than the first, and more spread out, its wings arcing forward as if to encircle its fleeing prey. There were no uniforms, and the riding was loose and furious, but the horses were fresher and the sun caught upraised blades flashing in the shimmering air. Despite the pace, several riders had risen in their stirrups, guiding their mounts with their knees as they fired carbines at their quarry ahead.

Dawlish felt a surge of delight. This would be his moment.

"Cast off, Mr. Holmes," he called, fighting to disguise his excitement. "Take her into midstream. Fast! Gunners to action stations!"

Holmes yelled commands and the British seamen, catching the mood, scampered to loosen the mooring cables. Egdean had taken the helm, having curtly dismissed the other quartermaster. If his Commander was sailing into harm's way then he would trust nobody but himself at the wheel.

"Signal the *Montelindo* to hold station," Dawlish ordered. "We'll deal with this ourselves!"

The *Toad* nudged out into the current and Holmes, standing to the side of Egdean on the platform below Dawlish, positioned himself between the engine-room telegraphs, his fists grasping the handles for the port and starboard engines. The gunnery indicator-dial stood before him.

"Bursting Shell," Dawlish called.

Holmes reached to the indicator and rotated its pointer across the inscribed brass plate. Down in the bows, unseen beneath the deck, on the gun-captain's platform, another pointer mimicked its movement across an identical dial. At the gun-captain's yelled command the loaders pulled their chain-hoist along its overhead rail to the rack of red and yellow-tipped hollow shells, each packed with two hundred pounds of powder. *Not ideal for use against cavalry*, Dawlish thought, designed as they were to gouge into the vitals of another warship before exploding, but sufficient perhaps for the purpose at hand.

Dawlish was counting mentally... thirty nine, forty... Holmes was holding the *Toad* almost stationary, her screws churning slowly in unison to keep her bow-on to the current. Seventy four, seventy five... now the rammer would be drawing back and the gun captain would be reaching for the elevator lever... ninety, ninety one... and the great Armstrong came heaving gently up through the deck and her muzzle jutted through the gap in the forward breastwork.

An electric bell sounded on Holmes' indicator. "Run out! Awaiting range, Sir!"

The riders were closer now and even with the naked eye Dawlish could distinguish the individual mounts against the backdrop of seething dust. Two thousand five hundred – no, twenty-two hundred yards, and closing fast. The gap between the clouds of dust – not more than one hundred and fifty yards, and by God, they were gaining! A miscalculation of even a hundred yards, a matter of two degrees difference in elevation, could wipe out the fleeing Guardia troopers.

Dawlish's mind raced, allowing the seconds for Holmes' reaction, for the port revolutions to slacken, for the *Toad's* bows to swing, for the thundering horseman to surge forward...

"Twenty-one hundred yards, Mr. Holmes. Your gun, your ship!"

Holmes lips moved silently, translating the range into elevation, compensating for the cold barrel that would drop the first round short and for the damp heat of the afternoon air. He reached forward, moved the indicator's pointer from the loading segment of the dial and across into the elevation scale, specifying the angle. The gun-captain, Morgan, exposed to view now, noted the corresponding movement on his repeater dial and opened the valve to the elevating ram. The squat barrel rose and steadied. Morgan's arm rose to signal elevation completed.

Dawlish's gaze was riveted on the rolling torrent of men, horses and dust. The pursuers were now closing the gap even further. Twenty-one hundred yards might be too much, but there was no time to correct.

Now came the moment of wrath for which Holmes had trained in dozens of bloodless exercises on windswept British anchorages. He reached for the telegraphs and signalled for half revolutions on the port engine and two seconds later, with the starboard still on full power, the *Toad's* blunt bow swung away from the current and arced across towards the southern bank. The craft's axis had not yet lined up with the second cluster of riders, and was still swinging, as Holmes' fist hit the knob before him. The sound of the electric bell on the gun-captain's platform was drowned by the roar of the Armstrong as flame and smoke blasted across the low bow. The *Toad* shuddered, then swung back into the current as Holmes signalled for full port revolutions again and as the huge black weapon sunk back beneath the deck to commence reloading.

Dawlish saw none of this and the trajectory was too flat for the round to be tracked, but his eyes were locked on the galloping target. He had steadied himself to withstand the jolting shock wave that lashed aft from the *Toad's* bows and he saw the skidding eruption of earth and brush where the shell hit the ground, gouged forward for fifty yards, drove among the riders on the right wing and erupted into a volcano of fire and smoke and clay and iron fragments and sundered limbs. The effect on the centre and right wing was instantaneous, sheering the majority of the horsemen off in panic to the right, away from the path of their quarry, hurling a few into headlong retreat.

The smoke on the impact zone was still clearing as the recharged Armstrong came heaving back through the deck. The range was shorter now - two hundred yards less - and again Holmes slowed the port engine. The bows swung across and the great muzzle again belched its torrent of horror across the Chaco. The second shell wrought even greater carnage than the first, scything a knot of horsemen into a bloody spray before it blasted itself into a short-lived inferno of smoke and flame. The charge disintegrated, scattering into small groups of survivors fleeing in headlong retreat on terrified mounts.

The *Toad* held further fire, her weapon worthily blooded.

The horses were blown, and the riders were dust and sweat-caked, when the Guardia patrol limped into the settlement. Sergeant Gelb clattered down the jetty, where Dawlish had stepped ashore when the *Toad* had again pulled alongside.

"You saved us, Commander." His voice was a croak and he rinsed his mouth from his canteen and spat before continuing. "A little more and them bastards would have got us. They got Lieutenant Hartshorn, and Navarro too."

"What are they?" Dawlish asked.

Gelb's voice registered controlled-fear, courage sobered by close escape from death. "Guaikurus, most of them – and, by Christ, somebody's been licking them into shape. They always could ride, but now they've got some discipline." He smiled. "I guess they still can't stand artillery though, and that's one damn big cannon you've got there, Commander."

"Where did they find you?"

"Took us in the rear, five, maybe six miles upriver. There's a fort there, huge damn mounds of earth along the shore. Cannon pokin' from 'em, like we had back at Magdalena."

He brushed aside Dawlish's eager query on calibres. "Didn't get near enough to tell you more - there's a swamp this side of it. Hartshorn wanted to skirt round, take a look if there was an approach over dry ground. That's when they hit us - came in from our left. They must ha' been sheltering in a grove of timber and the first we knew was when a shot dropped Hartshorn." He suppressed a shudder. "They're good, damned good. I turned our boys and ran – reckoned it more important to get word to you than slog it out with 'em."

"You did right," Dawlish said. And now he wanted to calm Gelb, take him aside, wring from him every detail he could remember of the fort before the memory blurred.

He nodded towards the huts on the foreshore. "Set your men to putting that settlement in a state of defence, Sergeant. Water the horses when they've cooled - no need for further patrolling. Our Reducción friends won't be back today. I'll see you on board here in ten minutes and then you'll tell me what you found."

Later, sitting with Dawlish and Holmes at the table in the *Toad's* tiny wardroom, drinking coffee and sucking on a cheroot, Gelb recalled more under gentle interrogation than he himself would have believed possible.

The earthworks themselves? Low, maybe eight, ten feet high, fresh earth, no growth on them to speak of on the forty-five degree sloping outer wall.

And thick? Hard to say, but from the view he'd had of one of the embrasures, perhaps fifteen feet.

And the location? Firm ground along the southern shore, six, eight, feet above river level, the bank steep, almost a low bluff.

He'd mentioned a swamp? Yes, on this, the downstream side, where a sluggish stream fanned out as it entered the river, an area low and waterlogged, two or three hundred yards across, with the higher ground rising beyond it. It looked as if the few trees and bushes growing in it had been cut down - that was why it was so damn difficult to get closer.

Dawlish's pencil moved rapidly over the pad before him, sketching each detail to build up a picture that became more sobering with every stroke.

And the layout? At least four sides, and probably a fifth, making a redoubt like a distorted pentagon, sixty, eighty yards per face. On the river side the sloping wall lay close to the bank and another ran parallel to the swamp's edge, while the face linking these lay at an angle of some forty-five degrees to the river. The two guns set in embrasures in this face dominated the river approach.

The face paralleling the bank? Hard to see, but at least one embrasure, though with no guns visible.

And the landward face? No artillery to be seen, but there seemed to be a more complex system of outworks, maybe trenches, and the ground in front was burned bare of scrub for a distance at least a hundred yards.

And there was likely to be another face, at right angles to the riverbank on the upstream side – if there was some entrance Gelb guessed it would be there. Hartshorn had tried to work inland to survey these inner faces from cover, and that was when the Reducción cavalry had struck. There had been rifle-fire from the redoubt as the chase had started, but it died away quickly and it was impossible to guess how many men might be inside.

And the river at that point? Straight for about eight hundred yards downstream of the earthworks, straight and narrow, fifty, sixty yards wide. A firm bank on the opposite side, the flow well-channelled.

The sketch was almost complete now, intimidating in the obstacles portrayed, impressive in the choice of location – a small, powerful swamp-shielded fortress, well capable of withstanding any land assault the Consortium might launch and of blocking any advance by water. And yet with Gelb's last detail Dawlish felt his first flush of elation.

Narrow and channelled meant a strong head-current but no sandbars – a clear river.

Dawlish stared again at the sketch, identifying himself with whoever – almost certainly Roybon – had directed the straining, ant-like swarm that must have heaped up that earthwork, ever-vigilant for the whistle blasts from downstream that would announce the arrival of the enemy before it was complete. The urgency would be great, the time short and effort would be concentrated where the threat was greatest.

His pencil hovered for an instant over the paper, then scratched out the wall perpendicular to the river on the upstream side, the side least under threat. It would be the last to be completed, if completed at all.

It would be a gamble, but... The panicked cavalry would be streaming back, their reports confused and garbled, telling of a land force and ships moving upriver. The Reducción commander – and here Dawlish could almost see Roybon before him – would be readying for an attack. A combined attack, by land and riverine forces, cautious, systematic, taking maximum advantage of the Consortium's manpower and artillery. An attack based on the reconnaissance report, an attack that would take time to plan and prepare.

An attack would be expected - *but not today.*

Dawlish checked the time. Just before two o'clock - almost five hours of daylight. He knew with sudden clarity what he must do.

"Signal the *Montelindo* to raise anchor and move upstream, Mr. Holmes," he said quietly. "The *Toad* will follow. You'll put us alongside the *Montelindo* and I'll cross briefly – I've instructions for Calles and Purdon."

Holmes was already on his feet.

"And another thing," Dawlish said, "warn Morgan to be prepared for action. Bursting charges and solid shot. Either could be needed."

He turned to Gelb. "Sergeant – I need you ashore. When Colonel Culbertson arrives tell him to hold the flotilla here until I send word. Tell him I've headed upstream to clear the river."

As Gelb jumped the gap that was already opening between the *Toad* and the landing stage, Dawlish heard the shrill whistle of the approaching *Ipora*. He would be far upstream, carrying the fate of the expedition with him, long before Culbertson and the rest of the flotilla arrived. There would be no endless conference in the *Tacuari's* saloon to sanction the assault he now planned, though the cost of any failure would be wholly on his own head.

Ahead, a bow wave was streaming from the *Montelindo's* low prow as she slowly got underway, and the *Toad* was rapidly overtaking her. When he saw her officers his orders would be simple. The *Montelindo* would parry – but the *Toad* would kill.

16

The last bend was rounded and the earthworks were a reddish-brown streak on the green-clad bluffs a half mile ahead and to port. The river was as Gelb had reported – a straight and rapidly flowing channel without bars or shoals, the current too fast to allow blockage by a boom and powerful enough to slow the passage of oncoming vessels clawing their way upstream under fire of the earthworks' guns.

The *Montelindo* was in the lead, a low, black, rust-streaked hulk that showed no exterior sign of human presence. Her sun-scorched decks were cleared of every obstacle to her guns' arc of fire and even her boats had been left moored to the bank downstream. Her turret was manned, its twin one hundred and ten-pounders run out and charged with bursting shell. Purdon and Calles had abandoned their exposed bridge and peered forward through the slits in the six-inch armour of the small conning tower, passing hushed orders to the helmsman standing behind them. The monitor crept forward relentlessly, making a good four knots against the current, her engines panting softly at three-quarters revolutions, fear palpable among the men who sweltered and trembled inside her armoured plates.

The *Toad* trailed her by a hundred yards. She too was cleared for action — as much as a lightly armoured craft that relied on manoeuvrability for protection could be. Dawlish had toyed briefly with the idea of moving to the small iron conning tower beneath the open steering platform, the only shielded position on the gunboat. He had rejected the notion almost at once — not only would visibility be hopelessly restricted when most needed but he would find it hard to look the Gatling crews in their exposed positions in the eye afterwards — if there was an afterwards. He stood therefore with Holmes and Egdean on the bare steering platform consciously ignoring his awareness of the total lack of protection. He forced himself to ignore the fear gnawing inside him — for this slow, steady approach was more terrifying by far than the horseback charge through the scrub — and made himself stand as motionless and as outwardly calm as commanders had done before him as their ships had crept forward under sail to break an enemy line.

Ahead of the steering platform, though slightly lower, a gunner and a loader stood by each of the two six-barrel Gatlings. Spare ammunition boxes stood open. Dawlish caught a gunner's eye. He remembered his name — Hilliard. The man smiled, saluted and spun the barrels with his right hand. They rotated with a satisfying rattle. Dawlish looked forward. The Armstrong was invisible below the deck but was already loaded for firing.

"Hold her here, Mr. Holmes." He hoped that the slight quaver of fear in his voice was not noticeable. "Hold her on the screws".

Holmes' hand moved to the engine telegraphs. The *Toad* dropped astern slightly, then stood still against the current. An eternity followed that Dawlish would never forget – the sun beating down on the still and parched Chaco on either bank, the green by the water's edge, the *Montelindo's* black shape ploughing steadily up the rippling surface of the river, the embrasured earthwork ahead, the silence broken only by the soft beating of the engines.

Dawlish focused his glass. He could see clearly the earthen flank that was angled at forty-five degrees to the river, and the gaps through which two vicious black muzzles protruded. They looked like rifled twenty-pounder Parrotts looted from Magdalena and it would take only one of their rounds to devastate the *Toad*. Foreshortening meant that he could see little of the sloped wall lying along the river but it seemed to have a single embrasure. A few figures were discernible on top of the mounds while the heads and shoulders of others showed below them.

The *Montelindo* was now five hundred yards from the fort and still forging ahead.

Bright flame flashed from the two visible embrasures, followed by rolling clouds of yellowish smoke. A double roar came washing through the humid air and then a fountain of mud and stone blasted from the bank upstream and to starboard of the *Montelindo* while a geyser of water erupted only yards astern. She was unharmed, and she pushed on as the spray fell back in the river in her wake.

"They're good, Sir" Holmes said. "Fixed aiming points, known ranges. They nearly had her."

The *Montelindo* was slowing now and her turret was creeping to port to find and hold her target. The last wisps of smoke were clearing before the fort's embrasures and the weapons there had been run in for loading. Tinsley had said a good British crew could do it in twenty-five seconds – but Purdon had been given only a few days to drill this crew. Dawlish had already counted to thirty four...

A black muzzle ran out from the fort's nearer embrasure, then another from the second. Behind those earthen walls gunners would have called new bearings and sweating men would be straining to slew the pieces around to bear on the *Montelindo*.

The *Montelindo* fired first. Two shells were hurled, not the solid hundred and ten-pounders she would have used against an armoured craft, but hollow hundred-pounders filled with bursting charges and fitted with impact fuses set for a five-second delay. One shell, slightly too high, skimmed harmlessly over the fort and was lost somewhere beyond but its mate gouged into the sloped earthen flank to the right of the embrasure nearer the river. The initial impact scooped a pit in the inclined wall and then, as the clay thrown up was falling back in a shower, the main charge detonated in an orange and black-streaked flash that tore a deep crater.

The monitor slowed almost to a halt, her engines barely holding her against the current. She was a sitting target now, her armour insolently defying the shore-based guns. Dawlish knew that in the coming minutes the critical factor would not be material – for the *Montelindo* was built to take punishment – but human. He had seen enough young officers like Purdon in his career to know that he could rely on him to the death, but Calles and his crew were a different matter. He could only hope that the Purdon's influence had gone deep enough among them. Inside the monitor's turret the bagged charges and shells were even now being rammed home and excitement must now be partly overcoming fear. The opening salvo had been excellent – but could they keep it up?

The *Montelindo's* initial hit might not have been direct, but the cohesion of the Reduccionista crew serving the weapon closer to the reeking crater was obviously temporarily disrupted. It remained silent while the Parrott further from the river opened again. The shell hit the river's surface in a shower of spray some thirty yards ahead of the monitor, bounced, and hurtled in to the scrub on the opposite bank, flinging up a furrow of dust and foliage, but not exploding. Solid shot, Dawlish recognised, probably incapable of penetrating the *Montelindo's* turret but well able of jamming its rotation – and more than able to tear straight through the *Toad*.

The *Montelindo* fired again. This time there had been the slightest depression of the barrels and both rounds found their mark along the earthwork's base, almost exactly between the two embrasures. There was the same preliminary plume of soil as they burrowed into the slope, followed by two enormous and almost simultaneous flame-tongued eruptions that tore a jagged, smoking ten-yard breach in the wall. The embrasures to either side were blotted out by a falling curtain of clay and debris.

"Now!" cried Dawlish. "Full revolutions".

Holmes ground both telegraph handles forward and seconds later the *Toad* surged ahead, her twin screws biting and her blunt stem ploughing a high bow wave. Dawlish felt his hands tremble but he forced himself instead to take out a cheroot, strike a match and draw slowly as the tobacco began to glow.

"Kindly order the Gatling crews to engage as we pass, Mr. Holmes," he said. "Targets of opportunity only."

The *Toad* worked up to top speed, a good six knots against the current. She was a hundred yards downstream of the *Montelindo* when the embrasured weapon closer to the river blasted again. The bearing was perfect. A running plume of spray ten yards off the monitor's port bow showed where the shot hit the water and bounced before striking against the low flank just aft of the anchor stowage. A clanging sound rang out and a cloud of rust and paint flakes rose above the point of impact. The monitor shuddered, but held position. She could endure a dozen such hits if only her crew could keep their nerve. The fort's second weapon fired immediately after, but the gunners must have been thrown out by the recent impact on the wall and their aim was wide and high. The round screamed somewhere above the *Toad* and lost itself on the opposite bank.

The *Toad* was almost level with the *Montelindo*, coming up on its starboard side, that furthest from the fort, when the monitor fired again. Muzzle flame and a shimmering, transparent shock wave radiated from before the turret ports and Dawlish clapped his hands to his ears too slowly to save them from the painful crash of sound that lashed across the water. The *Toad* was shrouded for a moment in the same sulphurous-yellow cloud that enveloped the *Montelindo*, then forged forward into clear air in time for the impact of the shells on the fort to be visible. They struck the edge of the breach made by the last salvo, blasting another smoking gouge in the inclined wall.

And still the embrasures had not been hit.

Monitor and gunboat were now abreast. Dawlish grabbed the lanyard of the steam whistle and jerked it. It shrieked and he held it down for ten, fifteen, twenty seconds, until thrashing white foam at the *Montelindo's* stern told him that Purdon had heard and had rung for full revolutions. The monitor gathered speed, digging her low bow down so that water ran up and over the forecastle, but still Dawlish knew she could not match the *Toad's* top speed. Reluctantly he ordered Holmes to reach for the engine telegraphs and ease them back.

Three quarters revolutions. Ten seconds, and the *Toad* slowed. Both vessels were moving upstream in parallel, Egdean carefully nudging the *Toad* as close as he dared so that her vulnerable hull was shielded from the fort by the *Montelindo's* ironclad flanks, though her higher superstructure was still nakedly exposed.

Dawlish swept his telescope along the damaged earthwork. The muzzles had been drawn back for reloading when the last salvo had landed and there was no sign of them running out yet – not that it would matter in another thirty seconds since the two advancing warships would by then have passed outside their training arcs. He saw figures outlined above the rim of the earthworks and for the first time was conscious of the rattle of small arms fire. A single screaming ricochet told of a lucky round reaching the *Montelindo's* turret but it prompted the first burst of Gatling fire from the *Toad's* gunners. Dirt spattered along the earthwork's top as they found the range and the figures there dived for cover.

As the spinning barrels fell silent Dawlish's attention was focused on the earthen wall running parallel to the river bank which he could now see clearly for the first time. It was no more than sixty yards long but there was a single embrasure – and Dawlish's vessels would have to pass in little over two minutes. If it contained a weapon then its crew would have had ample time to prepare for what must be a point-blank shot. He flinched as another small-arms round whined somewhere close and he pulled on his cheroot. Egdean's lips were moving in silent prayer and Holmes' knuckles were white as he grasped the telegraph handles. One of the Gatlings stuttered into life again, then fell as quickly into silence.

One of the embrasured weapons fired for a last time, but it was a desperate shot at the limit of its arc, and the round ploughed harmlessly into the river forty yards astern. The warships now came level with the corner where the riverside and inclined flanks of the earthworks met and Dawlish saw that the bluff they rested on was slightly lower than the platform on which he stood. A few heads poked over the parapet and shots were loosed wildly. An insane impulse drove him to sweep off his hat and wave it towards his assailants. The Gatlings chattered briefly again and the irregular rifle-fire died away.

The *Montelindo* and the *Toad* surged forward, bow level with bow, the monitor's turret now rotated to bear fully to port. Purdon had done his work well - so far the *Montelindo's* crew had performed superbly – and now the most critical moment of all was coming. Dawlish could see the riverside embrasure fully now – it was less than forty yards ahead – and a black muzzle was running out, ready to rake any passing craft on the broadside. He reached for both telegraphs and pulled them back – full astern. An eternity passed before the engines paused, then lashed into reverse, and the two great screws dragged the *Toad* to an almost instant halt. The *Montelindo* drew ahead of her, leaving the gunboat momentarily exposed to nothing worse than small-arms fire – and the Gatlings could handle that.

Flame and smoke blasted from the embrasure as the *Montelindo* passed it. There was a clanging sound as the shot screamed downwards, bounced across the wave-washed foredeck, tore through the breakwater and carried a bollard with it into the waters beyond. Almost simultaneously the monitor's turret weapons erupted in reply. The elevation was too low to carry the shells into the embrasure itself, but that did not matter, for they bored into the bluff below it before blasting a geyser of fire and soil below the twenty-pounder it contained.

Dawlish saw with mixed horror and elation how gun and mount and crew, and the earth and timbers that supported them, were hurled skywards from the fiery pit. There was a second explosion, a low rumbling one, as the gun's stored charges flashed into brief life. A rolling pall of smoke and dust enveloped the earthwork's side and then there seemed to be a moment of great silence in which he could hear only the *Toad's* panting. Then a shower of falling debris pockmarked the river and rattled on the decks of the passing *Montelindo*.

"Full speed!"

Holmes signalled for full ahead, following the *Montelindo* past the reeking havoc she had created. The *Toad* slipped past the upstream end of the earthen wall and Dawlish saw to his delight that his surmise had been correct. There was no bastion at right angles to the river on that side - the fort had one open face and he could dominate it.

Now the full destruction of the earthwork could commence.

The next bend was two hundred yards upstream and the *Montelindo* forged towards it. Men emerged from hatches and scrambled over her decks to release the anchors. She took station in midstream, blocking the channel against any threat from upriver. The *Toad* followed close astern, her speed slower now, seeking to find the ideal range from which to bring the mighty Armstrong to bear on the fort's exposed interior.

The open centre of the earthwork was on a slight incline and as the *Toad* drew upstream it came into view through the missing face. The cloud of smoke and dust was clearing to show the cluster of wooden huts and a corral of horses or mules in the middle. Beyond them lay the rear of the two twenty-pounders which now pointed uselessly downriver through their embrasures. Panic reigned, with figures scurrying to and from the smouldering pit at the riverside wall, dragging out injured survivors. Others struggled to free the horses from their pen. A single wagon was seeking escape, its driver lashing terrified mules through the crowd that blocked its path. A knot of figures was labouring hopelessly around one of the surviving guns to drag it round to bear upriver, across the inner space. For one fleeting instant Dawlish was sure he recognised Roybon among them. A few riflemen had kept their heads and had moved off the walls and were moving up along the bank at a crouch, pausing to fire at the *Toad*. The walls were no longer a defence, but a trap.

At Dawlish's order the two Gatlings stammered into life, barrels spinning as the gunners ground the firing cranks round, raking the fort's interior with short, savage bursts, interrupted only as they shifted target or as the loaders replenished the feed-hoppers. The clusters of panicking men disintegrated, each dashing to seek his own shelter. The fleeing wagon upended in a chaos of flailing hooves and bloody mules. The group around the twenty-pounder wavered, then broke and fled for cover through the embrasure. And still this was not the full chastisement, but only the means of keeping the victims cowed until the *Toad's* full vengeance could be invoked.

In the following minutes the long tedium of the *Toad's* repeated drills paid off as Holmes, under Dawlish's calm directions, used her like the fine-tuned killing machine she was. With engines slowed she crept up almost directly astern of the *Montelindo*, and then, with the Armstrong heaving upwards through the deck, loaded and at the elevation signalled by the indicator, the port screw was reversed and she spun to face downriver. As the bows swung towards the earthworks Holmes, judging the exact instant with an accuracy that was by now instinctive, hit the knob that sounded the gunner's electric bell. The huge muzzle belched fire and spat the hollow, powder-packed shell towards the fort's interior. As it burst, spraying fire and iron shards and fragments of debris, and scything down any living thing within twenty yards, Holmes was already working the telegraph, throwing the reversed port screw into forward again so that the *Toad's* turn was stemmed and she moved downriver. The Armstrong had sunk beneath the deck again and now, out of sight, polished metal pistons and sweating human bodies were swabbing and charging and loading the iron monster's maw. The gunboat dropped downstream for a hundred yards, the Gatling's stuttering adding to the agony within the fort, and then another reversal of one screw faced her upstream again so she could advance towards the *Montelindo* for the whole cycle of carnage to start again.

Six times the manoeuvre was repeated and six times the terrible red and yellow-tipped shells ploughed into the shambles that had been the fort, ripping deep furrows in its earthen floor before blasting flame-scoured craters, smashing the pitiful huts into matchwood, hurling the twenty-pounders from their carriages and erupting their stacked charges. Terrified men and beasts struggled across the inclined walls and disappeared in panic into the scrub beyond, leaving behind a charnel house of burned and torn bodies.

When the Armstrong had dropped to reload after the fourth volley Holmes turned to Dawlish. "Do we need to fire again, Sir?" he said. He looked pale, obviously horrified by the carnage. "It looks like those fellows have had enough."

Dawlish choked down his own revulsion but knew that victory here must be absolute, its morale effect terrifying. "Continue firing, Mr. Holmes," he said. He did not look him in the eye.

The slaughter ended only because Dawlish could see no more sign of movement. He looked at his watch. Almost six o'clock. It would be dark soon. Suddenly he felt drained.

"We'll anchor in midstream," he told Holmes, "but first send a boat downriver to the *Tacuari*. Send a good man. Let him find Murillo and tell him I've cleared the river."

He looked away from the fort, unwilling to see too closely what he had done.

17

But Dawlish could not keep himself away from the fort, and what he saw there spurred him to a desperate resolve.

It rained during the night, a downpour that soaked the lookouts straining for any sign of the *Torres* or of movement along the riverbank. There was none, though distant moaning, weak, and finally dying away, did reach them from the earthworks. Through the darkness the *Toad* and the *Montelindo* swayed at their moorings in midstream, crews busy inspecting engines and hydraulics and making the minor readjustments needed after the strain of the day's battle. At first light Dawlish had himself rowed ashore and approached the fort cautiously with a small escort. Wisps of vapour drifted across the muddy ground as the first sun began to boil away the night's rain.

Nothing he had seen yesterday from the *Toad* – not the flame-crimsoned fountains of earth or the rolling banks of foul yellow and black smoke, nor the scurryings of the tormented creatures that had blundered between them – had prepared him for the morning's sodden misery. The great furrows torn by the shells before they exploded, the blackened craters, the splintered and charred fragments of the huts – even bodies flung down and frozen in bizarre attitudes of death – these he had expected, and indeed had seen before.

It was the scale that overwhelmed him. The scale – and the human fragments.

The muddy pools that littered the red earth were scummed with a brighter crimson, highlighted here and there by a violent yellow or blue too dreadful to contemplate. He stepped aside, and began to choke when confronted with a naked and blackened leg, torn away at the thigh, but soon he saw that this was not the worst. Every other conceivable portion of human anatomy was strewn about the shambles. Black flies were feasting already and they rose in buzzing clouds at his approach. He pressed on, unwilling that the seamen of his escort should see him biting back his nausea, but as he did he heard the sound of one of them vomiting behind. A bird rose reluctantly from the flayed remains of a torso, the ribs exposed, and he wanted to believe it must be a dog's. The ruins of the corral was perhaps the worst of all, for a shell had fallen among horses, sundering their great bodies and hurling their organs over a huge distance. Behind him somebody spewed again and then stammered an apology.

Nobody still lived, though not all the victims had died immediately. Waterlogged tracks in the mud showed where wretches, some mutilated beyond comprehension, had dragged themselves towards some imagined succour and had there died. One was a woman, middle-aged, with grey streaks in her matted black hair, her clothing burned indecently away, her entrails clutched between her hands. Later he found others, some even more tortured. He passed on, ashamed, gorged carrion birds flapping lazily from his path.

The river was visible through the crater in the earthen wall where the *Montelindo's* fire had detonated a volcano beneath the embrasure. Dawlish looked for the gun it had once sheltered and finally recognised its muzzle protruding from the mud some fifty yards distant. Something white was smeared against it and he did not want to look closer.

There was a whisper behind him, an English voice, West Country, saying with quiet indignation "Not much to be proud of here," only to be stilled by Egdean.

"Pipe down, Hill," he said. "You don't want the Commander to hear you." And yet even in the voice of the faithful seaman there was a tone of discomfort, an implied reproof perhaps for the officer he worshipped.

But the remark stung. Dawlish forced himself to ignore his own rising sense of shame and to thrust from his mind the image of sleek men savouring brandy and cigars in a hotel in Sheerness. He climbed the earthen wall angled to the river and from the embrasures of which the two Parrotts had engaged the *Montelindo*. Portions still held their sharp profiles, the inner and outer sides sloped at forty-five degrees, the top a yard wide, the soil to build them scooped from now water-filled trenches before them. Other sections had been blown away or reduced to rounded heaps. He picked his way with difficulty to the landward face. In front of it, where the devastation had not reached, he found it was as Gelb had reported, with a complex of zigzag trenches, some roofed over with logs and soil, and the ground before burned bare of scrub but scattered with inclined stakes. Swampy ground stretched beyond. Any land assault across this ground would have been suicidal.

The fort had one weak-point and by a combination of inspired guesswork and quick resolution Dawlish had exploited it. But he knew that there would be more earthworks upriver – Culbertson had found out that much on his reconnaissance months ago – but it would be insane to hope that similar weak points would not now be strengthened. The Reducción's greatest resource was human muscle – and desperation. The labour that had been deployed to create this earthwork must have been immense. Its horrified survivors would already be spurring their friends upriver to remedy any deficiencies in the defences there.

There was movement beyond the swamp, horsemen, Gelb's troop retracing their steps of the previous day, and probing so as to come around the landward wall. Dawlish stood and waved his hat and in the distance somebody rose in his stirrups and waved back. He ought to have a flag flying above the shattered fort to signify is submission – but what flag? There were no Consortium colours that he knew of and worse, as that unseen seaman had remarked, there was little here to be proud of.

One of the twenty-pounder barrels had landed precariously on top of the wall. Dawlish sat on it, looked out across the devastation within the earthen horseshoe. This had been butcher's work. So too had it been at the Taku forts, and on the advance to Kumasi – and yes, on one flame-shrouded night in an African swamp that he never wished to remember, and at the rain-swept Georgian anchorage of Poti. But governments, whether representing the Crown, or Lords and Commons assembled, or the Ottoman Sultan, had ultimately sanctioned those slaughters, and there had been a national purpose, however opaque. That was somehow different to the Board of the Hyperion Consortium, no matter how exalted its members, sitting comfortably before a coal fire in the Railway Hotel, Sheerness, and planning to project murder into the heart of another continent.

There was another image too that disturbed him, glimpsed only minutes ago, but one he knew would unman him if he lived to take Florence in his arms ever again. He had not counted on killing women.

And this was only the start, the very threshold of the Reducción defences, and the horror could only grow worse. He had a sudden recollection of Aquino shaking his head when Tinsley had asked about prisoners on that ridge above La Garganta. It might take time, and losses, but Dawlish had no doubt that the flotilla carried the resources needed to grind down all opposition. He knew also with certainty that, however much he might recoil from this present moment's horror, he would play his role. He was a professional, and he had given his word. Whether or not promotion and a command lay at the end of the venture, he would stick to his bargain.

And yet... his position with the Consortium would never be stronger than at this moment. In an hour or two he would meet Murillo, Culbertson, Aquino and all that sordid crew. However they might begrudge it, they could not withhold admiration for this achievement. They would know that he was essential to the expedition's success, perhaps even be ready to indulge him to keep him co-operative. Had it been now that he had been pleading for Roybon he might have been more successful.

Roybon... Roybon, with his bruised face, and even more bruised pride, must be limping with the fort's survivors into Puerto Plutarcho, finding words to explain to El Pobre how his delaying tactics had failed at such cost, wondering how further disaster could be averted. He must know he was in an even deeper chamber pot than at Sedan – and yet his behaviour under questioning proved that he might care little for himself. But for the men who had laboured to create the Reducción, and for the women, and the children too, Roybon must realise that any accommodation would be better than an even greater charnel house such as this.

Even slaves were left with their lives – Roybon must acknowledge that. His was the one face that Dawlish could put on the Reducción, and it was a rational one. Roybon must surely have some respect for him after the interventions he had made for him...

Dawlish stood up and beckoned Egdean to him. "Go to the *Toad*, Egdean. "My compliments to Mr. Holmes and request him to come across. And to be so good as to bring a bed sheet."

"A sheet, Sir?" A look of amazement.

"That's right. A white bed sheet."

A whistle blasted downriver. The *Ipora* was rounding the bend, unmistakable by the raised drawbridge swaying above her towed barge. Culbertson would be fretting on her bridge, thinking up sarcasms. She was making slow progress against the current. The

Tacuari, Murillo's craft, was no doubt close on her heels. Dawlish knew he would have to be fast.

Gelb's riders had reached the open face of the fort. They paused there, silent on their mud-streaked horses, awed by the destruction. Gelb urged his mount forward towards Dawlish when he spotted him coming to meet him. The horse hesitated again and again, too dainty hoofed to tread on the offal beneath it.

"Look's like you've had the best of it, Commander," he said. "The place looks like a Chicago stockyard at close of business."

"Is Carmelita here?" Dawlish cut him short.

Gelb nodded. "Machado's riding her now."

"I'm taking her, Sergeant. I'll need her. And a Winchester, and a bag of fodder for her, and a canteen of water. Also one of your men who can find me the way overland to Puerto Plutarcho."

Gelb's eyes narrowed and he paused before he spoke.

"You figuring on deserting, Commander? Not wise, Sir, not wise at all. Those bastards upstream will fillet you slowly for what you've done here. And besides, Colonel Si wouldn't be none too pleased if I were to assist you. He ain't a man to cross."

Dawlish stiffened himself. "Are you querying the intentions of a senior officer, Sergeant? An officer of the Royal Navy?" He summoned his most icy quarterdeck manner. "Do you dare mention the word desertion in relation to a superior? Are you questioning my honour?"

"No offence intended, Sir. No offence," Gelb's hand moved to his hat brim in a half-forgotten gesture of deference.

"My mission has been agreed with Don Plutarcho himself," Dawlish lied, allowing a conciliatory note to enter his voice. "He believed that the rebels would be prepared to listen to reason once we'd destroyed this position. Don Plutarcho has appointed me his personal representative. You can check with him when he gets here."

"But Colonel Culbertson…"

"Colonel Culbertson." Dawlish shook his head slightly and allowed an arrogant tone to flavour his words. "Colonel Culbertson is an excellent officer. But he's not always privy to the deliberations of the Board of the Consortium."

"But I'd need an authorisation, Sir, a paper from yourself…"

"A paper to absolve you from all blame if one of Her Majesty's officers should prove to be a liar. Is that what you mean, Sergeant? Is that it?"

Gelb nodded silently, uncomfortably.

"Then you shall have it, by God," Dawlish said with mock fury, scarcely able to mask his satisfaction as Gelb groped in his saddlebag and eventually produced a crumpled scrap of paper and a stub of pencil. Beyond his horse's haunches Dawlish could see Holmes approaching, followed by Egdean carrying a folded sheet – and all the time he was aware of the *Ipora* beating upriver.

Haste was essential. He snatched the paper, scribbled a few phrases stating that Gelb had been acting under his instruction, and that his objections had been noted and over-ruled, and then pushed the paper back towards the embarrassed Sergeant.

"You can read, I suppose," he said with heavy sarcasm. "I trust that my wording is to your satisfaction, Sergeant? Good. Then be so kind to have Carmelita ready, and one of your men who knows the ground. If all goes well we'll be back by nightfall."

"It's suicide, Commander," Gelb said. "Them bastards won't give you a hearing." He pulled his horse about and returned to the troop.

Holmes had come close enough to hear him and his face registered disbelief. "You're not leaving us, Sir?" he said. "Not now."

Dawlish explained his plan briefly. He said nothing of his motivation, for indeed he would have found it difficult to define it. Until now the concept of duty had somehow always sustained him, but now he was conscious that something different was involved which he had not the time to analyse or to explain. But Florence would understand it, even if it meant his death, and that was a comfort.

"And you'll see Señor Murillo," he said, not envying Holmes the task. "You'll tell him I have every confidence in your ability to command the riverine component until I return – before dusk I should hope."

"And if you don't return, Sir?"

"Then I imagine you'll give Admiral Topcliffe good reason to be very appreciative of you, Holmes. I trust it'll be worth a promotion."

He took the bed sheet, and from the splintered remnants of the corral selected a long lath that might serve as a pole to hang it from.

"Let me come with you, Sir," Egdean's voice was glum with foreboding.

"You can't ride, Jerry," Dawlish said, touched. "And Mr. Holmes will need you at the helm."

Gelb approached, leading a lightly laden but empty-saddled Carmelita and followed by a squat, pockmarked half-Indian trooper.

"This is Romualdo," he said. "Speaks Spanish, Guaraní, some Guaikuru. He knows the ground." He dropped his voice. "He's got cousins in the Reducción, probably a woman or two as well. Either they'll skin him on sight, or fall on his neck like the prodigal returned. It ain't much, Sir, but he's your best chance."

There was a hint of concern in Gelb's voice, a memory perhaps of shared danger in that charge through the scrub that now seemed so distant. Dawlish regretted having to lie to him.

"Thank you, Sergeant," he said. "Wish us luck".

He nodded to Romualdo, handed him the sheet and lath and then swung himself into the saddle. He urged Carmelita into a trot and splashed through the mud away from the fort. He glanced down the river one last time. The *Ipora* was still far enough downstream that it would be ten minutes before Culbertson could be ashore. The story he had told Gelb might just take in the Colonel and delay pursuit until Murillo arrived to unmask it as a fabrication.

The ground was more open now. They broke into a canter, on into the Chaco beyond.

18

The going was difficult at first, the hooves sucking in the wet mud, but as the sun climbed the earth dried and the last wisps of mist cleared. The scrub-clad plain stretched out before them, brown and brittle and thorny. The ground was open, with patches of thicker brush, which they skirted, and isolated stands of higher timber. They rode diagonally away from the river, leaving it to their right, and at intervals their progress was slowed by shallow watercourses, still flowing with the remnants of the night's rain, which would have cleared by midday. None came higher than the horses' bellies and they struggled through without difficulty, Romualdo eager to show Dawlish how to seek out the best places to cross. With the opportunity of studying him more closely, Dawlish recognised him as one of those who had charged with him against the howitzers. At the next crossing he found an excuse to mention that he remembered him and to praise him for his riding that day. Yellowed teeth flashed pleasure in the pocked face.

They rode from the start with carbines at the ready, Dawlish copying but not equalling the easy grace with which Romualdo couched the weapon's butt in the crook of his right elbow, thumb and palm cradling the stock's neck, finger on the trigger. The trooper rode slightly ahead, his small dark eyes scanning every hummock and patch of brush for signs of danger, not hesitating to gesture to Dawlish to fall back at the slightest suspicion.

Twice they found dead horses, both scorched and gashed such that they could only marvel they had made it this far. Further on a hastily buried body, still fresh, had already been uncovered from its shallow grave and worried by scavengers. Occasional discarded items of equipment and clothing showed that the bulk of those who had escaped from the fort had come this way.

With the safety of the flotilla now so far behind Dawlish began to feel a chill of fear dilute his earlier optimism. The survivors of this trail of misery would be unlikely to accord him a kind reception. It was time to make use of the sheet. They dismounted and tied it to the rough pole taken from the corral and jammed it upright into Romualdo's bucket holster. The air was still and the sheet hung limp, hardly streaming as they cantered on, but providing a beacon of sorts to render them conspicuous above the low brown scrub.

Dawlish feared what was behind almost as much as what lay ahead. He knew it could only be a matter of time before his bluff was called, and Gelb's troop sent after him, and indeed by mid-morning there was an ominous brown smudge rising on the horizon behind. He had a head start, but much of the ground so far had been covered when it had been muddy and now, as the sun climbed, the pursuers had the advantage of drier ground. Puerto Plutarcho itself could not be more than a dozen miles ahead, but it was impossible to guess where the first outposts or patrols might be encountered. The horses were tiring, and the dust and the heat and the glare were combining to slow the pace. Dawlish envied Romualdo his leggings, for his own thin duck trousers gave scant protection against the rough grass and scrub that tore at his calves. There was no sign of life other than a spiral of birds wheeling around some other casualty of the night's flight.

And then, to the front, and to the left, they spotted a thin column of rising dust.

Dawlish repressed an urge to turn and gallop away from it. The ground here was scattered with clumps of shoulder-high brush. Better not to be found in such close terrain, but to spur forward to more open ground where he and Romualdo could be seen from a distance. He took the lead, breaking into a fast trot, until he found an almost-bare patch, cracked and seamed by heat, its surface naked for two hundred yards in every direction.

Still that column of dust grew closer.

"We wait here," Dawlish reined in and pushed his carbine into its holster. "Yours too," he added when he saw Romualdo hesitate. The man was frightened, but he complied and Dawlish hoped that his own fear did not also show as clearly.

"Lift the flag. Wave it slowly – that's it, slowly, back and forth."

The horses shook themselves and snorted, grateful for the pause. Romualdo continued to sweep the flag slowly from side to side. The sun beat down, insects shrilled and Dawlish felt the sweat running down his back and his hands shaking. The dust rose now from beyond the strip of scrub at the edge of the bare space they stood in, but still there was no sign of the riders who raised it. Dawlish noticed that the sheet had been patched, and there was an indelible Admiralty mark in one corner and he wondered if this was the last thing he would remember. But still they kept the horses stationary and Romualdo continued to sweep the flag.

Now the dust cloud paused and died. Dawlish knew that stealthy figures had dismounted and were creeping through the scrub. He was being watched and perhaps a rifle was being sighted on his chest this moment. He laid down the reins and raised his hands slowly. He waited an eternity like that, and his arms started to ache, but now he dared not lower them again lest he provoke the unseen watchers.

He became conscious of movement to his left, but he feared to turn. The agony of waiting continued, of dry mouth, and trembling, and sweat and aching arms and above all the knowledge that in the next moment he might be smashed from his saddle and from life by rifle fire he would never hear. And still Romualdo swept the flag to and fro across his mount, but slower now, for he too was tired and just as frightened.

Dawlish never heard the Guaikuru who padded from behind close enough to shove a muzzle into the small of his back.

"Come down, Señor," a voice said in Spanish. "Slowly, with your hands up."

He lifted his right leg across the saddle and slid to the ground. A hand reached forward and eased his Adams from its holster. Movements to his left told him that Romualdo was being put through similar paces but he could not risk moving his head to look across. The muzzle was removed from his back.

"Now turn around, Señor. Calmly."

A tall, lean Indian in a tattered leather shirt stood before him, aiming at his midriff. A wide-brimmed straw hat threw his face into shadow, but not enough to hide broken teeth glistening under a harelip. His eyes blazed hatred. A knife, wider than a bayonet but just as long, hung from his belt in a hide scabbard. His rank smell was almost overpowering and Dawlish feared him as he would a wild animal.

"I know you are an Englishman, Señor," the man said in a slurring whisper. "Even if the others do not, I will cut you up. Not now maybe, but later. You will plead with me to give you death, just like the other English did after we rose with El Pobre."

Beyond him two riders were approaching at a slow walk, carbines at the ready. The nearer wore a felt hat and a brown cotton jacket and had trousers stuffed into high boots. He did not look liken an Indian, unlike his companion, who was leather clad, like Dawlish's captor. Their remnants of military equipment – bandoliers, pouches and strapping – looked worn and ragged but their Martini-Henrys seemed well cared for and the same probably went for their sheathed sabres. Half-a-dozen other horsemen were now visible on the edges of the clearing, dusty and unkempt, all with the same air of effortless grace in the saddle.

A loud, slapping sound and a groan of pain to Dawlish's left told him that Romualdo had been knocked to the ground. Somebody laughed. There was another blow and they laughed again. For the second time that morning Dawlish knew that his only hope lay in a display of arrogant confidence.

"Is this how your Reducción treats ambassadors?" he shouted to the closer rider. "Does a flag of truce count for nothing?"

Romualdo was being kicked systematically and was gasping with pain.

"You are a spy, Señor," the horseman said as he reined in. His accent, not unlike Aquino's, told he was Paraguayan. "We are not fools. A rag on a pole doesn't change what you are."

"My mission is to El Pobre," Dawlish said with as much cold dignity as he could feign. "I've nothing to say to you, my friend. If you want to know more of me, then check with Señor Roybon."

"Capitan Roybon knows you?" the man said, obviously surprised.

"And I'll hold you answerable to him," Dawlish cut in. He noted that Roybon had promoted himself one rank since he left French service. "I'll hold you answerable for a start for attacking my escort. You can order your men to stop beating him. Now! Ahora mismo!"

The rider was young, not above twenty-five, and Dawlish could sense that he was unsure how to handle this situation. He did however snap a few words to his men and Romualdo was hauled to his feet and abused no further.

Dawlish locked his gaze into the rider's and said: "I'm lowering my arms now and I don't expect to be harmed. And you can tell your ruffian that I'll be expecting my pistol to be returned when I leave." He did not wait for agreement, but he moved slowly nonetheless.

"Your name, Señor?"

"Dawlish. Commander Nicholas Dawlish. And yours, Señor?"

"Gil. Lieutenant of Cavalry of La Reducción Nueva." For all his shabby appearance, there was a hint of pride in his tone.

"You'll take us to Capitan Roybon? The matter is urgent."

"And your business, Comandante? I'm sorry, your name, I cannot remember it." When told, he repeated it several times, as if intrigued by its strangeness.

"Our business is not for your ears, Lieutenant Gil, but it is serious, and urgent." Dawlish said. "Capitan Roybon will welcome seeing me, I assure you. But we must be fast."

Gil hesitated, looked over his shoulder and was clearly troubled by the column of dust rising above the scrub to the east. He gestured to it. "You are not the bait for a trap, Comandante? For Culbertson's locusts to surround us?"

"Not if we move fast, Lieutenant."

Gil looked nervously one last time towards the eastern horizon, then barked commands to his men on the ground. They took the Winchesters and sabres from Dawlish's and Romualdo's horses. Gil told them to mount.

"You will be covered closely. You'll follow Ramon here," He jerked his head towards the mounted Indian. "We follow. If you try to break loose, you will be shot down."

"You're taking us to Capitan Roybon?"

"In good time. We ride fast. In ten, fifteen minutes we stop and then we blindfold you. I tell you now so you do not think we play false. You understand that I cannot let you see the defences of La Reducción."

They moved off north-westwards into the sparse scrub at a fast trot, joined as they pressed on by another dozen horsemen who seemed to materialise from nowhere. Dawlish had an uneasy feeling that they were being watched, but it was only when crossing an almost dried-out watercourse that they were challenged by a group that appeared on foot from a thicket, and then allowed to pass. Unlike the Reducción infantry he had encountered earlier, those riflemen who had stood their ground above the Gullet and during the charge on the howitzers, these men were poorly armed. One carried what

172

looked like a muzzle-loading musket and several were equipped only with machetes and spears. The harelipped Guaikuru pointed to Dawlish as he rode past them and said something that made them laugh unpleasantly.

Another ten minutes and Gil called a halt. It was time for the blindfolding. Dawlish refused the filthy bandana first offered and insisted that his own handkerchief be used. It was still clean, though crumpled, and when doubled, then folded again, it effectively shut off all sight.

"I will lead your horse myself, Comandante," Gil said, "not fast. Do not fear. Hold the saddle before you."

But the experience was still terrifying, though Dawlish knew that Carmelita was moving only at a trot, and often falling back into a walk as some obstacle was negotiated. The sensation was of being out of control, and at a great height, and of moving at breakneck speed and liable to topple off at every turn, however slight. He forced himself to relax lest the mare, and worse still, his captors, sense his fear and yet the feeling of helpless vulnerability did not subside. There were sounds of other voices now, and of feet running as if to hurry to catch a spectacle, and expressions of surprise occasioned by the sight of him.

There was a sense of being spoken about as if he could not hear. "Yes," somebody said, "he is English. Another of Murillo's Englishmen. There is no end of them."

And then another voice, answering with a certainty that was chilling: "But even so, they will all die in the end. El Pobre has said so."

The pace was very slow now, with many twists and turns, followed by the jolting descent of a steep slope and then a climb up another, equally steep. Then a straight and level section for several minutes and afterwards again a succession of twists and turns, and another descent and climb that threatened to tumble him from the saddle. More voices, some in a language he could not understand, but sounding hostile and mocking until Gil stilled them. A piercing whistle sounded at a distance, the first impression being of a boat on the river, but then there followed the unmistakable chugging of a locomotive moving slowly. Dawlish knew that a narrow-gauge railway for moving produce had been under construction when the revolt had erupted. Somebody had obviously had the expertise – and the determination – to get it operational since. But why?

The sound dropped away and then came the smell of wood smoke, and cooking food, and women's' voices, and then these too were left behind and they rode on for a long distance on the level. Dawlish had lost all sense of time and distance and direction. He longed for vision and orientation again but he remained silent and straight-backed, conscious that he must retain respect at all costs. The sound of hooves, which then fell silent. A new arrival and a greeting.

Gil enquired about Roybon's whereabouts.

"Sleeping now, I think, in his quarters," another voice said. "But he was at the hospital until an hour ago. He would not leave until he was satisfied about the wounded he brought back with him."

The speaker must have gestured to Dawlish, for Gil then said: "An Englishman. From the Hyperion fleet. He came to us himself, under a white flag."

"A fool therefore," the other said, and laughed, and rode away.

Another five minutes and they halted finally. Gil removed Dawlish's blindfold, not ungently, before he dismounted. For a moment he was dazzled by the midday sun, and then found himself on one side of a dusty square faced by dilapidated single-story mud-brick and wooden houses. A row of withered saplings told of a long-neglected attempt to plant for shade. Two platoons of barefoot troops were trudging back and forth in a semblance of close-order drill and beyond them another was going through the motions of a volley-fire exercise. A scattering of ragged children looked on, showing as little interest as they did in the corpses that dangled from the crossbeam of a long gallows at the far end of the square. The structure was substantial and was built for more than the two victims who now graced it with placards draped around their elongated necks. Dawlish looked away quickly. He had seen enough to tell him that these wretches had been denied the mercy of a long drop.

Gil motioned him towards the nearest house, a large clapboard bungalow with peeling paint and a wide veranda. Missing shutters and smashed trellis told that it had once had pretensions to elegance. There had been a garden in front too, but only stumps of the palings remained, and a few overgrown clumps of flowers and greenery and the mutilated remains of a plaster statue of a nymph. Several horses were tied to a rail outside, swishing their tails against the flies that buzzed them. Beyond them a pony stood between the shafts of a shabby dogcart. One glance told Dawlish that the unkempt little beast was not a native, but a forlorn survivor imported from Britain, and that the broken-springed and paint-blistered vehicle it pulled had once been the pride of some Hyperion manager's wife.

Two heavily armed Indians barred their path as they mounted the veranda. Gil produced a paper. It was scrutinised with all the solemn respect reserved by illiterates for the written word. Then they shook their heads. They had their orders from the Señora that nobody was to be admitted.

Gil was embarrassed now, for a small crowd was gathering, some gesturing angrily towards Romualdo. It was important, very important, Gil said. He had brought a special visitor, and he could vouch for it that Capitan Roybon would want to see him immediately. His voice began to rise, and he started to gesticulate. Didn't they recognise him? Would he bother the Capitan with a trivial matter? Yes, he knew the Señora had ordered it, but even so...

"Even what?"

The voice was emotionless and cold and all the more threatening for being a woman's. The face might have been of granite. She pushed open the torn fly screen that masked the open doorway and stood before them, short and muscular, though not stout. She wore a nondescript grey dress and the sleeves were rolled up to show strong, sun-reddened arms.

"Is it not enough that our good Capitan has been earning his rest in the defence of our Reducción?" she said. "He must rest until sundown. His deputy is at Post Number Four. Go to him." Her Spanish was fluent but her inflexions betrayed her. She could only be French.

"It is Capitan Roybon I have come to see," Dawlish said. "I come from the Consortium flotilla, Madame. Capitan Roybon will not, I believe, hesitate to see me."

She turned to Dawlish for the first time, and leaned slightly forward to peer at him with pale blue eyes and he realised that she was accustomed to wearing spectacles. Her face must have been beautiful once, and was still unwrinkled, but it had tightened long ago into a mask of joyless intensity. Only her hair hinted at a remnant of vanity, for it was clean and well combed and piled up and tied with care. It was snow-white, though she herself could be little over thirty-five.

"One of the leeches." She looked at Dawlish with cold venom. "A hired bloodsucker. You may go back where you came from, Señor. You have nothing to say that we want to hear."

The quarterdeck manner would not help now. "I don't intend to argue the issues with you, Madame," Dawlish said quietly, "but I can assure you I did not risk my life to come here for mercenary reasons." The choice of adjective was unfortunate and her lips drew back in a sneer, but he pressed on. "I didn't meet Capitan Roybon under pleasant circumstances but I trust that he will not speak ill of my behaviour on that occasion."

"So you are the English sailor?" she said. "The Comandante Dawls? Indeed, Señor, he has mentioned you." The mispronunciation was the first hint of human frailty. "And your message Señor? That we must submit to Murillo's yoke or you will blow us apart? That these people must be slaves of the Consortium again?"

There was an almost hysteric edge to her voice now, but she seemed to realise it, and she checked herself. "Enter, Señor. You too, Lieutenant Gil." She motioned towards the doorway. Gil drew his pistol half-apologetically and covered Dawlish as they entered.

176

They passed into the stuffy gloom of what had once been a parlour but was now occupied by three paper-strewn desks at which shirt-sleeved men seemed busily at work. One entire wall was covered with maps, both printed and hand-drawn, some brightly coloured. More lay on a large table. Dawlish ached to see them closer but he looked deliberately away, unwilling to seem prying. The sight of this systematic staff work depressed him, just as so many other aspects of the Reducción's ruthless efficiency had before. He followed the short woman through an inner door to a smaller room containing a roll-top desk and a few battered chairs. A reproduction in a gilt frame showed Highland cattle grazing by a Scottish loch. The Frenchwoman bade him sit, and left Gil to guard him.

There was a short embarrassed silence before she returned. With her came Roybon, his eyes red-rimmed, one side of his face livid with a powder scorch, a robe clutched around him. Dawlish saw no warmth in his look of recognition, but there was something of respect.

"I don't know why I should welcome you, Commander Dawlish," he said in English. "First you destroy my howitzers, then my fort, and now it must be my sleep also."

But then he reached out and shook Dawlish's hand, the first that day to do so.

19

Puerto Plutarcho showed every sign of having been consciously laid out to be part town, part industrial site, with workshops, warehouses, stockyards and dwellings disposed on a rectangular grid. Now it had also become a camp, as whole outlying settlements had been evacuated to it ahead of the Consortium's advance. The once-neat bungalows of the Hyperion managers and supervisors, and the labours' huts and barracks, were now packed to overflowing. Every open space seemed occupied by hastily erected mud and thatch hovels, outside which Indian women squatted and cooked over open fires. There were children everywhere, some partly clothed, the younger totally naked. There was a stench, faint but pervasive, of smoke and cooking and excrement and decomposing rubbish.

Riding beside a silent Roybon, Dawlish had an impression of an ant-heap. The French officer, now dressed, had dismissed Gil's attempt to blindfold Dawlish again before they set off. What of significance, he asked, might their guest see between here and El Pobre's house? No further reference was made to their earlier meeting and the atmosphere was one of formal correctness. The white-haired woman – Madame Le Vroux, Dawlish learned – drove beside them in the dog-cart, not hesitating to crack her whip to keep at a distance the swarm of urchins running alongside. They passed several further bodies of infantry, some well-armed and obviously well-drilled, others equipped with little more than agricultural implements and only recently subjected to a semblance of military discipline. But there were many of them, very many.

In what Dawlish knew to be the direction of the river there rose higher roofs and walls of rusting corrugated sheet. Smoke and steam drifted from the chimneys and vents that pierced them. The pulsating sound of a large stationary steam engine and the rattle of overhead shafting and slap of drive belts told that the workshops were working at full tilt. They could only be producing weapons, however crude. Great mounds of cut logs lay close by, fuel for the furnaces. A line of bent figures was dragging another wagonload to augment the pile. There were no young men among them, but many women.

Roybon followed Dawlish's gaze. "Necessary, Señor Dawlish," he said. "Necessary, I fear. There is other work for the horses and mules these days."

The slipways up which the Hyperion steamers would have been hauled for maintenance must lie beyond the workshops, and there too would be the uncompleted canning plant and the cattle-loading jetties. The river was broad at this point, Dawlish remembered from the charts, sluggish and deep, wide enough for the steamers and their barge strings to manoeuvre. The river frontage must surely be defended, but the buildings ahead blocked his view.

The small cavalcade turned left at an intersection. A single gallows stood at the corner, guarded by two Indians. A corpse dangled from it. Dawlish forced himself to look and saw it was fresh. Black flies buzzed around the fouled cotton trousers and the bare and bloodied back. Hanging had not been enough – a flogging had preceded it. A rictus of agony was frozen above the placard proclaiming the victim a deserter and a traitor to La Reducción. High overhead a half-dozen birds spiralled patiently.

"Some of the human livestock you mentioned a few nights ago?" Dawlish said, turning to Roybon and seeing that he was looking away, as if consciously distancing himself from the horror.

But it was Madame Le Vroux who spoke.

"A man who had been given his freedom and did not value it." Her voice was raised enough to carry from her cart to the troopers who rode behind and it seemed all the colder for being a woman's. "A man who ran when his comrades stood and died to cover the retreat from the fort."

"Simone, be quiet," Roybon said in French. "The Commander is not a committee-meeting. He understands necessity."

They came to a large central square, its grass patchy, but devoid of the makeshift huts that had filled other similar spaces. It had the look of a badly kept parade ground. They halted before a large bungalow. The garden had been cleared and replaced with a courtyard surrounded by thatch-roofed, open-sided shelters. Whole families squatted there, some cooking by small fires. Children played in the dust in the centre. Several groups clustered patiently around sleeping or recumbent figures, fanning them against the heat and flies.

Half-a-dozen men guarded the veranda. A crippled old woman was being carried down the steps in the arms of a younger man and another woman was holding her hand and weeping. Behind them an officious-looking individual in a faded black suit was consulting a large ledger. He beckoned to one of the guards and spoke quietly to him. The guard turned and shouted the name "Dolores Mataca" towards the courtyard. An Indian woman rose to her feet from one of the groups and crossed to the veranda, carrying a baby.

"El Pobre heals the sick every morning from ten to twelve," Madame Le Vroux said as they pushed their way through the curious group that was gathering round. She uttered the name with a hint of reverence.

"So he's a magician as well as a prophet," Dawlish regretted his words as he spoke them, but the woman's air of righteous certainty had irritated him.

"No, Señor," she said with venom. "No magician. A man of science. A medical doctor, well qualified at the Paris Salpetriere. But a poor man, and the servant of the poor and so, despite all his other cares, he still makes time each day to exercise his profession for their good."

The guards on the veranda seemed more in awe of Madame Le Vroux than of Roybon. It was she who led the way into the house, into what had once been a parlour. All traces of decoration, even of comfort, had been removed. The walls were white and bare. A single desk and chair stood at one end, behind them a case of medical textbooks. At the other side of the room stood an examination couch and a glass cabinet containing bottles. Surgical instruments gleamed on a low table beside it. The Indian woman who had entered earlier stood by the couch and her child lay upon it. A tall man, clad in the white cotton shirt and trousers of a peon, but clean and snowy white, was bent over it, a stethoscope around his neck and his hands feeling the child's distended abdomen. He did not turn around as they entered. Another woman, in a poor imitation of a nurse's uniform, stood to his right.

The bustle left Madame Le Vroux. She stood quietly and, looking sternly to Dawlish and Roybon, held a finger to her lips.

The child whimpered weakly and its mother moved to pick it up. The tall man gestured her away, then rolled the infant over and began to feel its back. It wailed briefly, then lapsed into silence. The small torso was drenched with sweat and the mother was weeping. At length the man stood upright and Dawlish saw that he was as tall as himself, about six foot, his hair thick and grey. He turned to the woman and showed a long sallow face with sunken eyes.

"Your child is going to die, Dolores," he said, drawing her to him and embracing her. His voice was soft. "Perhaps today, certainly tomorrow. You can only make it easy for him, no more." The woman was sobbing. "You have been given this short time together. You must value it and remember it in the times to come. The memory of his love for you and of your love for him must sustain you."

He passed her gently to the nurse, then scribbled on a piece of paper and handed it to her. "Eugenia will see that you are given this medicine. It will not make your child well, but it will make the parting easier. I have no other solace to give you. You must find your own consolation in your love for your child. That will never die."

"Aguirre! We have an emissary from the Consortium." Madame Le Vroux's hushed voice was a mixture of reverence and affection as the woman was led away.

He turned and walked to the desk, ignoring their presence. He sat down, swivelled his chair to face the bookcase, studied the spines for a moment, then selected a tome. He placed it on the desk before him. He consulted the index, found a page and began to study it, his head supported by his hand, his eyes shielded. The silence in the room was all the louder for the distant crying of a child in the courtyard. He might have been alone.

Madame Le Vroux looked nervously at the others, then spoke again. "It is the Englishman, Aguirre. He who showed some mercy to Jacques, Comandante Dawls. He has a message for you."

"A message more important than the work of healing?" He did not look up and his voice was almost inaudible. "The Consortium has given us messages enough already. Must I hear another now during the hours of assistance?"

He turned a page and picked up a magnifier to study a diagram more closely. The nurse had returned and hovered respectfully before the desk. After another minute of silence he noticed her and nodded. She spoke a name.

"Ah yes, Eugenia," he said. "The good Pablo is next. Bring him, and we shall see if he makes progress." As she left he looked up and straight at Madame Le Vroux.

"You are still here, Simone?" he said with a quiet tone of mock surprise. "You have no other tasks but that you must disturb mine? Does the Reducción's wellbeing demand that you interrupt the examination of an old man's hernia?"

He had still not allowed his glance to fall on Dawlish and again he returned to his book.

"Aguirre, forgive me... I was not thinking," Madame Le Vroux began, obviously flustered, "We will go now. Perhaps later..." Her voice trailed off and she turned, arms outstretched, to shepherd the two men towards the door.

Roybon pushed past her and stood before the desk.

"You should listen to him, Aguirre," he said, "if only because he risked his life to come here." He turned and looked Dawlish straight in the eye and in his gaze and tone Dawlish recognised a respect and trust that he suddenly wished he could justify. "This Englishman showed himself to be a man of humanity and compassion when I was at Murillo's mercy."

"Compassion and humanity you would not have needed, my dear Jacques, had you not so unfortunately lost your howitzers and allowed yourself to fall into the hands of the enemy." Aguirre – El Pobre – was looking up now. His chill tone gave no hint of the warmth that had comforted the grieving mother only minutes before. "Compassion and humanity, dear Capitan Roybon, that were notably lacking when La Reducción's defenders were butchered in your downstream battery yesterday."

Roybon took a step forward, visibly angry, and Madame Le Vroux plucked at his arm to restrain him, but now El Pobre had risen and was advancing towards the decrepit peon whom the nurse was escorting towards the examination couch, ignoring his other visitors, once more the compassionate healer. Roybon turned angrily towards the door and Madame Le Vroux flustered behind, beckoning him and Dawlish to leave.

The old peon was sitting on the couch and El Pobre was assisting Eugenia to remove the shirt to bare the withered body, his voice tenderly reassuring.

Dawlish had felt his anger rise with each new negation of his presence and now it outweighed his fear and uncertainty. He had risked everything for this meeting and now he would have his say, he would be heard. He pushed past Madame Le Vroux, then planted himself in the centre of the room with the same assured stance with which he had learned to hide doubt and fear since boyhood.

"Señor Aguirre!" There was authority enough in his tone to make El Pobre turn. "Yes, Señor Aguirre, it's you I've come to see and you'll hear me whether you like it or not. I'm the last chance for every poor wretch here and, by God, you'd better listen if you don't want to see them all end like those in the earthwork yesterday."

"La Reducción has no need of your help, Señor," El Pobre said, not turning. "The enslaved of this earth have no need of the pity of their oppressors. The wretched need no longer live upon their knees and bow to the yoke of servitude!" His voice was metallic and had fallen into a rhythm, as if repeating a litany for the thousandth time.

"Yes! Yes!", Madame Le Vroux said from behind, her voice almost ecstatic. "Their day is now and their leader is here!"

"I've heard your sermon, Señor Aguirre," Dawlish said, "and now you had better hear some hard facts. The Consortium is almost upon you with a force strong enough to recapture this entire settlement."

"Impossible!" Madame Le Vroux hissed.

"It will not be easy, I'll grant you that, but in the end Don Plutarcho Murillo will be sitting in that chair of yours and General Aquino will be doing his bidding to the letter and Colonel Culbertson and his troopers will be riding down whatever stragglers make it out into the Chaco. You and your friends will have had your day of power and hundreds, maybe thousands, of innocent people will have been starved or slaughtered for nothing."

"And your alternative is the alternative offered by the tyrant throughout history?" El Pobre turned to him. "Submission and enslavement? Our servitude for your forbearance?"

"Never!" Madame Le Vroux cried. "One Commune was enough!"

"I'm asking you to bow to the inevitable," Dawlish tried to infuse patience in his voice. "The Consortium wants its investment back and would prefer to get it the easy way than the hard way."

"Investment – capital – before humanity!"

"For the Consortium, Yes! But if you negotiate now, then you've got intact herds and workshops and facilities to throw on the bargaining table. The Directors in London want profit above all. They don't want a shambles. They know there will have to be reforms in the way this business was run..."

"Their business, but our lives!" El Pobre's face was stony with contempt.

Dawlish ignored him "You will have to leave here, you and your friends – that I can negotiate. You can go where you wish, with papers, money and in safety – that I can secure for you."

"And the others? The peons whose blood and sweat have created these riches? The inheritors of so much oppression? What will they have?"

"Their lives," Dawlish said. "Not much, I grant you, but better than the alternative, as any one of the poor devils burned and flayed in the battery yesterday would tell you if they could speak!"

"You, who inflict it, speak easily of oppression as something to be endured, Commander Dawlish," Roybon said quietly, "but a man of your spirit would not endure it himself. Yet the common labourer feels enchainment as deeply as the officer and gentleman. I never learned that lesson until I found myself a state prisoner and felling logs with the humblest in the forests of Cayenne."

"Where without him we might never have endured!" Madame Le Vroux's voice had lost it shrillness. "Jacques and his brother went hungry that others might eat and bore floggings for others who could not. And when the time came for escape..."

"Quiet, Simone," Roybon said, seeing the surprise on Dawlish's face, "you confuse the good Commander. He can have little sympathy for officers who once disobeyed an order, even if it was to turn artillery on a rabble of desperate wretches in the last days of the Paris Commune!"

Dawlish suddenly comprehended Roybon's story – the link to those blood-drenched weeks, nine years before, when the army of the newly constituted French Republic had been used to quench socialist revolt in Paris. Still smarting from humiliation at the hands of the scarce-departed Prussians, the repression launched by Adolphe Thiers' government from its base at Versailles had been savage and merciless. Paris streets had run red with blood, whole sections of the city destroyed.

"Yes, Commander – that was my offence, my brother's too." Roybon's voice was bitter. "Young officers, fresh from the shame of a Prussian prison-camp, ordered to sweep the red canaille from the streets of Paris and sickening of the butcher's work. It was but a short and disagreeable step to the penal colonies of Guyana with the remnants of those we tried to spare. Perhaps I should be grateful. At least it was there where I gained my education in the true realities of life."

"The Commune's end was mild to what will happen here," Dawlish said. "If you indeed care for these people then let it be for their lives you care, and not some vague dream of a Jacobin utopia."

"Not Jacobin, Commander! Socialist!" Madame Le Vroux almost screamed. "The way of the future, the goal all history leads to!"

"The Commune taught me that I had to choose a side," Roybon said, "but Cayenne taught me that it was no mere cliché that death could be preferable to submission."

"True for a man," Madame Le Vroux added, with venom, "but ten times more true for a woman! Better death than slavery!"

"Paraguay has known hell, Señor." It was El Pobre, releasing the hand of the emaciated Indian on the couch. "Paraguay has been a hell since the Jesuits' experiment was quenched, a hell raked over by native tyrants, and lastly, when it was little better than a desert, raked deeper still by the Consortium's capitalist locusts."

He came nearer, his words so rapid that Dawlish had difficulty understanding. The hand clutching the stethoscope draped round his neck was trembling. "There was a dream here once, Señor, a dream that Paraguay might indeed become the paradise nature had given it the riches for. The Jesuits dreamt it, until they were expelled and their work was undone. Even the elder Lopez dreamt it when he sent me and others to Europe to study, that we might return to transform this land. That dream was my beacon when I walked the wards of the Salpetriere Hospital. But when I returned, a young doctor so full of hope, it was not to heal the sick of Asunción but to salvage human wreckage on the battlefield."

El Pobre was so close that Dawlish could see the passion burning in his eyes. "For years this land was scourged, its men slaughtered, its women abused, its children starved and eaten by disease, its rivers choked with corpses and its villages foul with the smell of death. I was in the midst of it. I knew what I should do and I could not do it. I lacked the simplest supplies that might have made my ministrations other than agony. Six years Señor! And then it ended. It ended when the men were all but gone and when there was nothing left to devastate."

A vein was throbbing on his forehead and his deep-sunk eyes held Dawlish's gaze with blazing intensity. His voice carried the terrible conviction of a man who had emerged from an abyss believing himself a prophet.

"And yet Señor, hope persisted, even after that end - hope that God was at last finished with us, that somehow we might claw back some comfort from the desolation. But God had not forgotten us! He sent us Murillo and his leeches, to build a new empire of slavery in a land too weak to resist."

He stopped and was suddenly aware of the old man lying impassive on the couch, his lined face a mask of hopeless patience. "Forgive me, Pablo," he said. "I will help you later. Eugenia, bring our old friend back in one hour." He helped assist Pablo to his feet with exaggerated care and Dawlish saw that he was trying to calm himself.

And Dawlish realised that the opportunity was slipping from him, perhaps that no opportunity had ever existed, that he had risked his own life coming here on the basis of a miscalculation. He could hope for no more than a few minutes in which to argue the impossible.

20

El Pobre moved to his desk and sat down. Madame Le Vroux laid a hand on his shoulder, the gesture at once reverent and protective.

"I'm not trying to justify the world to you, Señor," Dawlish looked El Pobre in the eye and hoped that his own tone conveyed absolute sincerity. "I would not have risked my life to come here for that. But I must tell you that the desolation you speak of will be here, and more terribly than before, if you do not take this chance to negotiate. Your people only have their lives, and you must leave at least that much to them."

"You think I do not know the Consortium, Señor?" El Pobre's voice was quiet now. "I who worked two years as its Medical officer? I who was fool enough to think I might do some good among the wretches Murillo's brigands enslaved? I saw them come with their steamboats and their workshops and their managers and their improved cattle breeds. I believed that here at last might be justice and compassion, if only because they would guarantee the Consortium a contented workforce. And what was the reality? That the cattle were worth more than the people! That the people were livestock themselves, though of a more worthless breed! They might herd the cattle, but

Culbertson's jackals were there to herd them in their turn. For two years I endured it, and when I spoke out at last..." He stopped, held up his hands, as continuation was futile.

"He was flogged senseless, flung in a stable and then flogged again." It was Roybon, his voice toneless, as if tired of the recitation of misery. "They shipped him downriver with the cattle and he spent another eleven months in a cellar in Asunción. They flung him on the street when they thought his mind was gone. That was where we found him."

"We?" Dawlish said.

Roybon smiled and there was a hint of pride. "Simone. My brother Michel, who died so well with the howitzers. Myself. One other. We were the last poor remnants of seven Old Communards who escaped the penal colony. We survived Cayenne, but we lost the others in Northern Brazil, yet because we had some skills between us we survived after a fashion and we found our way to Asunción."

"We survived – yes, we survived, but at what cost!" Madame Le Vroux sighed.

"We might be in Argentina now, or Chile, and with new identities, had I not recognised a familiar face on what I first took to be a beggar," Roybon said. "You see, Señor Dawlish, I knew Aguirre Robles before – when I was young, when my cousin also studied medicine in Paris."

"A lesser man would have been dead. It was I who had the joy of nursing him back to undertake his great work." Madame Le Vroux's tone mixed pride and love. El Pobre reached for her hand, caressed it and kissed it. She looked at Dawlish. "Meeting this man – this poor man, Comandante, this great man – gave meaning to all a poor Parisian schoolteacher had endured. He recovered. And he showed us the way forward!"

"To emulate the Jesuits? To recreate the Commune?" Dawlish was impressed in spite of himself by the conviction and ambition of these ragged insurgents. The puzzle was falling into place now, with a precision that would have delighted Topcliffe had he been present.

"More than the Jesuits ever created. More than the Communards dared dream of." El Pobre's voice sounded rational, yet the vision was messianic. "A self-sufficient state, remote and isolated enough to sustain itself against the world. A state inheriting modern industrial plant and scientifically bred livestock. A state with the weapons and the men and the professional leadership to repulse any threat. A state that will be a beacon to the wretched far beyond its borders. A state based on fraternity and dignity and common ownership of property."

Dawlish heard the quickening rhythm and growing feeling of the words, and sensed the power that must have swayed thousands to commit totally to La Reducción Nueva. And then he remembered the deserter still dangling not two hundred yards distant, a cloud of flies hovering about his lacerated back. Utopia was less than perfect. The Royal Navy still flogged, though rarely – a distasteful necessity, he knew, but essential in extremis, but bad enough to make him faint when he had first witnessed it as a boy – but not as a prelude to hanging, and not accompanied by preaching about brotherhood and dignity.

"So you returned to Puerto Plutarcho?" Dawlish asked.

"Not immediately," El Pobre said. "Not to the settlement itself until after its liberation. But I was outside, and moving constantly, and speaking to small groups who crept out to meet me on its outskirts. The oppressed were listening and spreading the message by mouth and the literate ones were passing our bills from hand to hand until they fell to shreds. The ground was fertile. Murillo and Culbertson had seen to that."

"And there were preparations far beyond the settlement," Roybon's tone was proud, "identifying every weapon worth having between here and Magdalena. I saw to that. But you must have guessed that, Commander – you're a professional and you'd plan just as thoroughly. Without the artillery, and the rifles, and the *Torres*, La Reducción Nueva would have been stillborn."

"And now its time is past," Dawlish said. "Your Reducción was an experiment – a bold one. It had its success and now its end is at hand. Like it or not, but the Consortium is back with the power to crush you. You cannot doubt that now."

"Never! Never!" Simone Le Vroux was shaking her head.

"You gambled on isolation and it has not saved you." Dawlish ignored her. "The forces that will destroy you have been delayed but they are upon you now. The real killing and the real dying – not just the men, but the women and children too – will start soon. If you care for these people you will leave them with their lives. Your position is hopeless."

"And yours, Monsieur?" A new voice, French and heavily accented, but cold and sarcastic. Dawlish turned to see the small man in white who had entered silently. "Are your lines of communication so short, and your supplies so secure, that you can afford to be lecture us?"

The newcomer's face was pinched, his nose sharp and his eyes dark. His black hair and beard were cut so close as to be stubble. "Are your troops so well trained, and so reliable, and so eager to follow their beloved commanders against any odds, that our defences need not concern you? Was your single encounter with our monitor so successful that you can regard the river as yours? It seems to me, Monsieur, that it is you whose position is more properly to be regarded as hopeless."

"I haven't had the pleasure..." Dawlish began, already half-knowing who this must be and disliking him already.

"No pleasure, Monsieur, I assure you." The little man's mouth was twisted in a sneer. "Neither now nor in the future." But he half-bowed nonetheless. "Alain Pannetier, sometime naval officer, sometime convict, sometime escapee and now a free man, unchained. A Socialist, Monsieur, a proud Socialist, and dedicated to stopping you and your associates re-establishing slavery."

Dawlish had the impression of hearing a formula the little Frenchman had perfected with frequent usage.

"I had the pleasure, Monsieur, of sinking two of your vessels further downstream." Pannetier smirked with obvious self-satisfaction. "I look forward with relish to sending the remainder to follow them."

"Another Communard then," said Dawlish, irritated by the Frenchman's naked animosity, and now himself on the point of losing his temper. "One bloodbath wasn't enough for you? You want your battles and your glory but it's these wretched Indians who will pay the price!"

Dawlish recognised that his sudden and intense dislike was not prompted by the tone of smug self-righteousness and sarcasm alone. This was the man who had dismembered the *Humaita* and the *Velasco* and who had left him floundering amid dozens of drowning men. The taste of failure was still bitter. This man was a superb professional, his own match and maybe more. And this was the man whom he must destroy if he were not to be destroyed himself.

"Liberty is never cheap, Monsieur," Pannetier said. "I do not boast but, like my comrades, I know the price."

Dawlish sensed, and loathed, that same smug pride in self-reformation that even Roybon was not wholly free of.

"It was no easy step from my command in the Seine Flotilla during the siege to hewing logs in Cayenne," Pannetier continued, "but like my comrade Roybon I could not stand by and see innocent Communards slaughtered! So No! Monsieur! I do not need your lectures about price!"

"But the price was high enough yesterday," Dawlish taunted deliberately, hoping for any insight that would aid him in the duel he knew awaited him with this man on the San Joaquin. "The Reducción could surely have done with your services, Monsieur Pannetier, while I was ravaging its redoubt!"

"The *Torres* cannot be everywhere," Madame Le Vroux cut in shrilly.

"Indeed not," Dawlish said, "and in fact your monitor has been nowhere since we saw it above La Garganta! Unarmoured paddlers seem more in Communard Pannetier's line than proper warships."

Pannetier's own visage was scarlet now with controlled rage. "You may expect me when you least expect me, Monsieur," he snarled. "This is no game for gentlemen of leisure, no duel over a social gaffe. I will find you when the time suits, and I will blast you and your crew of mercenaries into the oblivion you deserve."

"Once a Jacobin, always an assassin," Dawlish said with bow and was gratified by the Frenchman's obvious anger. Yet dislike him as he might, the Frenchman concerned him deeply. The use of the Seine Flotilla's gunboats to harry the Prussian flanks had been one of the few inspired features of the French defence during the siege of Paris. Pannetier had learned the art of riverine warfare in a merciless school.

Dawlish turned to El Pobre, forcing himself to speak calmly and slowly. "I came here as an honest man with nothing to gain. I ask you for the last time – are you ready to negotiate? If you have a message for Murillo then I will carry it."

"There is no message." El Pobre turned away. He moved to the desk, sat down, lifting the magnifier, making as if to consult his textbook again.

Dawlish looked towards Madame Le Vroux and she glared back silently with a mixture of indignation and triumph. Pannetier had moved to the window and turned his back. Only Roybon tried to communicate, lifting his hands palms upwards with an involuntary gesture of futility and dropping them again.

In that instant Dawlish knew what he would now do, without further hesitation, without more soul-searching, though with great remorse. He would complete the service he had committed to in the parlour of that Sheerness hotel, as the fire had crackled and the rain overflowed the gutters outside.

The sunlight was dazzling as he emerged on the veranda. A few faces, ill or bored, were turned briefly to him as he strode out past the shelters of the sick. The clerk with the ledger scurried from his path. Roybon followed, gesturing to a guard to untie the horses.

Dawlish heaved himself into the saddle. "You'll want to blindfold me again," he called as Roybon mounted alongside.

"It will be time enough at my quarters," the Frenchman said.

They rode in silence, the awareness that the last boundary had been crossed unspoken but palpable. The dangling corpse was passed again, consciously ignored, more portentous now than an hour before. Roybon's clapboard house was in sight before he finally spoke.

"El Pobre, and the others, they are right," Roybon said. "But it is no easier for that. Simple humanity is not enough, Commander. If there was another way then, believe me, I would take it. You cannot tell me that the Consortium offers anything desirable."

"No," Dawlish said, "but time does, and time means life. All I've tried to gain these people is time."

"Time for Murillo and the gentlemen backing him in London to suck them dry." Roybon's voice was weary, rehearsing old arguments. "Enslavement today, and progress perhaps to wage slavery in twenty years. In fifty more they might advance to the level of one of your Manchester drudges. England showed the world one way, Commander, but there is another."

There was a counterargument, Dawlish knew, but there was no time for it now and Roybon's ears had been stopped long ago in the streets of Paris.

They rode on in silence. Gil was waiting on the shaded veranda and Romualdo with him, smoking and laughing with a group of Reducción troopers as if nothing divided them. Only the hare-lipped Indian stood aside, his face grim with hatred. They fell silent as Dawlish approached and dismounted.

"Drink a cup of coffee with me before you leave," Roybon said and Dawlish felt enough respect for him not to refuse.

There was an endless interlude of silence while it came, real coffee, served in a chipped china cup, decorated with a picture of a shepherdess, a cup that must have carried an English trademark on its base. Perhaps it had belonged to Mrs. Hannah Farnsworth. Dawlish had remembered the name he had seen in Roybon's notebook.

He asked about her.

"A manager's wife," Roybon said. He sensed Dawlish's concern. "She escaped downriver with her little boy. The husband was killed." He paused, then said "A lot of regrettable things happened then."

"Did any of the wives remain?" The possibility that they might have done was unthinkable.

Roybon shook his head. "None living," he said. "There was a lot of bitterness."

They lapsed into uncomfortable silence until Roybon asked "Where did you learn French, Commander?"

"Pau," Dawlish said. "I was there as a boy. My uncle retired there. Many English did." The memory of those years was still a poignant one, the prelude to deep sorrow, even deeper humiliation, later. What had followed had nearly wrecked his career.

"A beautiful town, Commander," Roybon said.

The conversation died. Roybon broke the silence as they left by saying: "You're welcome to the hat. It fits you as well as it did me."

And again silence, and heat and sweat and faint wood smoke and the smell of refuse and excrement. On the square another weary squad was going through the motions of drill and beyond them were the gallows and its burden. Some dignity was now being preserved, for a barefoot youth had been posted to throw stones at the birds when they approached too closely.

Dawlish extended his hand before Gil applied the blindfold. Roybon's grasp was firm.

"Goodbye, Commander," he said. "You tried to do your best."

The last glimpse Dawlish had before the cloth blinded him was of the bruised eye sockets and powder-scorched face of a man he would have been glad to call a friend in different circumstances.

Then he was helped into the saddle. He turned his horse and hardened his heart to destroy that same man and all allied with him.

21

A single shot killed Romualdo as he and Dawlish crossed the open strip between Gil's patrol and Gelb's waiting knot of horsemen.

The blindfolds had been removed, and their weapons had been returned as their eyes adjusted to the glare. The jolting, sightless ride had been as unpleasant as that earlier in the day, the sounds and smells as vivid, the panting of the shunting locomotive a little closer, the impressions of passage through a maze of defences even more daunting now that there was no doubt that they would have to be breached the hard way. They halted by the Reducción picket line that had watched the Consortium horsemen in informal truce all day. Gil tipped his cap in the semblance of a salute as he returned Dawlish's pistol while the harelipped Guaikuru hawked and spat and watched with sullen hatred. The patched Admiralty sheet was produced, crumpled and without its lath, so that Romualdo could only wave it like an oversized handkerchief.

They urged their horses into a walk. The ground ahead was almost bare, broken only by scattered clumps of knee-high scrub. A thousand yards ahead four mounted men could be seen against a line of wispy trees that must surely shelter more. Dawlish ignored the possibility that Gelb, or even Culbertson, might be waiting there with orders to ensure that he would not return alive. He submerged the fear by imagining himself already in the *Tacuari's* saloon, defending his failed embassy, reporting his findings, somehow retaining his command. Around him now, in mid-afternoon, the warm air lay heavy on the baking Chaco and the only sound was of insects.

Romualdo rode slightly ahead of Dawlish, and to his left, clumsily flapping the white sheet across his body. The horses plodded forward, heads down, glistening with sweat, flicking their ears against the small clouds of flies escorting them.

The single heavy slug came from behind, catching the trooper in the lower back and blasting through his abdomen, throwing him across his horse's neck even as the sheet before him flushed crimson. He slid down the right flank as his mount panicked forward, dragging and bouncing him across the heat-fissured ground for fifty yards before his foot wrenched from the stirrup. He lay like a broken puppet, face up, eyes open and sightless, face already draining, as Dawlish cantered past, crouched low, heart thumping, almost palpably feeling the satisfaction of the harelipped Indian.

Dawlish swerved and wove as he raced forward, intent on spoiling an aim that might plough a furrow up his spine before he reached the cover ahead. Carmelita was as sure-footed now as when she had charged the howitzers. A whinny to the left told him that Romualdo's terrified beast was closing up and galloping alongside, eyes bulging, its shoulder blood-smeared.

He saw the low gully in front of the tree line almost too late, pulling Carmelita's head back and slowing her before she slithered down its inclined edge. The riderless horse cartwheeled over, limbs threshing, reins and stirrups flailing, a terrible scream terminating abruptly as it piled into the hard-packed floor of sand beneath. Dawlish kept his seat somehow but he was bruised and winded as he drew rein beside the still-quivering carcass. He looked about to see a half-dozen Guardia troopers staring at him from within the ravine. One was Gelb.

"A pity about Romualdo," he said as he approached. "He's one more score for us to settle."

196

*   *   *

"You took much on yourself, Commander Dawlish," Murillo said. "The Consortium is not paying you to act without instructions."

They were alone in the saloon of the *Tacuari*. For the first time Dawlish saw Murillo less than immaculately dressed, his shirt collarless and his waistcoat undone, as if awoken from an afternoon nap. On the table before him there was a large-scale map, hand-coloured, a blue snake bisecting it, a cluster of orange rectangles at its centre, contours exactly plotted close to the blue, but more sparse beyond – Puerto Plutarcho. Murillo might be displeased, but he wanted information.

"No disrespect, Señor Murillo," Dawlish forced an expression of pained regret, "but you are paying for initiative as well as professional skills. You know Britain like your own country. You must know the veneration in which the Royal Navy holds Nelson, whose victories were based on seizing opportunities regardless of prior instructions." He paused, his brow furrowed with feigned reluctance. "If I have offended you then I apologise," he said quietly, looking down.

"Hyperion engaged a two-eyed officer," Murillo said. "He would have to lose one if such insubordination were to be tolerated."

Dawlish looked up to see a slight smirk of self-satisfaction at this shaft of wit. "But this two-eyed officer delivered you the fort," he said. "He not only blasted it from existence, rapidly, efficiently, cheaply and without loss, but he did so without support of the land forces."

Murillo nodded, even muttered reluctant appreciation.

"I've been inside Puerto Plutarcho." Dawlish leaned across the table and planted his finger on the open space among the orange rectangles south of the river. "I've met El Pobre. I've met his commanders – not just Roybon, but his naval commander and a woman who may be more dangerous than either."

"El Pobre? What is he?" Murillo's eyes were hungry behind their thick lenses, his voice greedy.

"Like yourself, Señor, a Paraguayan. A doctor. A doctor called Aguirre Robles."

Murillo's face paled with shock and anger as the revelation sunk in.

"Him? So he returned?" His tone was cold with hatred. He was silent for a full minute, trembling as he sought to control himself, and then he said: "We should have hanged him when he first caused trouble." He looked straight into Dawlish's eyes. "The greatest errors, Commander, are those born of leniency. And the others?"

"French, like Roybon. Socialists, condemned nine years ago for their role in the Paris Commune, escapees from the penal colonies in Cayenne. The naval officer's an arrogant blackguard and the woman's a fanatic. I suspect she's done more to whip up enthusiasm than the rest of them put together."

"Topcliffe suspected something like this," Murillo said. "Without some outside influence to inflame them Culbertson could have kept them in line for a century. With these agitators eliminated it can be done again. And this time there will be no errors of leniency."

"They'll fight. They won't hear of negotiation."

"Nor will I, Commander, nor will I. And I have the forces to humble them."

"Only barely, Don Plutarcho. The settlement isn't just a fortress - it's an arsenal and a storehouse and a stockyard. Roybon is an artilleryman of genius and he's had months to build his earthworks. And I know to my cost how his sailor colleague can employ the monitor. And they have the railway working – God knows why, but the balloon will tell us. But it's not just the troops. El Pobre and his ladyfriend have mobilised the entire population."

"You saw this, Commander?"

Dawlish gestured towards the map. "I can't tell you the extent of the defences but if you draw a perimeter a mile outside the entire settlement you won't be far wrong. The earthworks are at least as formidable as the fort we destroyed because everybody fit to walk will have been working on them like ants. El Pobre's French supporters saw the end of one Commune and they won't shrink from dragging everything down with them into a similar inferno if the choice is between that and a Consortium victory."

"And you doubt our resources can achieve that?"

"I doubt it absolutely."

"And your solution, Commander? Not retreat I trust?"

"No Señor, nor siege neither. A siege would bleed us faster than it would bleed La Reducción."

For once Murillo did not balk at the word.

"The monitor I must destroy, and that I'll do – depend upon it," Dawlish said it with quiet determination. He had met Pannetier and the contest was now personal. "But on land you'll need a breach – a fast one – and you'll need troops inside before Roybon can reinforce it. Tinsley can give you your breach but then it will be up to Aquino and Culbertson, and I hope they've got men enough, and backbone enough in them, to finish the job fast."

"Here, tonight at six, we discuss further with the entire staff. Culbertson is reconnoitring the defences even now and we'll hear his report." Murillo dropped his eyes to the map again, ignored Dawlish for a moment, and then said without looking up: "You can return now, Commander, to the vessels you should never have left."

Dawlish stood and bowed, innerly satisfied that Murillo had accepted, however grudgingly, that he was needed. He was at the door when he was called back.

"The Consortium will need your written report, Commander," Murillo said. "Not just on Aguirre Robles and his scum but on your destruction of the fort. I understand there was considerable expenditure of munitions. It is essential that the records are maintained and books balanced."

Why bother? Dawlish thought, though he nodded assent. The Consortium had got her munitions, no less than the Toad herself, at scrap value.

He emerged into the sunlight and looked upriver. The *Montelindo* was anchored far upstream, smoke curling lazily from her thin stacks, the *Toad* five hundred yards astern of her. He checked his watch: four-thirty. It was time to get back to his command.

*   *   *

Culbertson's report that night on the defences along the Reducción's south-eastern and southern flanks – what his troopers could plot of them before being driven off – had been pessimistic. The morrow proved the reality to be even worse.

It took all night to fill the balloon. In the remaining daylight Dawlish had pushed the *Montelindo* and *Toad* cautiously several miles upstream. This brought them to a point eight miles in a direct line from Puerto Plutarcho, though three wide bends made the distance by water considerably longer. There was still no sign of the *Torres* monitor and the *Montelindo* and *Toad* again took up their blocking positions. The balloon's barge followed, Grinling scurrying busily among his crew, directing them in broken Spanish, linking piping to the retorts and flooding the first acid on to the broken scrap within to release hydrogen.

"It ain't the iron that's worrying me, Sir," he said when Dawlish had given him his orders. "God knows there's enough of that about. It's the blessed acid!" He gestured to the rows of straw-packed carboys. "I've enough for two fills, maybe three, and then that's your lot."

Culbertson's troopers secured a position on the southern bank, abreast of the *Toad*. Paddle steamers pulled alongside as darkness fell, their towed barges disgorging part of Tinsley's artillery and four companies of conscripts. A half-moon illuminated the conscripts' labour on construction of an earthen redoubt from which two ten-pounders could command any approach from upstream. Should the *Torres* appear, their effect would be no more than distracting, but every advantage, however small, would count.

The landscape was already reddening in the minutes before the sun rose over the eastern horizon when the balloon lifted from the deck. It ascended lazily, its charge scarce enough to lift its triple load through the dawn's coolness, and it would surely sink as the morning wore on, but Dawlish was eager to be aloft. Culbertson might once have been dismissive about such tomfoolery but once lodged in the swaying basket he looked nauseous. Aquino's square, flat face registered no concern at the experience and his field glasses were already sweeping westwards.

"As much rope as you can give us," Dawlish called to Grinling as they lifted. "The higher the better".

"But not enough to hang you, Commander, Sir!" Grinling shouted. His reddened bald-patch was shiny with sweat and his clothing was drenched after the night's exertions, but the nervous little showman was happy to be busy again.

Dawlish shivered. He had woken feverish and had recognised the stirrings of the recurrent malady that had plagued him since his Ashanti days. He had double-dosed himself with quinine, yet now the first wave of cold was replacing fever and his head was beginning to ache. "Not now, God," he prayed involuntarily to the deity whose existence he often doubted. "Not now. Let the malaria hold off for another twenty-four hours."

The horizon receded as they ascended – first the tops of the trees nearer the river, then the rim of brush beyond it, then the flash of water – and the colour changed from crimson to scarlet to brown and to dun as the sun rose behind them. Smoke drifted beyond the scrub to the west, not just the haze of cooking fires but three more solid columns vomiting from the Reducción workshops' brick chimneys.

At three hundred feet the clustered buildings were visible, and as they climbed higher the grid of streets could be discerned. White steam gushed and rose briefly among the rusted corrugated roofs of warehouses and workshops, and the sound of a whistle reached them seconds later, faint but shrill.

"Shift change," Dawlish said. "No different to the wage slaves of Manchester, Commune and Reducción notwithstanding"

The straining canopy lurched higher and all three watched intently as the ground stretching between them and the settlement was laid fully open to view. A jagged earthen stripe gashed southwards from the river, hewed and burned free of vegetation, its path roughly following the terrain's contours. Two miles into the scrub it jerked south-westwards, then west, its furthest limits lost in the scrub. Its surface was slashed by trenches, at places two in rough parallel, and linked by zigzags, and there were mounds at irregular intervals, their open-backed rhomboid shapes indicating artillery within.

"Hell 'n tarnation!" Culbertson spat over the side, "It's Petersburg all over – 'cept this time it's us on the outside."

"It's worse," Dawlish said, remembering how his destiny had once been linked to a hastily entrenched Bulgarian town that had resisted a Russian onslaught for half-a-year. "It's Plevna."

It was the work of months, yet still it was not complete, for swarms of human ants still laboured in places, black against the fresh earth they threw up. The nearest scattered buildings were a mile or more inside the trenches and broad patches of open ground between them were liberally dotted with cattle. Another whistle blast carried across the Chaco and a thin line of white smoke pinpointed a tiny locomotive pulling several cars parallel to the southern defences.

"Seem's they've got themselves the railroad runnin'. Smart." Culbertson could not disguise his respect. "Surprised they've rail enough though – we never received more nor two shipments."

"Wood," Aquino said. "Hardwood, plenty of it, just keep replacing it. They've got the labour." His glasses swept from the locomotive back to the trenches.

Dawlish shivered again, was grateful for the sun's growing warmth. He ignored his discomfort and concentrated on the defences. It was not the magnitude alone that awed, but the ingenuity of adaptation of fortification to landscape. The earthworks' bend towards the southwest was anchored on an expanse of swamp that extended along that distant face, stretches of open, slimy water visible among the low green vegetation and reeds. Even there, there was still a single trench line.

The nearby north-south face running inland from the river represented the most obvious point for attack, for here the flotilla's guns could be brought to bear to support the ground troops. Here the earthworks followed a low ridge and the shallow depression that lay outside it – a mile or more across – showed patches of stagnant water at its deepest points. Had that depression been fully flooded, the obstacle would have been unpassable. The scrub on either side had been burned and any approach towards it would be across a charred desert. Three major redoubts dominated this face, one at the point where the swamp commenced, the next half way between there and the river, the last at the river itself. Together they commanded the depression.

Dawlish swept his telescope towards the river. The earthwork anchoring the line there was massive, much larger than that reduced two days before. A twin on the opposite bank provided a similar function for the line of trenches that snaked north and west to protect the small part of the settlement lying north of the San Joaquin.

"I reckon they've got some of the Parrotts from Magdalena in them forts," Culbertson said.

Three Parrotts had been destroyed at the fort downstream, leaving twelve, probably three or four per river-fort and the remainder in the earthworks to the south. And somewhere upstream, secure behind their protection, the *Torres* would be lying among the corrugated sheds by the slipways.

But it was not the larger forts which aroused Dawlish's concern. It was not even the single detached fortification, much smaller than the others and positioned on the riverbank a mile downstream from them. It was the dry canal, six or eight yards wide, that extended from the depression towards the river, aiming at a point on the riverbank directly behind this smaller outwork. A double row of heaps of soil, a half-mile long, marked the sides of the canal that had reached within fifty yards of a pit that lay behind an earth and timber dam built into the riverbank itself. The small fortification served one purpose only, to protect the dam and the pit behind it.

Hundreds of people, maybe even a thousand, were slaving in those last yards of the canal, hacking the ground, scurrying to carry the spoil away in baskets on their heads. There were enough to make their arrival at the pit a matter of hours, not days – and when they reached it Dawlish knew there would be an explosive charge waiting, built deep into the dam, to blast it from existence and deluge the San Joaquin into the depression.

"Commander Nick,' Culbertson said. "Just get them boys to winch us down. You an' me and the Colonel here need a chat on the way down. If we're not standing on that dam before sundown then we might as well turn back for Asuncion."

*   *   *

The mounted patrols Culbertson sent into the scrub along the river, towards the canal, ran into concealed rifle fire when still two miles from it. The *Montelindo* moved upriver in rough co-ordination with the patrol but was itself exposed to a peppering of small-arms fire that rattled harmlessly off her plating. She dropped back a mile, then anchored again in midstream. Dawlish, on the *Toad*, held the gunboat never less than five hundred yards astern of the monitor, and in visual contact, painfully aware of the damage that even light artillery fire could wreak on his potent vessel's unarmoured deck.

Culbertson's patrols withdrew without loss, moved south to probe and outflank, but again ran into a sharp crackling from the thicket before them. The process was repeated twice more, and two troopers were lost – enough to confirm that the unburned ground between the Consortium forces and their objective was untenable for horsemen. They fell back to establish their own thin picket line in the scrub.

Aquino was already in action. One company of regulars, four of conscripts and two of Tinsley's ten-pounders landed just downstream of the *Toad*, at the furthest point that Culbertson's returning galloper could confirm to be out of range of Reducción fire.

"I don't like this, Dawlish," Tinsley had come across to explain Aquino's plan and relay his request for support. "It's rash in the extreme. The Colonel wants to use his men to drag my guns forward – the wretched mules aren't up to it, nor fast enough, he says. If my Spanish serves me, he wants me to blast a path through the brush with canister. Then he'll drive his troops forward until they encounter more of the scoundrels and then repeat the action until we get to the open ground."

"You'll have the *Toad* in support," Dawlish said. "I've seen what her bursting shell did to their cavalry, and back at the fort. Their infantry won't stand it any better. Aquino will be through the scrub before you know it."

"But there will be an open flank." Tinsley's mournful tone lent the term an aura of Holy Writ. "And the fort protecting the dam? Even if there's only light artillery there it will slaughter the infantry when they approach it across the open ground. Aquino's surely not expecting my weapons to make a significant impact on the earthworks? We should at least wait until we've landed the mortars."

Dawlish watched Tinsley return shorewards, his face still furrowed in concern and his whole demeanour that of an unheeded prophet. Dawlish's own earlier chill had disappeared, replaced by a low but undeniable fever. The ache in his head was a low throb, tolerable but threatening worse. He had taken more quinine.

And now, before action, he needed five brief, private minutes. The day ahead might well be his last. The ending of life did not in itself frighten him, though the idea of pain or mutilation did, badly, but the thought that he might never see Florence again was almost unbearable.

He scribbled a note for her in his tiny cabin, a single sheet, heartfelt, the words incapable of saying what he wanted to convey. He had lost her photograph, but her image was no less strong in his mind for that and it hurt to remember the simple happiness of that Southsea villa they had shared so briefly. He added a postscript, more businesslike, mentioning the Portsmouth solicitor who held a will that she knew no details of but which bequeathed her his Shropshire properties. He had agonised over the decision, but had resolved at last that Edgar, the infant half-brother whom his new stepmother had produced a year before, would inherit enough directly. The farms had come to himself from his mother's brother, that retired naval officer who had died of consumption in Pau, and their revenues had been a welcome supplement to his naval pay. Florence as a Lady of the Manor was a sight he would have gladly seen and he knew she would carry it off well.

He had a seaman bring the letter to Grinling for safe keeping, to be forwarded only in the event of an untoward event. He noted with wry amusement that he had shrunk from writing the word "death".

22

The *Toad* was already moving slowly against the current, the invisible Armstrong loaded and its crew standing to it, the Gatling positions manned. Shouted commands carrying across the water from port told of Aquino's companies being dressed into two lines.

On the steering platform Dawlish turned to Holmes. "Signal to *Montelindo*: Raise anchor and engage fort."

He scanned the southern shore as the *Toad* crept forward, Egdean at the helm, steady as ever. The San Joaquin's banks were firm and low here, never higher than eight feet above the water, and the current was steady across the eighty-yard width. From his platform he could see perhaps a mile across the scrub-clad Chaco, ground very similar to that over which he had charged the howitzers, open spaces interspersed with thickets. Roybon's riflemen would be there, fingering their weapons, ragged Indians with frightened brown faces, like those he had sabred in that nightmare charge, but determined and dangerous and no less ready to sell their lives dearly.

Aquino's forces were on the move now, and the telescope's disc of view revealed one of the ten-pounders bouncing forward, twenty men pulling on its traces, rifles slung across their backs. An officer on a horse was riding alongside, brandishing a revolver. The limber followed, its team similarly motivated. Tinsley rode little behind, crouched in the saddle, a Havelock flapping on his neck.

A rattle of fire upstream confirmed that the *Montelindo* had drawn level with Reducción riflemen on the southern bank. The *Toad* had her target.

"That tree – slightly rising over that clump – about two thousand yards. You see it?"

Holmes nodded and shifted the indicator. The ringing of the bell in the gun-well carried sternwards and seconds later the Armstrong surged up, the hydraulic pistons hissing as it settled into firing position.

"Run out! Awaiting range Sir!"

The crackling was dying away upstream as the *Montelindo* pushed forward unmolested but Dawlish's mind was concentrated only on the range to that tree.

"Eighteen hundred! Elevate! Ready to swing!"

The movements were well practised, the *Toad* and her crew acting like a single living organism, the sequence flawless as the bows swung to port and the great muzzle vomited fire and death towards the brown Chaco. Acrid, choking smoke billowed over the steering platform as the bows swung back again to breast the current. Dawlish had dropped his hands from his ears and was still raising his telescope when the shell landed a hundred yards short of the aiming mark. A shudder passed over the low thicket as the five-second fuse permitted the shell to plough a short furrow of rippling earth before blasting it into a rising spout of flame-cored smoke and soil.

"Hold Station!" Dawlish ordered. "Reload!"

The impact's sound washed back over the *Toad* and when it passed there was the noise of rifle-fire to port. Aquino's troops had encountered opposition. Whatever havoc the *Toad* might have wrought in their rear the Reducción riflemen in the forward positions were holding firm.

The Armstrong had risen into sight again, pregnant and deadly. Holmes called "Ready to Fire, Sir! Run out! Awaiting range!"

"Wait," Dawlish said, eye glued to the telescope, conscious that the store of bursting shell was limited. He saw a smoking crater, flames crackling in the low growth at its edges. Figures were falling back through the scrub, but at a few places groups were still heading forward to face Aquino's drive, their will and nerve strengthened by the resolve of some few humble heroes. He glanced upstream. The *Montelindo* had almost reached the shallow bend that would remove her from view as she drove on towards the dam-protecting fort.

A ten-pounder opened fire. Aquino's advance had stalled at a section of open ground commanded by a wall of thorn beyond but Tinsley's straining team had swung their piece around and three rounds of canister in quick succession tore a corridor through the thicket. Hundreds of iron balls lashed through the undergrowth, cutting down any rifleman in their path and driving the remainder rearwards in panicked flight.

The Consortium's first rank, conscripts mainly, surged forward across the parched earth and into the shredded foliage beyond, tasting unaccustomed victory, their bayonets plunging wickedly to finish any wounded encountered. The second wave, conscripts stiffened by regulars, followed closely and Tinsley's hauling team was moving forward with machetes to hack a pathway through the brush for gun and limber. Three hundred yards further south the second artillery piece was in action, driving back the opposition there also.

The scrub made the action all but invisible from the *Toad*, only the rising smoke and sound of gunfire locating it roughly. Dawlish could however see the expanse of open ground two hundred yards beyond it, across which small knots of Reducción troops, rallied from the impact of his first shell, were beginning to move forward to bolster the defence against Aquino's advance.

"There, Holmes - that patch!" His pointing finger indicated the rough oval of thorn into which the Reduccionistas were disappearing. It would be the next strongpoint that Aquino must storm. "One shot, then we move upriver to support *Montelindo*. Range thirteen hundred. Swing at your convenience."

Again the familiar drill. Again the indicators, the elevation adjustment, the telegraphs, the port revolutions slacking and the bow falling away from the current and Holmes' fist pounding the firing knob and the endless half-second before the Armstrong bellowed and then sunk into its well.

The shell screamed into the nearer edge of the thorn and exploded beyond. A scorching ball of light and smoke expanded from the impact, flaying and dismembering the troops positioned there and blasting out an expanding circular scythe of stones and sundered metal to cut down those whose stood rooted, horrified, on the open ground. Aquino's force surged forward again, butchering the dazed survivors.

The *Toad* was facing upstream again and the telegraphs called for maximum revolutions. She built up to a steady six knots. The *Montelindo* had disappeared around the bend, making Dawlish uneasy even while he watched with satisfaction the rout developing to port. The small-arms crackle had all but died away and what he could see of the Reducción forces were in headlong flight parallel to the river. Aquino's foremost troops had emerged into the open ground in a ragged line, a bayonet flashing here and there, some platoons running forward briefly to gain some minute intermediate objective, then falling back to a walk. The second rank followed and Dawlish's last glimpse before the intervening scrub and the *Toad's* forward movement blotted the scene from his view was of a ten-pounder being dragged into the open and Tinsley - yes, even Tinsley! - waving his cap from horseback to encourage his team.

Rifle-fire sounded further south but the second ten-pounder fired three rapid rounds and thereafter there was silence. The *Toad* had pulled level now with the point of her first shell's impact, but there was no firing from the bank. What defenders there had been here must by now be streaming back towards the canal. The gunboat's blunt bows pushed steadily forward, the sudden hush enhanced rather than broken by the steady panting of the engines, the wash of the water along her flanks, and the low rattle of Gatling barrels being spun for checking by their watchful gunners.

A double wave of sound rolled downriver, the crash of the unseen *Montelindo's* turret weapons opening at three hundred yards on the fort protecting the dam, followed an instant later by the dull "Whump!" of shells bursting in the earthen glacis. Blooded two days earlier at the downstream fort, knowing now the worth of Purdon's intensive training, the monitor's crew was oblivious of the rifle-fire that beat as harmlessly as hail on the iron plating. The captain, Calles, also invigorated by that earlier victory, now stood calmly by Purdon in the armoured conning tower, instructing the helmsman to keep the vessel dead-on towards the current.

The *Toad* rounded the bend. The *Montelindo* was visible now, smoke drifting aft from her black hull, still moving slowly upstream. A gap had been torn in the sloped wall of the small fort ahead. Of the embrasures visible – and Dawlish knew from the morning's balloon reconnaissance that there were six in all – two had muzzles protruding, not the twenty-pounders from Magdalena but nine or twelve-pounders looted in that same raid. Against the *Montelindo* they were worthless, but they could still wreak havoc on the *Toad* and could decimate Aquino's advance. The dam was just visible beyond the earthwork, its river-face fronted by timbers secured with a row of vertical piles. Figures were moving hesitantly across its crest to reinforce the threatened fort. In the unseen ground beyond it, and below the dam, the swarm of workers would be excavating the ultimate section of the canal – under threat of lash and noose, if Madame Le Vroux had anything to say about it.

All now hinged on the *Montelindo's* ability to eliminate the fort and clear the way for Aquino's advance before those last critical yards of earth had been gouged out and the dam destroyed.

"Hold station," Dawlish called, unwilling to risk bringing the gunboat closer. He noted remotely, as if of another person, that his fever had died and his head was clear. Perhaps the last dose of quinine had done its work.

At quarter revolutions, the *Toad* was almost stationary. He focused his glass on the small fort and held it as the *Montelindo's* guns roared again, one shell striking short and exploding harmlessly but the other tearing deep into the earthen glacis slightly rightwards of an embrasure showing a muzzle. A cloud of flame-shot smoke and dust cleared slowly to show a smouldering gap. But still no gun had been disabled and the fort, though bruised, was still potent. Some iron hand within – Roybon himself surely – was resisting the urge to retaliate uselessly against the tormentor on the river and was holding fire to repel the landward threat.

Retreating Reducción troops now dotted the open ground between the fort and the scrub held by Aquino's force. The General had halted his straggling advance and had pulled his men back into the brush to regroup for the next, most critical, rush. Tinsley's ten-pounder was firing from cover at the thicket-edge, the shell fuses cut back for airburst. The fleeing targets were too dispersed for the rain of shrapnel to cause significant casualties but it added to the terror of the rout.

Under cover of the scrub Aquino's regular sergeants were hastily organising troops that had become separated from their platoons in the headlong advance. Lines were being dressed, weapons checked, more ammunition distributed and water sluiced down parched throats. Even the conscripts had been elated by the ease of their triumph thus far but a quietness now stole over them as they looked across the bare, charred ground they must now cross. Four hundred yards lay between them and the low wall of fresh earth that marked the canal's bank. The routed Reducción riflemen were taking shelter there, their line anchored by the small fort at the river. It was taking its pounding from the Consortium monitor but there was no sign yet of its guns being eliminated.

Dawlish scanned the blackened ground, marked here and there by the hump of a tumbled body or, more pathetically, by the odd wounded wretch crawling hopelessly towards of the canal line. He saw, with mixed admiration and trepidation, that the open space was marked at intervals with red and white-striped stakes. Roybon had left little to chance – the fort's gunners had predetermined ranging marks. Unless the *Montelindo* could reduce the fort soon, Aquino's force would be scythed down before it had got half way to the canal.

The crash of the monitor's guns washed down the river again. She, and the fort beyond her, were half-obscured by a heavy pall of smoke and dust. Dawlish had lost count of her salvos but he hoped that the monitor's long-neglected and only recently overhauled turret-training mechanism and gearing could stand the continuous firing. It was time for the *Toad* to lend support.

He told Holmes quietly what he wanted, keeping unspoken his concern about the extent to which he would be risking the unarmoured gunboat. Accuracy – and brevity of exposure – would be everything in the minutes ahead.

The great Armstrong rose hissing from its well and into firing position before the *Toad* was launched upriver. Elevation was raised almost to maximum, and the charge reduced, for plunging fire at six hundred yards. The Gatling crews stood by their weapons, their Broadwell hoppers recharged. Dawlish felt his hands shaking. He pulled a cheroot from his shirt pocket, bit the end away and spat it over the side before ordering full revolutions. He hoped that Holmes did not notice the trembling flame as he lit up. The smoke gave a brief surge of pleasure as he braced himself against the *Toad's* acceleration.

Half the five hundred yards to the firing point had been covered before the first sporadic rifle-fire crackled from the scrub on the northern bank. Several shots whined close enough to be audible and one ripped into the bridgework before the indicator panel. Dawlish drew on his cigar, forcing himself to deny that he was the target and to scorn cover. "Steady, Mr. Holmes," he said, conscious of the quaver in his voice, "Stand by to hold her stationary by that tree leaning over the bank ahead? You see it? Range from there about six hundred yards."

More rifle fire from the north. Splinters flew from the signalling mast. The Gatling crews had swivelled their weapons to face the wisps of smoke drifting from several widely scattered points in the scrub. At Holmes' command the nearer mounting stammered short bursts towards them.

"Hold fire, Mr. Holmes," Dawlish snapped, "We'll conserve our ammunition for better targets".

He flinched as a bullet ricocheted with an audible "ping!" off one of the funnels directly abaft. But the *Toad* was still surging ahead at full revolutions, and they were carrying her beyond the immediate zone of danger. The ragged fusillade died as she forged onwards, Egdean grimly intent on maintaining the midstream and responding to Holmes's instructions as precisely as if this had been an exercise on the Solent.

The marker tree was a hundred yards ahead. The fort lay beyond like a huge brown slug. The *Montelindo* had crept forward so that only a narrow strip of water separated her from the riverside glacis. The low hull rolled slowly to starboard as another broadside vomited from the turret, then wallowed back, decks awash. Both projectiles burrowed into the mound ahead before erupting in geysers of flame and earth, tearing a thirty-foot gash. A fog of smoke and falling dust enveloped the monitor as the sweating crews in the oven that was the turret sponged and rammed, eager now for the kill.

And yet the fort still lived. Flame spat from an embrasure on the landslide flank. The trajectory was low, the *Toad* the target. The projectile hit the river surface a hundred and fifty yards ahead, skipped in a flurry of spray, then bounced downstream in diminishing leaps before sinking harmlessly some twenty yards off the port bow. Close.

The Roybon touch, Dawlish thought.

Level now with the leaning tree. Holmes rang for quarter revolutions. The squat hull settled in the water, barely making way against the current.

"More than six hundred," Holmes' gaze flickered between the leaning tree, now fast approaching, and the fort.

"No closer," Dawlish said. "Your ship, your gun, Mr. Holmes. A shell plumb in the centre will do very well."

Holmes moved the indicator a notch. On the mounting the gunner inched his elevation wheel forward and the great barrel crept upwards two degrees.

"Over!"

The wheel spun in Egdean's hands and Holmes ground the telegraph forward for full revolutions on the starboard shaft.

The bows nudged over, then swung faster as the screw bit. Holmes' fist smashed on the firing knob at the critical instant. The gunboat juddered under the Armstrong's discharge and the projectile was arcing into its parabolic flight as the mounting fell smoothly back into its well and its crew rushed to reload.

The *Toad* was beam on to the current, and still turning downstream, as the shell dropped. It fell nearly vertically, slightly short of Dawlish's objective, not in the centre of the earthwork, but even more destructively, on the inner slope of the landward wall. It bored fifteen or more feet into the soft ground before erupting. A shock wave rippled across the glacis in the instant before the earth heaved up, engulfing the nearest embrasure and lashing flame and debris into the cauldron formed by the enclosing walls.

"Hold station! We'll give it one more round" Dawlish was loath to drop downstream again into range of the invisible riflemen and was less concerned now by the threat to his gunboat from the fort. The

Toad swung to face upstream again, engines panting at low revolutions. A low cloud of smoke and dust had all but obliterated the fort from view and the *Montelindo* had crept upstream and was almost level with the dam. She should have fired another broadside by now, Dawlish thought, and again the cold fear of a gearing failure crept over him.

Shouting from the southern bank announced that Aquino was launching his attack. A line of conscripts moved at a trot from the scrub in open skirmishing order. The second line followed fifty yards behind. Their goal was the fort and as they came on they met a ragged fusillade from riflemen crouched behind the canal line's earthen walls. The fire was ineffectual at first, but as the range closed isolated figures began to fall. Tinsley's ten-pounder was being jolted forward by its human team and its twin was emerging from the scrub further inland.

Now was the time for what remained of the fort's guns to scythe down the attackers with shrapnel.

The murk around the *Montelindo* was clearing and now, at the very moment that her broadside could have been decisive, she seemed to be manoeuvring opposite the dam. Boiling froth at her stern indicated frantic juggling with the screws.

"The training gear, God damn it! It's stuck!" Dawlish saw clearly that Purdon and Calles were attempting to aim the weapons in the jammed turret by aligning the whole vessel.

But within the battered fortification the stunned gunners took advantage of the respite and weapons opened from the embrasures. One shell exploded in the air, a text-book shrapnel burst that cut down a dozen of Aquino's oncoming attackers. The other ploughed into the burnt earth closer to the scrub and threw up a plume just behind the second line, panicking those nearest. The painted stakes were showing their worth – Roybon had the range. Four hundred naked yards separated the attackers from the fort and a few more salvos must surely break their resolve. A report from just beyond the scrub line told that Tinsley's ten-pounder had been slewed around to give a measure of support, but its first round spent itself uselessly short of the earthwork.

Now only the *Toad* could support the advance.

The Armstrong lurched up again into firing position. Range unchanged, elevation identical. Again the bows swung over and again Holmes pounded the firing knob.

The mounting was sighing back into its well as the nine-inch shell plummeted into the closest embrasure. Its volcano of flame and steel and earth carried with it the shattered remains of a twelve-pounder and its crew and as its fiery breath expanded it set off a second wave of destruction as stored charges erupted. A swirling column of black and yellow smoke vomited upwards – and at this moment the *Montelindo*, aligned at last, added the broadside of her frozen turret. The shells tore into the riverside glacis, gouging huge smoking breaches and hurling searing metal fragments within to torment the stunned defenders.

Out on the naked approach Aquino's advancing troops cheered as they surged forward, elated by their sudden deliverance and almost oblivious of the staccato rifle fire from the canal line. Both of Tinsley's weapons were firing over them, the range now found, the rounds falling on or inside the fort's bruised walls.

"They've had enough, Sir," Holmes said.

His pointing finger carried Dawlish's eye towards the rear of the fort. A shambling rabble was starting to stream out towards the dam, some in outright flight, others slowed by wounds or dragging stricken comrades. The *Montelindo* stood by helplessly, its weapons too powerful to destroy them without endangering the dam – and it was the dam's preservation that now mattered most.

"Full speed upriver, Mr. Holmes. Gatlings to open fire on that mob when they have the range."

The *Toad's* squat hull pushed upstream. It was almost level with the fort as the first line of Consortium attackers reached it. Tinsley's weapons had fallen silent as Aquino's force drew closer, but their support was not needed now, for only a few isolated Reduccionista heroes still crouched behind the ruptured walls. They died there, still doggedly firing their rifles until overwhelmed by the victory-crazed flood that streamed through the still-reeking breach torn by the *Toad's* last shell. Nobody on the gunboat saw any of this, for her two Gatlings were now spinning and barking, hosing death over the exposed causeway of the dam's crest.

Holmes held the *Toad* just level with the fort, for the *Montelindo* was stationary now opposite the dam. The range was less than a hundred yards, enough to allow the Gatling crews to pick their targets. They cut down a group on the furthest upstream portion of the dam and worked back to slaughter those closer who were still too hesitant, or too disabled, to jump off into the shelter of the pit beyond and below it. The Gatlings jammed, twice, three times, but there was a bloodlust on the gunners and loaders and they tore fingernails and scorched hands in their haste to rip the stuck rounds from the breeches and grind the barrels back into rotation.

And then, while the last cowering defenders of the fort were dying under the bayonets of Aquino's regulars, and while the fugitives writhed under the Gatlings' lashing, the dam was blown.

The charges had been buried deeply, one at either end, and they were detonated only seconds apart. A shudder ran through the timber-reinforced earthen crest. Dirt spurted upwards and outwards and then the whole structure heaved inwards under pressure of the river towards the pit beyond.

Cries of horror and despair rose from the survivors on the quaking causeway, audible in the silence into which the detonations had shocked the *Toad's* gunners. For one brief moment the dam seemed to freeze in a concave curve that might yet hold back the river, and then, slowly, a fifteen-yard section collapsed into the void beyond. The waters surged through, a deluge that carried the screaming fugitives into the maelstrom and engulfed what were left of the Reducción's swarm of labourers who had been slaving to the last to extend the canal to the inner dam-face. The torrent tore at the sides of the breach, enlarging it further, and roared up the canal like a tidal bore to flood the low ground beyond.

"Full Astern!" Dawlish yelled, but Holmes was even quicker, dragging both telegraph handles back as the *Toad* was sucked forward towards the foaming maw. The screws bit, and the gunboat edged slowly astern, the river's flow past her flanks temporarily reversed.

The *Montelindo*, closer to the breach, was not so lucky. Her screw thrashed violently in reverse, but the velocity of the flood was beyond its power and she was borne almost beam-on towards the gap. The stern smashed into the downstream side of the breach, burying itself in the earth, and the bows swung round under the current so that the midships, just in line with the turret, impacted into the upstream side. The deck tilted as the torrent racing beneath her roared on into the canal and she lay pinned against the opening.

The *Toad*, powerless to assist, reversed further, then spun on her axis and moved downstream, below the fort. Aquino's troops, victory torn from their grasp at the last moment, lined the fort's walls and watched despondently as the floodwaters surged through the canal into the depression beyond. They carried on their muddy crests not only the broken bodies of the Reduccionista labourers who had been sacrificed in the dam's destruction, but the Consortium's dashed hopes of any easy approach to Puerto Plutarcho. The waters' velocity slackened as they reached the wider spaces beyond and filled the low-lying ground, fingers reaching out until checked by some slight rise. For hours more they would flow, ever more slowly, until at last the great water barrier had been completed.

Dawlish watched, fighting back a dull but growing sense of despair that this campaign must now drag on forever. And then a sudden crash from upstream tore his gaze from the welling depression towards something more threatening still.

Four hundred yards upstream of the *Montelindo* the Reducción's monitor, the *Torres*, had rounded the bend. She had already thrust though the smoke of her first salvo and her shells were erupting in rising plumes just short of the trapped and impotent *Montelindo*.

It was for this moment that Topcliffe had made his errand that rainy night in Southsea.

Only the *Toad* now stood between the *Torres* and the flotilla's defenceless paddlers. This was her moment – and Dawlish's.

23

"Armour piercing," Dawlish said quietly as he focussed his glass on the low, black hull of that same monitor, the *Torres*, which he had last seen escaping upriver after disembowelling the *Velasco*. She was five hundred yards distant, four hundred beyond where the *Montelindo* lay pinned against the breached dam by the waters that sucked beneath her like a millrace under a sluice gate.

The *Torres* was almost stationary, her screw churning in reverse to hold her against the dual impulse of the river's normal flow and the added rush of water towards the breach. The turret slits showed no muzzles – the weapons were run in for reloading – but the armoured cylinder was inching round to correct its aim on the helpless *Montelindo*. Dawlish could almost feel the smug satisfaction of the *Torres'* ex-Communard commander as he lined her up for the kill.

I'll wipe the sneer of your face, you French blackguard, he thought.

While the river still emptied into the depression beyond the canal Pannetier could not risk bringing the *Torres* any further downriver lest she too be drawn to the gap. In that period, while the ravenous flow towards the stranded monitor still separated them, the *Toad* – lightly armoured and vulnerable, but nimble, and massively powerful – would have her opportunity. For this she had been refitted in a Sheerness graving dock and knocked down as scrap to the Hyperion board. For this Dawlish had made his compact with Murillo, Kegworth and the rest of them, while Topcliffe had smiled knowingly. And it was this which would buy him a command and the next rung on the ladder of advancement.

Hidden in the well in the *Toad's* bows the gun crew was moving fast in response to Holmes' rotation of the pointer across the indicator dial. The crane arm was dragged across to the racks on the starboard flank where the two hundred and eighty-five pound red and white-ringed solid Palliser-patent shots nestled. The lifting tongs latched on a nine-inch diameter cone-nosed plug of hardened steel capable of punching through eight inches of armour plate at point-blank range.

"Double charge, Mr. Holmes," Dawlish said, "Low trajectory, maximum velocity."

Holmes' indicator registered the choice. Below decks the hydraulic rammer was already withdrawing from the barrel, leaving the silk-bagged charges compacted, and the massive projectile was being eased into the loading trough. Egdean was expertly edging the *Toad* slowly downstream, breasting the temporarily reversed river flow that carried water towards the thirsty mouth sucking beneath the *Montelindo's* canted hull.

"It will be tricky when we turn, Sir," Holmes's voice had a quaver of doubt. Like Dawlish, his eyes were riveted on that menace of the *Torres*.

"Can you manage it?" Dawlish asked Egdean. "I want her held stationary."

"Slow astern once we turn, Sir, quarter revolutions I'd say, if we're not to be pulled upriver."

"Very well, Egdean. Lieutenant Holmes – you'll fire on the swing? Good! Your eye has my total confidence! And range? Five hundred you'd say?"

"Nearer five fifty, but we'll drift on the turn. Say five thirty."

The Armstrong's massive cylinders heaved it from its well. Holmes swept the indicator arm to the range quadrant. Obedient to the repeater dial before him, Morgan, the gun-captain, eased his valve wheel open, bleeding fluid in briefly to raise the muzzle scarcely higher than horizontal. His arm moved up to signal elevation completed.

Flame stabbed savagely from the *Torres'* twin weapons in the instant that the juggling of the *Toad's* screws and rudders began to spin her to face upstream. The range was all but point blank, the aim perfect. A fountain of spray close to the *Montelindo's* bow marked where a solid projectile, similar but lighter to that just loaded into the *Toad's* Armstrong, bit into her iron flank. It tore into the space within, bouncing and tumbling and rending all before it, human or metallic, until its energy was spent. The second round struck almost at the bow. Its trajectory was higher, by inches only, but high enough to strike the inclined iron deck rather than the side, and to ricochet harmlessly across the *Montelindo* and into the canal beyond. Spray fell away to revel a neat half-moon at the waterline where the first round had smashed through. Already water was rushing in and unless the compartment could be isolated the vessel abaft of it would flood. A hatch on the foredeck was thrown open and two figures staggered out, dragging a blood-sodden third. Nobody followed.

The *Toad* was rotating now, all but on the spot, starboard screw full ahead, port full astern, helm fully over, muddy froth churning astern. When the blunt prow pointed at the northern bank, and was still turning, Holmes telegraphed for quarter reverse revolutions on both shafts. As the bow and the great weapon above it arced towards upstream the speed of rotation diminished slightly. The *Torres*, a smoke-wreathed iron fortress, was not yet fully in line with the gunboat's axis when Holmes, allowing an instant for the gunner's reaction to the bell, smashed his fist down on the firing button. The Armstrong blasted hardened steel and a sulphurous cloud enveloped the gunboat's bows.

Dawlish, hands clapped to his ears, oblivious of the thunderous wave washing aft, and had eyes only for the three extended plumes that marked the projectile's skipping progress. It first struck the water fifty yards short of the *Torres*, bounced in a flurry of spray, struck again, leaving five yards of clear water between the cascade and the monitor's bow and then hopped harmlessly on, to be lost in a final impotent flurry in the river beyond.

Near, but a miss nonetheless.

"We won't get her on the swing, not a fast one," Holmes said. "She's too small a target at this range, too low. We'll have to hold steady." He ended on a note of interrogation, a request for approval. Dawlish nodded.

There was movement on the *Torres*. A single brave soul – Pannetier perhaps – emerged on deck to take in more than could be seen through the conning tower's narrow slits. He stood for an instant, his gaze riveted on the gunboat, then disappeared back into the iron citadel. It would not take an astute intelligence to recognise which of the two Consortium vessels was the more important target. It would be *Torres* to *Toad* now, thick skin to thin, brawn against agility.

The *Toad's* weapon had sunk from sight and Egdean was holding station with both engines reversed, revolutions reduced as the pull towards the breached dam lessened. The water level was rising in the canal, and in the depression it fed, and soon the river's normal flow direction would reassert itself. Unseen below, another solid shot was sliding into the Armstrong's sponged and charged barrel. Upstream, in the choking confines of the *Torres'* turret, other gunners would be straining through similar movements.

Years of training and exercise, and the discipline of a British crew, brought the *Toad's* giant weapon heaving back into its firing position ten seconds before the twin snouts of the monitor's guns could be run from their gaping turret slits. In those seconds Egdean, under Holmes' quiet instruction, inched the bow across with rudders alone, nudging the gunboat's invisible axis towards its target. The great iron drum that was the *Torres'* turret ground around also, and its vertical slits were all but aligned with the *Toad*, and the twin muzzles were running out as Holmes punched the firing knob.

The Armstrong's barrel was hot from the last discharge and the hardened-steel shot carried further before bouncing once on the water's surface ten yards short of the monitor. The aim was dead-on, for as the shot skipped upwards at the shallowest of angles it gouged into the angle between flank and deck fifteen feet forward of the conning tower. Spray lashed outwards and skywards and the whole vessel shuddered and lurched.

A hit. A very palpable hit.

But now smoke and flame belched from the *Torres'* turret. *Some fool panicked into ordering fire,* Dawlish thought cerebrally, for accurate aim would be impossible on that heaving craft. There was a rushing noise to port as the *Torres'* missiles tore past – and afterwards Dawlish would attest to the accuracy of that clichéd comparison to an express train – and then two harmless plumes of water and mud erupted from the riverbank three hundred yards aft.

Smoke drifted around the *Torres,* then cleared. Her bows had swung to starboard, obscuring the point of where she had been hit, but she was still moving ahead, though erratically. Regardless of the degree of immediate damage inflicted by the *Toad's* successful shot, the massive impact would have jarred through the entire hull, flinging men from their feet, dazing and disorienting them, shearing rivets, starting seams and perhaps even jamming bearings. The *Toad's* next blow must be delivered before Pannetier and his officers could regain control.

"Closer, Mr. Holmes," Dawlish yelled, loud enough to hear himself with his own blast-deafened ears. "One hundred yards closer. Fire when ready and keep firing."

The *Toad* surged forward, the engine room responding instantly to Holmes' demand for full revolutions. The Armstrong had already sunk again from sight and then, sponged, loaded and rammed, rose again from its well and settled into firing position.

"Four hundred!" Holmes shifted the pointer across the brass dial and in the bows the muzzle depressed slightly.

Morgan's arm rose – Ready to Fire.

Upriver the *Torres'* bows seemed to have grounded on a sandbar and the waters astern boiled as her reversed screw thrashed to pull her free. Her axis lay some thirty degrees off the river's, exposing her port flank. The turret's muzzle slits pointed towards the bow and there was no sign of rotation. Dawlish found himself praying that it was jarred off its rollers.

Egdean, obedient to Holmes' shouted order, spun his wheel. The gunboat's bow swung to starboard, sweeping towards alignment with the grounded monitor and then the terrible Armstrong vomited its projectile upstream. The shot touched the river's surface a hundred yards short of the *Torres*, then skidded onwards in a running plume of spray and struck just aft of the bows. Dawlish, eyes smarting as they strained through the smoke drifting aft from the now-disappearing Armstrong, saw water cascading skywards from the point of impact and a ripple running aft across the deck. The *Torres* was in agony now, and inside her hull stunned and terrified men would be struggling dizzily to their feet.

The *Toad* swung back towards midstream and forged on. The stranded and impotent *Montelindo* was now just off her port quarter. The river still surged beneath the trapped monitor, dragging her against the breach in the dam, but the flow was weaker now and only the slightest correction to the *Toad's* helm was needed to keep her in midstream, clear of that hungry maw. The *Montelindo* was not just pinned - she was also down by the bow, the hole punched by the *Torres'* shot already submerged and water lapping on the deck as far aft as the anchor gear. A figure emerged from the conning tower as the *Toad* ploughed past – Purdon.

"The magazine's flooded, Sir!" he yelled, but neither Dawlish nor Holmes had ears for him, their attention riveted on the *Torres*.

Wounded and shaken the Reducción's monitor might be, but enough remained of the strength that a small army of Birkenhead shipwrights and Napier engine-builders had imparted to her fifteen years before to let her survive. And now she was mobile again. With her bows shocked free from the sandbar by the *Toad's* last hit, her stern awash with the foam lashed by her reversed screws, she was pulling astern into midstream. And there was worse. Inside that tortured hull Pannetier's leadership and hours of drill must be paying off, and dazed men must be overcoming their terror and performing well-rehearsed tasks, for the turret was rotating slowly and jerkily. Muscle-power straining on cranks was somehow grinding the heavy cylinder around.

The *Toad* drove forward, its weapon charged and ready, the range falling below three hundred yards. The muzzle was all but horizontal. Holmes' eye was fixed on the *Torres'* turret and his fist hovered over the brass firing-knob. The *Torres'* gun-slits were still not lined up on the approaching gunboat. In every painful second it would take the gasping crew beneath the turret to crank it round the range was narrowing and the *Toad* was all but assured of a hit.

And now again the urgent command, and the wheel slipping through Egdean's expert hands and the glass-hard shot blasting low across the water. A furrow of spray marked its passage towards the monitor. The range was little over two hundred yards and the shot struck on the port side, just aft of the turret, but almost parallel with the vessel's axis, so that the blow was a glancing one. The projectile skidded and bounced across the armoured surface and then tumbled on harmlessly into the waters astern.

Choking on the smoke that still wreathed the bridge, deafened by the report, Dawlish saw the looming *Torres* deadly before him. "To starboard, Mr. Holmes!" he shouted. "Get upstream of her!"

Scarcely a hundred yards now separated the two vessels, the monitor still thrashing astern in midstream, the gunboat, with two knots advantage, heading towards the forty-yard gap between her adversary and the bank to pass beyond. This close, the black and rust-streaked monitor seemed no less malignant and dangerous than when she had dismembered the paddlers on the lake. Rows of rivets stood out like warts on her mottled skin and before the turret the top and rear of the squat conning tower were blast-scoured to bare metal. The narrow, forward-facing viewing slits in that massive iron casting grinned wickedly and, somewhere within, Dawlish could almost feel the presence of Pannetier, brilliant and vindictive, desperate but resolute.

The *Torres'* run-out guns jutted from the turret's ports and were now almost lined up on the approaching gunboat. The *Toad's* Armstrong had sunk below the deck, and was reloading feverishly, but over a minute would pass before it would heave up again to render the gunboat potent once more. Within that minute the *Torres'* twin weapons could blast it to fragments unless...

"Gatling crews! Engage turret!" Dawlish yelled. "Aim for the gunports!"

The port weapon opened first, the second instants later. Soft, heavy .45 inch rounds spattered and ricocheted harmlessly against the monitor's plates but the flying chips of rust and paint they dislodged gave the marksmen their reference. The starboard gunner was the first to locate the turret, then hose his stream towards the slit of the nearer gunport. The helm was over and the *Toad* was shearing past the *Torres's* bows. Then Hilliard, on the port Gatling, also found the slit. Both gunners held their aim steady, swinging their weapons to hold the gunport under fire as the angle changed and the *Toad* slipped past. They milled the firing cranks round steadily as the barrels whirled and barked and as the loaders urgently fed fresh rounds into the rapidly emptying hoppers. The vertical slit, only partly blocked by the muzzle, was like a funnel in the ten-inch thickness of the turret face, concentrating the Gatlings' deadly torrent into the interior. It would be a slaughterhouse there, with screaming lead bouncing and ricocheting within its confines until velocity was finally spent or a target was found in bone and tissue.

The *Toad* might have passed totally unscathed had not some freak event within that shambles –
a Gatling round striking a firing pistol or a demented gunner jerking a lanyard in his final agony – triggered the turret's starboard gun. Flame and smoke vomited from the furthermost slit. The shot screamed close enough to Dawlish's right for the rush of its passage to throw him, half-stunned, to the deck. Above him the signal mast stood in empty air for a split second, a full foot of its middle sheared away to nothingness by the missile's passage. Then, pulled down by its still-intact stays, it crashed on to the steering platform. Aft, the uppermost eight feet of the starboard smokestack was sliced cleanly away and carried into the river. Dawlish scrambled instinctively to his left as the mast smashed through splintering planking. It tore one of the engine-room ventilators free and came to rest in a mess of cordage and rent timber.

By some miracle the telegraphs and helm were untouched but a stunned Holmes was on his knees by the binnacle. Egdean had been flung to the far side of the platform, felled by the whip of a sundered mast stay. "I'm winded, Sir," he gasped, "just winded."

Dawlish struggled to his feet. Blood ran from his nose, and his ears rang, but he realised that he had sustained no greater injury from the shot's screaming transit. Her rudders undirected, the *Toad's* bows were swinging over to starboard. The bank loomed ahead and in moments she would be aground. Dawlish fought his way across the tumbled mast and tangled stays and threw himself on the helm, spinning it frantically to carry the bows to port. The engines were still at full revolutions and the *Toad* swerved drunkenly away from the shore and up the passage left between it and the *Torres*.

Egdean joined him. "I've got her, Sir!" he said, taking the wheel. The black hull of the battered, aft-ploughing monitor was slipping past and now the *Toad* thrust into the clear water upstream of her. The Gatlings had fallen silent, deprived of their target as the monitor was masked from them as the gunboat drew ahead.

Holmes was supporting himself groggily against the telegraph. "I'm fine," he gasped, "I'll manage, Sir!" He brushed aside a thread of blood running down his forehead.

"Egdean has the helm!" Dawlish shouted, hoping that Holmes could hear better than he could himself. "The Armstrong is yours!"

Holmes nodded, then looked aft. The *Torres* was already almost a hundred yards astern, holding the midstream, its screw still in reverse, just enough to hold her stationary against the current. With the *Toad* upstream of her she was effectively blind as regards movement astern. The presence of the *Toad's* deadly Gatlings between her and Puerto Plutarcho meant that nobody could venture onto the afterdeck to con her sternwards upstream. She had one hope, and even that was a desperate one, to turn somehow by juggling of engine and rudder. Only then could she run upstream, steered from the low armoured conning tower forward of the turret.

Ahead of the *Toad* the river was clear for three or four hundred yards before disappearing in the long northerly bend beyond which lay the two Reducción forts revealed by the morning's balloon reconnaissance. Short of that bend the *Toad* could manoeuvre freely and batter the trapped *Torres* to destruction. Dawlish felt a savage delight as the charged and shotted Armstrong lifted into sight again. His craft might have sustained minor damage aft but the vital hydraulics and deadly armament that gave the *Toad* her venom were unscathed.

"I'm turning on engines, Egdean," Holmes called. "Steady on the helm!"

Less than two hundred yards separated the two vessels when Holmes reached for the telegraphs. He held the starboard handle on "Full Ahead" but drew back the port to "Full Astern". The squat gunboat's forward motion slowed and died. She turned slowly on her own axis, almost stationary in mid-river, as the two powerful screws worked against each other, pulling her anti-clockwise in stately rotation.

"Gatlings! Hold your fire!" Dawlish sensed how the gun crews, eager for action, braced themselves as the vessel came about. "Fire only if you see movement on deck! Conserve your ammunition"

The *Toad's* bows were lined up on the southern bank and still she was turning. Holmes was looking downriver at the *Torres*. His hand hovered over the range indicator, paused briefly, then moved back and closed into a waiting fist above the firing knob. The elevation would remain unchanged from the last shot.

And still the bows swept over, arcing away from the bank, facing downriver now, with the *Torres* coming in line with the gunboat's longitudinal axis. The monitor was attempting to turn, and more of her port flank was visible, but it was the turret on which Holmes was focussed. The *Toad's* rotation was smooth and regular, the gun-platform she represented rock-steady. The range was little over a hundred yards, for the current was carrying her slowly downstream. An instant before the Armstrong lined up on the trapped monitor Holmes punched the brass knob. For half a second the electric bell sounded in the bows and then the great weapon hurled its missile downriver.

The shot struck the massively armoured turret fair and square. It did not penetrate, but shattered, and fragments ricocheted from the point of impact, yet it drove a saucer-shaped depression into the curved surface that could be seen from the *Toad's* bridge. Not visible was the effect the shock might have had upon the turret's rollers and training mechanism, even assuming that enough of the gun crew had survived the Gatlings' lethal showering to take advantage of them.

"Dead on!" Dawlish was elated. "We'll head upriver and repeat the exercise."

The *Toad* was still turning, her bows now pointed towards the northern bank.

"There's a damned good chance her turret's jammed", Dawlish said. The Armstrong had already sunk for reloading. "One more shot on the turret to make sure of it, and then we go for the hull."

Both engines shifted into "Full Ahead" as the gunboat's bows swung into the current. Egdean held the midstream, glancing over his shoulder towards the wounded but still unvanquished *Torres*. Battered and perhaps inoperative its turret might be, but the monitor was still manoeuvring capably in midstream, still attempting to turn. The screw was being juggled rapidly in ahead and astern to hold her clear of the shallows by either bank. She was not yet beam-on to the current, but would be in another minute. Beyond her the *Montelindo* still lay helplessly against the breached dam. The situation should have been ideal, with the enemy trapped between two powerful vessels, but fate had intervened to make one of them impotent when it was most needed.

The sequence was as before. The *Toad* advanced upriver for two hundred yards until the Armstrong rose into its firing position again. Then the gunboat commenced its stately pirouette, drifting downstream as it did, its weapon sweeping towards its prey. The *Torres* was practically beam-on to the San Joaquin's flow and there were figures – three, four – flitting over the deck, calling information on position and direction to the all-but-blind helmsman in the tiny conning tower.

"Hilliard! Clear that deck!"

The port Gatling stuttered into life. Its barrels spun, clattered to a halt, ground around again, as the gunner sprayed the monitor's deck. A body jigged convulsively and collapsed across the *Torres'* ground-tackle but its fellows had thrown themselves down in time and had wriggled frantically behind the shelter of the turret. It was a poor haven, for at that instant the Armstrong vomited. The hardened Palliser shot struck the turret's curved wall. Deflected, it gouged a furrow along the armoured surface before flying off harmlessly into the river.

Dawlish felt frustration rising sourly inside him as this second point-blank impact failed to penetrate the massive drum. "The hull, Mr. Holmes," he called as the *Toad* swung away from the wallowing monitor to face upstream again. "Low, next shot! Hole her on the waterline!"

The gunboat drew upriver. Beneath her deck the sweating crew once more swung bagged charges and hardened shot into the loading trough and the hydraulic rammer plunged them into the sponged barrel.

"I can't hit the waterline from close range," Holmes shouted as Egdean steered upstream. "The mounting won't depress below horizontal. I'll need at least three hundred yards to drop the shot."

Astern, the *Torres* had pulled herself almost beam-on to the current. With her full port flank now exposed she now presented the best possible target. Dawlish tore his glance from her and towards the waters ahead. The *Toad* had advanced a full three hundred yards upstream and the bend was close. The river curved gently northwards until it was lost between low, brush-covered bluffs on either shore. It was time to turn, for beyond that curve lay the last two forts guarding the approach to Puerto Plutarcho.

Holmes rang for port full astern, then crouched by the firing panel. A slight rotation of the range indicator instructed the gunner to lower the barrel to horizontal. Water and glycerine bled from the elevating cylinder. Holmes' hand was poised over the firing knob, his eye aligned with the *Toad's* axis – and the Armstrong's. The bows dropped away from the current and the hull commenced its rotation. The turn was none too soon, for the *Torres* had at last managed to carry her bows slightly upstream and the exposed flank was already foreshortening. Another minute and she would be forging upriver towards the protection of the forts, steering possible again from the protection of the heavily armoured and forward-facing coning tower.

The *Toad* fired. The aim was deadly, Holmes' range estimation exact. At two hundred yards from the muzzle the shot had dropped far enough to touch the river's eddying surface, then skimmed forward in a cascade of spray, lifted clear for another fifty yards, then touched again and ploughed forward in a ripple of spume until it smashed into the monitor's port flank just ahead of the conning tower. The armour was thinner here – and less hard-faced to boot – and the impact was perpendicular. The solid shot punched through and buried itself in the ship's vitals, rending metal and crushing bone and gristle.

Heat and acrid smoke rushed aft across the gunboat's bridge. It cleared to show the *Torres* wallowing, bows already noticeably down as water rushed in.

"We can pound her to scrap from here!" Holmes's voice sounded far-off to Dawlish's deafened ears.

"Hold station!" Dawlish yelled, "I want *Toad* nailed to this spot!"

With both screws reversed at quarter revolutions the gunboat was almost stationary. The Armstrong slipped below the deck and as reloading progressed Egdean's gentle but continuous helm adjustments kept the vessel's axis aligned on the target. Dawlish's gaze was riveted on the *Torres*. The monitor might be stricken, but she was somehow still managing to crawl upriver towards them.

The great cannon surged again from its well and Dawlish felt his heart leap with it, confident that this next shot must surely cripple the monitor permanently. The gunner's hand had risen to signal readiness. Holmes' fist floated above the firing knob.

At that moment the *Toad's* fortune changed, transforming her from the monitor's remote and deadly tormentor into an embattled animal fighting frantically for her own survival.

Intent on the destruction of the *Torres*, nobody on the *Toad's* bridge or Gatling positions had seen the danger that came sweeping around the river's bend astern. They remained oblivious until a white plume rose only feet from the *Toad's* starboard flank, and with it the sharp report rolling downriver from a twenty-pounder looted from Magdalena.

Drenched by falling spray, Dawlish turned to see a vessel that looked like a floating barn come thrashing towards the *Toad*, scarcely two hundred yards separating them. The low raft-like bows and the foaming waters astern betrayed what she had started as, a Hyperion sternwheeler, but her upperworks had been transformed. From a point perhaps a quarter-length aft of the bows a sloping box of rough-hewn and unpainted timbers, two decks high, enclosed what had been the accommodation, freight and machinery spaces. It terminated in a semi-circular hump that protected the paddle wheel itself. The single funnel rose high above, showering sparks and wood smoke. The forward face had been more heavily protected by a layer of railway sections laid side by side. A single port had been cut in this inclined and crudely armoured glacis. From it the smoking muzzle of the twenty-pounder gaped for a moment before being dragged in for reloading.

Dawlish had seen drawings of such vessels in old illustrated magazines – "Timberclads" improvised by desperate Confederates on American rivers in a hopeless bid to slow the relentless advance of technically superior Union forces. They had seemed pathetic and slightly ridiculous to him then, but there was nothing risible in the hulk now bearing down on his gunboat. The *Toad* was trapped between two enemies and he had only seconds to decide which to engage first.

And the wrong choice would mean disaster.

24

The *Toad* and her weapon were still aimed downstream towards the *Torres*, away from the timberclad's oncoming menace. Holmes had turned to see the threat astern but his hand was still frozen above the firing button. Dawlish swept it aside.

"Turn!" he yelled. "Target astern!"

Egdean spun the helm, turning to port, and then Holmes ground the telegraph handles, one for full forward, the other for full astern. The screws bit and the *Toad's* rotation rate increased, turning within her own length to face upstream.

"Gatlings!" Dawlish bellowed. "Target astern! Aim for the gunport!"

The port weapon's hail of lead lashed the rail-armoured surface, seeking yet not finding the open port or the gun crew within. The second Gatling was still masked as the *Toad* swung over. Still the timberclad surged on, foredeck awash, two other ports now visible in her sloping port flank, though whatever they sheltered was blanketed from view. The *Toad* was beam-on now, still rotating, with less than a hundred yards separating the vessels. If the gunboat's turn to bring her adversary under fire were not completed by the time the timberclad's bows slammed into her then she could be cloven in two.

"One shot!" Dawlish called, unwilling to admit that there might not even be time for that. "Then we pass upriver of her! We'll take her from the rear!" A small voice within him whispered that even then the bend ahead should not be negotiated, that beyond it lay the Reducción's forts.

Eighty yards separation, and the *Toad's* bows were pointing obliquely upriver. Forty more degrees of swing and the Armstrong could be brought to bear. Dawlish was unconsciously calling the angle to himself, powerless to speed up the gunboat's rotation, and Holmes was crouched over the firing panel, poised to strike the firing knob.

Fifty yards separation. The timberclad's twenty-pounder emerged from its port. It jerked across slightly as the crew within heaved on tackles to bear it over to the gunner's aim. Then it was lost in an eruption of smoke and flame as it blasted.

Two seconds earlier, ten degrees of the *Toad's* rotation less, and the solid ball might have torn into the Armstrong mounting. Now however it shaved harmlessly past the gunboat's stem and was lost in a maelstrom of spray beyond.

Thirty yards separation – and the *Toad* was faced upriver now, bow to bow with its onrushing adversary. Holmes' open palm slammed down and then he reached for the telegraph – full ahead on both screws.

The range was so close that the timberclad's bows were scoured by the Armstrong's searing breath. The solid shot gouged diagonally into the starboard side of the glacis, just short of the gun-port, tearing away the corner of the slope-sided box. Twisted rails and splintered wood were tossed into the river beyond or pounded into the now-exposed gun-compartment, eliminating the twenty-pounder and its crew. The timberclad lurched drunkenly, its stern swinging into the path of the *Toad*.

As the *Toad's* twin screws churned full ahead, Egdean swung the helm to carry the gunboat along the timberclad's port flank, but through the thinning but still choking smoke of the Armstrong's discharge Dawlish saw that a glancing collision was unavoidable. He noted with relief that the *Toad's* Armstrong was already sinking back below the deck, all danger of its muzzle snagging avoided.

Timberclad and gunboat met with a grinding, scraping crunch, port flank to port flank. The *Toad's* riveted iron hull and breastworks ploughed splintering channels along the paddler's wooden side as the vessels ground past each other. The gunboat, massively built to bear her huge armament, was the better fit to resist and a loud report of cracking planks told of the other craft's agony. Egdean was knocked to his knees by the impact but he struggled up immediately, intent on throwing the helm over and carrying the *Toad* free into the open water to starboard. As he did the *Toad's* bows drew level with the aftermost of the two gaping ports in the timberclad's flanks. Something snaked out from it, then another. There was a glimpse of ropes falling across the gunboat's deck and over the now-closed and decked-over well into which the Armstrong had sunk. The lines snapped taut as the iron grapnels at their ends bounced and clattered over the deck and then caught, one on a mooring bitt, the other on the angle of a coaming. Another grapnel followed, then another, their hooks grasping on deck-fittings, their cables tightening to draw the vessels together. The waters astern of the paddler foamed as her hidden wheel reversed, then stopped, killing the vessel's forward way and locking it all the more firmly to the *Toad*.

"Gatlings!" Dawlish's words were lost as the gunners opened on the mob of howling men that now came bursting from the timberclad's side ports. These contained no guns but were no less deadly for that, funnelling two torrents of machete and rifle-armed men across to the *Toad*. The gunboat's bulwarks were higher than the ports and the boarders were forced to throw themselves upwards for a hand-hold on the top, or to scramble across the backs of their fellows below. The first to drag themselves over were scythed down by the hammering Gatling fire, jerking like bloody marionettes as they fell, but the press from below hurled more and more across.

Even in that extremity, years of Royal Navy firing drill told themselves in the short-bursts, six or eight rounds each, in which the gunners cranked their spinning barrels, shifting aim between, avoiding the jams that continuous fire would make inevitable. Torn bodies draped themselves across the bulwark, and others slumped to the bloody deck beneath it, but still La Reducción's boarders clawed over. Enough survived the heavy slugs that ripped splinters from the deck and ricocheted between the iron bulwarks to throw themselves behind protection or come scrambling aft. Some were clad in shabby cottons but others were all but naked, many with bright red and yellow streaks painted across their chests and faces. They howled as they ran, machetes or spears upraised, sprinting for the Gatling positions and the bridge.

The first priority was to break contact with the timberclad, and only then to deal with the boarders.

"Gatlings! Cut the cables!" Dawlish bellowed, but his words were drowned in the clamour. Something screamed past his left ear – an enemy rifleman had established himself behind cover in the *Toad's* own bows. Dawlish had instinctively pulled his Adams from its holster but he forced himself not to raise it. At this instant his brain was his – and the *Toad's* – most decisive weapon.

There was one priority now – to separate the two vessels as quickly as possible – yet in the storm of firing the gunners were deaf to orders. "To the port Gatling, Holmes!" Dawlish yelled. "Cut those cables!"

Holmes, revolver in hand, scrambled from the steering platform. A spear thudded into the woodwork to his side as he reached the deck and a screaming Guaikuru launched himself at him with a raised machete. Holmes blasted him from his path, then launched himself towards the vertical iron ladder leading to the port Gatling platform. He grasped a rung and started to climb. The weapon was still barking in deadly staccato, depressed to its maximum as it sought and pounded the scurrying boarders.

Dawlish saw this from where he crouched behind the plinth of the Armstrong's indicator panel, his Adams in his hand. Egdean was stooped over the helm, lips moving in prayer. The *Toad's* engines were still in full-ahead, and she was dragging the timberclad with her in a slow and drunken upstream course.

"Hold the midstream!" Dawlish yelled, for it was essential to maintain position in deep water until the cables were cut and the *Toad* could break free. Another bullet sang past and then the indicator plinth juddered as a round slammed into it. He peered around it as Egdean swung the helm to hold the two locked vessels away from the shallows.

The starboard Gatling's loader jerked upright, his face frozen in eternal surprise as he saw a spearpoint burst through his chest from behind before he toppled over the rail and crashed to the deck. The gunner, intent on hosing away the next wave of boarders clambering across the bulwark, neither saw nor heard the painted Guaikuru who heaved himself up the ladder behind him. The heavy machete that swung into his neck all but severed his head. His weapon's spinning barrels ground into sudden silence, drenched by the fountain of blood that engulfed them.

Dawlish saw this remotely, as if in another universe, and the seconds of the deadly little drama seemed like centuries. The Guaikuru at the starboard Gatling turned, his face a rictus of savage delight, but Dawlish's Adams was moving across towards him, the range less than twenty feet. Backsight and foresight aligned on the yellow-striped chest. The pistol jerked and the Guaikuru slammed back and tumbled from the mounting.

Holmes had climbed to the portside Gatling position. To his gesticulated command the gunner, Hilliard, swung his weapon from the shambles at the gunwale, where boarders still clawed their way across the bloody heap of their fellows, and directed it at the nearer of the grappling cables. It shredded and broke as the slugs tore into it. The taut cable next to it lashed free as a burst of lead found it also. Holmes was shooting aft with his revolver, blazing down at the desperate knot of boarders who had gained the cover of the boiler casing and were heading for the bridge ladder.

Hilliard shifted his aim forward but, as he swung, his loader spun around, clutching a shoulder seared by a rifle-round that tore his shirt but not his flesh. The Gatling stammered into life, then fell silent as the hopper emptied. Holmes turned, pushed the gasping loader aside and reached into the ammunition box. Inexpertly, he shovelled rounds into the hopper. Hilliard ground his crank forward again and the spinning barrels sprayed towards the remaining cables.

"Behind you, Sir!" It was Egdean, somehow still manoeuvring the helm from his crouched position.

Dawlish turned towards the access ladder at the rear of the steering platform, up which the first of the attacking group to reach the stern area was now climbing. A head appeared over the edge of the deck, just long enough to aim a spear that a bare arm sent whizzing harmlessly to Dawlish's right. He fired back once with the Adams before the hate-filled face ducked from sight, knowing instantly that he had missed.

Three rounds left in the cylinder, and the chance of reloading negligible.

Two figures hurled themselves simultaneously up the ladder and on to the bridge, one a screaming, half-naked Guaikuru, the other in filthy brown cottons. Both swung machetes. Dawlish fired instinctively, his first round catching the Guaikuru on the hip. The pistol's double action gave him an almost simultaneous second shot that tore into his attacker's chest and tumbled him to the deck. The second boarder stumbled across the prostrate body, his momentum lost. Dawlish stepped across and kicked the machete from his hand as he struggled to rise. He looked up, terror now on his round face as Dawlish brought the Adams up to it. He might have been pleading in the instant before he died.

Dawlish side-stepped the falling body and glanced down the ladder. A separate battle was in progress at its base as three of the *Toad's* stokers, as black and grimy as devils, had cornered the two surviving boarders who had got that far. Another lay at their feet, his head split by one of the coal shovels that the stokers wielded to such dreadful effect. Led by Wilcox, the banjo player, they had burst from the engine-room companionway as the boarders congregated round the bridge ladder, surprising them from the rear. The scuffle was short and brutal. Wilcox's shovel sliced into the arm that held the single survivor's machete and then the others chopped down and finished him.

"Forward Lads!" Dawlish shouted down to the stokers. "Keep 'em clear of the Gatling!" He moved back to Egdean's side.

"She's pulling us over!" the seaman said. Despite all his efforts the two locked vessels were perilously close to the southern bank's shallows.

The stokers surged forward, their bloodlust up. They emerged on the open deck between deckhouse and the closed-off Armstrong well as the surviving Gatling tore through the third grappling cable. It parted in an explosion of fibre and whipping ends. The one remaining cable was stretched bar taut as the *Toad* strained away from the timberclad. It strummed like a violin string, then parted with a loud crack, flailing

238

across the deck and dropping like a dying snake as the two vessels separated.

A howl of anger and horror rose from the isolated boarders still crouching uncertainly in the bows, sheltering in terror from the port Gatling's terrible rain. But now the aim shifted, for as the *Toad* drew away from the timberclad, Hilliard poured fire into the open port piercing the sloping side. Bodies were piled there and in the confines beyond the ricocheting rounds were making the interior untenable.

The remaining boarders at the bow, perhaps a dozen, half of them wounded, were shocked into immobility as the Armstrong came heaving from its well. And not just the great weapon burst from below, but six of its crew, wielding cutlasses. What they lacked in numbers they made up for in freshness and ferocity. Joined by the stokers running forward, and by Holmes storming with them, revolver in hand, they fell mercilessly on the winded and exhausted boarders. Separate small but deadly conflicts developed across the midships and bow areas, chopping, thrusting, kicking contests on blood-slippery decks. No quarter was asked or given. A single Armstrong-loader fell dead, cleft to the chin by a machete stroke, and a stoker, Niven, took a spear-wound in the shoulder that would finish his coal-heaving for ever, but it was the boarders that fared worst, hacked down, or despatched by Holmes' pistol.

The *Toad* had drawn slightly upriver of the now-drifting timberclad, and had almost reached the bend. Dawlish, upright now by the helm, reached for the telegraph and rang for quarter revolutions on both screws, hoping that there was still enough manpower below to respond to his request – Boyson, the artificer, must be alone there now. To his relief the engines responded seconds later. The *Toad's* speed slowed and Egdean held her almost stationary against the current.

Dawlish looked aft. The waters frothed by the timberclad's stern now, but she seemed to be stuck fast on shallows close to the southern bank. Four hundred yards beyond her the *Torres* was crawling slowly upstream. Her bows had sunk from sight and waters lapped in a white wave over her mooring gear as she crept forward.

Dawlish felt a feral surge of exultation. The *Toad's* decks might be bloodied, splintered and corpse-strewn and his crew might have taken casualties that he would mourn in a quieter time, but at this moment he had an intact and devastating fighting machine under his command and both his enemies were at his mercy.

"The deck's cleared, Sir!" Holmes shouted. "Every one of 'em accounted for!"

"Gun crew to their stations, Mr. Holmes! Stokers below with the wounded! And I'd welcome your presence on the bridge."

Holmes joined him, panting and sweating. Blood saturated a ripped left shirt-sleeve. "It's nothing, Sir", he said. "A scratch. I was lucky."

"First the paddler, then the *Torres*," Dawlish said quietly. "And the Armstrong?"

"Loaded. And bursting shell at that."

Once again, the worth of training and initiative. While the boarders had stormed across from the timberclad, and while a murderous melee had raged above them, Morgan had not only driven his crew through the routine of loading but had the presence of mind to specify an explosive round.

"Your weapon, Mr. Holmes."

Morgan's bellow carried aft: "Pipe down! Look to your duties!" The gun crew, elated from their orgy of killing, were at their stations again. Now they must calm again for a more methodical form of slaughter. Morgan's right arm rose – Armstrong ready.

"Helm steady, Egdean," Holmes said quietly. "We turn on engines only." He reached for the telegraph. Port astern, starboard ahead, increasing to half revolutions.

The *Toad's* bows swept round, arcing the Armstrong's murderous muzzle towards the grounded timberclad, little over a hundred yards distant. The stern wheel still thrashed beneath its drumlike wooden shield and at the two flank ports from which the boarders had stormed figures were dragging survivors from the water. Sparks and smoke still belched from the single tall stack and there were other figures atop the sloping superstructure, riflemen taking position to rake the *Toad*.

In that instant the timberclad was still a living, vital machine, however improvised and inadequate. Moments later she was a flaming shambles.

The Armstrong's bursting shell struck astern, almost axially. It punched through the stern wheel drum and gouged through the machinery beyond. It burst the boiler in its passage before it exploded in the heart of the sloped topsides. Flame raced and seared through the space within, blowing timbers outwards and erupting through the deck above like a volcano. A second explosion followed almost simultaneously as the charges stored for the vessel's twenty-pounder detonated. The after half of the sloped, barnlike upperworks had been reduced to a collapsed, blazing wreck.

There was no time to gloat. The *Toad* swept past the blazing wreck, intent on her second victim. The Armstrong had already sunk for reloading. Holmes had reached for the indicator dial.

"Armour piercing?" he asked.

Dawlish nodded. The indictor arm was swept across. Down in the bows the lifting tongs would now be grasping solid Palliser shot.

The *Toad* was moving slowly downstream towards the barely on-coming *Torres*. Holmes shifted the range pointer. "At two hundred yards," he muttered.

The Armstrong emerged. Further muffled explosions came from astern as the timberclad burned to its waterline and men leaped overboard, but on the *Toad's* bridge there were eyes only for the *Torres*.

Two fifty yards... two twenty... The monitor was dead ahead. Waters now lapped across her foredeck as far aft as the conning tower, the mooring gear fully submerged. She was hardly holding her own against the current. The turret slits could not be seen, indicating that the drum itself was jammed. The *Torres* was crippled and impotent, and yet in his heart Dawlish felt no mercy.

Holmes punched the firing knob.

For the last time on that long day the Armstrong spoke. It hurled its deadly missile into the *Torres* just aft of the turret, striking in a fountain of spray and punching through the now-inclined deck, deflecting on some massive casting beneath, tearing downwards and aft through bulkheads and destroying whatever integrity remained. Her frames tortured beyond endurance, her plates springing apart as rivets sundered under the shock, the monitor now admitted water in torrents. Her dazed and terrified crew, those not annihilated by the shell's passage, scrambled for escape from the rising flood, crowding and panicking at ladders and companionways.

Dawlish shook his head slowly when Holmes suggested another shot. "Take us downstream, but slowly. Quarter revolutions, if you please. We've come a long way for this."

It was satisfaction enough to steam calmly past the *Torres*. She was not just down at the bows but heeling to starboard as well, her twin screws stilled and lifting above the water as she settled. Her deck was crowded with terrified men who hesitated to commit themselves to the river, while others struggled to drag wounded through hatches. One had balanced himself on the now dangerously sloped turret and was shaking his fist and yelling in fury. Dawlish heard his own name, mispronounced, but still recognisable. It was Alain Pannetier, sometime naval officer, sometime convict, sometime escapee and now a free man, unchained – a Socialist.

"The Gatling could shut him up, Sir", Holmes said. His wound was painful now and he was in no mood for compassion.

Dawlish shook his head. He too had known failure. "He's a professional, Mr. Holmes", he said. "We're all members of the brotherhood of the sea. He's suffered enough."

The *Toad* moved downriver, leaving the *Torres* astern. With one final lurch the monitor rolled over, revealing her screws and rudder before they too were lost beneath the muddy waters of the San Joaquin.

It was a long way from the Birkenhead yard where she had taken form – almost as far as from the Sheerness graving dock where her nemesis had fitted out and where Dawlish had committed himself to her destruction.

He tore his gaze away from the heads dotting the river's surface. He suddenly felt both sad and weary – and chilly too, for he could not deny now that his head was aching badly and his temperature rising.

25

Dawlish was shivering violently. He was cold despite the late afternoon's warmth as the *Toad* moored in midstream, level with the *Tacuari*. The command vessel had moved cautiously upriver, in the wake of the land and river advance, and it now lay moored to the bank just short of the helpless *Montelindo*. Dawlish's head was aching hard enough to impair his vision and he knew that within an hour this chill would be replaced by fever. Now, when he least needed it, the scourge of the malaria that he carried within him was asserting itself. Three or four days of misery lay ahead. He swallowed two more glasses of Quinine wine, hoped they would somehow keep the fever in abeyance, and him on his feet, for a few hours longer. Then he gave directions for clearing the shambles on the *Toad's* deck.

The crew's elation of victory was fading fast, and a dejected mood would quickly set in as they came to terms with the death and injury of shipmates. It was essential to keep them busy if the *Toad* was to stay a potent fighting machine. The wounded had to be made comfortable, the corpses of the boarders thrown overboard, their own dead laid out for respectful burial – and it would have to be before nightfall, in this heat – the decks swabbed and, above all, the Armstrong mounting's hydraulic system checked. Packings would have to be tightened or replaced, glycerine and water reservoirs topped up. The weapon's barrel must cleaned thoroughly after its repeated firings. The damaged starboard smokestack must be extended if furnace-draught was to be maintained – but that could wait. It was more important to jury-rig the fallen signal mast. Restacking of charges and ammunition in the magazine so as to be closer to the loading gear could also wait. Replacements for the dead Gatling crew would need hasty training. A quick discussion with Holmes set priorities and allocated responsibilities between four separate working parties.

Boarders' bodies, simultaneously gruesome and pathetic, were splashing overboard as Dawlish crossed to the *Montelindo*. He was starting to tremble now. Soon the shivering would be wholly uncontrollable.

The canal and the depression beyond the sundered dam had filled up. The *Montelindo* was still jammed in the breach, her deck heeled along her length at fifteen degrees, her foredeck awash. As Dawlish boarded Purdon separated himself from the small group at the bows that was pulling a swimmer from the water.

"We're checking the damage, Sir. We're badly holed – it looks like the plates' edges are bent inwards. It'll be a devil to patch."

"Can you reach it internally?"

"We've closed off the magazine and the forward compartment – both flooded. There's one vertical hatch only."

"Did you get anybody inside?"

"One man, but there's such a tangle of wreckage down there that he couldn't reach the hole. Good pair of lungs though. He was in well over a minute."

"You're trying again?"

"To tell the truth, Sir, I'm not keen on sending another one in. There's a lot of blood and bits of bodies in there."

"Boilers? Engine? Steam pump?" Dawlish cut him short.

"We have steam, Sir. The engines seem fine but until we shift the stern we won't know if the screw is damaged. But the pump's functioning."

"Then start plugging, Mr. Purdon." The fire in Dawlish's head made him impatient. "Hammocks, awnings, whatever's to hand, blood or no blood. Then get pumping. Get a kedge laid out from the stern. The *Toad* will be available in addition to assist in the morning and I want you to come off stern-first. No sense in damaging your screw further."

Once in open water the *Montelindo* would have to be heeled to expose the hole for patching. It would take days, perhaps a week, days when the *Toad* must guard the river alone. And then, to his relief, Dawlish's hammer-beating brain told him that there was time now. The *Torres* was gone and if the Reducción had warships left they were limited to pitiful timberclads like the one he had demolished upstream. The *Toad* could cope alone for now.

He headed wearily for the *Tacuari*.

*   *   *

Dawlish subsequently remembered little of the night's conference because he collapsed before the end of it. All he could recall was that it was acrimonious, though it had started well for him.

Murillo came the closest to warmth that Dawlish had ever seen.

"Well done, Commander Dawlish." He grasped his hand limply. "Admiral Topcliffe did not overstate your capacities after all. You have justified handsomely the investment we made in the Rendel. The Board will be most gratified."

But success on the river had been matched by what amounted to failure on land. The Consortium had indeed forced its adversaries back into Puerto Plutarcho's fortifications, and had inflicted severe casualties while sustaining trifling losses. But the single setback, the failure to capture the dam before the canal was flooded, cancelled all the gain. Direct access to the fortifications was now made impossible by the flooded ground.

"A bit more of – you must know the fancy word for it, Commander Nick – a bit more eee-lan, that's the word! A bit more eee-lan would have done it." Culbertson's words were slurred with alcohol. "Five minutes faster to that little fort and we'd ha' been whistlin' Dixie this very minute under the very walls of the Goddamn Reducción." He glared at Aquino and Tinsley in turn, daring them to reply. "Five minutes? No, by Jesus! Just four! That would have done it!"

Aquino's black eyes fixed Culbertson with contempt, but he was silent. Tinsley was stung however, though not by the reflection on his professional capacity.

"I cannot hear the Lord's name abused, Colonel." His tone was pious. "We only court further setbacks by these continued blasphemies."

"Gentlemen!" Murillo brought them to order like a schoolmaster. "The reckoning can come later. We have arrived at Puerto Plutarcho. Now tell me how we take it!"

And there was no immediately obvious way.

Through a red haze of rising fever and blinding headache Dawlish heard the grim litany of depleted resources and tried to keep track of the figures. Four hundred and forty three conscripts already out of account, half dead, the rest too debilitated by sickness to stir themselves, leaving two thousand, six hundred and sixty fit for duty. Eleven hundred and sixteen regulars remained from the twelve hundred that set out. Culbertson could muster just over two hundred and seventy Guardia troopers, though by now he had mounts for only three-quarters. The artillery had suffered least and Tinsley could man all his weapons, field artillery and mortars alike. Reinforcements should be en-route by now via Magdalena, at least another two companies of regular infantry and half-a-dozen more of hastily-trained conscripts, if arms could be found for them, but nothing had been heard of them so far. Food was running short as well, for the anticipated supply of foraged beef had not materialised due to the

Reducción's efficient gathering of herds into the Puerto Plutarcho perimeter. Everything depended on the Asunción government's ability to mobilise more river transport – and most of what had been available to start with was already on the Rio San Joaquin.

"I make it about four thousand men," Culbertson drawled. "And there's at least five miles of entrenchments this side of the river alone. That's – let me see." He paused, the effort too much for his drink-dulled brain. "Major Tinsley, Sir, you cannoneers are always good at cipherin'. You tell us."

"More than two yards per head," Tinsley said coldly.

"It don't sound much, neither for a regular siege nor a storming, even if we could get across that goddamn inundation. An' thousands of the sons of bitches inside, and time enough for 'em to concentrate wherever we hit them." Culbertson threw back another glass and scowled in morose frustration.

"The Colonel summarises accurately, if not elegantly." Murillo's tone had an edge of fear. "And the river? Surely now that the monitor is sunk..." His words trailed off in a note of interrogation.

"Blocked." Dawlish's head pounded. Enunciation of even a single word was an agony. "The forts still block it."

He had a mental image of the two massive earthworks that he had seen from the balloon, anchoring the trench lines to the northern and southern river banks. Their sloped walls and deadly embrasures were the last things he contemplated before the furnace in his head reached white heat.

Then he fell forward on the table and remembered nothing more.

*   *   *

Two days later Dawlish became semi-conscious, and that was worse than the merciful oblivion that had enveloped him before. He fretted and tossed, alternately shivering with heart-piercing cold, then stewing in hot sweat, half-aware of Egdean pushing bitter-tasting quinine between his teeth. He was vaguely aware that he was on board the *Toad* and he babbled of the work needed to restore it for action. Holmes' soothing assurances only agitated him further before he drifted off again. Confused images tormented him even then: burned bodies in a wrecked fort, the *Torres* blasting flame, the timberclad's howling boarders, and a serene Florence in a silk gown, pouring tea into a china cup decorated with a picture of a shepherdess.

The fever left him on the third day. His legs were uncertain and he felt weak and exhausted, yet he tottered to his feet nonetheless. But his spirit felt reborn. He recognised the feeling from previous malarial bouts, a consciousness that he had come through an ordeal that made all other challenges seem petty. His clear head and cool body, even if weak, seemed like gifts. He welcomed life, even if his immediate preoccupation was with death and destruction. He felt a surge of almost maudlin affection and gratitude for Holmes and Egdean, who had cared so solicitously for him and who were so obviously happy to see him restored. Half-embarrassed, he covered his emotions with a display of gruff efficiency, demanding an immediate account of developments over a breakfast of coffee and biscuit. Afterwards he heaved himself, panting from effort, to the *Toad's* bridge, waving away any attempts at assistance. He saw with satisfaction that the gunboat was a fighting unit again. Even the damaged funnel had been restored to full height.

The river was secure. The *Toad* was moored in mid-stream slightly upstream of the breached dam. Her Armstrong covered the long straight reach up to the bend, beyond which lay the Reducción forts. It had taken a day and a half to get the *Montelindo* unjammed and afloat again and now she lay a mile downriver, heeled over by transfer of stores to expose the damage to her hull. Through a telescope Dawlish saw how a barge had been brought alongside to facilitate repairs. A small forge glowed, showing that rivets were being heated for the patch.

"And her armament, Mr. Holmes?" He snapped the glass shut.

"The turret can be trained by hand, Sir. It's slow, but better than nothing. The problem is the flooded magazine. Major Tinsley is bagging us powder charges from his own supplies but we'll have to wait until the magazine is pumped out before we can recover the shells."

"How long?"

"Another day at least."

"And propulsion, Mr. Holmes?"

"She'll move, Sir, but just about. Purdon reckons she'll make half revolutions. The engine's no worse than it ever was but one of the bearings is binding. She lost a blade on one screw but at low revs it shouldn't be a major problem."

So, in a day, Dawlish reflected, his offensive force would be restored – not completely as it was before, but enough to outgun and outfight anything El Pobre's forces could send down against him. But movement upriver – that was another matter.

The situation onshore, as he learned from Murillo when he had himself pulled across to the *Tacuari*, was still beset by uncertainty and lack of direction. Culbertson was absent, away to the south with a force of mounted troopers. He had ridden off in a large loop so as to skirt around the defences and probe the south-western flank. Aquino had cast derision on the idea. He had stated that, regardless of whatever weaknesses Culbertson might find, nothing could be achieved so far from the river and the supply-route, and the support of the *Toad*. Seconded by Tinsley, he was arguing for bypassing the inundation at the narrowest point, by crossing the canal behind the breached dam. Murillo had authorised commencement of preparations, but nothing else. The mortars were being landed to provide heavy support and work was already starting on the components of a wooden bridge. A trench system would zigzag from there towards the earthworks to avoid a direct approach across the open ground. The final assault would be at night, concentrating on a single point close to the river.

From the *Tacuari's* high steering-position the preparations were obvious, though to Dawlish they seemed half-hearted. More conscripts could have been allocated to cutting wood and driving the piles for the proposed bridge, and more still to landing the mortars. Too many seemed occupied in the construction of makeshift shelters in a camp further downstream. The Consortium, by default, was settling in for a partial investment.

"Do you support General Aquino's plan?" Dawlish asked.

"No final decision has been made as yet," Murillo said, "and Colonel Culbertson's opinion must be taken into account. He knows the area better than any other." Dawlish noted a tremor of uncertainty, even of desperation, in Murillo's voice.

And then Dawlish saw it clearly – Murillo was frightened, out of his depth. He must know in his heart that he was not being presented with a viable plan, not by Culbertson, and not by Aquino, nor was the river route an option while the forts dominated it. But he knew that something must be done. To sit here outside the Reducción, while it could still supply itself from the west, could only mean a slow bleeding away of the Consortium's forces through disease, demoralisation and ultimately hunger. Murillo was desperate. He had reason to be.

"Have you any better suggestion, Commander Dawlish?" he asked, almost plaintively.

A small voice inside Dawlish told him that this cold, heartless, book-keeping little tyrant deserved his humiliation and yet he could take no satisfaction in it, for he himself was equally lost for a solution.

"*No, Señor,*" he was about to answer. But then, suddenly inspired, he said instead "I could only answer that after a reconnaissance. I believe that Grinling still has enough acid to allow another ascent or two."

"Be assured of my support, Commander. Whatever you need, call upon it." Murillo's words were rapid enough to betray his desperation.

Most of the hydrogen had leaked away since the last ascent and the balloon lay on its barge in a crumpled, deflated heap. Grinling, sweating and harassed in a collarless shirt and forgotten by everybody else in the excitement of recent days, was genuinely delighted to see Dawlish.

"I was praying you'd get better, Sir, indeed I was. I didn't relish deliverin' that letter of yours to your good lady, Sir! Dear Me, No! I'd have visited you myself, exceptin' that I can't leave this blessed barge. Need two eyes in the back of my head, I do. These Dagos would steal the milk out of your tea if you let them. An' exceptin' you, Sir, nobody seems to know what to do with this here balloon of mine."

It would take six hours to generate enough gas to inflate it. Dawlish, already feeling exhausted from his exertions so far, resolved to return to the *Toad* to sleep until then. He turned back as he was about to board the *Toad's* gig.

"The balloon can carry a maximum of six I believe?" he asked.

"For low ascents only, Sir," Grinling said with an air of professional expertise. "For the garden-fete and country-show trade. The basket's big enough. Ladies don't generally choose to go very high – two hundred feet is usually it – and of course it helps the turnover. Why, I've even lifted eight once, but they was young ladies, from an academy, and light like."

"So with a single occupant, how high?"

"Oh high, Sir, very high. With the other gentlemen you was almost to four hundred the other day, so I daresay you'd make six, maybe more, if you was alone. But the rope's the problem. There's only enough for five hundred feet, and that's it."

"You'll have rope by midday," Dawlish said. "There's enough in stock. I'll send a few seamen from the *Toad* to help spool it on your winch."

"In the morning you'd get more height still – cooler air, Sir. More of a difference of density as we scientific men puts it. Could you wait until then, Sir?"

But he could not wait, and he was back at three in the afternoon, rested, and feeling the better for a meal. The balloon swayed gently, tethered to within a foot of the deck, its canopy taut. Dawlish checked the connection of the new rope carefully, fighting back an unspoken fear of a break leaving him drifting off into the unknown Chaco, or worse still, into Puerto Plutarcho.

Grinling helped him into the basket. "You're sure you want to go up alone, Sir?" he asked. "Nothing to be ashamed of, Sir, but if you don't know the ropes, so to speak, it can be a bit intimidating like."

Dawlish shook his head and settled himself in.

"This rope with the green mark, Sir," Grinling fussed. "It's for the release valve. You can bleed off gas if you need to come down. But the red one – don't so much as look at it. It's for the rip panel for releasing all the gas when you're down. Pull that and I'll be deliverin' that letter to your good lady, Sir!"

Lightly loaded, the balloon rose fast, pulling the rope off the winch so fast that the crew on the cranks were obliged to restrain it rather than pay it out. Dawlish did feel nervous, and the motion of the basket was more lively, and indeed slightly more sickening, than when more had occupied it, but as he rose higher interest in the scene below displaced all other feelings.

The panorama had changed only in one particular from that which he had surveyed with Culbertson and Aquino from this same vantage. It seemed like an age before. The muddy, straggling line of the flooded depression, nowhere except at the canal narrower than a hundred yards, barred direct approach to the fortifications. And, not unexpectedly, there were signs of greater Reducción activity along the stretch of earthworks directly facing the canal. Freshly turned soil indicated extra embrasures being cut and a slowly moving plume of steam showed where the narrow-gauge railway was being used to shift material – almost certainly cannon – towards that face. Applied in that area, Aquino's battering ram tactics could only lead to a massacre. Figures moved on the fire-step behind the parapets – there seemed more than previously – and a cloud of dust on an open space marked where a company was being put through its evolutions. The pall of wood-smoke above the settlement and the vomiting chimneys of the workshops in the far distance confirmed determined preparation. The twin forts flanking the river looked more menacing than ever, though there was grim satisfaction in the sight of the timberclad's burned-out hull in the shallows and of the dark streak close to midstream that marked the *Torres'* grave.

He was now at six hundred feet or more, and the river's sweep and Puerto Plutarcho's grid pattern and the baked Chaco surrounding it were more like a map than ever. He forced himself to ignore the details and concentrate on the overall scene. Somewhere on that landscape of untidy human settlement and winding river and parched scrub and massive earthworks lay the key to victory. Hidden below, perhaps even in such plain view as to be unrecognisable, must be some advantage to the Consortium, some vulnerability for the Reducción, that both had missed.

The river dominated all. Its winding sweep, first northwards towards the forts, then west and south and west again, enclosed the greater part of the settlement. The heart of the Reducción – the workshops, the wharf, the stockyards, the housing, and now the arsenals and fortifications also – all lay south of the river within that great loop. Only a few stockyards and straggling, makeshift housing, protected by a ragged line of trenches, occupied the northern shore. The prize was on the southern bank and from the east the flooding and the earthworks made it essentially unassailable by the Consortium's meagre forces. The fortified southern flank of the defences, where Culbertson was even now probing, looked still less promising. Any approach would be through thick scrub, which would demand tracks to be hacked for the artillery, but, most undesirable of all, it would draw the Consortium forces away from their river-base. Aquino had been right in that – a determined sally by the defenders could cut off any such force from the river. Only on the distant western flank, four, maybe five miles distant, now made more visible than previously by the balloon's greater altitude, did the defences peter out to nothingness.

And that was it!

Only on that distant western flank could the Consortium's resources be sufficient to force an entry. An assault from there would carry them through the rear of the defences and into the heart of the settlement. No siegeworks, no long preliminary bombardments, but a fast, murderous attack into La Reducción's heart. It must carry terror and confusion with it while the conscripts still did not realise the desperation of their position and before El Pobre and his Communard henchmen could somehow improvise a defence line. Success would have to be immediate and total.

The choice was stark: find a way to attack from the west – or fail.

The Rio San Joaquin was the key. It alone offered the route along which the men and artillery and supplies could be transported fast to the western flank. But that route ran between the two great forts that dominated the river and on past the settlement itself. The armoured *Montelindo* alone might brave that passage. But it was the fragile paddle steamers that must transport the men, artillery and supplies. Labouring slowly upstream against the drag of their towed barges, they would be shredded in minutes by the twenty-pounders nestling in the forts' embrasures.

Yet the forts could be reduced – slowly but effectively – by Tinsley's mortars directed from Grinling's balloon. How long? Days perhaps. But each falling shell would proclaim the Consortium's intention of forcing the river, and Roybon, brilliant strategist as he had already proved himself to be, would awake to the implied threat to the West and would start strengthening his defences there accordingly. The teeming human ants that Dawlish had seen scooping out the canal could be just as easily set to raising earthworks on the western flank.

And then the solution came to Dawlish, not as a flash of original inspiration, but as a memory from earlier reading. It had been a desperate and imaginative tactic once before, and not so long ago either, but it had been successful. With speed, energy and a ruthless willingness to risk serious loss it might just be successful again.

He stayed aloft for another hour, testing and retesting his hypothesis against the realities beneath him. He gauged distances, estimated times, allowed for setbacks and delays. He considered the role of each element of the Consortium forces, and their reliability and their ability to meet the demands upon them. He visualised the reactions and objections of Culbertson, Aquino, Tinsley and Murillo in turn and he determined how he might answer and convince them. And in the end he was still satisfied.

He signalled to Grinling to winch him down.

26

Nobody liked the plan. Not Aquino, of whose troops such speed would be demanded, nor Tinsley, of whom a timetable would be required that would admit no slippage, nor Culbertson, for reasons of his own. Murillo liked it least of all, for he realised that it provided only for absolute success or absolute failure.

"Failure would mean Hyperion's bankruptcy - you realise that, Commander Dawlish?" he said, frowning. "Our credit is at its limit in the City."

Several thousand of us will be facing worse than bankruptcy, Dawlish thought, *but you, you cold miser, you and Tinsley will be the only ones to whom the plan offers an escape route to Asunción.*

But instead he said "I'm equally concerned, Señor, as I'm sure Admiral Topcliffe and Lord Kegworth would be. That's why we need the next two days to reduce risks to the minimum. We must leave nothing to chance."

"And if we fail here, the whole country will be at Aguirre Robles' mercy." Murillo almost spat out the name he loathed. "You're asking General Aquino to sacrifice the last regular troops the Republic of Paraguay can rely upon."

"My regulars will do it," Aquino growled. "But the conscripts, they get frightened in the dark. They panic easily. They can lose their way."

"But that's why Colonel Culbertson's pathfinding is so essential," Dawlish said. "Nobody knows the ground better. His troopers will be serving as guides."

"No Goddamn use your trying to soft-soap me, Commander Nick," Culbertson sneered, "and the fact that Ulysses S. Grant pulled the same trick don't impress me none neither! Plenty Rebs faced the Goddamn son-of-a-bitch at the Bloody Angle and Cold Harbour and he didn't prove himself as nothin' but a Goddamn butcher of his own men."

"In all fairness, Colonel," Tinsley said solemnly, for once ignoring Culbertson's profanity, "the precedent that Commander Dawlish quoted was a somewhat earlier and more successful action of Grant's. But it did violate every accepted principle of warfare and there was a great element of luck involved." His forehead and brows wrinkled with concern as he sucked on his pipe, shook his head slowly and stated "No Gentlemen. It's dangerous. Dangerous and unconventional."

Yet none of them argued any alternative of their own with any conviction. The assault from the dam area, for which preparations were so sluggishly in progress, was quietly conceded to be a blood bath in the making. Culbertson's reconnaissances had only confirmed the near impossibility of an assault on the southern flank with the forces available. Shared between them, unspoken and undiscussable, yet palpable nonetheless, was the acceptance that every day diminished their strength. The first cases of conscripts deserting to the Reducción had been confirmed. More were inevitable. And all the time sickness and hunger would be reducing their numbers further. Already the daily record of deaths from fever and dysentery, high before, were beginning to climb towards levels which would paralyse the entire force..

Dawlish returned to the map once more, exhausted and slightly feverish again, yet aware that he must prevail this night, or not at all. Repeatedly he restated details, answered objections, incorporated the grudging suggestions for improvement that came first from Aquino, later from Culbertson and finally even from Tinsley. He knew he was making progress when Aquino sent for Prado, his own artillery major, to assess the feasibility of advancing the ten-pounders as the plan demanded. Dawlish himself answered a concern of Murillo's by calling Purdon in briefly to confirm the *Montelindo's* battle-readiness within forty-eight hours. Culbertson grudgingly conceded that the ground – which he knew well – would facilitate the manoeuvre. Merit was found with the preparations for Aquino's frontal assault, but now only as a diversion. Tinsley, drawn in by sheer professional interest, suggested how the mortars' true targets could be lulled into false security until the critical moment.

Dawlish made a show of mulling cautiously over each new proposal, making an initial show of reluctance, then allowing himself to be won over by step-by-step argument until he finally incorporated the idea enthusiastically. It was essential that the others must believe it to be their plan as well as his.

Three hours passed. Tinsley was now officiously recording the changes and suggestions, meticulously cross-checking their consistency with features discussed earlier. Culbertson was sprawled across the table, annotating the map, highlighting gullies and other features that could impede or conceal the advance, and Aquino and Prado were in detailed discussion of minimum supply levels. Even Murillo was drawn in, his keen bookkeeper's mind invaluable for reconciling movements and schedules.

By midnight Dawlish was again close to collapse, sustained only by willpower and quinine, but his plan – modified, fine-tuned and, he was forced to admit, improved – had been accepted. Murillo gravely recorded the fact in the Minute Book, requested them to sign it and the conference closed.

In three nights the final movement against La Reducción Nueva would commence.

*   *   *

Three days of preparation, of construction, of selection and overhaul of equipment.

Three days of ever-more detailed planning and scheduling, of labour, of vessel movements and loadings.

Three days of deception.

Culbertson's troopers reconnoitred again along the southward flank, taking care to be observed themselves, but not too obviously so. On the second day a plume of dust further south indicated a Reducción patrol's presence. They rode to head it off. There was a brief exchange of dismounted, long-distance fire across broken scrub before the enemy faded southwards into the Chaco. A single corpse marked the exchange.

The most visible activity was inland from the broken dam. On the far bank of the canal, on the side close to the Reducción, relays of conscripts were set to throwing up an earthwork as an obvious stepping-off point for a trench system to reach towards the grim fortifications. Behind it, two improvised pile-drivers rose and fell from shearlegs, their hammers raised and dropped by human muscle and their monotonous thumping beating out a rhythm for the efforts of the small swarm constructing the bridge across the canal. Others dragged timber cut further downstream from a barge moored nearby. Sunlight flashing on field-glass lenses within the embrasures of the Reducción bastions told of continuous observation of the activity. A few isolated shells exploded harmlessly in the open ground separating the forces, then ceased, taunting reminders that the approach from the canal to the sloped earthen walls could only be murderous. The conscripts worked in fear under the blows and abuse of the regular sergeants overseeing them, glancing uneasily at the threatening ramparts against which they believed they must soon be flung.

Tinsley's three Sevastopol mortars were installed in the abandoned fortification downstream of the dam. Three separate platforms, each of four layers of heavy timbers laid at right angles, had been dug into the open centre of the earthwork. A hastily-laid wooden track allowed the massive weapons to be dragged in from the river through a breach torn by the *Toad's* bombardment. By evening on the first day they squatted there like evil black slugs, rows of shells laid out to either side and their charges already stored in the fort's own bomb-proof magazine, which had survived intact the pummelling from the river. From a spindly-legged observation platform on one wall Tinsley, prismatic compass in hand, was calling back sighting instructions through a speaking trumpet to the crews straining to orient the mortars one at a time. During the night Grinling's barge would be towed upstream. At first light Tinsley would be giving yet more accurate orders from high overhead.

But the most urgent preparations were on the river. Vital though the *Toad's* role would be, she gave Dawlish least concern. Holmes saw to that. His efforts were matched by Purdon's on the *Montelindo*, which was ready for action on the second day, her hull patched and her flooded compartments pumped out and cleared of the pitiful human detritus that polluted them. Her armament's bagged charges were useless when recovered from the magazine. The soggy mess within was dumped overboard, but the bags themselves were dried on the sun-baked deck plates before being filled with coarse-grained powder from Tinsley's stores. The bursting shells could not be trusted after their immersion and the contents of some fifty of them were dug out laboriously and replaced with black powder. Their potency would be reduced, but there was no alternative.

Dawlish's heaviest task was downriver, among the cluster of paddle steamers and barges. Here he had no British officers or seamen to fall back upon, no shared assumptions of efficiency and discipline. The inflated pay offered the riverboat captains and crews might have seemed attractive back in Asunción but the battles of recent days and the melancholy procession of scorched and bloated corpses drifting downstream past their vessels had shaken their resolve. Suspicious and sullen, their response to every order was to explain how it could not be fulfilled, either at all, or not in time. And yet they were vital to the task ahead though none of them could be trusted until the last moment with details of what was demanded of them. Only the secondment of four of Aquino's junior officers, hard-faced regulars whose contempt for the rivermen was undisguised, gave Dawlish the means to enforce reluctant compliance with his orders for sorting barges into strings and for transferring essential supplies to the few paddlers he would employ.

A detailed inspection of the engines and boilers of all the steamers told Dawlish that only three offered the combination of speed and reliability that he demanded. The *Coimbra* was the largest. Freed from her towed barges she was good for five knots against the current. Culbertson's craft, the *Ipora*, was well maintained, since the Colonel himself had demanded it, and she alone would tow a barge in the coming operation, that same cavalry-landing barge with its raised ramps from which Dawlish had led the mad charge on Roybon's howitzers. The *Pilcomayo*, which normally towed Grinling's balloon barge, was the smallest, but the most manoeuvrable. Her handiness and slightly shallower draught could well prove useful. Murillo had reluctantly consented to the *Tacuari*, his own command vessel, being demoted to the task of towing Grinling's barge into position. Her machinery was the best maintained of all, but Dawlish knew that any attempt to wrest her from Murillo to risk in the approaching action would meet a closely-argued but determined refusal. The over-riding reason would not be mentioned – the requirement to provide a Director of the Hyperion Consortium with an escape route downriver in the event of outright failure.

The rapidly climbing sun was still burning mist off the river when the first mortar opened fire. Tinsley swung high overhead, accompanied by Grinling, a coir line running down from their basket to the fort below. The black spherical shell hurtled upwards, hung for a moment at its apogee, then began its screaming plunge towards the Reducción rampart directly ahead of the canal bridge. It fell a hundred yards beyond the embrasured wall, throwing up a geyser of earth and vegetation, spending itself harmlessly in unoccupied ground. A derisive cheer went up from the defenders, yet there was an uncertain tone to it. The balloon's presence gave the assurance that later shots would be more effective. Even now Tinsley's first correction was slipping down the line to the mortar crew. Ten minutes later an adjusted elevation dropped the second bomb directly behind the wall and twenty yards to the left of a gun position.

The first mortar fell silent as its consort was readied. It fired three times in just over an hour, and its third shot blasted a crater into the sloped wall. Then it too lapsed into silence and it was the third mortar's turn to speak. By midday all three weapons has registered on, or close to, the section of ramparts directly in line with the half-built canal bridge. The balloon was winched down and Tinsley, hot and sweating, but triumphant, thanked his crews.

260

"Eighty-three seconds, beam to beam," Purdon said, snapping his watch shut.

It was mid-afternoon and he and Dawlish were on the *Montelindo's* forecastle, watching the turret creep around. Invisible below, half-a-dozen crewmen were straining on a hand crank to rotate the iron drum within its bearings. Repairs to the hydraulic training engine had proved impossible in the time available.

"It will have to do, Mr.Purdon. Keep their strength up, though. We may need it tomorrow night! Don't stint their rations!"

Dawlish turned away, confident that the battered monitor could be relied on, gratified by the transformation that Purdon's discipline and care had achieved in her crew. Even entrapment at the broached dam under the guns of the *Torres* had failed to dent their new-won pride in the brutal efficiency with which they had dismembered the fortification and headed the upriver assault. Capitan Calles, now glimpsing glory for himself, had proved himself Purdon's willing supporter as long as the fictional relationship of captain and first officer was maintained. Even Cabrera, who had transferred so reluctantly from the *Tacuari* to pilot the monitor, seemed proud of having carried the vessel through such hazards. His greatest challenge was coming, Dawlish mused, and were he to know its nature he would turn tail for Asunción here and now.

Sheltered from the view of the Reducción's defenders by the river's gentle bend, the paddlers were busy until sundown, shifting barges upstream, shunting them into strings in predetermined orders, securing them by the southern bank, close to the improvised camp. Inevitably there was a grounding, necessitating the *Toad's* intervention to resolve it, and several minor collisions as well, but nothing serious enough to halt the momentum now gathering. Men swarmed over stores under the supervision of Aquino's officers, extricating specific items, setting others aside, shifting them across to other barges or steamers. Sergeants fussed over piles of weapons and ammunition, fixing allocations for each company. Heavier equipment remained on

261

the barges, or was shifted laboriously from one to another for purposes of concentration.

Yet despite these efforts, more conscripts were drafted to work on the bridge over the canal and on the earthwork beyond it. At intervals through the afternoon Tinsley's mortars flung a few more shells towards the Reducción's ramparts, still obviously ranging shots. At every discharge the sweating construction crews looked up from their toil and followed the screaming plunge of the shell until it blasted a pit in the sloped walls, or fell more harmlessly in open ground. There was fear in their eyes too, fuelled by the conviction that once this bridge was complete, and when the trench approach had crept close enough to those walls, these same mortars would be blasting the breach through which they must pour into the Reducción. The defenders that viewed them equally fearfully across the intervening ground knew it too. And they also were making their preparations.

It was all going exactly as Dawlish had conceived it in the balloon.

Night fell. The mortars fell silent but the sun's dying light revealed fresh crews relieving the labourers at the bridge, and the piledrivers' thumping reverberated through the darkness. Invisible in the scrub at the southern end of the inundation, Culbertson's troopers maintained a picket line, alert to any scouting probe from that direction. A reddish glow hung in the air above the dozens of cooking fires scattered among the hovels that constituted the Consortium's onshore camp. Regulars and conscripts alike ate and drank and slept, their curiosity about the barge and paddler movements dulled by fatigue. Guardboats moved over the water upstream with muffled oars, watchful for any other suicidal timberclad.

The *Toad* swung gently in midstream, her Gatlings manned. Dawlish slept in a net-shrouded hammock slung on her afterdeck, satisfied that the morrow would see the climax – for good or ill.

27

After three o'clock in the afternoon all steps were irrevocable. Only two outcomes were now possible – victory or rout.

Culbertson's mounted force showed itself conspicuously on the Reducción's southern flank during the early morning and then fell back quietly on the river, taking a roundabout course through the scrub. The troopers walked by their mounts, not just to rest them for the night ahead, but to avoid dust clouds that could betray their withdrawal. Their straggling column arrived at the camp before noon and settled down for a meal and brief rest. The *Ipora* already lay alongside, one ramp of its towed cavalry barge resting on the bank.

At the canal-bridge site the piledrivers thumped steadily and the construction parties shone with sweat as they hefted timbers and piled earth. Odd flashes from lenses on the ramparts beyond confirmed close observation of their progress. The Sevastopol mortars sent bombs plunging towards the fortifications several times during the morning, once blasting a satisfactory breach in direct line with the bridge. Within an hour a swarm of workers could be seen heaping a new rampart behind it until another expertly dropped projectile scattered them.

While the mortars erupted spasmodically Tinsley went aloft in the balloon, alone but for Grinling. The present fall of shot did not interest him, nor did their effect on their targets, engrossed as he was with compass and telescope. Ranges he could only judge by eye. He jotted down the figures in small, precise writing. As the balloon was winched down at midday he was already busy with triangulation calculations, his references to a small volume of mathematical tables impressing Grinling enormously. The work of retraining the squat monsters then commenced, dragging their massive bulk around to new headings. The third weapon blasted at the ramparts for the last time at two o'clock. An hour later it, like its fellows, would be lined up on a new and unseen target. Then three mortars waited silently. Their time was all but come.

The *Montelindo* manoeuvred clumsily in midstream, enough to confirm that she was mobile, though barely so, then moored. The *Toad* lay astern, now grimy, coal sacks piled high around her scanty superstructure. Most of her crew slept through the day, exhausted from the coaling and other preparations. Every packing in the hydraulic system had been replaced or retightened, every water and glycerine reservoir topped up. Powder and shot, with bursting shell to the fore, had been rearranged in the magazines. The Gatling platforms were stacked with the last reserves of ammunition – consumption so far had been huge. The engines and boilers had been checked, the bearings oiled, and all pronounced sound. The *Toad's* last refit in Sheerness, surplus to Royal Navy requirements or not, was still paying dividends.

But the greatest activity was at the camp. Here, shielded from Reducción view by distance and the river's bend, a snaking, straggling bridge of barges was being manoeuvred into position. Kedges dropped in midstream provided central anchorage and cables secured the craft at the extremities to trees on either shore. The barges ground and heaved against each other as two paddlers dragged and pushed them into position while windlasses improvised from logs and powered by muscle tautened the lashings. By early afternoon it was complete, a ramshackle floating causeway that bowed and rippled with the sluggish current, the gaps between its individual members precariously spanned by rough-hewn planks. The *Tacuari* was stationed on the downstream side, its wheel churning slowly to nudge it gently against the flow. It was crude and unstable and it would not resist the flood that even a short rainstorm would bring – but it was a bridge, a passage from the south bank to the north, across which almost the entire Consortium force could pass in under an hour. It needed only the briefest of useful lives and the sky was clear, with no threat of rain.

The majority of the forces slept fitfully and uncomfortably through the day in their improvised shelters. When awake they watched the floating bridge's growth with bewildered foreboding, then lapsed back into passive stupor until roused and mustered in mid-afternoon for the last distribution of rations and ammunition. A cordon of Aquino's regulars, hard-eyed and contemptuous, surrounded the camp, weapons ready, watchful for attempts by unwilling conscripts to slip away into the scrub. A full company of regulars already guarded the northern bridgehead and a second had fanned out into the scrub beyond, alert for Reducción scouts that never appeared.

And at three o'clock, with scarcely four hours of daylight remaining, the balloon rose.

Dawlish stepped into the basket beside Tinsley, nodded to the winch crew and felt the ground fall away. They rose sluggishly. The envelope was wrinkled, for much of the hydrogen had leaked. The last of the acid had been used and this would be the final ascent. Around four hundred feet the balloon wallowed to a standstill, but it was high enough for their purposes. Their gaze was fixed on the river's bend, a silver snake in the westering sun, flanked by the mounds of the two great riverside fortifications, the Reducción's last and strongest bastions.

"The southerly worries me the more," Dawlish steadied his glass against one of the basket's suspension ropes. "The heavier armament's there."

His disc of vision showed the fort's three twenty-pounders nestling in deep embrasures. They were positioned in a sloping wall that inclined at some forty-five degrees to the river's axis so that with traversing they could dominate any target from the moment it rounded the bend until it passed level with the fort itself. They were well spaced – no direct hit would take out more than one. Two smaller weapons were mounted in the wall paralleling the river, probably twelve-pounders, sited so as to fire broadside into any vessel that had survived destruction by their larger brethren.

"I've assigned two of the mortars to it, Commander," Tinsley said, "but at this range the precision will be low. We'll hit the fort once we've got the range, but it will be a matter of luck whether we hit the guns individually."

Dawlish shrugged. "It's enough if you spoil their aim." Yet the thought of the *Toad* scuttling towards and past those gaping muzzles chilled him. He shifted his focus to the fort on the northern shore. It was almost a twin of the other, though with one twenty-pounder fewer. The third Sevastopol survivor was dedicated to it.

"Satisfied, Commander?" There was suppressed excitement in Tinsley's voice.

Dawlish glanced back downriver. At the southern bridgehead Culbertson's troopers were strung out in lines, riders standing by their horses, ready to cross. Beyond them the infantry was being mustered by company into ragged black rectangles. The *Ipora* was anchored upstream of the bridge, the drawbridge ramps raised to vertical on either flank of the barge swinging astern of her. Its decks were packed, not with Culbertson's cavalry, but with most of the Consortium's artillery. The ten-pounders and their limbers were there, jammed wheel to wheel, and even Roybon's captured howitzers. Their mules were lodged beneath the palm thatching that had previously sheltered the Guardia's horses. The *Coimbra* and the *Pilcomayo* paddlers were also moored in midstream, below the *Toad* and *Montelindo*. They too were loaded.

"Satisfied?" Dawlish said. "As I can ever be. Let's commence, Major Tinsley."

Less than a minute separated the signal Tinsley waved down by green flag and the report of the first mortar. Dawlish forced himself not to look down towards the massive weapon and he fixed his gaze instead on the southern fort. He heard Tinsley say urgently "There it is!" as the sphere hung visible as a stationary dot at its apogee. Then it was dropping, one second, two, three... and there was the impact!

A geyser of earth and fire and shattered vegetation spouted skywards two hundred yards short of the fortification and a fraction to the right. Tinsley pushed a scribbled correction into a container and dropped it down the communication line to the mortar crew below. Dawlish swung his glass towards the earthwork and saw figures scurrying in alarm towards the nearer wall, gesticulating towards the drifting column of dust and smoke. Surprise had been total – and now it remained to be seen how quickly the fort's defenders could recover their wits and maintain their nerve under repeated pounding.

The second mortar was already prepared for firing. Correcting the lay and elevation was the work of six minutes before it too was hurling its missile skywards. The line of fire was exact now, but the range slightly too great, for the shell dropped just beyond the fort into the river, throwing up a muddy plume.

"Bracketed," Tinsley muttered, scribbling a correction.

Now the turn of the first mortar again, its aim and elevation adjusted. The fall of its shot was almost perfect. It pounded into the furthest wall of the fort, scooping a crater and scything debris and iron fragments across the open interior and towards the rear of the wall across from it. The figures atop that wall were scrambling for cover now, leaving several of their number behind like discarded toys. They scurried for cover, some to crouch in the meagre protection close to their guns, others towards what might have been termed the bombproof shelters. That description, Dawlish knew, was an overstatement when it referred to thirteen-inch projectiles plunging from fifteen hundred feet towards excavations roofed with logs and earth.

Five minutes later and the second mortar was again ready. There was little sign of life in the fort as the missile destined for it blasted skywards, for the defenders had taken what cover they could. This time the shell did not explode on impact, but the crater it pounded was in one corner of the fort's interior.

"A dud fuse," Tinsley said. "You can expect it. One in six, maybe one in eight if we're lucky."

"And you can keep dropping shells like that?" Dawlish did not need to add that his own life depended upon it.

"Just as we agreed, Commander. One every fifteen minutes initially and one every five, or less, once your vessels disappear around the bend."

And there would be no way of knowing the damage being inflicted once the balloon had been hauled down. As the unprotected *Toad* and the other vessels steamed out of cover and towards the forts Dawlish would not know whether the mortars would have succeeded in eliminating any or all of the twenty-pounders, or whether their crews had been so demoralised by the shelling as to desert their weapons. He felt fear growing in him, that familiar gnawing hollowness in his stomach that always came before action. He tried to ignore it, knowing that only activity could stop it mastering him.

"I think the Northern twin demands your attention, Major," he said, focussing his glass its brown walls and gaping embrasures.

With only one mortar dedicated, it took longer before range and aim corrections brought the second fortification under fire. By the time that three shells had impacted on or close to it, one on the rear wall, the others ahead and beyond the earthwork, though close enough to drive the defenders into shelter, Dawlish was reasonably satisfied that Tinsley's mortars could make the forts all but untenable in the hours ahead. He took one last look towards them and steeled himself to the knowledge that in less than three hours he would run the *Toad* between them. Only then, as he stood exposed on the gunboat's open bridge, would he know whether the ancient Russian weapons would have triumphed.

"Let's go down, Major," he said quietly. "I'm casting off in an hour."

Darkness was less than two hours away as the balloon descended. There was an awkward moment as they clambered from the basket. As Dawlish turned to go Tinsley extended his hand hesitantly.

"We may not always have seen eye to eye, Commander." He spoke with obvious embarrassment. "But you are a courageous man, Sir, and you can rely on me tonight. I will be praying for you as we go about our work. God bless you, Commander Dawlish."

Dawlish, touched, recognised a moment such as he had seen and experienced before, one of men in the imminent presence of death laying aside pettiness and spite. He grasped the proffered hand and shook it in both of his. "And you also, Major. I've no hesitation in entrusting my men's life, and my own, to your cover." He felt a surge of regret that he had not made more of an effort to understand and like this stiff, pompous, and yet decent, man. He turned away quickly before Tinsley saw his emotion.

The mortars fired in slow succession as he hurried back to the riverbank, their effect unseen and unknowable now. Downstream the crossing had commenced and he found Culbertson and Aquino by the bridge, agreeing final arrangements.

"I'll see you on the riverbank by two o'clock latest, Commander Nick," Culbertson said as he heaved himself into his saddle, "Three miles upstream o' the Puerto's jetties." For a heavy man he was surprisingly limber and his flabby figure carried some last trace of that jaunty assurance that had sustained the Southern Confederacy through four desperate years. He leaned down and grasped Dawlish's hand. "An' if I don't see you there, why, I reckon it'll be in Hell instead." He grinned, spurred his mount and trotted it across the flexing planks, the only man to cross the river on horseback, somehow communicating his confidence to his unblinkered and surefooted animal.

Culbertson's troopers followed, leading their blindfolded mounts across the rippling causeway, urging the frightened animals across the improvised gangways that linked the barges. Most went quietly but a few, terrified and quivering, plunged and whinnied before they were quietened so that the narrow column alternately bunched and straggled. At last they were across to the northern bank, a hundred and eighty of them, fodder slung in bags before their saddles, bedding rolls behind, each man carrying carbine, sabre and eighty rounds of ammunition.

This was the start of the great outflanking movement that would place the Consortium forces upstream of the Puerto Plutarcho. It would cut them off from their line of communication with Asunción and, unless Dawlish could pass sufficient transport steamers upstream past the defences, it would strand them on the opposite bank from the enemy's main force. Should Tinsley's mortars not silence or disable the forts, should Dawlish's vessels fail to pass them, then their situation would be hopeless.

It was a gamble that broke all principles of military prudence and challenged all precedents but one, Grant's audacious right hook around the Vicksburg defences in 1863. If what had succeeded with vastly superior forces on the Mississippi worked here on the San Joaquin then it would allow the Consortium forces to fight their way into the Reducción from the unfortified West.

Culbertson's force formed up quickly on the northern bank in four separate columns, the animals quiet again when they felt earth beneath their hooves. The baked Chaco was reddening as the sun fell yet further and the horsemen moved into it at a steady walk between the patches of scrub, heading northwards first. At nightfall they would be turning to the west in the great sweep that would carry them around the Reducción's north-bank fortifications and then south-westwards towards the river again. Individual scouts, Guardia troopers who had known this terrain intimately before El Pobre's revolt, had stealthily traversed much of the route earlier in the day and had found it unopposed.

The first columns of infantry now filed across the floating causeway, led by two regular companies. They followed the cavalry into the darkening scrub. Two mule-drawn six-pounders accompanied them, puny weapons in themselves, but capable enough of deterring any tentative Reducción investigation with a few blasts of canister into the darkness. Several more conscript companies followed, then regulars again. The bridge flexed and bowed with the current and with the varying, shifting, load but the *Tacuari* sternwheeler at midstream held it steady with its slowly beating paddle.

The sun's disappearance as a bloody sphere was an omen that depressed the more superstitious, but there was moonlight enough afterwards for the crossing to proceed unhindered. Units judged either more reliable or less so alternated. Among the conscripts there was a sufficient leavening of professional officers and sergeants to enforce quiet and discipline by any means necessary. Men stumbled and cursed as they negotiated the bridge, and one wretch fell and was lost, howling, in the dark waters but overall the crossing northwards went smoothly. The steady crash of Tinsley's mortars set a rhythm for the march into the scrub and duller explosions reverberated from the direction of the riverside-forts. Well before eight o'clock the last of the outflanking forces had passed into the darkness of the northern shore and the only Consortium ground unit left on the southern bank was the single lonely half-company left to protect Tinsley's mortars.

Dawlish was only remotely conscious of the activity on the bridge as the *Toad's* idle screws shifted to quarter revolutions. He scanned the squat gunboat as it pushed forward into the current, the windlass rattling as the anchor was weighed. The Armstrong was invisible under its covers, primed and loaded with bursting shell, and around it he could imagine the crew sweating in their assigned positions. The coal barge had been left behind and the usually immaculately holystoned deck was stacked with sacks which would serve as protection before the furnaces devoured them. They were piled two and three thick against the deckhouse and in a low palisade around the navigation bridge. The Gatling crews were half-obscured by the sandbags, topped with open ammunition boxes, that surrounded them to waist height. All ports and openings had been screened with blankets to shroud the vessel in darkness. It was already like a Turkish bath in the boiler and engine-rooms.

"Steady at quarter revolutions until we have the *Montelindo* and paddlers under way," Dawlish said quietly. Holmes nodded. Dawlish could sense the younger man's controlled fear, and hoped that his own was not as obvious. Egdean was at the helm, steady as ever.

"The *Montelindo's* making heavy going of it," Holmes said. The battered monitor was wallowing forward, a dark mass that was almost awash. Her panting engine was labouring and she was making less than three knots against the current. Dawlish had visited her earlier and knew that little more than Purdon's drive was keeping the injured craft and her half-trained crew in action. A figure was perched atop the conning-tower, Purdon himself, who would keep that position until danger forced him below to the confined view through the narrow vision-slits. The *Ipora* was doing better and though the ramp-barge she towed was fully laden, her engines were sound and she as well capable of a sustained five knots upstream. For now she kept station a hundred yards astern of the *Montelindo*. Sandbags and firewood were stacked against her wheelhouse and boiler-casing, protection ineffective against anything but small-arms fire. A single round from the twenty-pounders nestling in the upstream forts that were even now under mortar-bombardment would be enough to disembowel the flimsy paddler, or to wreak devastation on the artillery and mules crowded on the barge swinging astern. The artillery crews themselves were divided between steamer and barge, some quietening the animals, others mingled with the company of regulars that crouched, rifles ready, behind whatever scanty shelter the *Ipora's* upperworks offered. The two other steamers followed, each laden with regulars and with similarly meagre protection, neither with anything under tow.

The five vessels moved upstream towards the bend that hid the forts, the *Toad* leading, followed by the straining *Montelindo*, the *Ipora* and the other paddlers thrashing in the rear. To port a mortar's flaming breath briefly silhouetted the sheltering earthwork with a ghastly scarlet light. Tinsley was firing blind and Dawlish forced from his mind the knowledge that variations of temperature, wind and charge-quality might have shifted the point of impact of the shells by a substantial margin from the vicinity of the forts. A red glow coloured the sky in the west – a hopeful sign that something was burning at the forts, though how much damage was done would remain a mystery until they came in direct view.

He glanced astern. Astern of the vessels in his wake the floating bridge was like a solid barrier across the river. There was no sign of activity there now and Culbertson's and Aquino's forces had disappeared into the darkness of the Chaco. Below the bridge, he reflected with a stab of bitterness, Murillo would be sitting snug on the *Tacuari*, perhaps recording this critical moment in his beloved minute book, ready to drop downstream to safety at the first news of failure.

The *Montelindo* was setting the pace, and it was too slow for comfort. There was no help for it until the bend was reached. Dawlish chewed on an unlit cheroot and Holmes' fingers drummed a nervous tattoo on the telegraph pedestal. A metallic whirr sounded as a gunner spun his fasces of Gatling barrels. The urge to signal for higher revolutions was almost irresistible. The capsized wreck of the *Torres* slipped past to starboard, an arrowhead of ripples streaming from the rudder that still pierced the surface. The bend was only minutes away. Another mortar report, and another in quick succession. It was almost time for Tinsley's crews to intensify their rate of fire.

Now Egdean was sweeping the *Toad* into the bend in a smooth arc. The great expanse of moonlit water opened before them and then – there they were! Dawlish's gaze was riveted on the great dark, smoke and flame-enveloped humps of the twin forts more than a mile ahead. Fire raged inside the northern earthwork, tingeing the billowing clouds above with flickering red and casting a sinister light on the apparently intact installation on the opposite bank.

"Tinsley did it by God!" Dawlish exclaimed. "He hit a magazine!"

As the *Toad* forged onwards the three unseen mortars astern roared in quick succession. Somewhere overhead the bombs screamed towards the forts. They erupted in crimson-shot flashes that were quickly obscured by great gouts of soil and dust rising from their craters. Two fell on the southern bank, one to the north, and, though it was difficult to judge, none appeared to have hit either fort. It hardly mattered at this stage, Dawlish reassured himself, though he was trembling, for the effect of three hours of this on the semi-trained defenders must have been nerve shattering. The northern fort looked unoccupied, even untenable, but it was impossible to judge what damage its counterpart opposite had sustained.

The *Montelindo* had rounded the bend now and the *Ipora* was swinging into view in her wake. A hush had fallen over the river as the reverberations of the explosions rolled over the Chaco and died away. This was the moment of maximum danger, when the *Toad* and *Ipora* were at the mercy of any weapons still operative in the forts. From this point on the *Montelindo* would have to take her chances alone.

"Signal full revolutions," Dawlish said, moving to the rear of the bridge. There he twice raised and lowered the shutter of the aft-facing signal lamp. The vessels astern would know that the *Toad* was moving to maximum speed and starting her run. The *Montelindo's* turret began to grind painfully around to line up on one of the forts – Purdon had disappeared below and Dawlish hoped that he had seen enough to select the southern fort as his target. The three paddle steamers would shelter astern of the *Montelindo* until the moment when it seemed best for them to surge at full speed in the *Toad's* wake. Three of Aquino's most trusted lieutenants stood by each of the paddlers' masters, their task to ensure, at gunpoint if necessary, that there would be no hesitation.

"Full revolutions." Holmes pushed the telegraphs forward. The screws thrashed to maximum and the gunboat lunged forward. As she did, the darkness astern was lit by three closely successive flashes as the mortars spoke again. Their crashes rolled upriver seconds later but, while their bombs still hung in the air, the inclined face of the southern earthwork was illuminated by a single stab of flame. Yellow light washed over the *Toad*, and Dawlish grasped the rail, transfixed, knowing that at least one weapon was still in action in that fort ahead. Time stood still in the realisation that there was no option but to forge on regardless and there was no comfort in the shrill whine to starboard that told of the round missing the *Toad* by feet only. The range was shortening and if Roybon had a hand in it then the next round might smash down the gunboat's axis.

The mortar bombs fell. The first dropped inside the northern fort, adding to the inferno now clearly visible through the embrasures, but the second was lost somewhere beyond the forts. The third impacted short of the southern earthwork, its flash exposing the cratered face and a huge gap where one of the three twenty-pounders had been mounted. Rising billows of debris obscured the wall just as another tongue of flame spat from an embrasure – a second twenty-pounder was also still in action, for the interval since the last round was too short for a single weapon to have reloaded and fired. A plume of spray ran towards the advancing *Toad* as the shell skipped and leaped downriver. Egdean threw the helm over instinctively, but it was not that which saved the gunboat, for the bows had hardly started to swing, but rather the fractional aiming error that sent the projectile skimming past the starboard flank, showering the *Toad* with a fine rain. The vessel lurched back into midstream and there was no option but to plough on towards the deadly embrasures

One glance astern told Dawlish that the *Toad* was masking the *Montelindo's* aim. It would be minutes yet before a sufficient gap opened to allow the monitor to fire. In the battered but deadly southern earthwork the smoke-grimed gunners would have run in their pieces and be even now sponging and reloading. The next rounds might well rake the Toad from end to end. There was only one alternative. "The Armstrong!" he yelled and Holmes, as if reading his thoughts, was already reaching for the indicator arm.

The massive weapon heaved up from its metal pit as the southern earthwork opened fire again – but high, so that the round screamed harmlessly overhead and to starboard.

"Sixteen hundred yards!" Dawlish shouted. Holmes pushed the indicator over and an eternity later the barrel hissed to elevation. The gun captain's arm rose – all ready.

There was no time for juggling with the engines, for the second twenty-pounder must imminently be ready to fire. Egdean swung the helm at Holmes' command and the *Toad's* bows began to creep to port. Then, judging his moment with an instinct honed in the recent day's actions, Holmes pounded the firing button. The Armstrong belched flame and shell. Dazzled, throwing one arm across his face against the flash, deafened by the sound washing aft, Egdean swung the gunboat back towards midstream.

The shell, a conically-tipped cylinder of forged steel, filled with two hundred and twenty pounds of powder, screamed across the moonlit waters, never reaching a height of more than a hundred feet, then dropped slightly and punched into the earthwork's inclined face. It hit five yards to the right of the twenty-pounder about to fire, that nearest the river, and it burrowed a dozen feet into the packed soil before its impact fuse activated the main charge. The whole sloped wall lifted, almost intact, as a fiery sphere erupted beneath it. A searing hail of earth, stones and scorching metal fragments lashed across the gun and its crew, tumbling it from its mounting and carrying gouts of tortured flesh and rags of clothing with it. Only the internal subdivision of the fort saved the second remaining weapon, an inclined sheltering wall deflecting the deadly shower over its stunned crew.

But on the *Toad* they knew only that there had been a hit, square and accurate, for all the improvisation of the aim. The Armstrong had fallen again beneath the deck and the well-practised reloading drill was in progress. The gunboat forged ahead towards the twin forts, the northerly obviously abandoned to the blaze within, the southerly still obscured by a pall of flame-illuminated smoke. From astern the mortars rippled into life again, three bombs less than a minute apart, one falling spectacularly but unnecessarily into the blazing northern fort and the others dropping short again before the tortured earthwork to the south.

"Another shot, Sir?" Holmes called but Dawlish shook his head – the rapidity of the *Toad's* advance while the fort's gunners were distracted was now her best defence, that, and the two one-hundred and ten pounders carried by the *Montelindo*. The *Toad's* rush upstream had unmasked the monitor, and now it added its fury to the fort's agony. Smoke engulfed the *Montelindo's* turret as her twin cannons' shells sped upriver. They screamed to port of the *Toad*, one exploding on the riverbank two hundred yards ahead but the other, skimming low, smashing into the earthwork's glacis. It failed to explode but it rained earth and rubble on the hapless defenders. The *Montelindo*, almost stalled by the recoil of its weapons, lurched forward slowly to resume her wallowing advance.

The gamble was paying off. "Steady as she goes," Dawlish breathed to Egdean, then reached for the signal lamp and raised and lowered the shutter four times. A winking light acknowledged his instruction from the *Ipora's* wheelhouse. The sternwheeler accelerated, beating upstream to starboard of the labouring *Montelindo*, passing her just as her weapons erupted again. The shells' fiery impacts were close enough to the fort's scarred walls to deter return fire.

Dawlish spat out the unlit cigar that he had chewed to a pulp, reached to a breast pocket, withdrew another, lit it. The pinprick of light would make no difference now. In the lucifer's flare he saw that Egdean's hands had relaxed their white-knuckled grasp on the wheel.

Holmes caught his eye, and there was a hint of pleading in his voice. "We're going to make it, Sir, aren't we?"

"No doubt of it, Mr. Holmes!" Dawlish realised that, despite the hell around him, he was enjoying himself. "Nothing can stop us now!"

28

The *Toad*, followed closely now by the *Ipora* and her barge, ploughed into the blaze-reflecting waters between the flanking earthworks. To the north was a furnace of flame and irregular explosions as the shattered magazine burned itself out. There was no sign of human movement but in hideously backlit embrasures the outlines of tumbled artillery pieces told of havoc. With dreadful precision, and adding uselessly to the devastation, Tinsley still dropped shells into or around the blazing ruin at close to five-minute intervals. On the southern bank there was no blaze but the flickering scarlet light reflected from the rolling clouds of smoke overhead revealed how it had been battered, and continued to be, by the combined fire from the river and from the mortars. The vessels, bathed in crimson, forged on in line astern, their deafened crews astounded that they still lived.

Now the *Toad* was level with the landward wall of the southern fort, safe from any weapon on it still capable of fire. Dawlish's gaze was fixed on the wall running parallel to the river. The two embrasures there were deeply shadowed, but not enough to hide movement there. For all the bombardment's fury there could still be weapons nestling there, lighter than a twenty-pounder for certain, but enough to rake the *Toad* as she passed broadside. It was a hazard he had foreseen and feared, and the Gatling crews had been well alerted to it before departure. Now was their moment.

"Gatlings!" Dawlish yelled. "Embrasures to port! Keep firing until we've passed!"

High in their mountings the gunners swung their weapons over, adjusted their aims, and cranked the firing handles forward. The six-barrelled stacks stuttered into life, showering a lead into the nearer gap. As the *Toad* thrust forward the full depth of the embrasure was revealed and in the flickering light a single cannon was discernible. It remained mute and the heaps around it might have been sandbags or bodies.

"Shift your fire!" Dawlish shouted but the gunners were fractionally ahead of him, interrupting their fire momentarily to swing their weapons towards the upstream embrasure. Again the spinning barrels hammered, seeking, then finding the gap that widened steadily as the *Toad* moved closer, yet still not near enough for the lethal torrent to penetrate to the interior, so that it buried itself in the upstream wall.

The Reducción gunner, who had stood so resolutely by his piece through the night's bombardment, now panicked and jerked his firing lanyard. Flame and smoke rolled from the embrasure with an ear-splitting report and a solid twelve-pound ball tore through the *Toad's* raised breastwork on the port side, just aft of the Armstrong mounting. Deflected slightly by the impact, it ripped across the deck planking and shattered against a starboard mooring bit. Hot fragments clattered across the deck and arced past the Gatling platforms, and over the bridge. The multiple barrels had fallen silent in the shock of the report but as the *Toad* carried them dead level with the smoking embrasure, Hilliard, the port gunner, ground his weapon into life again. A metallic spray hosed into the flame-illuminated recess and as the gunboat passed, and as the Gatlings fell silent again, Dawlish had a brief glimpse of an upward-canted barrel, the wooden carriage shattered under the brief pounding.

"Well done lads!" he called. The loaders were already transferring handfuls of rounds into the Broadwell feed-hoppers from the open boxes around them.

And now there was open river ahead, a stretch of moonlit water eighty to a hundred yards wide that ran straight for a mile or more before being lost in the next bend to the south that hid Puerto Plutarcho itself. Dark banks, open for the most part, here and there dotted with scrub, lay to either side. Dawlish glanced astern – the *Ipora* was thrashing unscathed between the now impotent forts. Astern of her, five hundred yards or more, the *Montelindo* was still plodding resolutely onwards. A flash in the eastern sky, followed rapidly by two more, suddenly reminded Dawlish that Tinsley's mortars were still in action.

"The whistle!" he ordered. "A long blast."

Holmes jerked the braided line to the steam-whistle on the port funnel and it howled the ear-piercing message downriver that the mortars' fire on the forts was no longer needed. Their exhausted crews could now drag them round to hurl shells as deeply as possible behind the Reducción's defensive walls, dropping them randomly to sow confusion and divert attention from the threat that would materialise from the west.

"We made it, Sir! Just as you promised!" Holmes was grinning like a madman.

Dawlish, deafened but elated, shouted "Half Revolutions," and had to yell again before Holmes heard him. "Slow now, keep in midstream."

Cold reason was reasserting itself after the recent frenzy and he knew that an unfamiliar sandbank or a submerged snag could be no less deadly to the small flotilla than the forts themselves. Earlier that day he and Holmes had quizzed every paddler's master who had prior knowledge of this stretch of river, but the shimmering waters that swirled in gentle whorls disguised all too well the hazards they had been warned of. Darkness lay now on either side and somewhere to starboard, five or six miles to the north, Culbertson's troopers would be looping westwards around the scanty Reducción defences there and Aquino's infantry would be plodding in their rear.

There was a brief period of near-silence while the mortars were being realigned, a hush emphasised by the even panting of steam engines, the slow thrash of paddle wheels and the occasional dull thump of some last munitions exploding in the burning fort astern. But there were no sharper reports of gunfire from the Chaco to starboard, no sound of musketry rolling across the parched scrub in the night-air, no signal that the outflanking movement had yet been detected.

In minutes now they would sweep into the bend that would carry them to Puerto Plutarcho itself. Dawlish could sense the increased tension as the *Toad* forged towards the still-unseen goal that had drawn him and so many others across half the globe. Beside him Egdean was scanning the moonlit waters' shifting surface intently, the wheel slipping constantly through his hands as he avoided some real or imagined hazard. On their exposed perches the Gatling crews were nervously watching for any sign of movement on the banks, sometimes spinning their barrels to ward off the nightmare of a jam when they would be most needed. Ahead, crouched in their allotted positions around the huge bottle-shaped weapon they served like some industrial-age Moloch, the Armstrong's half-deafened crew were hidden from sight in their metal chamber, tensely waiting for the insistent ringing of the electric bell that would send the whole mounting scissoring upwards. Below, aft, confined with the unprotected boilers that would condemn them to a scalding, agonised death if breached, the sweat-bathed complement there would be blocking their minds to all but the feeding of the furnaces, the maintenance of pressure and the smooth beat of their engines, alert for the urgent chime of the telegraph demanding changed revolutions. Knowing nothing of their surroundings when maelstroms of gunfire and explosion engulfed the small vessel, their courage, Dawlish knew, was perhaps the greatest of all.

"The *Montelindo's* catching up, Commander," Holmes said. As the other vessels had slowed, the crawling monitor had come close astern of the *Ipora's* towed barge.

"That's good," Dawlish answered. It was better than he could have hoped. The closer the vessels were bunched in the coming minutes, the better. "Adjust speed as you see fit to shorten separation."

"No sign yet of ..." But Holmes words were lost in a rattle of rifle-fire to port, short tongues of flame stabbing in the darkness.

"Port Gatling!" Dawlish yelled, fighting down his urge to cower as something thudded into the signal mast. In the instant before Hilliard's weapon stammered into action there was the sound of further rounds screaming close by and of the high "ping" of ricochets off hard metal. The Gatling paused, shifting aim, then opened briefly again. When it fell silent there was no further reply from landwards. Somewhere in the brush frightened men were cowering, some grasping in incomprehension at bone-shattering wounds in the shock-dulled instant before their agony began, some turning over in horror comrades already torn and lifeless, others scampering rearwards in terror through the dark thickets.

"Cease Firing!" The *Toad* was in the bend and the sweep of river was opening up again.

There, a mile ahead on the southern bank, was the irregular jumble of machinery, warehouses and repair sheds that marked the core of Puerto Plutarcho, the citadel of industrial and commercial power that

Hyperion greed and enterprise had planted in the heart of a distant continent.

There, familiar from such-often studied maps, was the dark finger of the loading jetty jutting out from the wharves and the high, moonlit corrugated roofs of the workshops that El Pobre and his cohorts had converted into such an effective arsenal.

There were the high brick chimneys, smoke-wreathed even now as the furnaces beneath powered the great static engines driving the shafting and belting and lathes and millers and drills that sustained La Reducción Nueva's power to resist. These were the facilities that Murillo had been so insistent about in his last interview with Dawlish before departure.

"They represent an investment of six hundred and fifty thousand pounds, Commander," he had said, his tone close to reverence. "They cannot be damaged! Not the least merit of your outflanking proposal is that it will most probably resolve the issue well to the west of our principal investments."

Extending beyond the untidy cluster of taller industrial buildings were the lower profiles of the settlement's dwellings, the irregular scatter of the adobe and thatch huts that housed most of La Reducción's population, and, beyond them, the regular grid of metal-roofed bungalows that had lodged Hyperion's senior staff. Lights showed against the dark mass of the buildings, not only winking, static lights marking open windows and doors but frantically bobbing lights that showed that forces were being mobilised and that confused and frightened units were blundering into each other in the half-darkness.

The sky flashed crimson to the southeast. Seconds later a crash rolling across the Chaco told that one of Tinsley's Sevastopol mortars was back in action. As its projectile exploded somewhere inside the Reducción's eastern ramparts the second, and then the third weapon broke silence. And still there was no indication of any engagement on the northern bank. With luck the *Toad's* arrival would be interpreted as a diversion and the reserves being mobilised in the settlement would be moving towards the threat to the east where the riverine forts had fallen and the main defences were under renewed bombardment. The scattered group of buildings on the northern shore, mainly shacks clustered around the stockyards there, showed no significant signs of life.

The *Toad* was in the straight now, with the *Ipora*, *Coimbra* and *Pilcomayo* in her wake, and the *Montelindo* was lurching into view around the bend. Ahead, the jetty was clearer now in the moonlight and…

Was that movement ahead?

Some bulky object was detaching itself from the dark mass of the buildings' silhouettes and moving out into midstream. Then a flash to port, closer, from inland, somewhere short of the first houses and then the bark of an artillery piece, a six or nine-pounder, a light weapon, but potentially deadly for the *Toad*. There was the sound of an impact ahead and to port, a thud, no explosion, solid shot impacting on the opposite bank. The unseen weapon, wherever it was, had neither the range nor the bearing, but the next round might be luckier.

Dawlish's mind was as yet still cold and analytical. The minutes ahead might give him no further opportunity to weigh chances. That single artillery piece was a distraction, a nuisance to be endured and left to the supporting monitor. Far more ominous was that slowly moving bulk up ahead, and he wanted to close with it quickly.

"Three quarters revolutions, Mr. Holmes," he said, reaching for the whistle lanyard. Three short blasts were the pre-arranged signal for the *Montelindo* to bring the settlement under fire, and he hoped that Purdon had already got a rough bearing on that solitary artillery shot – and there it was again, a stab of flame in the darkness. The shot's fall was unseen, but clear of the now accelerating *Toad*, and of the *Ipora*, speeding up in her wake.

Ahead a thread of silvery water separated the slowly moving dark shape from the jetty's end.

"Another timberclad!" Holmes exclaimed. "A mate of the one we saw off before! We'll gut her the same way, Sir!"

Moonlight and the blood-red light reflected from the burning fort far astern revealed the vessel for what it was, a low pontoon, almost awash, with a truncated pyramid rising above it. It must be pierced with ports for one or more weapons, but they were invisible as yet.

"Range, Mr. Holmes?"

"Eleven hundred, Sir, and closing."

Astern the *Montelindo's* turret weapons smashed twin projectiles in the general direction of the artillery position. One hit fractionally ahead of the other, and a hundred yards shorter and both threw up harmless but impressive fountains of flame-streaked earth. This must have been close enough to have panicked the Reducción gunners, for no further artillery-fire came from the southern bank. The *Montelindo's* next broadside, delivered minutes later when she was drawing level with the first of the housing, was directed blindly on thousand-yard ranging. The shells came skidding among the wretched huts, shearing through adobe and logs before wreaking fiery and splinter-scything havoc among the close-packed occupants. Inside the blistered turret the gunners sponged and rammed, readying for the next volley while Purdon's instructions for retraining came echoing down the voice-pipe from the conning tower. There was no specific target, only the mass of hitherto unthreatened housing occupied by the Reducción's defenders and their dependents. The objectives were panic, terror and confusion pure and simple.

Dawlish ignored the *Montelindo's* random slaughter. The timberclad, the last pathetic manifestation of El Pobre's riverine power – pitiful, yet dangerous in its desperation – locked his attention. It was moving slowly downriver, solidly in midstream, its intent all too apparent.

"He's a cold-blooded scoundrel." Dawlish was unable to keep the admiration from his voice. "He'll either stop us, or he'll go down blocking the channel."

"The Armstrong, Sir?" Homes asked. "The range is about nine hundred. I'll guarantee a hit in another two minutes. Shall I raise it?"

Dawlish shook his head, absorbed in the decision. A single Armstrong round could rake the makeshift enemy stem to stern, neutralising it as a threat but running the risk of sinking it in midstream. There was no option but to close – and in the long minutes of the approach to expose the *Toad* to whatever armament the timberclad carried. The image of Pannetier, defeated but defiant, shaking his fist from the *Torres'* sinking hulk, flashed across his memory and he regretted his magnanimity in refraining from finishing him in a hail of Gatling fire. He did not doubt now that the same sharp, fiery intelligence had staked his last, and his all, on the timberclad's present stand.

"Full revolutions, Mr. Holmes," he called. "And weave from side to side as much as you dare as we run upstream. We're going to have to withstand fire."

"But the Armstrong?" Holmes strove to disguise his fear.

"Full revolutions, I said, Mr. Holmes." Nestled in its iron pit, the great weapon would be marginally less exposed.

The screws bit. The *Toad* surged forward, Egdean throwing the helm now to one side, now to the other, so that her forward motion was a series of long zig-zags that carried the bows as close as he dared to one bank before turning violently and heading for the opposite. There was small arms fire now from the banks, a low ripple at first, then a growing rattle as unorganised groups of Reducción defenders rushed towards the river. Somewhere astern the *Montelindo* was in action again, her guns hurling indiscriminate death into the squalid hutments. Thatch roofs were blazing from the fall of its earlier shot and casting an increasingly bloody hue over the river.

Flame and smoke engulfed the timberclad's bow. The *Toad* had just turned and was heading towards midstream. Egdean swung the helm instinctively to bring the gunboat head-on to its attacker but the shell was already whipping harmlessly past her bows. Rushing on, it sheared harmlessly past the *Ipora* so closely that its wind tore at the troops on the galleries.

"Twenty-pounder! They take…" Holmes yelled, then stiffened, and gasped. He crouched over the telegraph, his face drawn, teeth gritted. "God!" he gasped. "God, My Saviour, give me strength!"

"You're hit," Dawlish said. Another rifle round slapped into the deck close by and another, and yet another, thumped into the coal sacks stacked around the navigation bridge. "I'll support you," he said but Holmes gestured him away.

"It's nothing, Sir," he gasped, "A scratch." His face was blanched and he somehow pulled himself erect to brace himself against the gunboat's next swerve.

"Gatlings!" Dawlish shouted. "To port! Short bursts!"

The barrels spun again, firing blind towards whatever imagined movement might imply the presence of the unseen riflemen. Ahead the smoke was clearing from the timberclad's bows and her single forward-facing gun-port was clearly visible. Four hundred yards now, and closing fast.

"Up Armstrong!" Dawlish had to shout again to make himself heard over the barking Gatlings. Holmes, grimacing in pain, leaned forward and reached for the indicator panel with a shaking hand and launched the now-familiar sequence – the great cylinders thrusting the squat barrel up into the firing position, the fractional adjustment of elevation, the gunner's arm raised to confirm readiness, the *Toad's* bows swinging over under the twin rudders only and then the blinding rush of orange flame and rolling yellow-grey smoke hurling the shell upstream.

Flash-dazzled, deafened, choking on the fumes into which the gunboat was thrusting, neither Dawlish, nor Egdean nor the now-groaning Holmes saw the impact. Whether through luck or skill, the aim had been perfect. The missile smashed into the timberclad's open embrasure, hurling back the weapon mounted there in the seconds before the fuse activated the main charge. An expanding sphere of flame, shell splinters and fragments of the vessel's own armament roared through the interior, igniting stored munitions, blasting life from its path, tossing over machinery and beating down bulkheads. Confined, finding insufficient release through the embrasure and ports that spewed scarlet jets of hot gas, the terrible ball thrust against the frames and joists and timbers of the makeshift superstructure. It bulged for an instant in a last hopeless effort to contain the inferno within, then exploded in a fountain of scorching flame, blazing wood and flying fragments of metal and flesh.

"Steer straight for her!" Dawlish yelled, "She's got to be pushed aside before she sinks!" He had eyes only for the now blazing hulk, little more now than a raft level with the water, from which all traces of superstructure and machinery had been sheared. Debris rained down around the gunboat and fiery streaks were falling like miniature comets. Something thumped on to the deck ahead and clanged off a bollard and the starboard Gatling loader cried out and fell writhing across his ammunition boxes as a wooden splinter speared into his shoulder.

"Straight for her I said, Egdean!" Dawlish called again, conscious that the *Toad's* bows were drifting to port. Then he looked over to see the helmsman endeavouring to steer with one hand while the other strove to raise Holmes from where he had crumpled on the deck.

"It's only a scratch, Sir," Holmes gasped, as Dawlish also tried to lift him, but the sodden patch under his left armpit told otherwise. "If you get me up I'll be fine."

One glance told Dawlish that the young officer would never be fine again and that he could do nothing for him at this instant. The vessel came first. He lowered him as gently as he could against the rampart of coal sacks. Holmes was groaning and a trickle of blood ran from his mouth. "Rest a moment," Dawlish said, "you've done enough for now." There was no time for any greater comfort.

Still full revolutions, and Egdean was thrusting the *Toad* towards the burning derelict. It was scarcely two hundred yards away, drifting down midstream with the current, a blazing obstacle which, either afloat or sunken, threatened to block all passage. It was going to have to be nudged aside, but at the gunboat's current speed the impact of collision could be devastating. Dawlish reached for the telegraph and signalled for quarter revolutions.

The heat grew in intensity as they closed. Flames roared from the remains of the improvised warship, yet through them was audible the sizzle of the charred and glowing timbers settling ever further into the water. The Armstrong had sunk back into its trough but its crew must now be feeling the warmth through the hull plating and looking uneasily at the bagged charges surrounding them. They at least were shielded from the direct heat but Dawlish could only throw up an already-blistering left arm to protect his face as Egdean manoeuvred the gunboat towards the wreck.

"I've got her, Sir," he called as the *Toad's* stem crunched into the three-quarters submerged hull around what had been amidships, splintering and burrowing a notch into the flame-weakened timbers. Half-revolutions now, and the gunboat's squat hull slowly pushed the burning raft towards the northern bank. Paint blistered and the deck planking browned and began to smoke. There was no perception of motion at first and as the heat scorched through the thin cotton of his shirt Dawlish knew despairingly that neither he nor his vessel could sustain this much longer. He and Egdean ducked as far as they could below the shelter of the coal sacks. And they endured.

Slowly, the heat-broiled gunboat thrust the blazing, settling hulk into the shallows. A dull shock reverberated back into the *Toad* as the wreck ground into a sandbank. Dawlish glanced astern: the *Ipora* had already passed upriver through the floating debris and drifting corpses and the *Coimbra* was already level with the gunboat's stern and passing in her wake. The *Pilcomayo* was following closely and, four hundred yards downstream, the *Montelindo* was doggedly blasting into Puerto Plutarcho's blazing shanties as she wallowed upstream.

Blistered and parched, Dawlish signalled for half-astern. He noticed as he did, as something remote and distant, that Holmes had fallen on his side and that a long dark pool extended from him across the flame-lit planking. He had brought his beloved Rendel almost to its goal but it would be up to Dawlish and Egdean alone to navigate it to the final rendezvous upriver.

At one thirty in the morning, slightly ahead of schedule, the watch on the *Ipora*, now in the lead, picked up the flashing light on the northern bank that was the signal that Culbertson's troopers had reached the river. It was at a point five miles upstream from the centre of the settlement. Not only had the riders passed around the northern boundaries of the Reducción defences without detection, but the tumult on the river, which had drawn all attention in that direction, had ensued that the slower infantry who followed were also undetected. The first were expected long before daybreak.

The water on the southern side was deep almost up to the bank and it was possible to manoeuvre the ramped barge so close that landing of the artillery proceeded quickly and smoothly despite the darkness. The *Coimbra's* and the *Pilcomayo's* troops landed with similar ease and fanned out quickly to establish a defensive perimeter. By three o'clock, while the *Toad* and the *Montelindo* hovered in midstream, ready to provide support against any movement from Puerto Plutarcho, the *Ipora* was already operating the ramped barge as a shuttle to carry troops across from the northern bank as they arrived there at the end of their march.

The Reducción's defences had been outflanked. The final act could now commence.

29

The first contact with Reducción forces occurred on the western outskirts of Puerto Plutarcho shortly before sunrise.

A mounted Guardia troop had thrust eastwards in the darkness towards the settlement's centre by the main track that led through the open scattering of huts and stockyards. Two footsore companies of regulars and a four-gun battery of mule-drawn ten-pounders hurried in their rear. The Reducción troops, ill-armed and half-trained reserves who would have been deployed on the Eastern ramparts had they been of better quality, came blundering down the track towards them in a loose, shambling rabble.

Culbertson himself was leading the Guardia. He dismounted half his force to pour rapid carbine fire into the approaching mob while the remainder outflanked the wretched Reduccionistas and harried them from hutments to either side. They broke within minutes and fled in panic, or desperately sought shelter in the shanties and allotments around. Terrified occupants streamed from the shacks – half-clothed men, frightened women carrying babies, screaming children, all joining the rout. Mounted troopers plunged among them with bloodied sabres, making little distinction in the growing daylight between armed and unarmed, until a stuttering bugle recalled them. There was a brief regrouping and then the thrust eastwards continued.

By this time, at the landing point, the last of the infantry was scrambling ashore from the ramped barge, weary and bemused conscripts who had trudged with glum resignation through the night. Many had snatched an hour or so of comfortless sleep as they waited their turn to be ferried across from the northern bank and others had watched with mingled hope and fear the fires raging to the east over Puerto Plutarcho. On the southern bank the first troops discharged from the steamers had thrown up a ragged semi-circular perimeter four-hundred yards across, scraping shallow rifle-pits in the sandy ground. The artillery had been landed immediately from the ramped barge and positioned in hastily scooped redoubts, but the effort was half-hearted, for it was already obvious that no Reducción forces would arrive in time to menace the ferrying. Once the barge was cleared of artillery it was free to shuttle the Guardia cavalry across. Within two hours of arriving at the river the first horsemen, back on terrain familiar to most of them since long before El Pobre's uprising, had left the perimeter's shelter and were thrusting for Puerto Plutarcho.

Through the night newly landed troops re-formed companies on the southern bank, heartened by the relative ease with which they had somehow arrived here. The need for silence was past and commands that had been hissed on the night's march were now bellowed. The moonlight and the crimson eastern sky offered some light for the operation, yet even so chaos could have engulfed it had it not been for Aquino. He seemed everywhere at once, his staff scurrying behind and relaying his commands. Men stumbled over roots and crevices as they formed ranks, and mules brayed and kicked as the artillery was got under way. On the river the paddles lashed the river to froth as the steamers manoeuvred close to the banks and ramps thudded down and reverberated to hundreds of feet as men hurried ashore. Muscles screamed as boxes and sacks were manhandled from the paddlers, ammunition for the most part since the troops carried their meagre rations with them. To eat beyond the coming day they must find their victuals in La Reducción itself.

Downstream of the landing the *Toad* and the *Montelindo* hovered in midstream, stern-on to the current, screws churning slowly in reverse to hold them stationary. Repeated firing had jammed the monitor's blast-scoured turret and the half-suffocated and smoke-begrimed gun crews lay exhausted on the foredeck. Clanging from below told of efforts to shift the turret. Every hatch was open to draw air into the dripping and vapour-clouded interior. The monitor was back under full Paraguayan control again now, for Purdon had been recalled to the *Toad* to take Holmes' place.

Dawlish watched the river from the gunboat's bridge, fighting sleep, averting his gaze from the canvas-shrouded bundle by the bulwark. Holmes had always seemed larger in life.

A stern-anchor had been run out and the *Toad* oscillated gently in the current, bows directed downstream. Several of the gun crew, released for now from their metal trough, slumped in sleep against the breastwork. The Armstrong nestled below, loaded. A check of the hydraulic accumulators, packing and valves had proven satisfactory. The bunkers had already been replenished from sacks on deck and a brief visit to the engine-room had confirmed that other than a leaking gland there was no cause for concern in that quarter. A recruit from the Armstrong crew had been selected to replace the injured Gatling loader.

The *Toad* was once more ready to commit murder.

*　　　*　　　*

In the first two hours of full daylight one company of regulars and six of conscripts were pushed up the track to support Culbertson's now-faltering easterly drive. Resistance hardened as they moved into the denser housing on the edge of Puerto Plutarcho itself. This was no longer an area of flimsy huts but of more substantial structures of adobe brick, cottage-sized accommodation for the stockyard workers, stores and workshops laid out in a grid by some long-since slaughtered Hyperion engineer.

Reducción troops were now arriving in greater numbers, thrusting the mob of fugitives aside. They deployed under cover of the buildings, subjecting Culbertson's dismounted troopers to well-aimed fire that first slowed, then halted them. The ten-pounders were ordered forward to support the Guardia but the mule teams themselves took casualties from hidden skirmishers. The Reduccionistas made no effort to counterattack but long before the first regulars had arrived to relieve Culbertson's stalled troopers they had established a strong defence, a ragged line that extended off to either side of the track. Small groups of Reducción riflemen fortified huts, smashing loopholes to supplement the existing openings. They flitted between the buildings under cover of the cactus hedges that edged so many of the simple gardens surrounding them, or crouched in the dry and shallow drainage ditches, extending the line and thwarting Culbertson's attempts at outflanking.

With the arrival of the regulars and their less willing conscript reinforcements a systematic effort to maintain momentum commenced. The track remained the axis of attack. The ten-pounders, manhandled now by terrified conscripts, blasted solid shot into defended buildings and gave cover for the infantry to move forward in a series of rushes. They advanced ever more cautiously, sobered by the fury with which their fellows were hurled down by largely unseen enemies as they raced across open spaces. Dim interiors were cleared in brief, savage tumults as bayonets, machetes and sudden stabs of flame settled possession. A second battery came into action, punching jagged gaps in adobe walls and collapsing lesser structures in clouds of dust and straw. Rifle fire was continuous, rising to short crescendos as some small fortress repelled a rush of weary infantry or fell to a surge of terror-inspired valour. Men kicked and bled their last, sobbing and groaning, among the pathetic domestic detritus of the ruined gardens and homes, humble yet hopeful, of El Pobre's disciples – trodden clothing torn from drying lines, thatch-screened latrines, cooking pots and shattered earthenware vessels, vegetable plots and tottering awnings.

Culbertson's troopers were withdrawn and snatched an uneasy rest as more infantry moved up towards the developing battle, while from the east Reduccionistas were reinforcing the line of defended buildings. The first Reducción artillery came into action shortly before ten o'clock, unseen light howitzers, slowing the advance further. Other artillery followed. By midday the Hyperion thrust had halted. Threats and summary discipline could achieve only so much, for the officers and sergeants were themselves as exhausted as the men by the night's march. There was no option but to consolidate, snatch inadequate rest and prepare for a further push in the late afternoon.

*   *   *

But there was a second, less direct, Hyperion attack, with heavier forces, and it did not make contact with the enemy until mid-morning. Two columns, each more powerful than Culbertson's, each with a high proportion of regular infantry, and with two batteries of ten-pounders and a half-battery of howitzers each, struck inland, southwards, before swinging round, first to the east, then northwards, in a great right hook. Aquino was in overall command and a regular platoon brought up the rear of each column to dissuade stragglers. Their route took them clear of built-up areas, initially through scrub and then across the cleared areas where the Reducción's cattle herds had been gathered. The first exchanges of fire were shortly before nine o'clock when a Reduccionista cavalry patrol was scattered by several shrapnel rounds from a hastily unlimbered ten-pounder. The columns pressed on, to collide ten minutes later with well-trained Reducción riflemen deployed in the cover of an irrigation ditch that squarely blocked the line of advance. Beyond it lay the first of the stockyards and housing, and from this direction more Reduccionistas were hurrying in ever-larger numbers.

Aquino had a battle on his hands – a desperate one – and it would develop independently of the conflict that Culbertson was conducting closer to the river. The fate of La Reducción Nueva – and of the Hyperion Consortium – would be settled in the coming hours.

*   *   *

Dawlish found the burial service in a well-thumbed Book of Common Prayer that lay among Holmes' scant effects. Tears started to his eyes as he read the inscription on the flyleaf: *"To our beloved son John on the occasion of his Confirmation, September 15 1865, in the hope that his life will be one of Christian Virtue, Compassion and Duty"*. Later he must face the task of writing to the Wiltshire vicarage where the same proud parents awaited a young hero's return. And later he must ensure that Murillo would forward Holmes' fee and the promised six hundred five-shilling Hyperion share certificates, whatever they might be worth after the last night's work.

The burial could not be delayed, not least because afterwards, despite all loss, Dawlish knew he must snatch a few hours of sleep. The process was quick, but with as much ceremony as the circumstances permitted. A grave was dug far back from the river's likely flood-line, and a pile of stones heaped by it for shielding the body from scavengers once it had been laid within. There was no time for a coffin and the canvas-rolled corpse was lashed to a plank and carried from the *Toad* by four of the crew. Dawlish wished for an ensign to drape across it – as Holmes would have liked – but the *Toad*, no longer a vessel of the Royal Navy, carried none. Arms locked over each other's shoulders, the seamen lurched over the uneven ground – deck, engine-room, Gatling and Armstrong crews all represented following the request of a solemn delegation led by Morgan the gunner, his eyes brimming.

"He always looked after the men before himself, Sir," he said.

There could be few better epitaphs.

The dull boom of artillery punctuating the almost continuous rattle of rifle-fire to the east was far enough away not to drown the words of the abbreviated service. Dawlish's voice caught as he read *"I am the Resurrection and the Life, saith the Lord, he that believeth in me, though he were dead, yet shall he live."* He wanted to believe it, as he regarded the pitiful heap before him.

Now the body was in the grave, and a stoker was down with it, laying stones gently on the canvas. Then it was time for the dry red earth to be shovelled on top. A small firing party discharged their shots. They filed back, deflated, saddened, to the squat, nimble and deadly gunboat that had been Holmes' pride and passion.

Too tired for emotion, Dawlish ordered to be called in three hours. Sleep was immediate but only minutes seemed to have passed when he was being shaken into aching wakefulness by Purdon.

"It's a Sergeant Gelb – from the Guardia, claims you know him," he said. "He won't be denied – says Colonel Culbertson sent him and it's life and death".

The distant rumble of the artillery seemed almost continuous, the rifle fire unrelenting, as Dawlish emerged blinking into the early afternoon sunlight. Gelb, sweat-stained, dust-grimed, and with a bloodied rag wrapped around his left forearm, was slumped on a mooring bit. Somebody had put a steaming mug of tea in his hand and it smelled strongly of the rum it had been laced with. He lurched to his feet as Dawlish approached. At that moment a heavier artillery report rolled across the scrub, followed an instant later by the dull thud of a large explosion. There was a lull in the rifle fire and then it resumed with increased intensity. It seemed closer than it had done before Dawlish had retired.

"That's the problem, Sir." Gelb gestured wearily towards the settlement. "They've brought up something big. Must be from the defences downriver. God knows how they've shifted it so fast. They're tearing into us, pushing us hard."

"The Colonel sent you?"

"Told me to tell you he was holding on by his eyebrows. We've still got a line through the huts and buildings, but most of our artillery's knocked out. They've got something heavy there, a Parrott maybe, an' it's tearing whole houses apart. It's powerful, whatever they have, and it's out-ranging us. An' we can't see nor a damn sight of it."

"Show me". Dawlish gestured towards the ladder.

But from the bridge there was scarcely more to be seen, just a long steak of scrub, broken here and there by trees and by sunlight reflecting from distant corrugated roofs. Smoke drifted up in lazy, billowing columns to form a grey canopy overhead. Isolated tongues of flame licked beneath. From this vantage, or indeed from the few feet extra that the signal mast would provide, it was impossible to distinguish anything of the battle in progress.

"Over there, Sir." Gelb pointed wearily. "About a mile inland from the river, I'd say." He seemed overcome by the hopelessness of identifying any exact position.

"How long can the Colonel hold?"

"An hour, he says, maybe less. The only thing keeping them conscripts in line is Colonel Si himself. They'd have run by now if our troopers weren't to the rear o' them."

"And General Aquino? Any news?"

"A galloper came about an hour back. The General's into the settlement, southern sector. Making progress, he says, but it's slow going, getting slower. But not much enemy artillery there yet."

The map of the settlement formed itself almost physically in Dawlish's brain. He could visualise Aquino's force gouging its way from the south through the stockyards and hutments towards the workshops by the river while Culbertson's thrust eastwards, potentially the shorter, was faltering and threatening to collapse. The Reducción forces would now be flooding across from the eastern ramparts that had been so effectively bypassed the previous night. They would be footsore and weary – though less so than the Hyperion forces – but they would be fighting with the savage determination of men defending their homes and families. If Culbertson fell back, the force that repulsed him would be turned on

Aquino's columns, and there was no way of predicting how the resultant grinding battle among the stockyards could develop.

Speed and momentum, the factors that had underlain the entire outflanking strategy, were bleeding away by the minute and once the lines congealed the advantage would lie with the Reducción's numbers.

And now there could be only one other decisive factor.

Artillery.

Merciless, bowel-loosening, flesh-rending, terror-inspiring artillery, concentrated at the right point, as El Pobre's was concentrating at this moment.

Artillery that would shatter the resolve of men who might withstand rifle and bayonet.

Artillery heavier than the twenty-pounder that the Reducción commander – probably Roybon – had somehow transported quickly over six or eight miles from the eastern ramparts.

The advantage had passed from the Hyperion forces. Only the *Toad* could reclaim it.

Culbertson knew it too. "He needs the *Toad* in support," Gelb was saying, "Bursting shell. Colonel Si said you'd know what he meant, Sir."

As he spoke the obstacles were raising themselves in Dawlish's mind – the Armstrong's low trajectory, the impossibility of firing blind, the inability to spot fall of shot and correct the aim, the difficulty of... He stopped himself. The list was endless.

"I know exactly what he meant, Sergeant Gelb," Dawlish said quietly, "and I'll deliver it." In his mind he added the word "*Somehow*."

He turned to Purdon, hoping that his voice conveyed confidence. "I want two bow anchors kedged out immediately, another stern anchor also – a firm four-point mooring, bar-tight. Then get the Armstrong crew to their stations."

"And then, Sir?"

"All other crew-members to be mustered on deck. And you, Mr. Purdon, will be taking command of the *Toad* in ten minutes."

And in those ten minutes he must find a solution. Somehow.

30

Only the harsh proof of implementation would show if the solution Dawlish found would be adequate.

By the time Dawlish heaved himself into Carmelita's saddle – for Gelb had somehow found her, and brought her, like some timid bribe – the *Toad's* port anchor had been dropped in midstream and the starboard was being rowed to a point close to the southern bank. Once the second stern anchor was also in position, the four anchors by then deployed would transform the gunboat into a fixed platform that could be trained by warping on the capstans.

Two of the half-dozen troopers that had accompanied Gelb had located a mule and on its back Egdean was loading a jute-wrapped bundle.

"No sign of the other mules, or of the limber," Dawlish said, "But we can't wait."

"I sent Peralta. He's a good man," Gelb answered. "He'll find them, get them here, if anybody can. And he's got three men with him to do the persuading."

Mounted again, Adams revolver holstered against his thigh and thirty rounds in his pouch, a box of lucifers stuffed in his shirt pocket, Dawlish ached with exhaustion and his eyes burned in the afternoon glare. He glanced apprehensively at the flurry of activity on the *Toad's* Gatling platforms, choked down the fear that progress there was too slow, acknowledged Purdon's salute, then pressed Carmelita's flanks.

297

Gelb moved ahead of him, leading through the scrub towards the vital track, and the two troopers followed, one leading the mule with its precious load.

Once they reached the track they managed a fast trot, slowing only to avoid the wounded limping back towards the landing area, or to overtake the supplies and scant reinforcements still being hurried forward. Soon they were among evidence of the first clashes of the previous night –wrecked huts, trodden fences, discarded bundles, a shattered cart, and already-bloating corpses scattered among the debris. A smell of burning hung in the air, underlain by the slightest hint of growing corruption. The sound of gunfire swelled.

"Better dismount here." Gelb halted at a charred cluster of half-collapsed shanties. "We're close now and they may have worked around the ends of the line."

Leading their mounts, they moved forward, pistols drawn. Rifle fire barked to a crescendo over to the left, riverwards, then died down again to a sustained low crackle. The slow, irregular boom of the artillery reverberated like some great drum pounding a dead march. Now they were among the rearward positions. There dazed and already-bloodied troops who had pulled back from the front had established a fallback defence. They were knocking loopholes in adobe walls and raising barricades across the track. One glance at their bewildered, red-rimmed eyes and haggard faces told that these men were near their limit. One more determined assault by La Reducción would scatter them in terror.

They left horses and mule in the shelter of a burned-out warehouse. Waiting there were a Guardia corporal and a conscript, sent to guide them along the track to the right. Thick patches of waist-high growth alternated with a grid-pattern of adobe cottages and more solid bungalows, many tumbled and burned. The sullen conscript struggled behind on foot, pressed into carrying the mule's light but bulky burden. The ground at several points was cratered and scoured by shellfire. Slumped bodies littered around told their own story of desperate attack and counterattack.

Their progress was blocked for several minutes by a small but vicious contest concentrated on a group of thatch-roofed huts, their gardens defined by cactus hedges. Within them a half-company of conscripts, stiffened by a handful of regulars, was holding off a local Reducción thrust. White-clad wraiths flitted briefly from cover and were gone again in a burst of rifle fire. From somewhere ahead a light howitzer was blindly lobbing shells that burst in fountains of earth and greenery. A lucky hit collapsed a hut into a dusty mist. A regular lieutenant was urging a ten-pounder forward to spray canister into the line of shacks and vegetation that sheltered the half-invisible attackers. Frightened conscripts dragged at the traces and strained on the wheel-spokes, crashing the weapon through fences and bouncing it over drainage channels. One fell, his trouser leg already blood-sodden and he was left, screaming in pain and despair, as the piece was manhandled into a firing position between the buildings. It blasted twice in quick succession, then fell silent, waiting for ammunition. The limber had been abandoned somewhere to the rear and supplies were being hand-carried forward. Brown-clad conscripts were hustled ahead to seize a hut half-hidden in the shredded foliage of a thicket, the target of the short bombardment. There was a crackle of rifle-fire, a brief glimpse of reddened bayonets and a piercing scream that rose and fell for an endless ten seconds before it was cut off abruptly.

The line had been stabilised for now. More conscripts were pushed forward to reinforce this new strongpoint, eyes blank with fear and exhaustion. One dropped, dead before he hit the ground, another collapsed moaning, hands grasping a crimson gouge in his side, victims of unseen riflemen on the right flank.

Dawlish felt fear tightening his stomach, fought down the urge to find some excuse to withdraw, hoped nobody would notice how carefully he held himself in the angle of a wall that offered only an illusion of cover. It was a relief when Gelb said "Too Goddamn hot here. We're going to have to loop around".

They skirted behind the line, conscious of just how thin was the screen holding the Reducción thrust, how hard pressed – and how steady, if irregular, the Reducción artillery. The dull "crump" detonations of the rounds flung by the invisible twenty-pounder that

Gelb had warned of were somehow more frightening than the sharper reports of the smaller shells.

They found Culbertson in a bullet-pocked bungalow. Bodies in the garden and the shallow ditch outside indicated an earlier battle for possession. He was huddled in conference with a Guardia captain and two regular lieutenants. His uniform was rumpled, filthy and sweat-sodden, his bulk seemed flabbier than ever with fatigue, and he smelled strongly of alcohol, but the eyes were as bright and sharp as ever. Dawlish had an immediate impression of a man somehow in his element, far from beaten.

"Never thought you'd fail me, Commander Nick," he said. "I need you sore now, mighty sore. An' I need that damn great gun of yours a sight worse."

"No promises, Colonel." Dawlish voiced the doubt that had gnawed and grown ever since he had left the track. He had lost all sense of distance from the *Toad* as his small group had flitted from cover to cover. "It could be as dangerous for us as for the enemy."

"Couldn't be worse than them folks, Nick," Culbertson said, "and I reckon I'll take my chance sooner on you than on El Pobre's sons of bitches."

"You're holding?"

Culbertson's answer was a sweeping motion of his arm that drew Dawlish behind him as he scurried, his limp more pronounced now, out of the building and along the shelter of the wall. He gestured for a pause at the corner, glanced carefully from cover, and then dashed for the protection of the next bungalow. Dawlish followed. The door had been knocked from its hinges and four troopers occupied the interior. A corporal guided them cautiously through the half-wrecked house, crouching beneath window openings. A gaping hole had been beaten into the end wall and here they paused again. An artillery piece opened somewhere far to their left, presaging another burst of rifle fire there. Dawlish and Culbertson dashed forward again, now towards the cover of the next hut, this one held by half a dozen frightened conscripts.

Two more such rushes carried them to a substantial building, two-storied, a combined store and office perhaps, now half-ruined. The portly Capitan Cardozo defended it with ten conscripts and regulars. He led them to the upper floor. The corrugated roof had been partly blown away and through the gap there was a marginally better view than before over the confusion of bushes, vegetable plots and shacks that constituted the battleground.

"Keep in the shadow, Commander." Culbertson pushed a small pair of field glasses into Dawlish's hand. "One flash o' light on them lenses and some Guaikuru buck will be drillin' your skull."

Rust-streaked metal or brown-thatched roofs sprang into sharp focus against the greenery as Dawlish adjusted the focus. Smoke drifted lazily upwards and he was somehow aware of movement and stirring, though no figures were immediately visible.

"To your left, Commander. See them huts by the tall trees? And beyond? A hundred yards or so?"

And there was movement enough there, though half-screened by the intervening bushes and housing, far enough behind the immediately disputed zone to give shelter to the Reduccionistas being marshalled into some semblance of order there.

"Several companies." Dawlish forced himself to ignore the growing fear knotting his stomach. The *Toad's* reassuring presence suddenly seemed very far away. "And more arriving from the east." He swung the glasses slightly. "Hurrying up in ones and twos. But somebody there is organising them into units."

"Somebody smart enough not to send them directly into the line and spread 'em too thin." Culbertson's voice had a hint of admiration in it. "Concentratin' to attack."

A crash from rightwards caused Dawlish to drop the glasses and jerk around to see a column of flame-shot earth climbing from the disintegrating remains of a shack fifty-yards distant.

"Lucky shot. It's a twenty-pounder, I'll wager," Culbertson said calmly. "Can't see the damned thing but it's somewhere yonder, firing blind." The confused mix of bushes and huts he gestured towards provided total cover. "It's got to be one of the pieces they had mounted on the eastern earthworks but I'm damned if I know how they got it here this fast. I just..."

His words were cut off as a rifle bullet slammed into the beam to the left of his head. Cardozo caught Dawlish by the arm, pulling him to his knees.

"Getting' unhealthy here, Nick," Culbertson said. "Time to go down."

There was a table in a backroom that had once been an office. Culbertson produced a sweat-sodden map from a breast pocket and laid it out, smoothing the creases. It was a meticulous piece of draughtsmanship, with every contour and track and bungalow and warehouse and stand of bushes exactly delineated. Albert Eastley of the Hyperion Survey Department, Puerto Plutarcho Office, had proudly completed and signed it on September 21st, 1878, six months before blood and fire had brought his ordered world to an abrupt end. The sepia ink with which the housing had been crosshatched had run but the map was more than adequate for the purpose at hand.

"The sons o' bitches are massing here." Culbertson stabbed with a grimy finger. "You've seen them. My guess is that there's more on the way and they'll wait for them a little longer, but they'll be coming over soon, and that Goddamn Parrott will be blastin' a path for them. They'll be coming right through here and they'll be heading for the landing." His finger swept a straight line towards the spot on the extreme left-bottom corner where the pale blue snake that was the river intersected the track from the settlement. There, marked earlier in pencil at a planning session on the *Tacuari*, was the perimeter secured immediately after the night crossing.

"Reserves?" Dawlish asked.

"Four companies, here." Culbertson indicated an oval a few hundred yards behind the present position. "One of regulars, three conscripts, a troop of my own boys. All jaded and bloodied but they've had two, maybe three, hours rest. Can't be any worse than them peons El Pobre is getting hustled into line. Ammunition's low though. And I've given orders to thin the line here" – he indicated the extreme left – "and concentrate 'em here. God help us if I've chosen wrong."

A crash somewhere close enough to shower dust from the ceiling on to the map. The twenty-pounder again, its rate of fire high enough to keep the defenders on edge, low enough to conserve its ammunition for the storm that would precede the assault to come.

"They're as stretched as we are." Culbertson spoke half to himself. "They're as weary and they're probably more confused and if they hadn't got that Goddamn twenty-pounder and a half-dozen lighter pieces to back it they'd have run by now!" His face was only inches from Dawlish, his words urgent on his whisky-sodden breath. "If I can hit them before they make their move they'll run like scalded cats! But I need you, Commander Nick! I need that damned great gun of yours to put the fear of God in them when I send my boys in!"

Dawlish fished in his shirt pocket, produced a stub of pencil, placed a cross on the spot that was as close as he could guess to the *Toad's* mooring point. "And the twenty-pounder – your best guess?" he asked, handing the pencil to Culbertson.

Another cross, this one in a cluster of sepia buildings. The pencil laid lengthways along the scale beside Albert Eastley's flourish, Dawlish's thumbnail marking the hundred-yard mark. The distance stepped off between the two crosses – a more accurate measurement could wait for now. Forty-three hundred yards. The Armstrong's extreme range for bursting shell was forty-eight hundred.

Culbertson was looking at him expectantly and Cardozo was glancing nervously from one to the other, aware that his hopes of survival to nightfall were dependent on Dawlish's next words.

Forty-eight hundred yards maximum range. And that, a small voice inside his head told Dawlish, was on delivery ex-works and at standard atmospheric pressure and temperature on a British firing range, before repeated firing had scored the barrel and eroded the rifling and before bagged propellant charges had been exposed to months of passage through the North and South Atlantics and up a steaming tropical river and before...

He stopped himself. God only knew what the maximum range was now, but if it was substantially less than forty-three hundred yards then there was a damn good chance that the *Toad* would save El Pobre's forces the effort of an all-out assault and wipe out Culbertson's force itself.

Again the twenty-pounder's report and the sound of rifle-fire from the front of the building. It rose in fury, then died again. The pressure was already intense and would not decrease until one side or the other made its move. And Dawlish knew that there was only one answer that he could give.

"We'll do it," he said.

And then, suddenly remembering Holmes, he added: "The *Toad* will do it, one last time."

31

El Pobre's ragged forces struck first, while Culbertson's reserves were being brought forward for the assault and before Dawlish's preparations were complete.

Not one, but two twenty-pounders opened the attack, blindly smashing explosive shells at drum-fire rate into the Hyperion front line and supplemented by a shower of plunging howitzer fire. Aiming or close targeting was impossible in the maze of buildings, gardens and bushes but the sheer volume of shot and noise and flying splinters that was concentrated within that warren would have shaken more seasoned and better-rested troops. It was enough to panic into flight perhaps half of the conscript forces holding the jagged line of huts and drainage ditches that constituted Culbertson's frontal position even before the Reducción infantry came surging from cover. These roughly aligned lines of riflemen were held back until the first storm of artillery fire had spent itself and then they advanced in open order as the exhausted gun-crews drew breath. They struggled forward through cactus fences and drainage ditches, encouraged by the meagreness of the resistance they encountered. In places brief defiance from some knot of defenders more resolute than the rest held them up momentarily, but always they moved on again, inexorably, bayonets bloodied and faces smoke-grimed, exultant in this moment of victory. A half-organised mob followed, armed with little more than machetes and axes, older men and boys, and wild-eyed, desperate women in hitched-up skirts.

Dawlish and Culbertson had already moved rearwards and so missed being caught up in the brief battle that raged around the storage building where they had but lately pored over the map. The outlying huts were taken quickly but Capitan Cardozo knew his business and his men maintained an iron firing-discipline until the last, littering the ground before the store with Reducción dead and wounded. The small fortress might have held out longer had a light howitzer not been manhandled forward and its trail raised to allow horizontal firing at point-blank range. Three rounds smashed a breach through which the Reduccionistas poured, bayoneting and chopping at the dazed survivors within. Two minutes sufficed and then they were lunging onwards to the next objective, leaving Cardozo's plump body for a half-dozen women to mutilate gleefully.

Culbertson's line collapsed over a distance of perhaps two hundred yards and on the edges of this gap troops who might otherwise have stood firm began to waver, and ultimately to retreat. Here and there a determined officer or sergeant held his men at their posts, either by example or by threat, and these kept up a galling fire on the flanks of the Reducción advance. Two ten-pounders were over-run, but the others guns held steady, protected by regulars or Guardia troopers, and these were slewed round to pour fire blindly into the area taken by the advancing enemy torrent.

The reserves Culbertson had so carefully gathered had been almost ready to advance when the storm broke. Now they were hurried forward to hold ditches and huts, rapidly establishing a new defensive line against which the leading Reducción attackers, by now tiring, blundered. Dawlish was by Culbertson as he stood barking deployment commands in the lee of a hut, bullets whipping small dust clouds to left and right of its shelter. A track flanked by a ditch on its far side ran past the shack. Into this shallow trench a whole company of regulars was poured. Open ground lay beyond, normally a last night's grazing for cattle awaiting slaughter in the settlement's shambles, and it was fringed on the opposite side by huts and vegetable plots. The regulars crouched in this half-sodden ditch, rounds in the breech, knowing that at any minute the Reduccionistas must surge towards them.

Dawlish anchored the map on the ground by four pebbles and oriented for azimuth with a hand-compass as best he could. His present position was marked by another pencilled cross, all but on a line linking the two previous crosses that marked the *Toad's* station and the suspected location of the enemy twenty-pounder. He used a strip he had torn from the map's edge, and on which he had marked off one-hundred yard steps from the scale, to measure off the distance from his present location to the *Toad*.

Thirty eight hundred yards – a comfortable margin of safety, he hoped, especially as he was going to be directly in the line of fire.

"Now, Commander Nick! Now! They're coming" Culbertson's tone was urgent. He was glancing round the corner of the hut, watching a solid line of stumbling, cheering Reduccionistas emerge from the cover beyond the grazing ground. From the ditch came the bellows of regular officers ordering their men to hold their fire.

"It's now or never then, Colonel," Dawlish said.

The ungainly canvas bundle had been opened and the signal rockets it contained spread out, sorted by the colour bands around their bodies, white and green and red. Dawlish selected a white one – white for marking line of fire – and propped it against the open channel of the light metal firing frame that he had set up to point almost vertically.

He pulled the lucifers from his breast pocket, selected one and struck it against the abrasive on the box-side. He thrust the small flame against the blue touch paper then stepped back as the glow ran up into the rocket's body. It rose in a shower of sparks over the roofs and foliage to burst in a searing white ball almost directly above.

Thirty-eight hundred yards away, on the *Toad's* bridge, Purdon had been waiting for this signal and even now he would be bellowing orders to warp the gunboat's bows around to line up on the distant and swiftly falling incandescent blob.

Another rocket in the channel now, red this time, "Maximum Range" according to the simple code Dawlish had hastily agreed with Purdon. As the deck crew pushed on the capstans, straining and slackening the cables that would orientate the *Toad* within her four-point mooring pattern, the gunner would be sending water and glycerine hissing into the pistons to elevate the Armstrong. Dawlish forced from his mind the fact that the weapon would be blasting blindly straight towards him. An error on his range assumptions would mean annihilation.

Yelled commands, and then rifle-fire crashing out along the line of the ditch. The Reduccionistas were half-way across the open ground now, but falling and stumbling as the volley smashed into them. Some were breaking and running rearwards, others, suicidally, were clustering into wavering groups. A handful still surged forward, heartened by the lull as the defenders in the ditch reloaded rapidly.

"We'll hold the bastards this time!" Culbertson shouted. "But I need your Goddamn fire, Commander! Where's the *Toad?*"

"Soon! Soon!"

Dawlish despatched another white rocket, and then another, before the incandescent white dot had fallen earthwards. The gunboat must be in the final stages of lining up by now and Purdon would need all the guidance he could get. Dawlish sent another red-banded cylinder hurtling skywards, emphasising maximum range once more, fighting down his own fear that the *Toad's* fiery breath was a greater danger than El Pobre's ragtag soldiery dying not eighty yards distant.

An eternity passed, an eternity of firing and of thrusting bayonets as the exhausted survivors of the Reducción assault reached the ditch. Rifle-fire erupted to the left, as another thrust that had skirted the open ground crashed into a cluster of huts hastily loop-holed by dismounted troopers.

Then the *Toad* spoke.

The Armstrong's report came rolling from the river just ahead of the shell that rushed overhead, low and dropping as it howled past, slightly to the right of Dawlish's position. A brief moment of near silence and then a roar somewhere beyond the Reduccionistas' line, a fountain of earth and flame and smoke rising beyond the clutter of huts and bushes. Another wave of attackers was breaking from the cover beyond the open grazing but the massive explosion to their rear, and the shudder rippling through the ground beneath their feet, gave them pause.

"On track, but over!" Culbertson yelled. "Can you shorten?"

"How much?" Dawlish shouted. The impact looked maybe four hundred yards beyond their current position – he had been correct to fret about the maximum range.

"Two hundred yards!"

Green for reducing range, each rocket a hundred yards. Two in immediate succession, and then, knowing that the barrel would be warmer for the next shot, tending to lengthen range, a third.

Down three hundred – risky for himself but potentially deadly for the attackers. The Armstrong, newly charged and loaded, would be settling into a slightly lower elevation now as Purdon, glasses clamped to his eyes and fixed on the falling green flares, signalled to the gunner.

Culbertson bellowed to an aide to carry orders for the remaining reserves to come forward. Reducción rifle fire rippled again as the half-stunned attackers screwed up their courage for a new surge across the open ground. To the left the improvised fortress manned by the Guardia troopers was holding its own. Further to the right a group of attackers collided with a regular-stiffened conscript company that held a small complex of tanning sheds.

The unseen *Toad* blasted again. Some variation in roundness or balance of the shell itself, or some slight loosening of the gunboat's mooring lines, shifted the projectile's trajectory leftwards of the former track. Its passage was almost directly above Dawlish and Culbertson and it was low enough for its rush to cause them to cringe involuntarily. It fell among the huts, just beyond the open ground, hurling flame and earth and shattered bodies upwards and outwards.

The defenders in the ditch were cheering. The new assault wave that has been gathering half-heartedly beyond the corpse-strewn grazing patch was breaking into bewildered groups that scattered to left and right, trapped between the rifles lining the ditch before them and the inferno that had exploded to their rear.

"Purdon will keep firing on this line until he's told otherwise," Dawlish said.

"Three shells more . No! Four." Culbertson's voice was elated. "Then another three or four about two hundred yards yonder, " – he pointed to the right – "same range. Then we'll go in with all we've got. You can manage that for me, Commander Nick?"

"In line with those sheds, Colonel? I'll get across there directly."

"And get back here then, Nick! You hear me now! I need you!"

There was less danger now breaking from cover, dodging at a stoop down the track that ran alongside the ditch, heading for the next cluster of huts. Dawlish led, his Adams in hand for reassurance, his near-exhaustion forgotten as he trotted forward, closely followed by two frightened conscripts carrying the bundle of rockets and the firing frame, a hard-eyed Guardia trooper bringing up the rear. They paused to take breath half way in the shelter a clump of bushes as the next Armstrong round hurtled over. It exploded just beyond and to the right of the previous impact. Two more rounds, Dawlish realised, and the ground there would be scoured clear. Then he followed the others in a crouching scurry along the ditch, conscious of bullets hitting the track to his side as he moved forward.

They gained the cover of the tanning sheds. The last assault here had been repulsed, but barely, for corpses of attackers who had crossed the rail fences that linked the buildings lay crumpled in the yard. A regular lieutenant and the best part of a company held the position, peering over their rifle-barrels through roughly smashed loopholes, waiting nervously for the next wave.

It was time now to change the *Toad's* line of fire. The trooper who had carried the launching frame had the initiative to start setting it up in the shelter of a shed, albeit at a crazy angle. Dawlish jerked the channel to the vertical and pulled a white-banded rocket from the bundle. "Sort them, God damn you! By colour!" he yelled to the conscript who had carried them, and who now cowered behind a wall.

As he fumbled for the matches in his pocket he realised that he was himself on the brink of hysteria. He forced himself to slow his movements, to breathe deeply, to ignore the weakness in his knees and the ache in his bladder. He laid the rocket carefully against the channel and struck the lucifer with still-trembling fingers.

A brief splutter and then the signal to *Toad* for change of firing axis soared upwards. He counted silently to twenty, ignoring the racket of rifle-fire erupting again from beyond the sheds, then set off another. He counted slowly again, visualising as he did so what would be the disciplined effort at this moment on the *Toad* as her bows were warped across to the new heading. The thought of that steadiness comforted him as he lit the third white rocket's touch-paper and called "Rojo!" over his shoulder. The conscript pushed a scarlet-banded cylinder to him and presently it too shot skywards. Now he could only wait for the *Toad's* response.

The lieutenant was hovering nearby. "I want to see the situation to the front," Dawlish told him. "Bring me there now! Ahora mismo!"

He was led into the dark shed, which smelled powerfully of hides and tannin. Wounded men moaned in the shadows. The air was thick with powder-smoke through which the light from the firing slits punched in the adobe walls lanced in silvery beams. The firing had died down as the survivors of the last Reduccionista assault fell back to the cover of a large field of man-high corn some fifty yards distant. The defenders fingered their weapons nervously, alert for the first indication of a renewed onslaught.

"They're there, Señor." The lieutenant pushed a defender aside and gestured through a rough firing port. "In the maize. And they'll come again."

The *Toad's* missile came roaring overhead somewhere to the right, so low that its onrush rattled the shed's corrugated roofing. It fell two hundred yards beyond, blasting a crater to the rear of the Reduccionistas pushing forward through the corn, scything splinters and stone and earth among them, scorching the parched maize stalks into a blaze. Dazed and terrified, the attackers stumbled forward, away from the crackling inferno that grew behind them, and towards the edge of the field. The first who blundered into the open triggered a ragged volley from the sheds that grew in intensity as more unfortunates struggled forward to escape the flames behind.

The crash of rifles in the enclosed space was deafening, and the smoke choking, but Dawlish had detached himself and was waiting for the *Toad's* next round. There was no need for correction for on this heading maximum range was sufficient. Another Armstrong shell tore overhead, adding fresh chaos to the disintegrating Reducción assault. Still the slaughter continued, a mixture of bloodlust and relief overtaking the sheds' defenders as they poured merciless fire into smoke-smothered, heat-scorched attackers at whose hands they had feared death only minutes earlier.

Dawlish was back by the rocket-frame, three red rockets to hand, as the fourth shell skimmed across on this heading. He fired them in rapid succession - the "Cease Firing" signal. He smiled grimly. It was time for counterattack and he wanted to be part of it.

For though the *Toad* had prepared the way, she had yet, he hoped, one more sting to unleash.

32

The last shell from the *Toad* exploded in the rear of the bewildered Reduccionistas as Culbertson launched his reserves forward. Exhausted, filthy and hungry as they were, nerve-shattered by hours of exposure to gunfire and close combat, the sight of the enemy breaking and retreating somehow roused them. The main thrust by the reserve companies was directly across the open grazing ground that had recently witnessed such slaughter, the blazing corn to the right and a slow, steady advance to the left by the dismounted troopers neutralising any threat to their flanks.

There was little opposition as they entered the gardens and shacks ahead, only the odd group of half-hearted defenders that turned and ran at the lightest probing. They pressed on past the *Toad's* still-smoking craters, pausing to bayonet wounded and to disarm, cuff into total submission and send rearwards those quaking Reduccionistas who approached with uplifted arms. Culbertson's orders had been unequivocal – flogging for the man who killed an unwounded prisoner. The victorious Consortium would need labour.

By the time Dawlish arrived back at the hut where he had last seen the colonel the third wave of friendly forces was already moving across the corpse-strewn open grazing. The ditch that had sheltered the riflemen was empty now, its occupants gone ahead. A regular captain with an arm in a sling was hurrying forward a half-company composed of men stripped from elsewhere in the line. Few looked in much better shape than the captain, but they too seemed to sense victory and to be wearily eager to finish the job.

"Colonel Culbertson? Where is he?" Dawlish asked.

"Gone forward, Señor." The captain waved towards ground ahead. The sound of rifle fire was growing there, irregular, staccato – yet ominously heavier than it had been a minute or so before.

Then, heart-breakingly, hope-destroying, a crash rose above the barking of the rifles, louder, more ominous. A twenty-pounder, still somehow in action. And then the staccato rising to a new crescendo as if the Reducción defence had been revitalised by that single shot.

It was not over.

"Any more reserves, Lieutenant?"

"These are the last, Señor. There's nothing more."

Son los ultimos, Señor. No hay mas. Dawlish saw the fear in the eyes of the wounded captain and the full impact of the words sunk home to him. He felt despair rising in him like nausea.

And at that moment the *Toad's* last venom was delivered.

"Commander Dawlish! We've made it, Sir!"

Dawlish turned, recognising the voice of Hilliard, the Gatling gunner. He was puffing up the track on foot in the wake of three mounted gendarmerie troopers. Bouncing behind him, hauled by four-mules led by Egdean and a half dozen of the *Toad's* crew, was a ten-pounder's limber. A Gatling was mounted atop, its frame secured by hastily improvised iron strapping passed around the box structure and locked with bolts. A crude platform of planks, large enough to accommodate gunner and loader, had been lashed in position with rope and it carried two boxes of ammunition. Boyson, the grey-haired engine-room artificer, was panting alongside and his face broke into a grin of pride as he saw Dawlish.

"Like you asked for, Sir!" he gasped as the contraption slewed to a halt. "Rough and ready, Sir, but solid as the Rock of Gibraltar!"

"And we're ready too, Sir!" Egdean heaved for breath. "Ready for anything!"

The seamen clustered around Dawlish, the normal reserves of discipline and rank loosened momentarily in the unfamiliar surroundings. Hilliard's loader, McCreevy, was there, and Wilcox the banjo-player, and another stoker and an able-bodied deckhand, all festooned not just with Sniders and bandoliers but with the cutlasses and boarding axes without which no bluejacket ever seemed to feel comfortable ashore. Dawlish glanced up at the six-barrelled weapon, high on its carriage. It was a brave man who would mount such an exposed position, but courage was hardly rare in this group.

"You've done well, Lads." He meant it. The removal of the weapon from the *Toad* and the improvisation of a mobile mounting – not to mention getting it here - was no inconsiderable feat. Smiles greeted him. Then he added "But the real test is yet to come. Are you with me?"

"We'd follow Old Nick to Hell, wouldn't we, Lads?"

The cheers lauding Wilcox's query drowned the protests of a Boyson shocked by the familiarity.

"Not as far as Hell, Lads! Just to Puerto Plutarcho will do for now!" Dawlish said, gesturing towards the firing. He saw that wounded participants in Culbertson's attack were starting to straggle back over the open grazing. The rifle-fire from the unseen battle amid the buildings and vegetable plots beyond was continuous now. Another report from the twenty-pounder told that it was still in action. At this moment a single round from the *Toad's* main armament might be decisive, but the advance ruled out calling on it. It was down to the Gatling.

"Colonel Culbertson's attack has hit opposition," he said, "and we're going to clear it! We're going to get this limber as close as we can to support him. We'll take the mules as far as we can and after that it will be Jack-power! Are you game?"

A chorus of "Ayes", and then they were moving forward.

Doors dragged off hinges in a nearby building bridged the ditch before they clattered across the grazing ground. The sound of firing was closer now. Swinging cutlasses cleaved a path through cactus fencing and garden palings.

It was difficult going, broken by huts and yards and drainage gutters and vegetable patches. The mules' eyes were straining from their sockets, their rumps raw from flogging, and men heaved on the wheel-spokes to force the ungainly limber forward. Spent bullets whined overhead or dropped in the dust to either side. They were near the firing line. The unseen Parrott twenty-pounder crashed out again and they were close enough now to hear officers' shouted exhortations to hold steady. They were encountering many wounded, the luckier hobbling rearwards and the more serious cases slumped in pain and despair in whatever illusory shelter they could gain.

A familiar figure approached – Gelb, unscathed but at the limits of exhaustion, sent back by Culbertson to locate Dawlish. His expression told of the gravity of the situation.

"Colonel Si – he's to the right, Sir – beyond them huts and trees. There's two slaughterhouses there, and stockyards beyond, and they've got more artillery there. The Colonel thinks two pieces."

"Could you see them?"

"Just the smoke and the muzzle flashes, Sir. They're between the sheds."

"And our forces, Sergeant? Pushing forward?"

"Stopped dead! Them Goddamn cannon knocked the fight out of them and El Pobre's bucks are pressing 'em hard."

Here was the Gatling's objective. The limber was brought lurching obliquely to the right, but the maze of housing and gardens was soon too congested to allow further use of the mules. They were unhitched and now it was up to the seamen and dismounted troopers to propel the ungainly vehicle further, manoeuvring it around corners, crashing over vegetable plots, slewing it between obstacles. Dawlish strained with the rest, his weight thrown against spokes or his shoulders braced under the limber box as it was half-lifted, half-dragged, over some ditch or fallen tree. The ragged volleys of Culbertson's force, now again defenders, crashed ever closer and unseen bullets clipped foliage from the bushes around.

And then, somewhere ahead, Culbertson's line broke.

At first there were no more than a few terrified men scuttling towards them, their weapons discarded, abject terror stamped on their gaunt faces, conscripts mostly. They stumbled and fell in their haste, glancing furtively back towards the crash of gunfire behind, then picked themselves up and blundered onward. The flood grew, no longer only conscripts, but regulars also, and even a corporal or two, and a single fear-crazed sergeant whose nerve had broken. They blundered unheedingly through cactus and crops and flowed like a torrent around every obstacle, obsessed only with survival. Their fear seemed contagious and Dawlish himself felt the fleeting urge to join them and saw even his own seamen exchange furtive, shame-faced glances. He knew that there was only one way to halt the madness.

"Over there! In the lee of that hut! Slew her round Lads!" he yelled, drawing his Adams. "Hilliard! McCreevy! Prepare for firing!"

The crewmen manhandled the clumsy limber towards the hut while the gunner and loader clambered up to their makeshift firing-platform and ripped the covers from the ammunition boxes. The shack provided minimal cover against any assault from the front or rightwards, and none from the left, where the ground was covered by yucca plots and stands of maize. Beyond, eighty yards beyond, was the crackle and smoke of rifles and a ragged black line was emerging from cover – Reduccionistas driving before them, on a frontage of two hundred yards or more, the terrified remnants of Culbertson's attackers in this sector.

Dawlish strode towards a knot of retreating conscripts, a few still carrying their rifles. Among them was a regular corporal who had thrown away his cap and was tearing off his tunic as he ran. Terror haunted his features. Dawlish grabbed him by the neck, swung him round and rammed the Adams under his jaw. The others paused. Two resumed their flight, but the remainder stood uncertainly, watching the unfolding drama.

"You're a corporal, not a coward!" Dawlish shouted. "You'll tell these men to go back! Pick up their weapons! Join me here!

Understand?" He jerked the hammer back with his thumb. He could smell the man's terror as he stopped squirming. Out of the corner of his eye he sensed a conscript raising a rifle but he ignored it and yelled "You'll take them back where you came from! Tell them gather their weapons!"

Something slumped to the ground to his left, a conscript stupid enough to raise his weapon in protest and more stupid still to hesitate, felled by a blow on the temple from the hilt of Egdean's cutlass. The huge seaman stepped behind Dawlish, covering his back. "All clear astern, Sir!" he growled.

Dawlish ground the muzzle under the corporal's chin, lifting him on to his toes. *"Uno! Dos!"* he shouted and before *"Tres!"* the terrified man was beseeching his men to run back to pick up their discarded rifles, any rifles. They hesitated for a moment, looking fearfully at Dawlish, then each other, and then moved reluctantly. Seeing them heading back towards the firing slowed the other fugitives. Egdean strode towards them, bellowing, slicing the air with his cutlass, oblivious of the spent bullets now raising small spurts in the dust around. His Spanish might have been rudimentary but his intent was obvious.

A conscript, stooped, picked up a weapon, and then, almost miraculously, walked towards Egdean and stood by him, his face towards the oncoming attack. *"Estoy contigo,"* he said. "I'm with you." It was as if his words had broken a spell. Another followed his example, and then another, and another.

Dawlish did not release the corporal until Egdean, now joined by Boyson and the stokers and deckhand, had hustled more than twenty men into forming a thin defensive line in a ditch to the left of the Gatling. The man had sunk to his knees, his crotch and trousers wet with urine. "Get up!" Dawlish snarled. "Find yourself a rifle and join your men." Sobbing with relief, the corporal scurried forward and joined them.

The firing was intense now, most rounds screaming too high overhead as the oncoming Reduccionistas paused in their forward rush through the crops to blaze wildly at the inadequate string of

317

defenders before them. The last retreating conscripts were flinging themselves into the ditch with Egdean and Boyson's improvised force, and the *Toad's* crewmen were forcing them to load, and hold to their fire.

A crouching run brought Dawlish back to the Gatling. He found that Gelb and his troopers had also halted some fugitives and had established a slight defensive position to the right of the hut. Hilliard and McCreevy were balanced on their firing platform.

"Loaded, Sir!" the gunner called.

"You see that patch of corn to our left? Two hundred yards? Yes? Line up on it." Dawlish's voice was steady. The position was ideal, allowing a line of fire all but perpendicular to the line of Reducción advance, while yet sheltering the Gatling from view. In the ditch to the left Boyson's thin line of defenders would serve as the bait to draw the attackers onwards.

"Ready, Sir!" Hilliard's hand was on the firing crank.

Dawlish peered carefully round the hut's sheltering corner. The Reduccionistas were close now, hardly fifty yards from that invisible line stretching from the Gatling's six-muzzled snout. They loped forward through the knee-high yucca in a ragged line, eighty or a hundred scarecrows in dirty cotton, flushed with success, oblivious of the danger on their flank. Perhaps half carried rifles and the remainder made do with machetes. Here and there a rifleman dropped to one knee to loose a round to keep heads down in the ditch they could now clearly see ahead. Another line followed twenty yards behind, as many men again, but bunched in groups with larger intervening spaces.

Bunched around the men with firearms, a small cold voice inside Dawlish's head told him. They're scraping the barrel.

"Hilliard! Hold your line of fire. Drop your aim towards that bush. You see it? About fifty yards." Dawlish's words were slow and deliberate. There must be no ambiguity. "On my command you'll commence firing. Three short bursts. Then lift your aim. Fifty yards further. Three more bursts. You understand? Then lift again. I'll tell you."

Rifle fire crashed out to the right, beyond the hut. On that side, blind to Dawlish, Gelb and his men were opening on the advance.

"Boyson! Egdean!" Dawlish yelled. A brief glimpse of heads bobbing above the edge of the ditch. "Fire at will!"

Heads and shoulders rose briefly from the ditch, rifles blasting towards the oncoming rabble, only the *Toad's* seamen keeping nerve enough to aim before they jerked back into cover. In the leading line two Reduccionistas were thrown down, but the others were enraged rather than cowed and they surged forward, yelling, bayonets extended and machetes upraised.

"Hold it! Hold it!" Dawlish said quietly, sensing the tensing of Hilliard's arm as the leading attackers crossed the line of fire and thrust towards the ditch.

And then the full weight of the assault was following. It was time.

"Fire!"

Hilliard pushed the crank around, a full revolution, six rounds, paused, then rotated it deliberately again, another burst, and the heavy .45 slugs tore into the nearest group of attackers, and then a third burst, jerking and convulsing them like crazed puppets. The Gatling bucked on its high and flexible perch, spraying widely around the aiming point.

"Up fifty!" Dawlish yelled. Some of the attackers were pausing, bewildered, but others still stumbled forward and the second line was blundering behind them into the killing swath. The barrels were rotating again, stammering leaden death, falling silent, grinding round again. The loader, McCreevy, was scooping fresh rounds from the open box at his feet, feeding them expertly into the hopper to avoid jams. Out among the yucca the Reducción assault was dying in a storm of hot metal and shattered bone and torn flesh. From the trench before them Boyson's small force poured fire into the few attackers who had advanced beyond the Gatling's slaying ground and these wretches, bewildered, paused, caught between two fires, and so died.

Up another fifty yards now, the Gatling vibrating on its precarious mount with every discharge, showering death into the assault's remnants. Dawlish was half deafened by the weapon's hammering, but not so much that he did not hear the screams of pain and shouts of despair as the onslaught broke. Men who minutes before had been thrusting forward elatedly in the wake of a defeated enemy were now themselves turning and dashing rearwards, abandoning their butchered comrades.

Another burst and then "Cease Firing!" The hot barrels juddered to a halt. Egdean and his men had risen to their feet and were firing into the backs of the fugitives.

Dawlish bellowed for them to join him. Seconds later they were manhandling the limber out from the cover of the hut, Hilliard and McCreevy struggling to keep their balance as it lurched into the open.

A near-silence fell in the wake of the retreating enemy, a momentary hush broken only by the more distant sound of firing on the flanks. Dawlish recognised it for what it was, a moment – perhaps the last he would get – of opportunity.

And so, into that hush, and across the uneven ground ahead, Dawlish threw his tiny force.

33

Boyson and Egdean led their ragged skirmishing line forward, recently panicked troops who had thrown away their weapons in their flight. Now they picked up rifles from the dead and wounded strewing the ground ahead. Terrified conscripts who had flung themselves into ditches and remained hidden until the Reduccionista charge had passed now emerged and joined the advance. Gelb's force was keeping pace to the right, also growing in numbers.

The limber jolted in their wake, a dozen seamen and conscripts dragging on the shaft and straining on the wheels, alternately pushing forward or backwards on the spokes under Dawlish's bellowed commands to swing it around obstacles. High and exposed, Hilliard and McCreevy fought simultaneously to keep their balance and to refill the feed-hopper, swearing as bare flesh was thrown against the Gatling's hot barrels. Progress was little more than walking pace, for even the smallest tussock or ditch was enough to necessitate ungainly manoeuvring.

A hundred and fifty yards to cross until the first cover, a clump of thorn and cactus which Dawlish had selected as the next firing point. At each endless yard he expected the silence to be broken and for the heaving, panting knot around him to become the focus for some resolute rifleman. But their luck held, and when the now-ominous hush was finally broken it was by Boyson's group clearing a ditch ahead of its handful of trembling defenders.

The thorn thicket lay just behind the ditch and the limber was pushed into its lee. The crew drew breath as Dawlish joined Boyson, whose force now crouched in the cover of the dry channel, looking nervously at the open ground beyond.

"They've halted there, Sir," There was fear in the old artificer's voice and Dawlish was uncomfortably aware that, however determined until now, he was a skilled tradesman, not a fighting seaman. "They'll be waiting for us."

"They'll run again, never fear." Dawlish hoped he sounded calm. "We have the Gatling." No less reassuring was the sight of Egdean, his bayonet bloody.

Three huts were clustered ahead, two-roomed adobe shacks with thatch roofs, and around them trodden plots of beans and yucca extended towards a line of rail fencing fifty yards distant. Figures moved there - impossible to say how many, or how resolute. Beyond, an open space and the black-walled, corrugated-roofed sheds that must be the slaughterhouses.

And there, between the sheds, the twenty-pounders now revealed themselves. Gelb's group, to the right, had already moved forward beyond the ditch, the sergeant himself at their head. They were moving ahead at a shambling run when two unseen cannon fired simultaneously. One shell fell buried itself harmlessly among the crops further to the right but the other, though it neither killed nor wounded, fell perfectly to stall Gelb's advance. It landed short, fifty yards or more ahead of the sergeant and his men, its flame-streaked plume rising before them like a defending spirit. They paused – and one even began to scurry rearwards – and though Gelb's urging carried them onwards again, there was a reluctance, a timorousness that had been absent before. Rifle fire crackled for the adobe huts ahead, light at first, then growing. A man spun and fell. His companion to the left froze. The pace slowed still further.

Among Boyson's men in the ditch Dawlish felt the unease.

"*Ahora somos perdidos!*" It was an anguished whisper of despair from a knot of conscripts, instantly silenced by a growl from Egdean, but the very sentiment could be contagious – and deadly. Only action could counter it.

Dawlish's instructions were brief: every rifle reloaded, bayonets fixed, the *Toad's* crewmen spread evenly to enforce discipline. He scrambled from the ditch and back to the limber.

Hurried orders to Hilliard and the manoeuvring crew. A glance towards Gelb's halting advance – by sheer force of example the sergeant was somehow keeping his small force moving forward despite the rising fire. A nod from Boyson confirmed that his men were ready.

The limber lurched from cover. An eternity of slewing and heaving. Then branches shoved beneath the wheels to block them and provide some semblance of a steady platform. Again the reports of the two twenty-pounders in quick succession, but no time to look for their effect. Hilliard traversed the Gatling towards the huts, tapping up the elevation, locking it.

"Ready, Sir!"

"Fire!"

The weapon stammered and clouds of brown dust enveloped the huts as the heavy slugs tore into their adobe walls. Boyson's force rose from its ditch and rushed forward, the laggards driven on by the *Toad's* seamen. They pounded forward, Egdean leading, unscathed by any fire from defenders stunned by the Gatling's sudden torrent. Gelb's group, now depleted by a twenty-pound shell that had dropped close, was somehow maintaining its momentum to the right.

The Gatling jammed but McCreevy had the stuck round free in seconds and Hilliard could again thrash the huts. An empty ammunition box was tossed down and eager hands passed another up. McCreevy shovelled rounds into the hopper and Hilliard ground the firing lever forward, measuring his bursts. The aim shifted again, this time towards the line of fencing, driving rearwards the thin screen of Reduccionistas that had sheltered there.

And now it was time for the Gatling to fall silent as Gelb's and Boyson's parties neared the dust-obscured cluster of shacks and crossed the rail fence. The rifle-fire was sporadic, the defence first half-hearted, then disintegrating, as the few Reduccionistas who had stood firm now turned and ran for the corrugated sheds. Heartened and amazed by their success, the panting force of conscripts, seamen and dismounted troopers fired into the rear of the fleeing defenders.

There was movement between the sheds. Dawlish stood on a spoke of a limber-wheel for a better view. Strangely, incongruously, in the distance beyond the slaughterhouses, there was a plume of white smoke – no, too white for smoke, more like steam – rising vertically. He noted it, but absently, and then dismissed it, his attention diverted by a twenty-pounder being manhandled forward from cover and swung to bear on the huts now occupied by Gelb's and Boyson's forces.

Hilliard had seen it also. "I've got it, Sir!" he yelled even as Dawlish's pointing finger identified the target, and he was already loosening the elevation-locking screw, tapping the barrels higher, sighting along them, then tightening again.

The barrels rotated and spat, half-a-dozen rounds that raised a brief storm of dust just short of the sheds. The Gatling fell into abrupt silence while Hilliard made a fast adjustment, tapped the elevation higher, locked it and grasped the firing crank once more. As he did the twenty-pounder blasted a shell towards the adobe shanties, collapsing the nearest in an eruption of smoke, flame and glowing shards. Through the clearing murk Dawlish glimpsed a rammer thrusting a sponge down the reeking barrel, loaders raising charge and shell to feed its hunger, but then the Gatling was barking again and suddenly those figures were jerking and falling. Another burst, and another, scything down the gunners, chopping splinters for the weapon's nearer wheel so that, weakened, it collapsed, hurling down the barrel.

It was now that Culbertson, on the right flank, launched his remaining forces forward from the positions in which they too had been stalled. Dawlish was first aware of this from the rising wave of rifle-fire from beyond the hedging and fencing that obscured his view in that direction. Soon there were signs of a full retreat as Reducción forces, plainly in disorder, began to stream across the yucca plots towards the black sheds. A moment later Culbertson's first brown-clad line, ragged yet with some semblance of order, emerged into view. It moved forward haltingly as groups were steadied to fire towards the retreating Reduccionistas, then reload deliberately and surge forward again.

The limber lurched and bounced forward, now to take station by the still smoking ruin in the adobe cluster. Dawlish was remotely aware of foully injured men calling hopelessly for assistance and of the smell of scorched flesh and of blood, but his attention was riveted on the black slaughterhouses, their function cruelly apt. Boyson was nowhere to be seen but Egdean and Gelb were urging their combined forces forward towards the sheds. They moved cautiously from one patch of cover to the next, while Culbertson's larger force converged from the right. The volume of rifle-fire was rising steadily as the retreating Reduccionistas were somehow regrouped behind the fencing of the surrounding stockyards. Unseen, hidden among the buildings, the remaining twenty-pounder blasted again, hurling a shell among Culbertson's advancing troops, opening a gap in the line.

Dawlish was straining on the limber wheel, helping slew it round in accordance with Hilliard's shouted directions as he shifted his aim back towards the slaughterhouses. The remaining twenty-pounder must be somewhere behind the nearer building's flimsy protection.

"The ammunition's nearly done, Sir!" McCreevy was pouring the last rounds into the hopper.

Dawlish thought quickly. "Finish it!" he shouted. "Keep firing until our people reach the sheds!"

The Gatling's final bursts hammered into the now-perforated structure, then stuttered into silence as the first of Gelb's men reached it. The remaining Reducción twenty-pounder vomited death one last time but then the attackers were upon it. Isolated shots rang out but screams and the flash of bayonets and machetes told of closer work. Culbertson's larger force came swarming in from the right, flowing around the farther shed to take the defenders in the rear.

"Right Lads!" Dawlish shouted. "We're going after them!"

Eight men were clustered around the limber, Wilcox the stoker and seven conscripts. Hilliard and McCreevy were scrambling down from their perch. Beyond his own Adams and Wilcox's Snider there was hardly a weapon between them, but Dawlish could sense that their blood was up. "Pick up what rifles you can over there!" he ordered.

Revolver in hand, he jog-trotted towards the sheds, Wilcox keeping pace. The sounds of combat were dying ahead, with only the occasional shot and then a noise hitherto unheard that day, yells and cheers of triumph. To the right Culbertson's force was streaming beyond the wreckage of the sheds.

The slaughterhouses had maintained their purpose to the last. Dawlish clambered across tumbled timber and zinc sheeting to find bodies slumped in every conceivable position, many torn and ripped by the Gatling's lashing, others transfixed in the dreadful hand-to-hand combat that had settled possession. A cowed and bruised knot of surrendered Reduccionistas was being prodded rearwards.

Dawlish shut his ears to the sounds of moaning and turned his face from the sight of evisceration, exposed bone and crimson flesh. Wilcox offered him a water bottle stripped from a fallen gunner. The tepid water, faintly metallic, told him how great his thirst had been. He knew he must press on – the advance had passed the ruins of the sheds and was pushing, slower now, towards the line of shacks, two hundred yards or less ahead, that represented the edge of Puerto Plutarcho's inner core. Beyond them were the higher roofs of the main workshops. They glinted in the sun like parodies of Christian's sight of the Celestial City.

He picked his way carefully through the wreckage and there, under the partly collapsed roof of a loading bay, he suddenly saw how the artillery had been shifted so rapidly from the distant downriver ramparts. There was a double stretch of railway track here – narrow gauge, three-foot – which merged into a single line at a switching point beyond the building. The track led die-straight across the open ground towards the settlement. And then he remembered that rising cloud of steam only minutes before – and also the sound of the whistle and of the chugging locomotive when he had first ridden blindfolded into El Pobre's domain. He had ignored the signs, and now the dawning truth gouged his stomach with fear. Long before the revolt, Hyperion engineers had laid a rail-system to link the settlement's shambles, storehouses and jetties. Afterwards, El Pobre – or Roybon, more likely – had extended track to run behind the ramparts, ready to rush reinforcements and munitions to any point under attack. And now the system was working in reverse, drawing reserves from the unmolested eastward defences and hastening them towards the settlement's threatened heart. If those reserves – and those fearful Parrott twenty-pounders – could be rushed back quickly enough then the Consortium's last-gasp thrust might still be crushed.

Dawlish's small force moved forward beyond the buildings, a small and random group, united momentarily by the Gatling's triumph. The ground was open, bisected by the railway line, dusty and bare of grass. Cattle had awaited here their turn in the shambles and now Reduccionista corpses littered it, silent witnesses to rout. Shooting crackled ahead, minor compared with the earlier tempest, but from far to the right – from two or three miles distance, Dawlish estimated – was a new sound, the low rattle of sustained rifle-fire, punctuated by the report of artillery. Aquino's force was also nearing the settlement, smashing opposition and thrusting for Puerto Plutarcho's vitals.

From the right a drumming of hooves – and there was Culbertson, grimed and sweating, slouching in his saddle and yet looking as if he belonged nowhere else. The sabre hanging from his pommel was bloodied. Three troopers flanked him, their drawn faces and red-rimmed eyes still drunk with the joy of killing.

The Colonel drew rein and reached down his hand. "You never failed me, Commander Nick," he said. "Seems I misjudged you in times past!"

Dawlish took his hand. For one fleeting instant he could smell the whiskey on Culbertson's breath, feel the callous on his palm – and in the next he was being hurled back by a blast of earth and flame. Flung from his plunging mount, the Colonel's bulk smashed into Dawlish, saving him from the worst of the searing blast, and beyond him there was the brief sight of one of the troopers literally disintegrating into a spray of blood and flesh. Dawlish was on the ground, stunned and half-deafened, blood drawn from his nose and ears. He fought to push Culbertson's weight from him. There was a sound of screaming – the dead trooper's disembowelled horse thrashing in agony – and the no less dreadful sound of the stoker, Wilcox, scorched black where he was not flayed raw by earth and fragments, realising the fact of his blindness. Three of the limber party lay crumpled in crimsoned mounds of rag and flesh. Culbertson's horse, the reins of which he somehow had hung on to, plunged and reared, its flanks and neck blood-streaked, its eyes protruding in terror.

Somebody was pulling Dawlish free – a stammering and bloodied McCreevy – and Culbertson himself was struggling to his feet, the clothing shredded, bellowing with anger, then quietening suddenly and soothing his horse with surprising gentleness. Dawlish found he could hardly stand for his legs were weak and shaking. He looked

327

quickly away from the smoking crater and the carnage around it. The surviving troopers were a little distance away, calming their terrified mounts and turning them back to the horror from which they had bolted. Whatever conscripts had survived the shell-burst were running rearwards towards safety. Hilliard lay in motionless in a bloody heap. Glancing away from him McCreevy shook his head in answer to Dawlish's unasked question.

"The bastards!" Culbertson croaked. "The sons of bitches! They've got another goddamn cannon up there. Another goddamn twenty-pounder!"

"The railway." Dawlish's voice was a hoarse whisper. "The narrow-gauge! They're using it to shift artillery from the ramparts." He was ashamed at the lateness of his insight. It seemed so obvious now that this was how the heavy weapons had arrived so quickly on the settlement's open flank. He was almost sick with anger against himself – one detail overlooked, but that detail the one that could yet tip the scales.

"We've got to take it, Nick," Culbertson said, no hint of bravado now in his voice. "You and me, and whoever's got a horse left to carry him. Otherwise the bastards have us beat." He bellowed towards the troopers. "Bring them horses here!"

Dawlish and Culbertson heaved themselves painfully into the saddles of the uninjured beasts, Dawlish's an unfamiliar mare, leaving the dismounted troopers to lead McCreevy and the blinded stoker rearwards. As they rode forward, towards the rear of Culbertson's advancing force, another shell landed, blasting a gap in the second line. Bodies fell and, more ominous still, several men, already tried beyond endurance, broke and began to run rearwards. It would take little more to send the whole force scurrying in their wake. And that fear could be contagious. Dawlish knew that he himself was also near his limit, aching and dizzy as he somehow held his still-frightened and unfamiliar mount in a canter, exhaustion sapping his strength. Culbertson rode ahead, slouched but indomitable, his uniform bloody, sabre in hand, unlikeable but splendid, Dixie's last cavalier.

They caught up with the second line as another shell blasted a gap to their left. Hurried consultation with a dazed sergeant – he thought that the Guardia troopers, what remained of them, were further to the right, close behind the foremost line of advancing troops. It was just short of the line of shanties ahead from which growing rifle fire barked. The unseen artillery piece roared again. Dawlish caught again the sight of rising steam and, in a brief instant of silence he heard the distinctive chug of a slowly moving locomotive. It was near, somewhere beyond those huts.

Another spurt, drumming across the dusty ground to where a grove of low trees sheltered a dozen horsemen, waiting for the infantry to clear a path through the huts eighty yards ahead. They looked hardly less exhausted than their mounts. Dirt-encrusted and sweaty as they were, Dawlish recognised Navarro and Plowright, who had charged with him so long ago to capture the howitzer, and there too was Neruda, the good shot. Culbertson's twenty-four carat sons of bitches. Now he would make one last charge with them.

Culbertson growled orders. A galloper was despatched to gather more horsemen. An infantry company, or what was left of one, was drawn out of the second line to the right and reformed behind the trees. Another joined it, exhausted and haggard, conscripts leavened with regulars. The remaining ammunition was redistributed equitably, weapons loaded, a man who had slumped into sleep on his feet shaken awake. They moved onwards to occupy the huts ahead, now cleared.

Swaying from fatigue, Dawlish fought down despair as he watched these weary scarecrows plod forward, for it seemed inconceivable that they had any fight left in them. From the left came the steady report of the twenty-pounder, blocking advance on that front. Another half-company, regulars and dismounted troopers, came shambling up and then a ten-pounder and its limber, dragged by two mules and by a dozen gunners and conscripts. They joined the reserves massing at the newly captured huts.

A whistle blast, piercing and wailing, rose loud over the rattle of gunfire. Beyond the huts ahead a plume of white steam rose and billowed, its root moving slowly. And at that moment another thirteen Guardia troopers arrived.

"It ain't much," the Colonel said, "and them Goddamn horses are near blown, but they're all we've got. Time to go now, Commander Nick!"

34

Afterwards Dawlish could remember but little of Culbertson's last assault, only its climax.

The ten-pounder hurled several rounds towards the thin Reduccionista screen in the huts to the front, and then the last reserves stumbled forward in a single lumbering wedge. Exhausted attackers encountered no less weary defenders among the shacks, but numbers were momentarily, and locally, on their side. The initial ripples of half-disciplined rifle-fire died down to individual shooting as the range closed and as bayonet and machete dominated the close combat. For three, four minutes the balance swayed to and fro before the improvised Reduccionista position collapsed and its defenders started to fall back.

And now it must be all or nothing, for the infantry was spent.

Culbertson launched his troopers. They had moved forward cautiously in the wake of the attack – less than twenty, Dawlish included – but as they passed between the newly-captured huts the old Confederate rose in his stirrups, raised his blood-smeared sabre and urged them into a full gallop. They drummed in a compact mass across open, sun-parched ground, ignoring and flowing around the fleeing remnants of the Reduccionista defence. Culbertson was yelling incoherently, and others took up the cry and the horses, jaded and listless moments before, caught the excitement and pounded onwards with flaring nostrils and staring blood-shot eyes.

Dawlish rode a little to the left and rear of Culbertson, trusting him for direction, his own weariness forgotten. He grasped the Adams in his right hand, leaving the sabre hanging on the pommel, and he was conscious of movement ahead, and of a light ripple of rifle-fire. To the left a fountain of earth rose up and the crash of a twenty-pounder shell washed towards him, but he was more intent on pulling his mount across to follow Culbertson's swing rightwards and to avoid collision with Neruda, riding knee-to-knee with him. A horse stumbled and cartwheeled, tossing its rider, but he had no eyes for that, only for the objective indicated by the colonel's outstretched sabre.

For there was the locomotive.

It stood, panting steam, surrounded by a milling group, at the rear of the four flatcars that it had pushed towards the cover of a partly-masking grove of trees. Small and pot-bellied, grey with encrusted wood ash, the small tank-engine had a homely look, a machine better suited to a Welsh slate-quarry than a South-American battlefield, yet for all its incongruity its mission was lethal. Three of the flatcars were empty – two of the twenty-pounders they had carried were already captured while the third was still blasting resistance somewhere to the left – but the fourth wagon still carried its deadly load. Balks and planks were stacked by its side as a makeshift ramp and men were straining to manhandle the cannon down it. Many were glancing in horror towards the oncoming horsemen, ignoring the frantic instructions of the gun-crew who knew that salvation could only lie in getting the weapon into action.

A hundred and fifty yards. A crackle of ineffectual shots from figures on the locomotive and flatcars, too few to slow the onslaught. Panicking men breaking from the crowd by the ramp, and running rearwards, the cannon lurching downwards wildly and then somehow restrained.

A hundred yards now, and still less, and Dawlish found himself howling with the rest as he urged his mount towards the flatcars and cocked his pistol. Steam plumed skywards as the engine's whistle shrieked in a vain attempt to terrify horses already too excited to hear.

The twenty-pounder lurched the last feet down the ramp. The crew was slewing it to bear. The mass of men around it was dispersing, some seeking shelter behind the cars, others surrendering to headlong flight. Only a small, dedicated knot remained to serve and defend the weapon. A rammer was pounding in the charge and to his side a loader was ready with the shell.

Fifty yards.

From the corner of his eye Dawlish caught sight of some figures crouched in the space between the engine's fender and the flatcar ahead of it. Something screaming close past his head caused him to duck but in that instant he realised that they were attempting to uncouple the engine. They had to be stopped. He pulled his horse across behind the charging mass of troopers and headed for the locomotive.

The Reduccionistas who had kept their nerve had turned to face the horsemen, machetes and bayonets raised in defiance. The shell was in the cannon's muzzle and the panic-stricken rammer was forcing it home.

It was too late.

The riders smashed into the compact mass, sabres swinging in slicing arcs and pistols blasting. The rammer and loader fell to Culbertson's blade. The gunner was already sprawled in death, his face blown away at point-blank range and his mate, hacked and bleeding, writhed beneath the gun carriage. The majority of their companions were pinned against the wagon, hopelessly defending themselves or equally hopelessly crying for mercy. Others scrambled across the flatcars or wriggled beneath them, but several of the troopers had ridden around to meet them on the other side and butchered them pitilessly.

Dawlish skirted the chopping, screaming mob and drew rein by the gap between locomotive and wagon. Three men crouched there, two intent on unhitching the connection while the third, an Indian, paralysed with fear, gaped with great staring eyes at the slaughter only yards away. Dawlish's mount, frightened, backed and tried to shy. He fought to control it as he swung his pistol across its neck. He ignored the Indian and fired down at the figures bent over the coupling. Jarred by his mount's jerking, his aim was wide, but the report alerted his victims.

A face was raised – pinched and sharp-nosed, smoke-blackened and ash-besmirched – framed by a close-cropped beard and hair, the eyes dark with anger and hatred. A face seen only twice before, but never to be forgotten – Alain Pannetier, who had fought the *Torres* to a wreck, whom Dawlish has spared as he had screamed defiance from its sinking hulk and who had now somehow survived the timberclad's fiery end the previous night.

There would be no quarter this time. Dawlish cocked and fired, but his horse was plunging and the slug caught the Indian rather than Pannetier, throwing him back with blood spouting from his chest. Pannetier reached for the mare's head, grabbed her reins and was carried off his feet by her momentum. He hung there, his weight pulling her round to the left and dragging her back to a stamping walk. She snapped at him, eyes bulging, as he tried to regain his feet and disengage his right hand from the reins. Dawlish, pulled forward, fought to regain control, tried to draw a bead on him, but the horse's neck hampered him.

Almost too late he saw the third man lunge upwards with a bayonet from his right. He turned, fired instinctively, almost blindly, saw his attacker go down. The mare plunged, momentarily lifting Pannetier from the ground, for he still clutched her reins. She dropped again, and he staggered free but held his ground before her. He had a knife in his right hand now, held like a sword, thumb extended along the blade. It was long and broad and now he advanced, sweeping it in fast, wide arcs towards her nose.

The mare backed instinctively, unwittingly giving Pannetier the opportunity to slash at her neck. She whinnied and plunged and spurted bright red over him as he darted past along her right flank. Dawlish could not keep his seat and came tumbling to the ground on her left.

He landed with a crash, dazed and bruised, knowing that he had dropped his revolver. Above him he could see only the blinding sun and the mare's bulk and stamping legs but the knowledge of the proximity of that dreadful broad blade brought him struggling to his hands and knees. His right hand found his pistol lanyard and followed it to the butt but before he could raise it Pannetier was above him and kicking into his chest.

"English bastard!" he screamed. "You destroyed my beautiful *Torres!*"

Dawlish snapped back in agony, head and face raised. An arc of bright light flashed horizontally before him at throat level, a fraction short of finishing him. To his left the pain-crazed mare screamed and kicked, forcing Pannetier to shift his footing.

It was Dawlish's chance. Still on his knees, he flailed blindly with the pistol. The knife hit it and bounced across his knuckles, opening them to the bone, not that he noticed yet, for he had one thought only, to get his finger on the trigger. Pannetier raised the knife again. He froze for an instant in that position as Dawlish's shot tore through his stomach, then toppled backwards, his expression of fury transformed forever into one of surprise.

Knees shaking, his head light, Dawlish staggered to his feet, suddenly aware that the sounds of battle were faint now, the firing sporadic. Culbertson's troopers still circled the wagons and guns, but all resistance there had ended. And then to one side there was movement, a single figure breaking free, momentarily unnoticed, and blundering painfully on foot towards Dawlish and the engine, his right shoulder a crimson mess. But now a trooper had seen him, and was spurring after him, sabre upraised, and still he stumbled on, still undefeated, Jacques Roybon, late Twelfth Regiment of Artillery.

"He's mine!" Dawlish yelled at the trooper, raising his pistol, firing in the air. The man reined in.

Roybon's strength left him and he sunk to his knees. Only now did he see Dawlish advancing towards him. Eyes met in recognition. There was no sense of hatred, rather one of two old friends meeting after long absence.

"Is it over?" he whispered.

"All but over," Dawlish said wearily. He took him in his arms, laid him down gently, then added "It never did have a chance. You knew that."

An attempt at a shrug, stilled by pain. "There was no option," Roybon sighed. "We had to try, no matter what." He waited for a wave of pain to pass. "One day, somewhere, it will succeed. Without me though."

His shoulder was shattered, the exact nature of the wound invisible under the blood and torn clothing. Dawlish staunched the flow as best he could with the remnants of his own shirt. Roybon was silent now, intent only on fighting pain.

Hoof beats announced the arrival of Culbertson and half a dozen troopers.

"So you got the sons of bitches, Nick!" Culbertson yelled, swinging himself from the saddle, "and there ain't none of them left up the track neither!" He regarded Roybon with interest.

"He's alive," Dawlish said.

"Alive enough to shine at a necktie party," Culbertson said without animosity, stating a fact.

"I'm taking him back to the *Toad*," A memory of an earlier encounter lent Dawlish's weary tone a defiant edge.

"You like the son of a bitch, Nick, don't you?" There was a note of understanding in the Colonel's voice. "I won't argue this time. You can have him for all I care. It's all over anyway."

Dawlish rose to his feet and took in the scene around. Jaded horses and exhausted riders clustering by the engine – a brass plate on the boiler identified it as the *Lady Agatha* – and a stillness of corpses by the flatcars a few hundred yards up the track. The force that had stormed that way was now pressing deep into the settlement.

But it was in the opposite direction that Culbertson directed his gaze.

335

"Look yonder, Nick," he said, "beyond the trees."

A dark mass of troops was moving there, driving the last remnants of opposition before it, driving them deep into the dying heart of La Reducción Nueva.

"It's Aquino." Culbertson said, "He's broken through and he's got the bastards on the run. If they've any sense they'll run up the white flag now."

And so El Pobre's dream ended.

35

Over.

It was the first thought that entered Dawlish's mind as he struggled into wakefulness. *It was over at last*, he told himself.

And was deceived.

A night had passed, of dreamless oblivion for Dawlish, of pain and intermittent delirium for Roybon and of merciful death for the blinded Wilcox. The *Toad* swung lazily in midstream, her magazine almost emptied, the Armstrong's worn-out barrel creaking slightly as it cooled through the hours of darkness. Only a skeleton watch guarded her as the exhausted crew lay sprawled in sleep, oblivious of the flame-tinged smoke rolling skywards downriver as Puerto Plutarcho endured its hell of looting, rape and murder.

Dawlish ached in every joint, and his bandaged left hand tormented him. He dashed water in his face, looked quickly away from the haggard wreck that confronted him from the glass and went on deck. Purdon was in control – decks were being swabbed and the *Toad* was already returning to its usual state of smartness.

A ship without a purpose now, Dawlish thought, as he listened to the report and commended actions in hand.

Then the butcher's bill. McCreevy had led a party to recover the bodies. Hilliard's lacerated remains were carried back in a blanket. They found Boyson among the slaughterhouses, shot and bayoneted, but with two Reduccionista corpses half-covering him. The old artificer, who had loved his compound engines so well, had died fighting. Sewn into canvas, their bodies lay where Holmes had lain twenty-four hours previously – could it be so short? – in company with Wilcox, who had charged so manfully beside them.

Dawlish was sick of it all now, was revolted by the slaughter, by his own part in it. He wanted to be gone from here, to be abandoning the *Toad* and all she had wrought and to be dropping down with her crew to Asunción and the Plate beyond in a Hyperion paddler. He knew he could never want to confide Florence the whole of what had passed or of his part in it for he feared the loss of her respect. He felt a rising surge of self-loathing and knew that he must suppress it for now. He must delay surrender to it – and purging himself of it – until he was on the steamer headed north from Buenos Aires to Britain. He knew it would be hard, very hard.

And now again the words of the burial service in that bare patch amongst the scrub. Three open pits in line with the single wooden cross that marked Holmes' grave. Again crewmen with arms linked across each others' shoulders trudging across the uneven ground, carrying loads that seemed to have no connection with comrades suddenly absent.

There was less urgency than there had been for Holmes, no battles left to fight. There was time enough to ask Purdon to read the Thirty-Ninth Psalm, though his voice weakened and failed as he came to the end. *Oh spare me a little, that I may recover my strength, before I go hence...*

Then Morgan, the gunner, reading haltingly from Corinthians, and other men weeping, for loss, for relief, for unspoken guilt that they had survived when others had not. *Therefore my beloved brethren, be ye steadfast, unmoveable...*

And so too they had been, Dawlish thought, though Murillo and Kegworth and the whole Board of Directors might care more for the havoc that they had wrought for them.

It was time for him to speak again. *Man that is born of woman hath but a short time to live....* The bodies were being lowered. Men were down in the graves with them, piling the stones carefully. *Thou knowest Lord the secrets of our hearts...*

And my secret, Dawlish thought bitterly, *is the ambition that brought you all here.*

A young seaman sobbed. Egdean was helping McCreevy out from Hilliard's grave, his face streaked with tears.

The earth was being cast in and Dawlish read: *Forasmuch as it has pleased Almighty God of his grace...* As he did he was conscious of movement to his left.

It was Aquino, mounted, who had drawn to a halt, spruce and cleanly uniformed, a dozen riders behind him. Beyond him, incongruously, a regular private held the pony that stood between the shafts of Simone Le Vroux's ramshackle dog-cart. It was empty.

Dawlish continued to read, *Ashes to Ashes, dust to dust,* but he looked disapprovingly towards Aquino, angry at his intrusion on private grief, wishing him gone. The General gestured with a wave that he should continue.

The last spadefuls were tossed. Three wooden crosses, names and dates of birth and death already scorched into them with a hot iron. The firing party forming up, no blanks but ball cartridge that would arc harmlessly into the vast Chaco. The shots rang out.

Purdon looked expectantly at Dawlish, awaiting the word to dismiss the parade.

"Have them reload, Mr. Purdon," Dawlish said quietly. "No dismissal yet." He walked towards Aquino, who dismounted as he approached.

"I imagine you've restored order, General," Dawlish said. "I haven't had time to congratulate you on your success."

"*Ahoro tranquillo*," Aquino said. "It's quiet now."

Dawlish knew instinctively, but did not want to imagine, what those words meant.

"It wasn't pleasant last night, but we had to let the men have something after their efforts." Aquino paused, then added "But without you, Comandante Dawlish, we would have failed yesterday."

Dawlish acknowledged the compliment, but knew already that this was not why Aquino had come. He guessed what was coming before the words were out.

"Now you have Roybon, Comandante Dawlish. Don Plutarcho wants him."

"And if don't give him up?" Dawlish fought to choke down rising anger.

Aquino refused to be drawn. "He'll have him, Comandante. Don Plutarcho rules here now and what he wants, he'll get."

"So Murillo's come up river at last? Now that his own skin isn't threatened?"

"Listen to me, Comandante. He'll take what he wants. He doesn't need you anymore." There was no tone of offence, only of patient explanation.

And it was true. And he had known that it must always end this way. There was but one card to play. Dawlish gestured over his shoulder. "Who do you think those men will obey? Murillo – or me? What's to stop me taking Roybon downriver in the *Toad*?"

"Señor Grinling."

"Grinling?" Dawlish could not disguise his incredulity.

"Don Plutarcho had him arrested last night. Two troopers will swear that they found him raping a woman. And that first he killed her

339

child." The very neutrality of Aquino's tone told that he knew it was a lie. He added, almost as an afterthought, "There was much like that last night."

Dawlish found himself almost laughing at the outrageousness of the accusation. The nervous balloonist's relations with women began and ended with the wife and two daughters of whom he spoke with the awed reverence of a Roman slave for a benign master.

"Damned nonsense, and Murillo knows it," Dawlish said. "And anyway, was he not downstream with Major Tinsley?"

"Murillo insisted that Señor Grinling come up to the settlement with him last night." Aquino looked Dawlish steadily in the eyes. Unemotional, stating facts, a man whose mission it was to act and never question. "Either you hand over Roybon or he'll hang Grinling. Publicly, with three conscripts who did worse. It will be a gesture of reconciliation for the people."

An eternity passed.

"So it's the Devil's Rosary again?" Dawlish's voice was harsh with failure and dread.

"No need for that anymore. It will be fast this time."

"You know he's wounded? Badly. He won't last till sunset.""

"That's why we brought the cart." Once the pride of some Hyperion manager's wife, now a tumbrel.

"He won't survive the journey," Dawlish said. His brain was racing. "I'll see Murillo myself."

"You won't hand him over, Comandante?"

Dawlish shook his head. "You can have me for security. I'll ride back with you." He felt himself trembling. "And I'll send the *Toad* downstream to Puerto Plutarcho. He'll be on board."

Aquino looked hard at him. "It will do no good, Comandante." He shrugged and Dawlish sensed he wanted no part of this. "But as you wish. Bring him on the *Toad*. You'll have a horse."

Dawlish turned to Purdon, took him aside and spoke quietly and rapidly. Then he mounted. He had never felt more wretched.

*   *   *

The cavalcade cantered towards the settlement up the track along which Culbertson's troopers had first smashed into the Reducción's defenders, past discarded equipment, burnt-out shacks, dogs and birds worrying bloated corpses. Cowed women and silent children, dead-eyed and hopeless, hovered like wraiths among the ruins.

Soon they were in the grid of streets and company sheds and stores and bungalows of the settlement proper, all pervaded by a smell of doused fires, smouldering embers and unburied bodies. The silence was oppressive, the skulking occupants flitting towards cover at sight of armed men. They passed the crossroads where Dawlish had seen the deserter dangle from the gallows. Now seven wretches hung from the collapsing structure, like turkeys in a poulterer's. No dwelling seemed to have been spared. Only a handful had been wholly destroyed, though many were partly burned, but the majority had doors and shutters ripped away and the pathetic contents lay strewn among the trampled vegetable patches. Only the industrial structures seemed intact, the rusting corrugated-iron workshops and stores, each with its guard of bored conscripts.

There was a sound of murmuring ahead, of low, fearful whispers from thousands of throats. It was interrupted once by a single shot. Total silence followed, and then it grew again.

Dawlish could already guess what was coming, for he recognised that they were close to the open square before El Pobre's house. They emerged on to it and here at last was Murillo's triumph.

The vanquished Reduccionistas, impossible to judge how many, but surely three or four thousand – men and women, ragged, filthy, exhausted and terrified – knelt there in the broiling sun. They knelt upright, not resting their buttocks on their heels, because the troopers who ranged on horseback through the open corridors left between the rough oblongs of prisoners lashed out with whips at any who did so. Some had fallen senseless, but so close was the packing that they scarcely touched the ground. Along the edges of the square regulars were drawn up, one every six or eight yards, bayonets fixed and levelled towards the crowd. The captives faced towards El Pobre's house and along that side four ten-pounders were spaced, slightly depressed, pointing straight into the hive of misery. There were women with whimpering babies among them, and old men, and wounded, tormented by flies and radiating the stench of human waste.

At first the murmuring seemed wordless, like the rising humming of insects, but as the column moved through the main passage through the crowd, Dawlish realised that though some were praying for mercy, whether to God or to the equally unseen Murillo, the majority pleaded only for water. The noise died suddenly as one of the horsemen pulled his mount stamping rearwards into a group of women, and, laughing as they crawled free, fired his pistol into the air.

Dawlish forced himself to confront what he had first turned his gaze from as they had entered the square. He looked deliberately at the improvised scaffolds on each of the four sides of the square. They had been knocked together from random planks and beams, some blackened and scorched, rickety platforms that stood ten feet above the crowd, and higher still were the uprights and sagging cross-beams of the gallows themselves. Each carried its ghastly freight of five or six bodies, crotches stained with last evacuations, eyes bulging incredulously. Gil was among them, the proud young lieutenant of Reducción cavalry, but he seemed infinitely old now. He still wore his brown cotton tunic but somebody had taken his boots and his bare feet were bloody.

Dawlish did not look closely at the last gallows, that outside El Pobre's house, until he dismounted, but he knew already what it carried.

There had been no long drop. They had been pushed from the platform and left to strangle, their necks elongated, flayed raw by the chaffing of the noose as they had kicked and struggled, heads bent grotesquely to the side by the enormous knots under the right ears. Simone Le Vroux's white hair had been chopped off close to the skull – there were patches of blood on it – to avoid interfering with the rope. Quite grotesquely, she still wore a pair of spectacles, one of the lenses smashed. In life Aguirre Robles's face had been sallow, and the eyes sunken. Now that face was livid and the eyes, bloodshot, frozen in agony and horror, protruded like an iguana's. The Poor Man and his adoring mistress had died as the poor had been condemned to die through history. A third noose, still unburdened, hung to their right.

And Dawlish felt ashamed, degraded by his own victory.

Murillo, immaculate as ever, sat at El Pobre's desk, a ledger before him and others already stacked in the case that had so recently held medical textbooks. The examination couch and surgical instruments were gone. He did not rise as Dawlish entered but he extended his hand.

Dawlish ignored it. Murillo affected not to notice.

"I've had no time as yet to thank you for your efforts yesterday, Commander Dawlish," he spoke neither with warmth nor the pretence of it. "The Board will be grateful."

"So it should be," Dawlish said.

"You have brought a prisoner for me, Commander Dawlish."

"I've brought you none, Señor." Dawlish forced calm into his voice. "But I've come for Grinling. And when you've handed him over I'll wish you good day and consider my service to the Consortium at an end."

Murillo's eyes blazed behind their thick lenses but he was obviously fighting to restrain his fury. "Bring me Roybon, Commander. Only then will the Board be advised of my satisfaction and will you be remunerated accordingly."

"Roybon's a brave man who deserves honourable treatment – no less than those poor wretches in the square," Dawlish said, but Murillo's look told of impatience and incomprehension. "You've won, Señor", Dawlish continued, shamed by the hint of pleading and desperation he could not keep from his tone. "It costs you nothing to show mercy."

Murillo ignored him. "You would get everything, Commander," he said. "The basic fee, the allocation of shares and the bonus agreed for successful termination of the campaign."

I managed without this wealth before, Dawlish thought. *I can manage again.*

"And I believe you might have had some other arrangement with Admiral Topcliffe as well," Murillo continued, "but of that I know nothing."

A little young for Captain in peacetime but it's been known before now. That was worth all the rest combined.

But the murmuring was growing again in the square outside, a thousand voices pleading as one. Had Florence been here she would have been pushing past the guards – Dawlish had seen her face oppressors just as terrible in Thrace – to carry succour to the weakest. And he remembered that he had contracted himself to match a Rendel against a monitor, to exercise his profession and fight armed men by land and water. Now he knew that the bargain had been a bad one, the price offered too low. It could never have been high enough for the real service demanded – or for his honour.

"The *Ipora* will be put at your disposal," Murillo was saying. "All the way to Buenos Aires. You and any of your men who want to accompany you will be en-route downstream by this evening."

"And Mr. Grinling?"

"And Grinling too, Commander Dawlish, violator and murderer though he may be." He paused, and gave himself the satisfaction of a smile. "But first of course you'll watch the Jacobin hang".

"And those people in the square?"

"People?" Murillo smiled faintly. "I'd hardly use that term, Commander. But I wouldn't worry about them if I were you. I'd rather worry about a future in which your hopes of advancement and promotion might be distinctly limited."

"You're a damned blackguard," Dawlish said. He ached to strike him.

"I'm a businessman." Murillo sat back, smug in victory. "And you. Commander, are in no position to negotiate. I expect Roybon within the next two hours or Mr. Grinling hangs."

Dawlish bit back his anger and contempt. "You'll have Roybon, and be damned to you," he snarled, then stormed from the room.

And now the cup now must be drunk to the last, bitter dregs.

36

The *Toad* lay alongside a jetty by the great workshops that fronted the river. Dawlish reached it through devastated streets and spoke briefly with Purdon. Instructions to the men followed, unobtrusively, to knots of three and four.

Aquino's riders, uninterested, smoked and lounged on the wharf. "My crew is escorting me," Dawlish told the General when he rejoined him. "I'm damned if I'm trusting Murillo."

"As you please, Comandante." Aquino shrugged. He too seemed sick of the business.

The dismal procession was led by Aquino's horsemen. The dog-cart followed them, flanked by the gunboat's entire remaining complement. Dawlish rode in the cart, supporting the partly conscious Roybon as best he could. Sweat stood on the Frenchman's face in great droplets and blood seeped through the bandages strapping his shoulder. Dawlish himself had extracted the bullet the previous night, probing inexpertly and grappling with a forceps, sterilising the wound with diluted carbolic. The cleansing had been inadequate, for the sickening scent of gangrene was growing, not that it mattered now. Before they left the *Toad* Dawlish had explained everything, though he doubted how much Roybon understood in his near-delirium. But of one thing Roybon appeared certain, that he was going to die, and he was resigned to it.

Only once did he speak. In a vegetable garden by the track two weeping women were scratching out a shallow grave beside a man's swollen, fly-encrusted body. Three uncomprehending children watched, one a girl of four or five holding an infant on her hip. The hut behind was gutted by fire.

Roybon saw, and tears ran down his cheeks.

"They were nothing. before. And now they're nothing again". He sounded weary. "Always the same."

The *Toad's* crew, marching alongside, oppressed by the smell and desolation, seemed to catch something of his despair. And Dawlish felt fear clawing within himself, fear worse than he had endured and suppressed on the river, or in yesterday's battle, fear and disgust for the spectacle he knew he must now witness, fear most of all that his courage might fail him in the ordeal ahead.

They passed into the square. The captives still cowered there under the cannons' mouths, still whimpered for water, and the troopers still ranged among them. Many recognised Roybon. The sight of him, pale, wounded and weeping unashamedly as he tried to hold himself upright in the dog-cart, confirmed to them that all hope was gone. Some cried out to him as he passed and from their sorrow for him Dawlish knew that this was what it meant to be loved. And as Roybon was loved, so too were he and his crew loathed. He could feel the frustration of his own men like something palpable, and he avoided the confused, unhappy glance that Purdon shot him. He forced himself to survey the full scene of anguish, to take in the brute suffering, but looking quickly away as his gaze met the despair in one or other pair of dark Indian eyes.

The dog-cart, pulled by the forlorn little English pony, carried him through the silent hatred of the crowd, and it steeled him further. And all the time his own hatred of Murillo's cold avarice and cruelty grew stronger, and he let it grow, for it fed his resolution for what must be done.

Roybon looked at the gallows and its burden. He glanced away, unable to suppress a shudder. Dawlish reached out and squeezed his hand, wishing that he had killed him yesterday. By the pressure of flesh on flesh he tried somehow to ask forgiveness for what was to come.

"You listen to me, Jacques! To me only! You understand?"

Roybon nodded. Dawlish thought he heard the whispered word "*Ami*".

Aquino had ranged his troopers between the dog-cart and the crowd. Dawlish sensed a movement at the house – a door being opened, nobody emerging yet. The moment could not be delayed. He uttered a short word of command to Purdon and the *Toad's* seamen stood by the cart. Egdean and McCreevy assisted Roybon down. He moved slowly and painfully, yet with immense dignity. Cries rose from the square, prayers and exhortations brutally stilled by a single pistol shot. Dawlish motioned to a spot close to his right and Roybon was held upright there between the two seamen, not ungently, sweat streaming from his pain-wracked face.

An infinity of waiting and of silence broken only by the crying of an infant.

Murillo emerged at last, preceded by half a dozen guards with rifles, and with a smirking and drink-befuddled Culbertson following. Behind, unbound but dishevelled and plainly terrified, came Grinling, walking unsteadily between two regulars. He had already vomited down his shirtfront and Dawlish thought he was going to do so again as his eyes moved unwillingly but uncontrollably towards the dangling bodies and the empty noose. He began to blubber in relief as he saw Dawlish.

Murillo's white linen suit was spotless, starched and pressed. Beneath the broad-brimmed hat that shielded his bald head from the sun, behind the sparklingly clear pince-nez, his cold eyes gleamed with venom and with triumph. He advanced, his entourage aligning themselves to either side, Culbertson lazily raising a hand in salute, Grinling looking fearfully to his escort and longingly to his countrymen.

Murillo looked directly at Roybon, his thin lips curling in contempt and hatred. The Frenchman looked past him as if unwilling to accept his existence.

Now the last card must be played, coldly, deliberately, systematically.

"Bring Capitan Roybon here," Dawlish said quietly to Egdean.

The doomed man was supported forward two paces between Egdean and McCreevy. The pain of movement drew a low gasp from him.

"*Ecce Homo*," said Dawlish.

"Here, Commander," Murillo said. "Bring him here."

"First I want Mr. Grinling."

Murillo jerked his head. The terrified aeronaut was pushed forward roughly. He looked around, confused, at first disbelieving that he was free, then stumbled towards Dawlish.

"God bless you, Sir," he babbled, "God Bless you, Sir!" but Dawlish motioned him behind him.

He could hear his own heart pounding. His stomach was hollow with fear and his hands trembled. Forcing the movement to seem casual, he turned his head to watch Grinling join the seamen.

An eternity passed.

The furnace heat of midday. The palpable gaze of the unseen prisoners, more terrible for their cowed silence. The mute testimony of the hanging bodies, steadfast unto death. Culbertson swaying, grinning stupidly. Aquino somewhere behind, efficient and lethal. Roybon, a man already dead, consumed by sorrow for what might have been. And Murillo, avarice triumphant.

"Now, Purdon!" No more than a whisper, but the agreed signal as Grinling reached temporary sanctuary. The hurried plans agreed while Roybon was fetched from his sickbed had been desperate but exact.

Dawlish did not shift, but in an instant Purdon's rapid order drew the *Toad's* crewmen into a miniature square around him, each man facing outwards, rifles swinging up to shoulders, a tiny knot of defiance that might survive less than a minute. But in that minute, Culbertson and Aquino would die, and they knew it too as they gazed in shock at the formation that had surprised them, for each looked down the barrels of rifles aimed directly at them. And Murillo would die before any, for Purdon's revolver had arced up and was pointing directly at him with the hammer raised.

In the seconds it took for Dawlish to reach him Roybon realised what was coming.

Horror registered on McCreevy's face and Egdean was whispering urgently; "Have faith, Sir, the Lord is with you, God is merciful..." but the prisoner hardly heard him but rather looked at Dawlish with something like gratitude.

Roybon's mouth was opening for thanks that would be forever unspoken as Dawlish pushed the pistol into his left side, gouging up beneath the rib cage with a violence that had no malice in it. He looked him straight in the eyes and pulled the trigger.

Blood spattered Dawlish and the others as Roybon slumped between them, then fell on the reddening ground beneath.

A moan rose from the unseen crowd, women wailing, men crying out. Movement behind Murillo, a guard, raising a rifle, an action instantly stilled by a barked order from Aquino.

Dawlish dropped his revolver to swing harmlessly on its lanyard and raised his hands as he turned to Murillo.

"I'm leaving, Señor." He spoke in English, his tones loud enough for a suddenly sobered Culbertson to understand, "and my men are leaving with me. If I don't have your word then Mr. Purdon will kill you. And if I do have your word, then Colonel Culbertson is accompanying us to the jetty. Any trickery, and Purdon kills him."

Murillo was fighting to maintain composure but he could not disguise the anger and impotence and fear in his voice. "The Board will hear of this, Dawlish," he hissed. "Kegworth and Mellish and Topcliffe – yes, Dawlish – Topcliffe! He'll..."

"Let the son of a bitch go, Don Plutarcho." It was Culbertson, moving across slowly, voice wheedling, but his eyes on Dawlish, pleading for time. "You've got what we came for, Señor, the whole damned settlement. There's nothin' to be gained by pushing Commander Nick, Señor, nothin' to gain and everythin' to lose."

Behind the trembling, rage-flushed face Dawlish could almost see the cogs and gears of Murillo's mean-spirited bookkeeper's mind grind out a fast calculation of profit and loss. And all the while the vocal mourning from the square and the controlled terror of disciplined men waiting for the order to fire and die.

"You have my word Commander," Murillo snarled, "but remember! The Board will know how to reward you!"

"Thank you, Señor Murillo," Dawlish said. "I wish you Good Day."

"Look's as if you and I are going to take one last turn together, Commander Nick." Culbertson mopped his brow and stepped past Roybon's prostrate body.

And so Dawlish marched from the square at the head of his men, their heads held high, England half a world away but suddenly in every mind. Several pistol shots rang out behind them as the wails of mourning and despair were quelled. The citizens of La Reducción Nueva were once more the chattels of the Hyperion Consortium.

And could it have been different? Dawlish wondered, as he passed between the corrugated sheds and spoiled hovels and dog-worried carrion.

Something mourned inside him for what might have been, a remote island of compassion and freedom and generous plenty. But against it a cold, hard voice told him that this day – and maybe a worse one – would have come anyway, under an El Pobre driven to insanity by power, self-certainty and messianic vision, a Robespierre of the Chaco. Roybon might have resisted for a while, but the end for him would have been the same.

Logic told Dawlish that it was so, that the dream could never have been, that it could never be.

And it was no comfort.

The End

Review Request

You know how important good reviews are to the success of a book on Amazon or Kindle. You also understand why this review request is at the back of *"Britannia's Reach"* and why it's on its own page!

If you've enjoyed this book then I'd be very grateful if you could post a positive review. Your support does really matter and I read all reviews since readers' feedback encourages me to keep researching and writing about the life of Nicholas Dawlish.

If you'd like to leave a review then all you have to do is go to the review section on *"Britannia's Reach"* Amazon page. You'll see a big button that says "Write a customer review" – click that and you're ready to get into action.

Thanks again for your support and don't forget that you can learn more about Nicholas Dawlish and his world on my website www.dawlishchronicles.com.

You might also "like" the Facebook Page "Dawlish Chronicles" or want to follow my blog on dawlishchronicles.blogspot.co.uk

Yours Faithfully: Antoine

p.s. If you haven't encountered Dawlish previously you may enjoy *"Britannia's Wolf"*, which deals with his service in the Ottoman Turkish Navy during war with Russia. A taster is provided on the next page. I hope you like it.

Britannia's Wolf

The Dawlish Chronicles
September 1877 - February 1878

Dawlish has taken a small Turkish gunboat, the Burak Reis, into a Russian anchorage...

... the Russian guardship was a thousand yards distant and the range was closing.

By Dawlish's side Onursal relayed his orders and the quartermaster swung the helm. Then he was shouting by hailing trumpet to the Krupp crew forward and he also set the Nordenveldt's crew to strip its oilskin covers away. The marine manning it was adjusting his sights and his loader was checking that its vertical feed-tracks were fully charged.

The *Burak Reis* lunged to port in a wide, smooth sweep, speed eight knots, rock steady in the calm waters, broadside-on to the advancing Russian.

A sharp report and a puff of smoke from the guardship told of a three-pounder, a pitiful counter to the wrath bearing down on her. A tiny fountain rose fifty yards off the *Burak's* port bow but the Krupp's muzzle was edging across, the layer's eye glued to his backsight as he spun the brass traverse wheel. Still the Russian came on, driven forward by some desperate hero, ramming now her forlorn hope.

"Atesh! Fire!"

The Krupp barked and its foul yellow discharge obscured its target. Already the breech was swinging open for sponging and the loading numbers were standing poised with the next bursting-shell and separate powder charge. As the smoke wreaths drifted clear of the *Burak's* bridge Dawlish heard a dull explosion and saw black billows, shot with flame, rolling upwards from the guardship. She lurched

353

drunkenly to port, her flank exposed, her forward superstructure shattered and burning. Dazed men stumbled on deck. Dawlish knew he could afford no pity.

"Nordenveldt!" Onursal called, directing the gunner to rake the deck.

The gunner rocked the crank of the five-barrelled weapon, each forward motion feeding and firing, each return ejecting empty, smoking cartridges. The heavy rounds lashed the Russian, scything bodies and splintering woodwork. And the Krupp was ready to fire again.

"Atesh!"

Another shell slammed into the dying guardship, gouging into the side beneath the funnel before erupting there. An instant later the dull "whumf" of the boiler's rupture tore the hull apart. The vessel rolled over as men flung themselves overboard, and its back broke. The bow disappeared immediately and the upturned stern submerged to the stilled propeller and jutting rudder. A score of men struggled in the water, as the *Burak* steamed past, turning now towards the merchant steamers.

One was getting underway. The barges alongside had been cast adrift and the anchor struck free. The vessel was moving slowly seawards. Smoke vomiting from the stack indicated frantic efforts to build up steam pressure. She was moving at little over two knots as the *Burak* pulled on to a parallel course, revolutions minimised, at a cable's separation.

Both Krupps blasted, their shells tearing jagged holes at the waterline. The steamer began to list. A boat was being lowered amidships, and men were dropping into it, others throwing themselves into the sea as she rolled further. All forward way had been lost and steam blasted from a relief pipe at the funnel.

"Leave her," Dawlish said. "She's finished."

The *Burak* headed for the remaining steamer in a wide, slewing turn, again at half-revolutions. The steamer was high in the water - the unloading must have been almost complete - and she still was firmly anchored. Her two boats were heading shorewards, laden with crew and stevedores from the barge still secured alongside.

"One shot should do it, Onursal Mülazim," Dawlish said.

The *Burak Reis* slowed. The range was two hundred yards, close enough for the forward Krupp to place a shell in the hull directly below the funnel. For one instant Dawlish saw the neat circular black hole that was punched in the rust-streaked flank, then orange flame came jetting back through it as the shell exploded within. Hull plating heaved, rivets sheared and fissures opened. A second later the wooden deck above splintered and rose as the boiler burst. Steam and flames gushed from the chasm it tore and the thin funnel whipped and toppled. The gunboat surged ahead, saving itself from the falling debris and from the glowing coals scattering like tiny meteors from the wrecked furnace. A fire was taking hold, blazing brightest in the remains of the midships deckhouse and licking forward and aft.

Onursal circled the gunboat around the burning steamer to bring the laden wooden barge on the other side under fire. One end was stacked with jute sacks, the other with barrels. A shell at the waterline did for it, disintegrating the structure and dumping the cargo in the water in a cloud of flour from splitting sacks.

The *Burak* headed now for the remaining victim in the roads, the anchored brig, from which the last boat was pulling hastily away. A feathery plume of water suddenly rose some hundred yards to port. The boom of the artillery piece ashore that had caused it came reverberating across the intervening water. Then another plume was rising, also short, and astern.

"Field-guns," Dawlish said, "light, but they'll be troublesome as we move inshore. Get another man aloft with the lookout. We need to locate them"

They must be standard Russian weapons, he thought, probably nine-pounders. The rating was deceptive, a convention based on the weight of spherical ball for the weapon's calibre. But those pieces would be throwing elongated, conical-nosed, explosive shells, twenty-four pounds each, well capable of wreaking devastation on the *Burak*.

He scanned the town and the open ground to the south. For an instant he saw the bright stabbing tongue of a muzzle flash from what looked like an earthen redoubt...

Made in the USA
Middletown, DE
09 February 2018